CARVER'S TRUTH

Nick Rennison is a writer, editor and bookseller. His books include *Sherlock Holmes: An Unauthorised Biography*, *Robin Hood: Myth, History, Culture*, *The Bloomsbury Good Reading Guide* and *100 Must-Read Historical Novels*. He is a regular reviewer of historical fiction for both *The Sunday Times* and *BBC History Magazine*.

CARVER'S TRUTH

NICK RENNISON

CORVUS

Published in paperback in Great Britain in 2016 by Atlantic Books Corvus,
an imprint of Atlantic Books Ltd.

10 9 8 7 6 5 4 3 2 1

A CIP catalogue record for this book is available from the British Library.

Paperback ISBN: 978 1 84887 181 6
E-book ISBN: 978 1 78239 408 2

Printed and bound in Great Britain by Clays Ltd, St Ives plc

Corvus
An imprint of Atlantic Books Ltd
Ormond House
26–27 Boswell Street
London
WC1N 3JZ

www.corvus-books.co.uk

To my family in Berlin –
Wolfgang, Lorna and Milena

PART ONE

LONDON

CHAPTER ONE

The street was not smart but the vehicle which turned into it was. Costermongers' carts were far more familiar here than broughams, and passers-by stared with unaffected interest at the brightly painted carriage, seemingly fresh from a Long Acre workshop, which came to a halt outside one of the terraced houses.

A young woman, dressed in blue, emerged from the basement area of the house and stepped into the street. She was wearing a veil, also blue, which hid her face from the group of idlers that had swiftly gathered to admire the brougham. Its driver sat impassively on his box seat at the front as the door to the carriage was opened from within. The woman in blue moved towards it, the small crowd parting to let her through. A gentleman in a grey morning suit alighted from the carriage and politely handed her into it, following her into the carriage's dark interior after she was safely settled into her seat. The door closed, the driver flicked his whip above the horse's head and the brougham moved off, making its way towards the parts of town where its appearance would cause much less of a stir.

The loiterers on the pavement watched it go and, as it rounded the corner of the street and disappeared, began to speculate idly on the reasons for its visit to their dull corner of north London.

* * * * *

Adam Carver, sometime traveller, intelligencer and occasional photographer, was surprised to see the man from the Foreign Office at the burial of Mr Moorhouse, his long-standing and fond acquaintance from the Marco Polo Club. He could think of no reason why the Honourable Richard Sunman should be there, standing in a remote corner of Kensal Green Cemetery, as the old man's body was committed to the ground.

It was a cold but bright spring morning and Adam knew why the other people gathered around the newly dug grave were present. The large, middle-aged lady to his right, weeping noisily behind her black veil, was Mr Moorhouse's niece and sole surviving relative. During their conversations at the Marco Polo, the old man had occasionally spoken of her. Although Mr Moorhouse had been far too much of a gentleman to say anything directly, Adam had gained the impression that his friend had thought little of this niece. 'Flora,' he had once said as they were both sitting in the club's sitting room, 'is a woman who observes all the social proprieties.' His tone of voice had suggested that he might have warmed to her more if she had not. Today, Adam thought, her loudly expressed grief sounded much more the result of respect for funereal convention than genuine loss. He doubted if she had seen her uncle more than a handful of times in the last years of his life.

The thin and sour-faced woman on Flora's right was her companion. Her hand was clutching the niece's arm as if she was arresting her and taking her into custody. Adam had been mildly surprised to see the two of them. Women did not always, or even usually, attend funerals. Moorhouse's niece had not entirely observed the social proprieties on this occasion. He guessed that the lives of Flora and her companion were so starved of drama that they could not bring themselves to miss the ceremony, even if the strictest etiquette demanded that they should stay away.

Grouped in a semi-circle to Adam's left were Moorhouse's other friends from the Marco Polo. Baxendale, the club's secretary, was shifting uncomfortably from foot to foot and looking as if he would rather be anywhere else in the world than Kensal Green. Duncan Farfrae – a man whose chief claim to fame in the club was that, as a small boy in Edinburgh, he had once sat on the explorer Mungo

4

Park's knee – was gazing mournfully into the middle distance. With Moorhouse's death, he had become the Marco Polo's oldest member and he looked as if intimations of his own mortality were preying on his mind. There were, perhaps, a dozen other men Adam recognized from his regular visits to the club in Pall Mall. He was surprised that there were not more. Mr Moorhouse, he had always assumed, had been a popular member of the Marco Polo. He had certainly been an almost permanent fixture in its smoking room since before many of the other members had been born. Everyone had known him but it seemed that only a handful of people had been prepared to make the journey to the West London cemetery to mourn his passing.

Sunman had not joined the group around the grave. He was standing some fifty yards away on one of the paths that criss-crossed the cemetery. Whenever Adam glanced in his direction, he appeared to be inspecting an elaborate monument on which two stone angels were playing harps and gazing heavenwards.

It was only when the ceremony was over and Adam, his commiserations offered to the still-weeping niece, was making his way back to the main entrance of the cemetery that Sunman approached. He was immaculately dressed in a black frock coat and looked as calm and collected as he always did. It was as if the two of them had met while strolling along Piccadilly rather than in a burial ground in the further reaches of the London suburbs. 'Poor old Moorhouse,' he said, reaching out to take Adam's hand in greeting. 'He was quite a friend of yours, I understand.'

'We met frequently at the Marco Polo. A gentleman of the old school.'

'He was, indeed.'

'I had no notion you knew him.'

Sunman waved his hand in the air as if to suggest that there were few people in London he did not know.

The two men began to walk in the direction of the Harrow Road, and Adam found himself wondering just why his companion had engineered this meeting. He had known Richard Sunman since his schooldays but never very well. Early in his Foreign Office career, the young aristocrat had informally recruited Adam, then about to travel to European Turkey, as an off-the-record agent to report on his journeys through this especially sensitive part of the Ottoman Empire. The previous year, on his second and more eventful expedition to that part of the world, Adam had again supplied Sunman with his thoughts and impressions on what he saw. His friend had seemed to set rather more store on them than had Adam himself. However, since Adam's return from a journey that had ended in betrayal, murder and the extraordinary death of his former Cambridge tutor, Professor Burton Fields, there had been little communication between the two men. Now Sunman, a creature of Whitehall and the West End, had turned up unexpectedly in an out-of-town cemetery. Adam was intrigued, but the man from the Foreign Office gave no indication that he was ready to explain what he was doing in Kensal Green Cemetery. The two of them walked on.

'Well, would you credit it?' Sunman came to a sudden halt. 'I knew this chap. I had no idea he'd joined the great majority.' He moved to the left of the path and pointed his malacca cane towards a red granite memorial, which looked to have only recently been erected. 'Well, Pater knew him. I met him. That's probably a more accurate way of putting it.'

Adam leaned forward to read the inscription: 'Sacred to the memory of Mr James Henry Dark who died 17th October 1870, aged 76. For many years Proprietor of Lord's Cricket Ground.'

'Pater was doing something for MCC,' his companion continued. 'Sitting on some committee or other back in the early sixties. This fellow wanted them to buy the lease of the ground from him.'

Adam, who had never heard of James Henry Dark and certainly never met him, could think of nothing to say. His thoughts had returned to Mr Moorhouse, whom he had known and much liked. His companion continued to gaze at the memorial.

'The paths of glory lead but to the grave, eh, Carver?' he remarked. He did not sound unduly troubled by the prospect. Perhaps he thought that, in deference to his social standing, he would be excused from treading them.

Adam nodded his head in brief agreement. He was certain that his friend from the Foreign Office had not travelled all the way to Kensal Green simply to indulge in commonplace observations about the inevitability of death. But the languid young aristocrat showed no signs of being in a hurry to divulge his other motives, whatever they might be. Instead, he turned away from the last resting place of Mr Dark and continued to amble along the path.

Adam followed him. The only sounds were the crunching of gravel beneath their feet and birdsong overhead. When a minute had passed and Sunman had shown no sign of disturbing the silence of the burial ground, Adam felt constrained to speak. 'I am surprised to see you here, Sunman. I would have thought you rarely strayed this far west of town.'

'I wished, of course, to pay my last respects to Moorhouse,' Sunman said. 'He was at school with pater, you know. Sixty years ago.' He shook his head as if he could scarcely credit the idea of his own father once being a schoolboy. 'Pater would have been here himself. But the gout . . .' He shook his head again, leaving it to Adam's imagination to conjure up thoughts of just how crippling that affliction might be. 'I did, however, have another reason for travelling out here. What you might call my ulterior motive.'

The two men had now emerged from the main cemetery gate. A black and yellow landau, looking impossibly elegant and out of place, was standing just outside. The coachman, when he saw his master approaching, leapt from his driving seat and hastened to open the door to the carriage. Sunman gestured towards its interior. 'Let me take you back to town, old man.'

Adam had intended to walk the five miles back to Doughty Street accompanied only by his memories of Mr Moorhouse, but he could see no polite means of refusing Sunman's offer. He climbed into the landau. His friend gestured in silent command to the coachman and followed him. They settled into the plush upholstery of the carriage's interior as it began to move in the direction of the distant city.

'I wished to speak to you in private, Carver.' As Sunman spoke, he was brushing near-invisible specks of dust from the sleeves of his frock coat. 'And I knew that you would be attending the interment of our poor friend Moorhouse. The occasion seemed opportune. I thought we could talk on the way back to town.'

'I am happy to do so. I do not think we have seen one another this year.' In truth, Adam thought, he and Sunman had not spoken since a brief meeting in St James's Park shortly after his return from Athens in the autumn of 1870.

'This is rather more than a social rencontre, old man. Delightful though it is to see you.' Sunman smiled briefly and perfunctorily, before reaching into one of the inner pockets of his coat and pulling out a photograph. He handed it to Adam. It was a cabinet card showing a pretty blonde woman. She was sitting in a photographer's studio, holding an unfurled parasol above her head. 'Her name is Dolly Delaney.'

Adam was puzzled. Why would Sunman be interested in someone named Dolly Delaney? He turned over the photograph. There was nothing on the back of the image.

'She is an actress.' Sunman spoke as if he was referring to some exotic species of creature such as a platypus or a manatee that he had heard described but never himself encountered. Perhaps, Adam thought, he hadn't. 'And a dancer.'

'An enticing young lady. Doubtless she graces any stage on which she appears. But why are you showing me her *carte de visite*?'

'We wish to speak to her.'

'We?'

'Certain people in King Charles Street.'

'In the Foreign Office?'

Sunman nodded.

Adam remained bemused by the turn the conversation had taken. What possible connection could there be between the upper echelons of government and some pretty ingénue on the London stage?

'Can you not find her at the theatre where she works?' he asked, after a brief pause.

'She has disappeared. She has not been seen at her lodgings or at the Prince Albert theatre for nearly a week.'

'Why should you and your colleagues be interested in the girl?' Adam looked at his friend in puzzlement. He waved the photograph that was still in his hand.

'I regret I cannot tell you why. I can only say it is imperative that she be found.'

There was silence in the carriage. Adam looked again at the young woman on the cabinet card. She was overly made up but she had a pleasant, attractive face. She seemed like a girl with whom it would be fun to while away an evening at Gatti's or a music hall . . . Adam realized suddenly what linked her with the Foreign Office. Some gentleman there had been doing exactly that. Could it possibly have been Sunman himself? He glanced at his companion, who was staring thoughtfully out of the landau's window, as if memorizing the route they were taking. Adam decided that he was an unlikely candidate for the role. If Sunman had his *affaires de coeur*, which he probably did, he would be far too discreet to allow them to impinge on his work for the government.

'Why are you telling me anything at all about her?' Adam asked eventually.

'I have suggested to my colleagues that you might be able to help us in locating her.'

'I? But surely the police would be able to trace a missing person?'

'It is better if the police are not involved in the affair. The fewer people who know that Miss Delaney is of importance, the happier we shall be.'

'But is she of importance? How is she of importance?'

'In herself, of course, she is not. However, we believe that she is in possession of information that gives her a significance she would not otherwise have.'

'And what information is it that you believe she possesses?'

'Alas, that I cannot divulge to you, Adam.' Sunman smiled politely, almost apologetically.

Adam noticed that Sunman had begun to use his Christian name.

9

Although they had known one another since their school days, he had rarely felt entirely comfortable with the young aristocrat, previously detecting various degrees of condescension in the other man's conversations with him. He saw now that Sunman, by his standards, was eager to ingratiate himself. 'One of your colleagues has been squiring Dolly around town, hasn't he?'

Sunman inclined his head in the faintest of agreements. These were not the kind of words he would use himself, he managed to convey, but they were essentially true.

'He has been indiscreet in his entertainment of her, has he not?' Adam almost laughed as he said this. He was rather enjoying the situation. Another thought struck him. 'The girl is not *enceinte*, is she?'

'That would be an added complication, but it is not one that we believe we need to include in our calculations.'

Adam made to hand Dolly's photograph back to his companion, but Sunman shook his head. 'Keep it,' he said. 'You will need it to help you in your search for the girl.'

Adam took one last look at the *carte de visite*. She really was a most attractive young woman. He took his wallet from his jacket pocket and slipped the photograph into it. 'Why have you chosen to ask me to find her?' he asked. 'Not that I am not flattered that you thought of me.'

'We need someone we can trust. We need someone with connections in the – ah – bohemian world in which Miss Delaney lives.'

'Again I am flattered. Although I am not certain that my life is particularly bohemian.'

'You have written books,' Sunman said, as if this was almost sufficient proof in itself. 'You live in Bloomsbury. You are close friends with that chap, Jardine – who is working as a scene painter in the very theatre where the young woman was last employed.'

'Perhaps you should ask Cosmo to look for her.'

'We do not trust him. Whereas, in that unfortunate business in Turkish Greece, you proved yourself entirely reliable.'

Had he, Adam wondered, proved himself entirely reliable? He

smiled inwardly at Sunman's euphemism. The murderous madness of Professor Fields had certainly been 'unfortunate' at the very least. He debated whether or not he should accept this dubious commission. Did he truly relish the prospect of tracking down the whereabouts of some missing actress, however pretty she might be? He was not about to set up business as a private enquiry agent. And yet the months since his return from Greece had not been busy ones. Too often fruitless thoughts of Emily Maitland, the girl he had loved and lost the previous year, had troubled him. Perhaps this was the distraction he needed to take his mind away from her.

'I will do what you wish, Sunman,' he said. 'I will look for this elusive young lady.'

'Capital,' his friend replied, as if he had never doubted for a moment that Adam would.

'I assume that,' Adam continued, 'however much you may mistrust him, I am free to approach Cosmo with questions about the young lady.'

'I would suggest that it would be easiest to speak to him before you speak to anyone else.' Sunman nodded his agreement. 'Although the theatre is a large one and employs many people. There is the possibility that he did not meet the girl or take notice of her.'

Adam thought about the blonde girl in the photograph. 'Oh, I believe Cosmo would have taken notice of her,' he said.

CHAPTER TWO

Adam gazed up at the vaulted roof of the German Gymnasium, its vast timber beams arching overhead. Today, the gymnasium was not as busy as it usually was but there were still more than a score of men in the main hall, engaged in a variety of activities. To Adam's left, one was swinging himself back and forth on the parallel bars; to his right stood several pommel horses, over which young men dressed in loose-fitting white shirts and trousers were leaping. In the centre of the hall, three pairs of boxers exchanged blows. A railed walkway ran all around the main hall and half a dozen spectators were leaning on the wooden rails, looking down on the athletic activities below.

It was a place he had only recently discovered. Rogerson, an acquaintance from the Marco Polo and a fervent advocate of the philosophy of *mens sana in corpore sano*, had recommended it to him: 'Best location in town for a bout of fisticuffs, old boy,' he had said. 'Always someone there prepared to go toe to toe with you.'

Adam, however, had disclaimed any interest. 'I think,' he had replied, 'perhaps I had enough of the noble art when I was at college.'

Rogerson had looked surprised, as if it was impossible that any man might tire of the joys of punching another, but remained undeterred. 'Not just boxing, old boy. Parallel bars, horizontal bars, Indian clubs, wrestling, fencing. Everything to harden the body and improve the mind. All for a negligible fee. You should toddle along and see what they have to offer.'

It was the last activity that Rogerson had mentioned which had caught Adam's attention. He had fenced for a short time in his final year at school and enjoyed it. He had occasionally, in recent months, thought it would be a good idea to take it up again. Here was the opportunity. He had made his way to the German Gymnasium, built and opened only a few years earlier in Pancras Road, and joined the ranks of its members. In the months since he had done so, he had become a twice-weekly visitor to the place.

'We have crossed our blades enough for the day, Señor Carver.' The man with whom he had been fencing bowed gravely in his direction and removed his face mask. Adam unfastened his own and returned the salute. Not for the first time, he wondered about the past history of his fencing instructor. Juan Alvarado was from the Argentine city of Buenos Aires – or, at least, he had several times spoken of it with the easy familiarity of someone who had lived there, but he had been obliged to leave the country and come to Europe a decade ago. His reasons for leaving were shrouded in mystery. Alvarado never spoke of them. Adam suspected that they were connected to the civil wars that had plagued Argentina for most of the decades since its independence from Spain. Alvarado had probably finished on the losing side in one of the many conflicts and decided that it was safer to travel into exile. Adam also suspected that the serious and distinguished-looking gentleman in early middle age who taught him fencing had found adjustment to a new life in London difficult. He spoke English fluently, if occasionally eccentrically, and hinted at the existence of a wife and children living in lodgings in Highgate with him, but he seemed, to Adam at least, a solitary, reserved man who had long ago decided that the best of life was behind him.

Now Alvarado bowed once again and, with the briefest of polite farewells, walked briskly out of the hall. Adam, carrying his rubber-tipped rapier and mask, followed him into the corridor. The Argentine had already disappeared from view. Only rarely did he linger for conversation after their practice.

Adam made his way to the changing rooms. Within half an hour, he was dressed in his own clothes and sitting in the comfortable library which the gymnasium also provided for its members, idly flicking through the pages of *The Cornhill Magazine*. He came across a fresh instalment of a serial about a character named Harry Richmond and began to read it, but his attention soon wandered. He had read none of the previous instalments and the prose of the story's author, a gentleman named Meredith, seemed curiously convoluted.

After a few minutes, Adam put the magazine to one side and leant back in his chair. Why *had* he agreed so readily to do what Sunman had asked of him? The truth was, of course, that he was bored. Since he had returned from Greece the previous autumn, he had had little to occupy his time. The weeks of searching for the gold of Philip of Macedon, which had culminated in Professor Fields's savage attack, had been difficult and dangerous but never dull. Coming back to London had meant a descent into an everyday normality which he had, he now realized, found hard to endure. He had taken up photography again but the recording of London's architecture, which had once fascinated him, proved a chore rather than a delight. He had put pen to paper to record his experiences at the monasteries of Meteora and in the hills of Turkey in Europe, but he had discovered that much of the truth about them needed to be omitted, and he had grown weary of the process. His world had all too rapidly become one of tedious routine. He had even begun to ask himself what he intended to do with the rest of life. And then, out of the blue, there was the Honourable Richard Sunman offering him an escape from that same routine. It might, of course, turn out to be the simplest of tasks to find the girl but, for some reason, Adam doubted it. There was more to her disappearance than Sunman was telling him. And whether the search proved brief and easy, or long and difficult, it would be something different to do.

Adam returned the copy of *The Cornhill Magazine* to the rack in which he had found it. He glanced briefly around the almost deserted library of the German Gymnasium. A red-bearded gentleman whom he recognized vaguely from previous visits nodded in his direction. Adam returned the salute and left the library with something of a spring in his step.

* * * * *

A newspaper boy was standing by the gates at the entrance to Doughty Street, bellowing about ''Orrible murder in 'Ackney'. Adam stopped to pay a penny for the late-afternoon edition of the *Daily News* from the urchin before turning into the street. Nodding to the porter in his wooden sentry box, and with the paper tucked under his arm, he walked fifty yards, took out a key and unlocked the door to the Georgian house in which he rented a set of first-floor rooms. Alert to the possibility that Mrs Gaffery might be in residence and intent upon conversation, he took the stairs at a gallop and was in front of the entrance to his own domain within seconds. He had no wish to listen to his formidable landlady expound her ideas on the ills of the world. Mrs Gaffery was a woman who knew her own mind and was not one to allow ignorance of a subject to get in the way of expressing a strong opinion on it. Adam was not always, or even often, in the mood to stand by the door to her rooms, nodding his head repeatedly as she told him what she thought of Mr Gladstone and Mr Disraeli, the recent marriage of Princess Louise, and the reasons why the French could never be trusted.

Safe now, he took a second key from his pocket and let himself into his rooms. As he entered his sitting room, Adam placed his hat on top of the sideboard and threw his coat and the newspaper he had just bought into an armchair. When he heard the sound of wood scraping on the floor in the next room, he realized was not alone.

Adam's manservant, Quintus Devlin, was already at home. He was sitting on a stool in the kitchen, reading a cheap edition of *David Copperfield* with a frown of concentration on his forehead. Quint was not a regular reader, nor was he a swift one. To Adam's certain knowledge, he had been reading the Dickens novel for the last four months and he had still not progressed much beyond page 200. His habit of returning to re-read again and again passages which had caught his attention was slowing him down, and Adam suspected that the one book might last his servant the rest of his life. Quint was clearly intrigued, however, by the imaginative world of The Great Inimitable. He would occasionally deliver his opinion of certain of the novel's characters, sometimes speaking of 'them days' after the last time he had been looking at the book, which meant that Adam would initially be puzzled by his remarks: 'This cove what can't keep his 'ands on his rhino,' Quint would say. 'This 'ere Micawber,' he would continue, noticing Adam's raised eyebrow. ''E's a prize duffer, ain't 'e? What a bleedin' juggins and no mistake. I reckon 'e got some kind of knock in 'is cradle. 'E wouldn't know 'ow many beans make five if 'e could count 'em on 'is fingers.'

On this occasion, Quint looked up as his master entered the kitchen. 'Working with bottles ain't that bad, you know,' he remarked.

'Whoever said it was, Quint?'

'The Copperfield bloke.' The manservant waved the book in the air. 'Whining on about 'ow he 'ad such a time of it when 'e was a lad, pasting labels on bottles in 'is old man's warehouse.'

'His stepfather's warehouse, was it not?'

Quint shrugged. 'Father, stepfather. Ain't no matter. The point is I done it. Worked with bottles. And it ain't that bad. I've done much worse.'

'I don't doubt it, Quint.' Adam could well believe that his servant had, in the course of a chequered career, faced more unpleasant tasks than the labelling of bottles. Abandoned as a baby on the steps of the St Nicholas Hospital for Young Foundlings in Ely Place, he had been christened Quintus by the Reverend Malachi Merridew, spiritual director of the institution, who had already been presented with four other orphaned infants that week and had turned to the Latin numbering system in his search for names for them. 'Devlin' had come from a label on the blanket in which he had been wrapped when he had been left in Ely Place. 'The property,' the label had read, 'of Devlin's Boarding House, Ardee Street, Dublin.'

Adam had met Quint on his first foray to European Turkey. Adam had then been a gentlemanly companion to Professor Fields, much interested in the Ancient Greek past; Quint had been an ungentlemanly servant, interested mainly in drinking and brawling. However, they had formed an unexpected alliance and, on their return to London, Adam had offered Quint the position of man-servant. Quint, rather to the surprise of both men, had accepted. He had accompanied his master to Athens and Macedonia once again the previous year and been a witness to the terrible crimes and strange death of Professor Fields. Now he was perched on a stool in rooms in Doughty Street, regaling Adam with his views on David Copperfield.

'This is no time to be discussing the finer points of Dickens's work, Quint.' The young man took the novel from his manservant's hands and placed it carefully on the kitchen table. 'Nor your past history of employment. We have work to do. We have a young woman to find.' As swiftly and concisely as he could, Adam explained the commission he had been given the previous day. He did not mention Sunman's name, although he assumed it would have meant little to Quint had he done so.

His servant listened, chewing stolidly on a plug of tobacco.

'I ain't sure I've got this,' he said, once Adam had finished. 'If some cove wants to cure 'is horn by bedding a dollymop, why's anyone worry about it?'

'The affair is not quite as simple as you seem to think, Quint. The gentleman in question is, I suspect, in a senior position in the Foreign Office. He cannot be jumping in and out of the arms of such as Dolly Delaney without causing trouble.'

'Even swells need a bit of fun.'

'Yes, but their fun must be discreet fun. And, in this case, it seems it has not been.'

Quint shrugged, as if acknowledging that the ways of his betters were a mystery to him. 'So we got to lay our 'ands on this Dolly mort?' he asked.

'In a manner of speaking, yes. Tomorrow you will make enquiries in the pubs around Drury Lane. Stand a drink or two. Find out if anyone knows anything about the girl.'

'And you'll be doing the round of the boozing-kens as well?'

'No, I shall not.' Adam headed towards his sitting room. 'I shall be visiting my old friend Cosmo Jardine.'

CHAPTER THREE

Adam thought about his long friendship with Cosmo Jardine as he and Quint made their way towards Covent Garden. He and Cosmo had known one another for years, both at school and at Cambridge. Like Adam, Cosmo had left college without a degree. Adam had been forced to do so by the death of his father and the disappearance of the family fortune; his friend, much to the outrage of his own father, the dean of a West Country cathedral, had been too idle to pursue his studies and more interested in painting and sketching than in reading Homer and Cicero.

Jardine had decided he would be an artist. Settling in London with little more than the lease on part of a cheap studio in Chelsea and a letter of introduction to John Millais, Cosmo had proved himself surprisingly committed to his new profession. He had even had some small successes. Works had been accepted at the Academy, although they had been hung so high that opera glasses had been required to view them. A Yorkshire mill-owner with a taste for nude women in the kinds of classical settings that made them respectable rather than shocking had commissioned a 'Judgement of Paris' from him. Paintings of Cosmo's own preferred subject matter – Arthurian legend – had been less easy to sell. A huge canvas of King Pellinore and the Questing Beast still languished in the Chelsea studio. Cosmo's debts had mounted. Eventually, as his creditors clamoured for legal action to be taken against him, he had been forced to take up painting scenery for a theatre. Much to his own astonishment, he had discovered he enjoyed the work and now, although the need

19

to earn money was less pressing, he continued to make his way to Drury Lane most mornings.

After saying farewell to Quint, who disappeared swiftly into a pub on Long Acre, Adam found his friend in a corner of one of the large props rooms at the back of the Prince Albert theatre.

Cosmo Jardine was standing at the edge of a huge backdrop, depicting what looked like Derby Day at Epsom, which was stretched flat across the floor. He was dressed in an ancient white frock coat, liberally speckled with paint, and was dabbing at a distant corner of the set with a long brush. He was so absorbed in his task that Adam was at his shoulder before he noticed him. 'Hullo,' he said in surprise. 'What brings you to this dark corner of Drury Lane? I believe this is the first time you've deigned to visit me in my humble place of work.'

'You are right,' Adam said. 'I have not been here before.'

'You were once so regular a visitor to my studio that I began to think I would have to ask you for a contribution towards the rent. But, since I became an artisan toiling away in the theatre, you have deserted me.'

'I apologize, Cosmo, I have been guilty of neglecting you.'

'You have indeed. But I forgive you.' The painter swung the enormous brush he was using away from the backdrop and propped it against a wooden trestle. The brush dripped red paint onto the floor. Jardine wiped his hands on his white coat as he looked at his friend more closely. 'However, I harbour a strong suspicion that there are other reasons for your visit today beyond mere sociability.'

'Is it so obvious?'

'Only to one who knows you as well as I do. Come, tell me what motive you have for bearding me here in my den, beyond the mere pleasure of seeing an old friend.'

'I'm looking for a girl who has gone missing. Her name is Dolly Delaney.' Adam took out the cabinet card which Sunman had given him and showed it to his friend.

'Ah, Dolly,' Jardine said, glancing briefly at the photograph. 'Who could forget her? I thought I hadn't seen her for a day or two. She's only been here a few weeks but her presence has noticeably brightened up the place.'

'You knew her, then?'

'Alas, not in the biblical sense. She is one of the chorus girls here.' Cosmo looked hard at his friend. 'But is there a reason why you are employing the past tense in speaking of her?'

'As I say, she has disappeared. That is all.'

'Good. I would hate to think that anything unpleasant had happened to her. She is a sweet thing. But why are you in search of her? Why are you charging around like a paladin in a medieval romance, intent on rescuing his lady?' Jardine looked sidelong at his friend. 'Ah, I have it. You *knew* her yourself.'

'Your mind runs on such predictable tracks, Cosmo.' Adam smiled. 'I have never met the girl. I did not know of her existence until two days ago.'

'So, what other reasons could there be for your interest in the fair Delaney?' Thumb and forefinger under his chin, Jardine eyed Adam in a parody of a man engaged in deep thought. 'I know,' he said, snapping his fingers. 'She is, in truth, a runaway from some landed family, fleeing her ancestral home to avoid an unwanted marriage. And her noble father, for reasons best known to himself, has employed you to seek her out and drag her back to the altar.'

Adam laughed. 'I don't suppose there are many daughters of the gentry employed in London's theatres.'

'You would be surprised. Actresses will happen even in the best-regulated families,' Jardine said off-handedly, turning to look once more at the backdrop on the floor. His thoughts were clearly centred more on his work than the fate of the missing girl. 'And dancers. You would be surprised by the backgrounds of one or two of Dolly's colleagues in the chorus here. I am told that we even have a vicar's daughter. Although that may be nothing more than rumour and calumny.'

Their conversation was interrupted by two stagehands, who passed behind Adam and his friend. A few moments later, they were staggering and grunting under the weight of a vast Chesterfield sofa,

21

labouring noisily to move its red leather bulk out of the props room and into the corridor outside.

'However,' the young artist continued, watching the men disappear through the door with their burden, 'I do not think that Dolly's family would be found in Burke's or Debrett's. Or even in Crockford's Clerical Directory. More likely to see her kinsfolk on the passenger lists of boats from Dublin to Liverpool.'

'I'd assumed from the name that she was – is – Irish.'

'In origins, I'm sure – Dolly herself is as Cockney as they come. To listen to her drop her aitches is an education in the language of the ordinary Londoner.'

'But no aristocratic branches of the family.'

'No, I think not. So that explanation of your interest cannot be correct. Perhaps she has fallen from virtue and you have been employed by one of the do-gooding societies to rescue her from the consequences of her sin?'

'You are wrong again, Cosmo. I have not found work with a charitable organization.'

'I am glad to hear it. Unlike the maiden ladies who run these societies, I do not believe for a moment that the majority of the tarts in London are woebegone Magdalens, forever preparing to throw themselves off Waterloo Bridge.' Jardine now noticed the red paint, which was continuing to drip from the brush. He moved towards the trestle, picked up a rag from the floor and wound it around the head of the brush. 'Most of them are quite happy to practise their trade, and find it advantageous to do so. They may well be better off than they would be working as maidservants or factory girls.'

'Perhaps you are right, Cosmo. Although many must be wretched enough. But we are digressing from the subject of Dolly Delaney.'

'I'm still in pursuit of the reason for your sudden interest in her.'

'It is a long story, Cosmo, and not one with which I can entertain you at present.'

'Have you no better means of employing your time, old chap?' Jardine hoisted the brush, its head now covered with the rag, and carried it across the room. He propped it against the wall, where a dozen similar brushes stood like soldiers on parade. 'Nothing better to do than run around town after a missing girl? She will turn up again shortly, I am sure.'

'I am told her disappearance may be of more significance than we can imagine,' Adam said.

'I have often wondered why you do not take another excursion to Thessaly,' Jardine said, ignoring his friend's remark entirely. 'Did you not once say that the manuscript you found in the monastery there held clues to the location of some treasure? Macedonian gold, was it not? Why not go in search of that, rather than touring London in pursuit of Dolly who, however decorative, is no more than a dancing girl. Dancing girls are ten a penny, whereas gold is a thing of beauty and a joy for ever. I would join you in looking for it myself but the climate in Greece would not suit me.'

'The manuscript is useless, Cosmo. I thought I had said as much to you long ago. Fields had it strapped to his body. When the gun went off and shot him, it was shredded. The little that remained legible told us nothing of gold or treasure.'

'Perhaps there is another manuscript. Gathering dust in the library of a Greek monastery.'

Adam had no chance to respond to his friend's suggestion. From the bowels of the theatre a penetrating soprano voice suddenly erupted into life, singing an aria from Meyerbeer's *Robert le Diable* as if her life depended on it. 'Who in the devil's name is that?' he asked, looking at Jardine in astonishment as the singer's high notes continued to echo around the props room.

The painter had moved away from the row of giant brushes, wandering over to his backdrop and dropping to his haunches. He was staring intently at the bottom left corner. 'That will be Letitia von Trunckel,' he said over his shoulder. 'Tizzi to her friends – of whom there are few. She entertains audiences here on Wednesday nights and Saturday matinees with her renditions of the classical repertoire.'

'A powerful voice,' Adam said.

'Not so much *bel canto* as "can belto", you might say.'

'If you were a *Punch* hack in desperate search of a pun, you might.'

'There are worse occupations than writing for *Punch*.' Jardine rose to his feet. 'I have even thought of trying my own hand at comic verse sometime.'

'Perhaps you could set them to music and persuade Fräulein von Trunckel to sing them in the music halls. I am sure they would be a great success.'

'Oh, never in the halls,' Jardine said in mock disgust. 'What do you find in most of them? Dull songs. Jokes so old they have grey whiskers. Stale sentiment. The only pleasure is to be found in admiring the ladies on promenade.'

'Is that not the case at most places of entertainment? Is it not true of this theatre?'

'You are correct, of course, my dear chap. Half of our evening's entertainment here is nothing more than a leg drama. The audience, or certainly the male portion of it, comes to see the girls in the chorus dancing, not to hear the thespians prating. And Tizzi's charms lie as much in her *embonpoint* as in her vocal cords.' Jardine sighed ostentatiously. 'No one, but no one, comes to admire the splendour of the painted backdrops. My talents are wasted here. And I an artist whose works have graced the Academy walls.'

'Oh, what Philistines people are,' Adam said, smiling. In truth, he knew, his friend was a sociable creature and happier here amidst the hustle and bustle of the theatre than he had ever been in his isolated Chelsea studio. 'But I ask you again about Miss Dolly Delaney.'

In the distance, the very loud sounds of Letitia von Trunckel rehearsing had ceased and been replaced by the quieter ones of a pianist, slowly picking out the tune of a Chopin *valse*.

'You are persistent, Adam, if nothing else. The person to whom you need to speak is McIlwraith.'

'The manager of the theatre?'

'He has a more enviable responsibility – he is the man in charge of the dancers.' Jardine paused as the Chesterfield sofa, last seen exiting the door, came back into view and, borne by the two sweating mechanics, made its way across the props room again. 'Although, taking his cue from his dour and doubtless puritanical Scottish ancestors, he shows little signs of admiring the female form divine. Doubtless that is why he was selected for the job.'

'This man McIlwraith is here now? Perhaps I could speak to him?'

'There is no show tonight. I doubt he will be in the theatre. But he will be here tomorrow.' Jardine examined his watch, which he was carrying loose in a pocket of his paint-bespattered white coat. 'It is approaching five,' he said. 'I have laboured long enough for one day. It is time to divest myself of this coat of many colours and lay down my brushes. I shall be dining at Verrey's tonight, Adam. Perhaps you would care to join me?'

'I cannot this evening, Cosmo. Another time.'

'You are becoming a recluse, my friend. Skulking in your Doughty Street garret, eating bread and cheese and drinking cheap ale.'

Adam laughed. 'Nonsense,' he said. 'I dine at the Marco Polo at least twice in the week. Not all of us can afford the extravagance of Verrey's.'

'Of course, a man can dine at his club more cheaply than elsewhere,' Jardine conceded. 'In truth, I cannot afford Verrey's myself, but I allow my creditors to worry about the expense.'

'I promise you that we shall both dine there before too long. I shall begin to put aside monies for the occasion immediately.'

'I shall hold you to your promise. Meanwhile, I shall speak to McIlwraith and tell him to expect a visit from you soon. Tomorrow?' Adam nodded. 'I am sure he will be able to shed some light on the mystery surrounding the lovely Dolly's whereabouts.'

* * * * *

The following morning found Adam once more at the theatre where Dolly had been working. Quint had again been despatched to the pubs of the neighbourhood to find out what he could. He had not seemed reluctant to go.

As Adam climbed the few stone steps to the Prince Albert's

entrance, he could not help but notice, hanging on either side of the main doors, immense placards, which advertised in glowing colours the thrills and delights to be experienced inside. One depicted Letitia von Trunckel in the famous mad scene from Donizetti's *Lucia di Lammermoor* – dishevelled and enormous, the soprano was shown wandering through a baronial hall in her wedding dress. Adam wondered briefly if Cosmo had created the poster but decided it looked too crude to be his friend's work.

Adam pushed open the door of the theatre and looked about him. There was no one in sight. The foyer was large and marble-floored. A wood-panelled box office stood to the right. It had not yet opened. The theatre, Adam thought, had the strange, slightly eerie atmosphere that all such establishments have when they are not in use. He moved forward, his shoes clicking on the hard floor.

A figure emerged from behind a green velvet curtain and hurried towards him. Adam was about to speak to him but the man, raising his hat briefly, was past and out into the street before he could question him. Adam approached the curtain and pulled it aside. A dark corridor led into the bowels of the theatre and he followed it. About twenty yards along the corridor, a gas light attached to the wall was giving off a dim light. A small boy in a crumpled red jacket and black trousers was standing beneath the light. He had a mouth organ pressed to his lips and he tootled a half-tune on it before staring malevolently at Adam.

'You lookin' for someone, mister?'

'Mr McIlwraith.'

'We ain't open, you know. 'E'll be rehearsing the tarts.'

Adam peered further along the gloomy corridor. Was there nobody here apart from this oddly menacing urchin? 'I appreciate that the theatre does not open for some hours, but Mr McIlwraith is expecting me.'

The boy sniffed noisily as if to suggest that he doubted the truth of what he was being told and continued to gaze unblinkingly at Adam. A good ten seconds passed and Adam was about to speak again when the child jerked his thumb over his shoulder. 'Big room down there,' he said. 'Second door on the right.'

Adam nodded his thanks and walked past the boy, who scowled at him as he did so. When the young man reached the door that had been indicated, he turned and looked back. The urchin was still there, leaning against the wall. He saw Adam watching him and stuck out his tongue.

Adam pushed open the door and went into the rehearsal room. It was flooded with light from a row of high windows. After the gloom of the corridor, the contrast was blinding and he was forced to shield his eyes briefly with his hand. When he was able to focus properly, he could see that this room, in contrast to the rest of the Prince Albert, was a hive of activity. A dozen young women stood in a row, holding a bar that ran along one wall, and swinging their left legs in the air. A man was watching them intently.

As Adam walked towards the centre of the room, several of the dancers noticed him and ceased their exercises. The man with them looked over his shoulder and saw that they had a visitor. 'Carry on, girls,' he shouted, and crossed to where Adam was standing, trying not to stare too closely at the legs on display.

'You must be Mr Carver,' the man said.

Adam acknowledged that he was.

'McIlwraith, sir. Hamish McIlwraith. Delighted to meet you, Mr Carver.' He shook Adam's hand energetically. 'Any friend of Mr Jardine's is a friend of mine. Surprised you could find us, tucked away as we are.'

Adam explained about the small boy who had directed him.

'Ah, Billy Bantam. He ain't no child, sir. Older than the devil he is, I sometimes think, and twice as wicked. He's a dwarf, Mr Carver, a performing dwarf. Been on the stage since Macready's day. Don't you go getting the wrong side of Billy, Mr Carver. He's a bad'un when he wants to be.'

Adam said he would be wary of the little man if he saw him again and Mr McIlwraith beamed with delight, as if Adam had promised him a rare and costly present. The dancing master bore little resemblance to the caricature of the dour Scotsman Cosmo had painted.

27

He was, in fact, short and plump and markedly jolly. He was also perspiring freely. He smiled amiably at Adam from a brick-red face and reached out to pump his hand again with great energy. He did not sound any more Scottish than he looked. To judge from his voice, he hailed from the city in which he worked. 'Mr Jardine tells me as 'ow you might be interested in our Dolly.'

'I would welcome the opportunity to speak with the young woman, certainly.'

'Ah, there's plenty of men interested in Dolly.' McIlwraith winked ostentatiously. 'There's a gentleman by the name of Mr Wyndham, for instance. He was round the stage door for weeks asking after 'er.'

'Wyndham?'

'He's what the Frenchies call a bow idle, Mr Wyndham is,' McIlwraith went on. 'Very handsome man. All the girls was most impressed. But it was Dolly as began to walk out with him.'

'Might Miss Delaney be with this gentleman now?'

'She might be.' McIlwraith took a white handkerchief from his waistcoat pocket and mopped his brow. 'She might not be.' He tucked the handkerchief back into his waistcoat and continued to grin broadly at Adam.

'But I am correct in thinking that she has not been here at work for some days—?' the young man said.

The dancing master's face became suddenly serious. 'She's a delicate flower, Dolly is,' he said. 'She come to me last week. "Mac," she sez – they all call me "Mac", the girls – "Mac", she sez, "I'm feeling all of a flutter. I ain't at all well." "Dolly," I sez, "you're as thin as a rasher of wind, and as pale as a candle. You don't look the ticket at all. You'd best get yourself off home." So, no, she ain't been at work of late.'

'But you have no reason to be concerned for her? Beyond the fact that she was unwell?'

McIlwraith looked puzzled.

'She has not been seen at her lodgings in the last week,' Adam explained.

The dancing master puckered his lips and blew out a breath of air. He stared at the floor as if the answer to the question of Dolly's whereabouts might be written on its wooden boards. 'Maybe she *has* been with young Wyndham,' he said eventually.

One of the dancers, a tall girl with dark curls and a willowy figure, had detached herself from the group practising their steps and moved across the room. She was now standing behind McIlwraith and listening to the conversation. 'You ain't goin' to find Dolly with that time-waster Wyndham,' she said. 'Whatever 'e sez.' She jerked her thumb contemptuously at the dancing master.

'Get off with you, Hetty,' McIlwraith said, turning around and seeing her for the first time. He now seemed much less jolly. In fact, he looked close to furious. 'The gentleman don't want to be bothered with your nonsense.'

'Dolly wasn't interested in a little mama's boy.'

'As I said before, Mr Carver, Mr Wyndham is a very 'andsome man.' McIlwraith, doing his very best to ignore the girl, returned his attention to Adam. 'Much like your good self, if I may be so bold.' The dancing master aimed an ingratiating smile in Adam's direction.

''Andsome is as 'andsome does,' Hetty said. 'And what Wyndham does is try to get his fingers in your frills. The girls knows all about 'im and the likes of 'im. No money, but all over you like an octerpus. And 'e ain't that much of a looker, anyways. Dolly wouldn't go with him.'

'You'd do best to keep your mouth shut, my girl,' McIlwraith snapped, rounding on her again.

'Do you know where Miss Delaney is now?' Adam addressed his remark to the girl. She shook her head. 'So, for all you know, she might be with this gentleman named Wyndham?'

'I tell you, she ain't with 'im.' The girl looked Adam in the eye, ignoring the dancing master, who was fussing and fretting at her side.

Adam would have welcomed the chance to speak further with Hetty but he felt constrained by McIlwraith's presence. He said no more.

'Well, if you ain't interested, you ain't interested,' the girl said after a pause, and flounced off to join the other dancers.

Adam watched her go. He would have to talk to her again when she was alone. He turned once more to resume his conversation with McIlwraith, who seemed to have recovered his good humour.

'Hetty's a lively one,' the dancing master said, with what looked very much like a wink. 'Always jumping around like a pea on a griddle. I wouldn't take too much notice of what she says, if I was you.'

'Well, perhaps I could speak to this gentleman named Wyndham. Do you have an address for him?'

McIlwraith waved his arm vaguely in the direction of the door leading to the outer corridor, as if he suspected that Wyndham might be lurking there. 'He lodges somewhere north of the Park, I believe. Tyburnia. A coming area, I've heard.'

'But you do not know exactly where.'

The dancing master shook his head.

'Well, perhaps I could write Miss Delaney a note and leave it here with you,' Adam said. 'I would like very much to speak to her and know that she is safe and well.'

'Lord, Mr Carver, you might just as well send a letter to a milestone on the Dover road.' The man could scarcely contain his amusement, wheezing with the effort of attempting to do so. 'Dolly can't read letters, sir. Not even what the Frenchies call billy deuces. She can't read anything at all.'

* * * * *

Adam stood in the marble-floored foyer of the Prince Albert and wondered where he should go next. The theatre was no longer eerily deserted. The box office was open, and people were coming and going through the heavy swing doors that led out to Drury Lane. The young man watched them for a while as he considered whether he had learned anything of interest. McIlwraith had seemed eager to point his finger at the man Wyndham as a possible beau for Dolly; the dancer Hetty had been equally adamant that her friend would have had nothing to do with him. He would have to speak to Hetty again when McIlwraith was not present. As he pondered the matter, he noticed a familiar figure enter the theatre. It was Cosmo Jardine.

'Ah, the very man,' the painter said as he saw his friend. 'I thought perhaps you would be here. How was our Caledonian dancing master? Was he able to enlighten you as to the whereabouts of the fair Delaney?'

Adam shook his head. 'All he knows is that he sent her home last week because she was feeling unwell. He has not seen her since. But I have also been told that Dolly has not been at her lodgings these last few days.'

The painter took his friend by the arm and guided him to the street. 'Let us take a stroll towards Long Acre,' he said, pointing down Drury Lane with a flourish. 'I have news for you myself.'

The two young men ambled arm-in-arm through the city crowds. Adam waited to hear what his friend's news was but Jardine seemed in no hurry to impart it. Instead, he launched himself into a denunciation of the Prince Albert's manager. 'The man is impossible. No sooner have I finished my Herculean labours on a dozen flats for the next production than he asks, nay, *demands*, that I should create another for a scene he has inserted at the last minute. I wouldn't mind, but it is only what we call a carpenter scene.'

'Which is . . .?'

'One which exists solely so that the carpenters and stagehands can put up the sets for the next act. Why does he need an artist for such work? Any Tom, Dick or Harry could do it.'

Jardine was full of mock indignation but Adam was not listening to him very closely. 'I don't suppose you know a chap named Wyndham, do you?' he asked, as the painter paused briefly to take breath.

Jardine looked puzzled.

'Some stage-door Lothario who pesters the girls,' his friend went on. 'Who pestered Dolly.'

'Ah, *that* Wyndham.' The artist took a step to one side to allow a smartly dressed woman with a pug dog on a lead to pass him.

'I thought for one horrid moment you meant Ben Wyndham of Lincoln's Inn.'

'And who might Ben Wyndham be?'

'A lawyer to whom I owe a trifling sum. I have no desire to talk of *him*.'

'What of this other Wyndham?'

'What is there to say? Perfectly ordinary fellow. Comes from a highly respectable Berkshire family.'

'This highly respectable family in Berkshire—?'

'Place near Newbury, I believe.'

'This highly respectable family with a place near Newbury. Would they be delighted to hear of their son and heir making eyes at a Drury Lane dancer?'

'Probably not. As I say, far too respectable.'

'Might they pay the Drury Lane dancer to vanish from the scene?'

'It is possible, I suppose,' Jardine said slowly. 'But it is not very likely, is it? And why should Dolly accept the money? She would see more long-term advantage in keeping her talons firmly in the flesh of young Wyndham – that is, always assuming that she wished to marry into respectability. Truth to tell, Dolly never seemed to me the mercenary kind. Her friend Hetty perhaps, but not Dolly. No, I think you are barking up the wrong tree there, old man.'

'I have met Hetty.'

'Quite the harpy, is she not?'

'She seemed a young lady of strong opinions, certainly.'

'Has she no notion where her friend has gone?'

'I had little chance to speak to her. I shall question her again when McIlwraith is not with her.'

'It may not be necessary. After you left yesterday, I made my own enquiries about the absent Dolly.'

'That was kind of you, Cosmo.' Adam was surprised. It was unusual for his friend to go much out of his way to assist others.

'No trouble, my dear chap,' the painter said airily, as they made their way into Long Acre. 'Always happy to oblige if I can.'

'Did your enquiries prove fruitful?'

'In a manner of speaking. I asked questions of another young lady in the chorus. Lottie Granger.'

'And Lottie had something to tell you?'

'She was not initially forthcoming. No woman wishes to hear a man talk too frequently of another. Particularly not in the intimate circumstances in which our conversation took place.'

'She was in your bed,' Adam guessed.

Jardine inclined his head slightly. 'You put it with uncustomary bluntness, Adam, but yes, she was. Lottie is a young lady whose company I have been enjoying for some weeks past.'

'And what did Lottie have to say? When you were not whispering sweet nothings into her shell-like ears?'

'That ours was not the only theatre to be benefiting from Dolly's beauty. She was also working from time to time at some cheap leg shop in the East End.'

'A penny gaff? What on earth was she doing there?'

'According to the lovely Lottie, she was very badly in need of money. It is not easy to find one job, leave alone two, in the West End, but a girl with Dolly's charms would be welcomed with open arms further east.'

'She would be paid little enough there.'

Jardine shrugged. 'True,' he said, 'but Lottie was adamant. Dolly was desperate and was willing to work wherever she could.'

'What is the name of this low theatre where she found employment?'

'Sadly, Lottie could not remember. It is in Whitechapel. That was all she could recall.'

'She said nothing more?'

'Our discussions took a different direction. We left Dolly behind. But there cannot be very many theatrical establishments in Whitechapel, can there?'

'I think you might be surprised, Cosmo.' Adam knew little more of the East End than his friend, but he suspected that the area was home to at least as many places of entertainment as the West End. They would just be smaller, cheaper and dirtier. It would not be as easy to find the one in which Dolly was moonlighting as Cosmo thought.

The two men walked a little further, turning left out of Long Acre and into Bow Street. They stopped opposite the Magistrates' Court and gazed idly across at the policeman who stood outside it, beneath the gas lamp and the carving of the royal arms.

'So a young lady called Lottie has been warming the cockles of your heart of late,' Adam said. He felt almost envious of his friend; he had enjoyed little female company himself in recent months. 'I did not know you had developed a taste for dancing girls.'

'What are men such as ourselves to do, Adam?' Jardine asked. 'We are young and full of animal spirits. Abstinence is out of the question. And the kind of woman one might think of marrying would not dream of indulging our male needs before the ring is on her finger and the honeymoon in Venice has begun. What, I repeat, are we to do? Are we to become pale, unhealthy celibates? To whom are we to turn?'

'Your questions, I am assuming, are rhetorical ones?'

'They are, old man, but I will take it upon myself to answer them even so. The last one, at least. Ladies of the chorus. They provide the solution to our problems. They are long of leg, lovely of feature and untroubled by the constraints that make their sisters in society such dull company. I am surprised it has not struck you before now.'

'I shall bear your words of wisdom in mind in the future,' Adam said.

'I would certainly advise you to do so. Here's your man.' Jardine nodded in the direction of Quint, who had just emerged from the door of a pub and was crossing the road towards them. 'I am due at the theatre. I shall leave you to ponder what I have said.' Cosmo waved his hand briefly and was gone.

Quint approached, breathing beery fumes. 'I done what you asked,' he said. 'Been standing drinks in there' – he jerked his thumb over his shoulder at the pub he had just left – 'like Lord Muck on election day.'

'With successful consequences, I hope.'

34

Quint took off the battered hat he was wearing and ran his hand through what little remained of his hair. 'Mebbe,' he said, replacing his hat. 'Better'n yesterday, anyways.'

The two men began to make their way through the Covent Garden market. It was approaching noon and much of the business of the place had been done hours earlier, but the piazza was still thronged with people and the mingled scents of flowers and fruits hung in the air. The noise was such that Adam had to bow his head slightly to catch what his manservant, though never the quietest of conversationalists, was saying to him.

'Place is called the Admiral Rodney,' Quint went on. 'I'm standing at the bar, rinsing my ivories with a pint of half-and-half. Got myself talking to two coves next to me. Blow me down, if they ain't both manservants like me, looking after gents like you. Now, one of 'em ain't no use at all. 'Is bloke's some kind of old lawyer, rooms in the Temple, never been to the theatre since Joey Grimaldi was alive.'

'An ancient indeed, then.'

Quint nodded but, intent on continuing his story, wasn't really listening to his master. 'The other one, though – 'is name's Dobson. Red-faced, lazy eye, ugly as a bear. 'E's swallering the beers I buy him like his insides is on fire.'

'But he has a tale to tell.'

'Turns out 'is bloke's at the Prince Albert most nights in the week. Idlin' around the stage door and lookin' goats and monkeys at the dancing girls as they come out. Dobson reckons 'e's got a partickler fancy for a blonde. Sounds like our mort.'

'Let me hazard a guess,' Adam said. 'The name of Dobson's master is Wyndham.'

''Ow the 'ell d'you know that?' Quint said indignantly.

'I have my own sources of information.' The young man smiled benignly at his servant, who continued to look disgruntled. 'If we did but know where to find this Wyndham, we might call the morning a success.'

'Ah, well, then that's where I'm one up on you,' Quint said, with a sudden note of triumph in his voice.

'You have an address for him?'

'The name of 'is club. Accordin' to Dobson, if Wyndham ain't round the theatre with his tongue 'anging down to his chest, 'e's at the C'rinthian losing his tin at billiards.'

'The Corinthian?'

'I ain't 'eard of it neither,' Quint said. 'Somewhere the other side of Piccadilly, far as I can tell from what the man said.'

By now the two men had passed through the market. As the church bells began to strike for midday, they turned north towards Doughty Street and home.

CHAPTER FOUR

T he room was dark and shadowy. It was early evening and the spring sunshine had faded. The gas lights had not been lit and only the flickering flames of the fire provided any additional illumination.

'This is Harry Vernon, Carver.' Sunman gestured towards the man standing by the fire. 'He is the gentleman of whom I spoke. The gentleman is as interested as we are in locating the whereabouts of Miss Delaney. Harry, may I introduce you to my old friend Adam Carver, who has been kind enough to undertake the task of finding her.'

Vernon was in early middle age. Plump and round-faced, he looked like an overgrown baby improbably stuffed into evening dress. When they shook hands, Adam could feel the softness and slight clamminess of Vernon's skin. The man was trying to maintain his sangfroid but he was clearly nervous and embarrassed.

All three of them were in a private room at Adam's club, the Marco Polo. To the young man's immense surprise, Sunman had told him that he was also a member of the club, which was located in a large Italianate building in Pall Mall. One of the requirements for membership of the Marco Polo was extensive travel in some far-flung region of the world. Adam had not been aware that Sunman had fulfilled this requirement; nor had he ever seen him in the building. As diplomatically as he could, he had said as much to his friend. The young aristocrat had merely shrugged – there was much, the slight raising of Sunman's shoulders unmistakably said, which Adam did not know.

'It's a pleasure to meet you, Carver,' Vernon said, looking as if it was anything but. 'I have heard much about you. I am hoping – we are all hoping – that you will soon be able to let us know where Dolly is. There is no word of her as yet, I presume?'

'It seems likely that she is working in a theatre in the East End, Mr Vernon.'

'The East End?' Vernon sounded baffled. 'Why would she be in the East End?'

'Because she no longer wishes to be seen in the West End?' Adam suggested.

'You must track her down there,' Vernon said hurriedly. 'The girl must be found.'

'The girl will be found, Harry.' Another voice entered the conversation. Adam turned in surprise to see a gaunt man with dark hair and beard rise from an armchair facing the fireplace and move towards him. The man was probably in his late thirties but looked older. He held out his hand. 'The name is Waterton. Gilbert Waterton. I am a friend of poor Harry here.'

Adam, who had had no notion that anyone else was in the room, took Waterton's hand. In contrast to Vernon's, it was as dry and rough as sandpaper.

'She has deserted Drury Lane in favour of Whitechapel High Street, has she?' the newcomer to the conversation remarked. 'Can you be certain of that fact?'

Adam glanced briefly in the direction of Sunman, who nodded, almost imperceptibly.

'Not certain, no,' Adam replied, 'but it looks to be a strong possibility. I spoke to people in the theatre where she was working. Most of them had no idea where she had gone, but one of her fellow members of the chorus thought that she had a second job in a penny gaff out east.'

'A penny gaff?' Vernon sounded horrified. 'What in God's name would she be doing in a penny gaff?'

'Much the same as she was doing in the West End theatre, I would guess,' Waterton said drily. 'Displaying her legs for the delectation of the audience.'

Vernon began to pace restlessly around the room. The others watched him. Adam noticed Sunman and Waterton exchange a glance, and he wondered how to interpret it. Were they sympathetic to the plump man's plight? Or were they irritated, even angry, with him for his imprudence? Probably both.

Vernon came to a halt by the fire, staring into it as if in search of comfort in its flames. 'I have made the most terrible mistake of my life,' he said flatly.

'You must not blame yourself, Harry.' Waterton stepped forward and placed his hand lightly on his friend's shoulder.

'There is no getting away from it, Gilbert. The fault is mine. I allowed myself to indulge in an affair with this wretched girl.'

'A peccadillo, my dear Harry, a peccadillo. Many a man has allowed his passions to get the better of his discretion.'

'But my sin – my *sin*, Gilbert, not my peccadillo – has not only put my soul in jeopardy' – Waterton waved his hand dismissively and Adam could not be sure whether he was making light of Vernon's sin or of his soul – 'but has put the interests of the nation at risk,' the plump man continued. The room was by no means warm, despite the fire in the hearth, but he was now sweating. 'It may have done terrible damage to my queen and country.'

In his pacing, he had now come to a high-backed Queen Anne chair that was pushed against the wall. He sank into it and, leaning forward, rested his head in his hands.

'You grow melodramatic, Harry,' Waterton said. 'Mr Carver does not wish to hear this. We will talk of your concerns later, if we must. For now, we should concentrate only on finding Miss Delaney.'

Vernon remained in the same position, face hidden. Adam was puzzled. Something in the man's elaborate *mea culpa* did not quite ring true. Adam felt as if he was in the audience at a theatre, watching an actor perform the role of a penitent. And yet there was surely no reason to doubt that Vernon did regret what had happened. How could he not?

Sunman, whose presence in the room Adam had almost forgotten, now stepped out of the shadows into which he had retreated. 'I

39

hope that we can still place our trust in you, Adam,' he said.

Adam briefly wondered what his further involvement might entail but he nodded his head to indicate that they could.

'Good,' Sunman said, rather peremptorily. 'You must scour the dreary streets beyond Aldgate until you find this woman. It remains of paramount importance that we locate her.'

* * * * *

'You are walking towards the Strand, perhaps?' Gilbert Waterton was standing outside the Marco Polo when Adam emerged from the club, nearly an hour after the meeting in the private room had come to an end. Vernon's friend had been staring up at the mosaic portrait of the old Venetian traveller above the building's portico like a connoisseur about to offer a sum of money to take possession of it, but now he turned his attention to Adam.

The young man agreed that he was heading in that direction.

'I have a dinner engagement in the Adelphi,' Waterton said amiably. 'We can walk together for a while.'

The air had grown chilly in the time they had spent in the club and Waterton, now wrapped in a black frock coat, was clapping his ungloved hands together to warm them. He looked like a bored habitué of the opera, half-heartedly applauding the debut of a new tenor. Adam stepped down into the street from the Marco Polo's portico and they set off down Pall Mall towards Trafalgar Square. For a while, they walked in silence.

'I am so pleased that you have agreed to help us with this unfortunate business,' Waterton said eventually. 'Sunman speaks very highly of you. He has told me several times of your exploits in Turkey in Europe.'

'I am sure he exaggerates. In truth, I did little enough.'

The two men waited for a small procession of cabs to pass before crossing the road into the square.

'No false modesty, Mr Carver, please,' Waterton said as they made their way towards Landseer's stone lions. 'You faced a series of difficulties and dangers far from the comforts of home and civilization,

40

and you overcame them all. You should be proud of what you did.'

Adam glanced at his companion. This flattery seemed sincere enough. Did Sunman truly speak so highly of him? he wondered. The young man from the Foreign Office had given Adam himself little indication that he did. They continued across the square. The vast bulk of Northumberland House loomed to the right as they came into the Strand.

'I say this not to embarrass you,' Waterton went on, 'but as an indication of the trust Sunman and I are putting in you to find this Delaney girl.'

'I hope I can justify that trust.'

'So do I, Mr Carver. Harry Vernon is a dear fellow but he has behaved very foolishly. There is a chance to rescue him from the consequences of his foolishness, but success depends on finding that girl.'

'Vernon is lucky to have a friend such as you are proving yourself to be, Mr Waterton.' By unspoken consent, they had come to a halt at the corner of Villiers Street. 'Not everyone would go to such troubles to extricate a man from a mess of his own making.'

Waterton waved his hand before his face like a man chasing away a troublesome fly. 'It is little enough that I am doing,' he said.

'I cannot agree. I admire you for your loyalty to your friend.' Adam raised his hat. 'And now I must leave you.' He made as if to continue along the Strand, but Waterton reached out a hand and held him by the arm.

'One word further, Mr Carver.' His grip on Adam's forearm was strong. 'Harry is inclined to the melodramatic at the best of times. And these are certainly not the best of times for him. All this talk of putting the nation at risk, of damaging his queen and country . . . I would not pay it too much heed. Harry exaggerates the consequences of his imprudence.'

'I shall bear that in mind.'

Waterton released his hold. 'The only person Harry truly risks harming is himself. And we must all endeavour to save him from his foolishness. Find the girl, Mr Carver. Find Dolly Delaney.'

'I shall try my best, sir.'

'Excellent.' Waterton raised his own hat and, turning away, began to walk down Villiers Street in the direction of the river.

Adam, wondering exactly what to make of the conversation, watched him go until the older man was lost in the evening crowd and the thin mist rising from the Thames. Then he strode off along the Strand in the direction of home.

CHAPTER FIVE

he Corinthian was not one of the smartest of gentlemen's clubs. It was tucked away in a side street off
St James's Square, and looked to have been erected
some time in the very early years of the previous century – and not to have been renovated or redecorated since. The
paint on its walls was peeling in places and its carpets were shabby
and threadbare. The attendant in the entrance hall who agreed to
guide Adam towards the billiards room was quite clearly drunk.
He meandered from side to side as he led the young man along
a dark corridor and, at one point, felt the need to stop and cling
briefly to a marble-topped side table before continuing. Adam
could not help but compare the atmosphere of the Corinthian with
the well-ordered tranquillity of the Marco Polo and thank his lucky
stars that he was a member of the latter.

Eventually the tipsy attendant stopped at an open door. 'In there,
sir,' he slurred and, attempting to gesture into the room, lurched
sideways. He reached out a hand to steady himself on the wall and
belched loudly. Adam found a small coin with which to tip the man,
who stood upright to pocket it and, struggling to make a salute of
thanks, poked himself in the eye. Adam left him nursing his injury
and entered the billiards room.

Adolphus 'My friends call me Dolphie' Wyndham was not at all
the Adonis-like figure McIlwraith had suggested he was. He was
a thin and gangling young man with a high forehead, pink cheeks
and a protuberant Adam's apple that appeared to possess a life of its
own, bobbing rapidly up and down his throat as he spoke. 'Dolly,'

he said. 'That's the blonde one, isn't it? Quite a stunner, I should say. Might have had a look-in with her if it hadn't been for her pal. Bit of a harridan, her pal, if you know what I mean.'

'Hetty.' Adam hazarded a guess at the harridan's identity.

'Is that her name?' Wyndham said absent-mindedly. He had moved away from the billiard table to speak to Adam, but his thoughts were obviously still on his game. He kept turning to look over his shoulder to where his opponent, a large young man in a tight-fitting dinner suit, was potting balls with great rapidity. 'Dark-haired girl. Breathes fire at a chap if he so much as lays a finger on her. Positive dragon! Much preferred the fair Dolly.'

'But you have no notion where the fair Dolly might presently be?'

'Sorry, old man, not a clue.'

'Your shot, Dolphie,' the plump man at the table called.

'When did you last see the young lady?'

Wyndham, whose eyes had drifted back to the billiard table, turned and looked blankly at Adam. 'Dolly?'

'Yes, Dolly.' Adam was struggling to keep the irritation out of his voice.

'Oh, days ago. At least a week. To tell you the truth, old man, I've rather got my eye on a redhead at the Alhambra. Haven't been seeing much of Dolly.'

'I say, are you all right, Dolphie?' Wyndham's opponent had moved the markers on the wooden scoreboard and was now standing by it, leaning on his cue.

'Right as ninepence, Smithy.'

'Well, cast an optic over here. Can't you see it's your turn on the baize?'

'Hope you don't mind, old man,' Wyndham said to Adam, 'but I've got half a guinea riding on this game. That wretch Smithy won the first out of three and if I don't pull this one back, I'll be emptying my pockets to pay off his bar bill. And I haven't exactly been in funds since last autumn – dropped twenty sovs on the Leger and have been close to stony for months.' With these remarks, he nodded politely to Adam and ambled towards the billiard table.

Adam watched Wyndham pick up his cue and stretch himself inelegantly across the baize to pot a white into the top right-hand corner. He turned and left the two Corinthians to their game.

* * * * *

Beneath the arch of the railway bridge stood a wooden cart. A banner unfurled behind it proclaimed: 'Thy word is a lamp unto my feet, and a light unto my path.' Standing on the cart, a street preacher was addressing a handful of passers-by who had been attracted to his temporary pulpit.

Adam and Quint skirted around the edge of the small group and emerged from underneath the bridge. Above them, a train heading out of the City rattled across it. The noise drowned any attempt at conversation.

'She'll be using some gammy moniker, won't she?' Quint remarked when the train had disappeared into the distance. 'Not Dolly Delaney. Something we ain't ever heard on.'

'Probably she won't be using her own name,' Adam agreed. 'She won't want to run the risk that her employers in the West End might discover she's working in a cheap penny gaff out East. I doubt they would approve.'

'So all the time we've been asking for Dolly Delaney, we've been wasting our breath, ain't we?'

Adam and his servant had spent several hours trailing along Whitechapel High Street, and the many streets that branched off it, in search of the missing dancer. They had found, as Adam had suspected, that the area was not short of theatres, although not many of them would have been recognized as such further west. None of the people to whom they had spoken in these music halls and penny gaffs had ever heard of Dolly Delaney.

'You forget that we have the photograph of her,' the young man said. 'Her name might have been unfamiliar, but her face would have been recognized.'

The manservant made a noise that suggested he was far from

45

convinced that they were not on a wild goose chase.

'Here is one more temple of the muses to try,' Adam said, pointing to a squat and square brick edifice set back slightly from the thoroughfare. On either side of its main entrance were two large but crudely painted banners. It was difficult to guess what they were intended to depict. Was it a love scene the artist had endeavoured to create? Or a fight of some kind? He peered at them, but remained unsure. Across the top of both banners, the words 'TONIGHT AT 7' were scrawled in foot-high lettering. 'Perhaps we shall make it the terminus for our journey today.'

Quint looked up at the crumbling and grubby brickwork. 'I ain't sure my togs are right for a nobby place like this,' he said sarcastically.

'They will have to forgive us our lack of evening attire,' Adam replied. He pushed open the door and entered, followed by his servant.

They found themselves immediately in the main body of the building. The light was low and a there was a faint smell of fish in the air. The place had once been some kind of large shop or warehouse but it was now gutted and bare of all but two dozen rows of solid wooden benches. At one end was a makeshift stage: no more than a small platform raised a couple of feet above the floor.

There was a door in the rear wall and a man emerged from it. He was wearing an ancient and stained canvas jacket, and around his neck was a dark red kingsman. A pipe was rammed into his mouth but it was unlit and looked as if it was usually kept so. His hands were in the pockets of a pair of black trousers. 'Can I help you gents with anything?' he asked out of one corner of his mouth, the pipe remaining firmly in place in the other.

'I do hope so,' Adam said. 'Am I speaking to the proprietor of this fine establishment?'

The man with the pipe inclined his head warily, as if to indicate that he might, in certain circumstances, be prepared to admit that this was the case.

'We're looking for a young lady who has gone missing,' Adam said, holding out the photograph of Dolly. 'We were told that she might have occasionally graced your stage here.'

'I ain't seen 'er,' the man said instantly, not even bothering to look at the cabinet card.

'Perhaps you could look more carefully, Mr—?'

'Beasley. And I ain't seen 'er.'

'The lady's family is very concerned about her disappearance, Mr Beasley. There might well be a financial reward for any information leading to her discovery.'

'All well and good, but no use to me. I ain't seen 'er.'

'Are there other people in your theatre who might recognize the lady?'

'Grimston and the others are getting themselves ready. They won't want disturbin' just to look at some tart's face.'

Adam could hear noises from behind him. He turned to see that the main door and two side doors had all been flung open and a steady stream of people was now pushing its way through them. He took his watch from his waistcoat pocket and glanced at it. It was 6.30. The audience for Beasley's show was beginning to arrive. 'Perhaps I could speak to them after tonight's performance,' he said.

'Waste of time. They won't have seen 'er neither.'

'That may well be the case. But I should like to ask them myself. May we stay and watch the entertainment?'

Beasley shrugged. 'Anyone as pays his penny can watch,' he said. 'For tuppence, you can 'ave a seat with a cushion.'

Adam and Quint positioned themselves on the front row, paying the extra penny each and taking the cushions.

Soon the makeshift theatre was filled with people, the noise increasing tenfold in five minutes. Friend bellowed raucously to friend across the room. Heat, rising from the growing crowd, gathered in its four corners. The smell of sweating bodies mingled with that of the beer that was now being sold from a temporary stall at the rear of the hall. Turning in his seat, Adam could see three barrels sitting on trestle tables. Beasley himself had tapped one of them and was pouring out pints. A confederate with a red face and straw-coloured hair was handing them out to the surrounding scrum of

47

would-be drinkers. A large, ugly man with a badly mended broken nose and cauliflower ears was standing by the barrels. His muscular arms were folded across his substantial paunch and he was scowling at everyone Beasley and his associate served.

'Not the friendliest soul in the place,' Adam remarked, noticing that his servant was also looking at the man. 'He bears the most striking resemblance to the gorilla Monsieur du Chaillu saw in Africa and described so vividly in his book.'

'I know 'im,' Quint said, a hint of contempt in his voice. 'Charlie Wethers. Fought the Whitechapel Wonder in '62.'

'I wouldn't care to stand toe to toe with him.'

'The Wonder walloped 'im. 'E may look vicious enough now, but 'e couldn't beat a carpet when 'e was in the ring.'

'Not the most obvious devotee of the theatrical arts.'

''E's 'ere as a chucker-out, ain't 'e?' Quint said. 'Any coves make trouble while the ale's being served and Wethers is supposed to 'ave them out on their arses afore they can say knife.'

They both turned back to the stage. 'I do believe the entertainment is about to begin,' Adam said.

The first part of the proceedings was a playlet called 'The Seven Steps to Tyburn', the title written on a placard and propped on an easel at the side of the stage by a bored-looking girl in a blue blouse and skirt. The audience hooted and yelled its approval as she did so, but the girl's blank expression of ennui never changed. The drama itself consisted of little more than a series of *tableaux vivants* depicting the downfall of a rich man who lost his fortune, and eventually his life, through his taste for gambling. Driven to robbery and murder to gain the money to support his habits, he ended on the gallows. It seemed very dull to Adam but the rest of the audience clearly liked it, clapping and shouting with delight at each change of scene. Several acts now followed in quick succession. Some were greeted with great enthusiasm; others were booed from the moment they stepped onto the low stage to the moment they stepped off it. A man who told comic stories was met with stony silence, another singing melancholy songs of death and despair with uproarious laughter.

More than an hour passed and the temperature within the hall was still rising. The fug of smoke from dozens of pipes and cigarettes now mingled with the smells of beer and sweat. A sense of anticipation was in the air. It was time for the lion of the show. This beast at last emerged from the rear door and clambered onto the stage to bellows from the audience. From what Beasley had said, Adam guessed that this was the Grimston who could not be disturbed. He was a huge man: well over six feet tall and at least twenty stone, his jowly face decorated with a flourishing walrus moustache. Dressed in a battered dress suit that was bursting at the seams, he planted his feet apart and held out his arms to the audience. They redoubled their shouts with delight. With surprising grace he pirouetted on his feet and, turning away from them, flipped up the tails of his suit. The crowd shouted again.

'Christ Almighty,' Quint hissed. "'E's got an arse the size of a Regent's Canal barge.'

Grimston swivelled back to his audience and reached out his arms to them once more. 'Tonight,' he bellowed at them, 'I will be singing that well-known melody, "The Pork-Butcher's Bride".'

There were roars of approval from the benches. 'Give it 'ell, Grimston,' came a cry from the back rows, rising above the general hubbub. This was clearly a popular choice. More cheers rose from the audience. One man sitting near Adam was almost overcome with excitement and was clutching convulsively at the woollen comforter around his neck. Adam wondered briefly how he could bear to continue wearing it in the heat.

As Grimston began to sing, in a raucous baritone voice, of the difficulties faced by a young butcher in finding a suitable bride, Adam allowed his attention to drift from the stage. This was surely, he thought, not a venue in which the young dancer for whom he was searching would be found. He had, in a strange way, enjoyed witnessing these performances at a penny gaff, so different from anything he had ever seen before, but he was no nearer to finding the woman Sunman wanted him to find. Perhaps Cosmo's chorus girl had been wrong about Dolly looking for work in the East End?

Certainly he and Quint had visited so many places like Beasley's without success that this seemed likely to be the case. He would have to come up with a different plan.

Adam's idle thoughts were interrupted by yells from the people around him. Grimston had finished his first song. Judging by the noise in the hall, the audience had enjoyed it, and the performer showed no inclination to leave the stage.

'And now,' he roared, his voice battling against the surrounding clamour, 'I give you a back-er-nalian ditty, a ballad what 'ymns the joys of everybody's favourite liquor.' He paused and there was a sudden hush in the room. 'BEER!'

Pandemonium ensued. The audience hallooed and yelled, and some threw their hats in the air. The man with the woollen comforter appeared to have passed out with excitement or, possibly, the heat. Grimston launched himself enthusiastically into a song that poured scorn on the pleasures of wine, as drunk by effete foreigners, and lavished praise on the health-giving properties of beer, the honest English working man's drink of choice. The song was tuneful and rhythmic and many in the audience were soon clapping along to it. Even Quint, moved perhaps by a paean to his own favoured tipple, looked close to enjoying Grimston's performance.

The burly singer roared out two more numbers – one celebrating the physical delights of a girl named Gertie, and another which told of English soldiers bravely facing certain death on a distant field of battle – before stepping from the stage. The audience was unwilling to see him go. It howled its enthusiasm and Grimston returned briefly to repeat his beer song. He waved graciously at his admirers, shook his sizeable backside in their direction one last time and was then gone. No amount of braying and bellowing from the audience would bring him back, and Beasley came forward to announce that the evening's entertainment was over. Beer would continue to be served for as long as the barrels lasted.

There was a general stampede in the direction of the temporary drinks stall, and Adam found himself at the back of the crowd, standing next to two men. The taller of them had a pipe clamped between brown teeth; the other was chewing a wad of baccy. They were both staring at him as if he had arrived as a visitor from the moon. When they saw that he had noticed them, the shorter man nodded guardedly in his direction.

'Good evening, gentlemen,' Adam said, raising his hat. 'Perhaps you can help me.'

They looked at one another, as if surprised by his ability to speak.

'Wotcher want, cully?' the baccy-chewer asked.

'I am looking for a young woman.'

'Ain't we all?' the man said.

'A very particular young woman. This one here.' Adam held out the photograph to the two men.

They gazed at it, the man with the pipe leering over the shoulder of his companion. 'Pretty face,' he said, with the air of a connoisseur of female beauty. 'She ain't got much flesh on 'er 'aunches, though.'

'Well, you know what they say, cully,' his friend remarked. 'The nearer the bone, the sweeter the meat. I'd crack 'er tea-cup and no mistake.'

'She ain't goin' to give you the time o' day, Hobbs. Not a looker like her.'

'I've had better-lookin' than 'er.'

'Garn! You ain't telling me that you've fit end to end with anything like this girl!'

'Dozens of 'em. May my bleeding eyes drop out if it ain't the truth, cully.'

'May your bleeding cods drop off, more like.'

'Gentlemen, gentlemen, please.' Adam waved the cabinet card in front of Hobbs and his friend. 'I need only to know if you have seen this young lady in the theatre. Or in the neighbourhood.'

The two men looked at one another. The desire to continue boasting of their encounters with the opposite sex was strong but it was counter-balanced by the feeling that, in this case, it might be easiest just to tell the truth. They shook their heads.

Adam sighed. Showing them the photograph had been a long shot. He slipped it back into the inside pocket of his well-tailored jacket.

'I seen 'er,' a voice said. It belonged to a shrivelled, bony man in clothes several sizes too large for him who had been loitering on the edge of the group as Hobbs and his companion blustered and bragged. 'I seen another pitcher of 'er.'

'Are you certain, sir?' Adam took the cabinet card from his pocket once more. 'Are you certain it was this young woman you saw?'

The bony man reached out a grubby hand for the photograph. Reluctantly, Adam allowed him to take it. The man peered at Dolly's face, wheezing as he did so. 'Sure as eggs is eggs,' he said. 'Mate of mine 'ad pitchers of dozens of judies. This one 'ere was one of 'em. She looked a bit different then, mind.' He began to laugh throatily but was suddenly overcome by a coughing fit. He turned away and spat on the floor.

'Different?' Adam was puzzled. 'You have just said it was the same young woman.'

'It were.' The man had ceased coughing but his voice was croaky. 'I never forget a face. Nor a judy's body.' He handed back the photograph and launched himself into more rasping laughter. 'She were different cos she'd dropped 'er drawers. She was naked as the day God made 'er.'

'You have seen a study of this lady in the nude?'

The man nodded. 'Quite a study she was, an' all.'

'Where was this? Who was your friend? And where did he obtain his photographs?' Adam was surprised to find himself angered by the thought that some backstreet idlers had been gloating over a picture of Dolly *au naturel*.

The bony man, taken aback by the asperity in Adam's voice, retreated a pace or two. 'Ain't so much a friend,' he said. 'More of an acquaintance.'

'What is his name?'

'I ain't sure. Bert something.'

'And how would Bert something have come into possession of these photographs?'

'How the 'ell would I know?' The man was becoming indignant. 'Look, mister, I was jest tryin' to be helpful. I don't know where he got 'em. These pitchers of naked judies is everywhere.'

Adam was about to ask further questions but the man turned and walked quickly into the crowd. Adam took a step forwards, as if to follow him, but realized that it would be futile.

'The cove's right, guv,' Quint said. 'There's thousands of dirty pictures out there. Millions maybe.'

'How can we discover who took the one of Miss Delaney?'

Quint looked at his master and shrugged. 'Prob'ly we can't. Anyway, we got other things to worry about.' He nodded towards the stage.

A delegation was heading in their direction. It did not look to be a friendly one. Beasley, flanked on one side by the huge Grimston and, on the other, by the cauliflower-eared Charlie Wethers, was making his way across the room.

The three men came to a halt in front of Adam and Quint. ''Oo the blue blazes is this pair of muttonheads?' Grimston asked in a tone that did not suggest friendliness.

'I ain't got no idea, Bill,' Beasley said. 'They was askin' questions afore the show, that's all I know. About some chit of a girl.'

'Questions?' The large man was outraged. 'There ain't no call for questions 'ere. What you mean coming 'ere with questions?' He jabbed a fleshy, sausage-like finger towards Adam.

The young man took a step back. He did not wish to become involved in a brawl, but he was not prepared to be prodded in the chest by an overweight baritone. 'Gentlemen,' he said, holding up his hands in a placatory gesture. 'There is no cause for disagreement. My man and I were merely making enquiries about a girl who has gone missing. Her friends are anxious to find her.'

'Bleedin' young toff,' Grimston snarled. 'Coming out east to look down yer nose at us. I ought to set Charlie 'ere on you.'

The former prizefighter made an odd, strangulated bark, like a terrier straining to get at rats, and took a step forward.

Adam took another step backwards and continued to make soothing noises.

''Oo's this bleedin' tart you're so interested in?' Grimston growled, punching his right fist into the palm of his left hand. 'Sounds like trouble to me. If you're after trouble, we can give it to yer all right. In bucketloads.'

A space had grown around the group as the drinkers at the beer stall realized that a fight might be in the offing and shuffled out of the way of those who might be doing the fighting.

'We want no trouble, Mr Grimston,' Adam said. 'We are merely—'

'Sod you, you little 'alfpenny swell.' The singer interrupted him. 'I ain't interested in 'earing any more of your gab. Put 'em on the street, Charlie.'

Wethers took a step forward.

'Watch out, guv,' Quint shouted. ''E's got a chiv.' A knife with a vicious-looking blade had indeed appeared in the old prizefighter's right hand. Clearly he no longer trusted the power of his fists alone to impose his authority. Quint moved with sudden and decisive speed, lifting his leg and booting the man firmly in the crotch. Immediately Wethers sank, howling, to the floor. He dropped his knife, which skittered away across the floor.

Before either of his friends could react, Adam stepped to his left, seized hold of one of the wooden benches on which the audience had been sitting and propelled it in the direction of Grimston and Beasley. It struck the larger man on his knees, making him yelp with pain and anger.

Adam and Quint exchanged a quick glance. They turned as one and ran for the exit into Whitechapel High Street.

* * * * *

'Not the friendliest of places, Whitechapel,' Adam remarked.

'There's worse out east,' his servant replied.

The two men had passed Aldgate Pump and were making their way down Leadenhall Street towards Cornhill. The sudden scuffle with Grimston and his cronies had exhilarated both of them, and they were walking with a definite spring in their step.

'Why, I wonder, was Grimston so swift to take offence?' the young man asked.

'Prob'ly thought you was out to peach him for selling liquor. A penny will get you a pound that 'e ain't got a licence to be flogging beer.'

'What about the man who claimed to have seen Dolly in the revealing photograph?'

Quint shrugged. 'Maybe 'e did, maybe 'e didn't.'

'He was a dirty and dishevelled rogue, was he not?' Adam said. 'His clothes looked as if they were made for someone else. And he had surely been wearing them to bed the previous night.'

''E 'adn't 'ad a bath since Balaclava, if that's what you mean,' Quint said. 'And I ain't too sure he'd got a bed to go to. Not unless you count the twopenny rope.'

'The twopenny rope?'

'In the cheap padding-kens. They just sling a rope between two hooks and the poor buggers hang over it.'

Adam looked aghast. 'How on earth do they sleep in such a position?'

'Most of 'em don't. Mind you, some of 'em are so bloody corned, they'd sleep if they was standing up to their chops in horse crap.'

Not for the first time in Quint's company, Adam was suddenly aware of vast realms of London life of which he knew little or nothing. He tried to think of what it must be like to have no bed in which to rest one's head each night, but his imagination baulked at the prospect. It was too far outside his experience. He could only conjure up nights under the stars in European Turkey, and those had been rather pleasant experiences. Sleeping rough in London streets must be very different.

'These daguerreotypes of women in the nude,' he said, returning to the original subject. 'They are sold under the counter in shops throughout town, are they not?'

Quint grunted in agreement.

55

'And yet the sale of them must surely be against the law?'

The servant made another noise, perhaps indicating uncertainty about the legal status of such pictures.

Adam continued his train of thought aloud. 'If they are illegal, then the police must be interested in the places that sell them and the photographers who take them. They must have knowledge of both. And we have a friend at Scotland Yard, do we not?'

'I ain't got no friends among the peelers,' Quint said, with some vehemence. 'Anyways, I thought you said your toff chum didn't want the blues to know anything about this girl.'

'There is no need to tell Inspector Pulverbatch anything much about Dolly.'

'Didn't we see enough of that bleeder Pulverbatch last year?' Quint asked.

Adam ignored his servant's question. 'We shall invent some story to explain our interest in her.' He thought for a moment. 'We shall say that she is your niece.'

'I ain't got no niece.'

'That she has run away from her respectable home in Peckham and that your sister is worried to death at the thought of what might have happened to her.'

'I ain't got no sister.' Quint's tone had become quite aggrieved.

'Particularly since word has reached her that her poor child has fallen into bad company and that she is in danger of losing her virtue. She has been obliged to pose for the most disgraceful daguerreotypes. Your sister is worried half to death.'

'I tell you, I ain't got no sister nor no niece.'

'We are going to speak to our old friend Pulverbatch,' Adam continued, taking no notice of Quint's protests, 'in the hope that he might be able to point us in the direction of the black-hearted villain who is preying upon the innocence of this sweet girl.'

'Why can't it be your bleedin' niece who's posing in the buff?'

'That is not very likely to be the case, is it? The inspector would not give credence to such a story.'

'Why the 'ell not?'

It was Adam's turn to sound aggrieved. 'No relation of a gentle-man such as myself would be so far reduced in circumstances that she would be obliged to remove her clothing for money.'

'But my niece and sister'd be as naked as an Indian's back as soon as you showed 'em a silver sixpence, I suppose.'

'I said nothing about your sister posing for such photographs, Quint. Merely that she was worried about her daughter's virtue.' Adam was growing exasperated. 'In any case, the question is entirely hypothetical. We have already established that you have neither sister nor niece. Cease making difficulties. I shall write to Pulverbatch as soon as I get back to Doughty Street.' The young man picked up his speed as they reached Cheapside. Quint fell into a grumpy silence.

The two men continued up the street, servant a pace behind master. The London evening crowds swirled about them. When the vast bulk of St Paul's was silhouetted against the moonlit sky on their left, Adam came to a halt and turned to Quint, who had also stopped, and was staring moodily into the middle distance. 'There is no need for you to accompany me to Doughty Street, Quint.' Adam, aware that he had offended his servant by impugning the virtue of his non-existent relatives, attempted to speak in a concilia-tory tone.

Quint merely grunted.

'If you wish to take some time off, I shall not need your services before breakfast tomorrow.'

Quint grunted again.

'A drink, perhaps? Are there not pubs hereabouts where you would be a welcome figure at the bar?' Adam was aware that there were few, if any, streets in the capital where Quint was not close to a hostelry of which he was a sometime patron.

'There's the Jolly Waggoners,' Quint conceded. 'Off Carter Lane. It'll be open till after midnight. I could mebbe find time to sink a pint or two of their pale ale.' He spoke as if by doing so, he would be bestowing a favour not only on the landlord of the Jolly Waggoners, but on Adam as well.

'Well, there you are,' his master said. 'The Jolly Waggoners it is. And I shall make my way back to Doughty Street alone. I shall see you at eight in the morning.'

Quint still looked unconvinced.

'For God's sake, go and have a drink, man,' Adam said. 'Enjoy yourself whilst you can. We shall have plenty of work to do in the next few days.'

His manservant said nothing but nodded briefly, like a man acknowledging a distant acquaintance across a crowded room, and disappeared into the night.

* * * * *

'Your name Carver, guv?'

Ten minutes had passed since Quint had left him. Adam had thought briefly of hailing a cab but it was a fine night and the prospect of a walk had been a pleasant one. He had strolled along Newgate Street and turned down Snow Hill, heading for Farringdon Road. As he approached the junction with Cock Lane, a man standing in a doorway addressed him.

The crowds that had been thronging Cheapside had been left behind, and there was no one else in sight.

'Who wishes to know?' Adam asked, peering into the dark.

'Summ'un with a friendly message for 'im.'

The man was tall and broad, dressed in a dark greatcoat and a long muffler which was looped several times around his neck. He was holding a stick with a silver top which glinted in the moonlight. The top was shaped, Adam could see, into the likeness of some animal's head. A fox, perhaps? The young man clutched his own walking cane a little tighter.

'Well, perhaps you should deliver it, sir, and then we can both be on our different ways. My name *is* Carver, but it is rather late in the evening to stand here and exchange pleasantries.'

'Oh, I'll deliver it right enough, guv.' The man laughed unpleasantly.

Adam was about to speak again but he had no chance. He was

struck suddenly from behind and staggered a few steps towards the doorway.

'You ain't felled 'im, you fool,' the man in the greatcoat hissed.

Adam was struggling to recover his balance. Greatcoat held his fox-head stick like a club and swung it into the young man's legs. Adam cried out with pain and was thrown to the ground. The unseen assailant behind him seized the collar of his jacket and began to haul him into a narrow alleyway that ran between the buildings at the beginning of Cock Lane.

Adam, more than half dazed, was unable to do much to resist. He threw a couple of feeble punches, which the man easily evaded; he tried to kick out his legs, but they seemed to be unwilling to obey the instructions from his brain. He was pulled into the alley and thrown, half lying and half sitting, against a brick wall.

Greatcoat knelt by his side. With a flick of the wrist a knife blade appeared in the man's hand. He held it against Adam's throat. 'Now, you want to hold yourself very still, guv. One slip and this 'ere chiv'll be right through your neck.'

Even in his half-stunned state, Adam realized that he should obey the man. 'What the devil do you want, sir?' he whispered. 'Take the money from my purse if you must.'

'Well, I might at that,' Greatcoat said, the knife in one hand still at the young man's throat. 'Seeing as 'ow you invited me to do so.' He used his other hand to rummage in Adam's jacket. He found the purse and pocketed it. ''Owever, that ain't the main reason why my pal and me stopped to talk to you.'

'You have my money. What more do you rogues want with me?'

'Like I sez, cully, a nice friendly word. A message from someone what 'as your best interests at 'eart.'

'I doubt that.'

'You've been asking a lot of questions about some tart named Dolly Delaney, ain't you?'

'I have no notion of what you mean.'

'Oh, I think you do, guv. I think you know exackly what I mean. Now, my friendly message is this. You can forget all about Miss

Dolly Delaney. You ain't 'eard of 'er. You don't want to 'ear of 'er. And you partickly don't want to be a-looking for 'er. You got that?'

'I am perfectly capable of understanding simple English sentences.' Adam was recovering from the sudden assault. Any fear he had felt when initially attacked was being replaced by fury that these brutes should dare to knock him to the ground. 'Even when spoken in your Cockney cant.'

'You're a mouthy one, ain't you? For a cove what's got a knife to 'is gargler, that is.' Greatcoat moved the knife very gently across the skin underneath Adam's chin. The young man could feel a tiny trickle of blood start down his neck. 'You can look down your nose at me all you want, cully. It ain't going to bother me. I'm the one with the chiv. But you keep on asking about young Dolly and you'll end up dead as a dog in a ditch.'

The man's face, wrapped in his muffler, was unrecognizable. His eyes, gleaming in the dark shadows of the alleyway, were all that Adam could see. He moved the knife closer to one of the young man's eyes.

Adam could not stop himself from flinching and shrinking back against the wall.

'Dead as a dog in a ditch,' Greatcoat repeated. He stood up, then suddenly and violently kicked the young man in the ribs. Then he and his companion turned and left the alleyway.

CHAPTER SIX

'**M**ebbe we should give up looking for the tart like the man says.' Quint had just carried a plate of bacon and eggs into the room and was idly looking out of the window as his master breakfasted. 'Ain't no point getting a blade in the bread-basket just cos some high-kicker's gone missing.'

'I am disappointed in you, Quint,' Adam said. He placed his knife and fork carefully on his plate and dabbed at his mouth with a napkin. He winced as he did so. His body ached from the blows he had received the previous night. 'And I will be damned if I allow some loutish ruffian in a dirty greatcoat and muffler to frighten me. Far from ceasing our efforts to find Dolly Delaney, we shall redouble them. I said to you last night that we would communicate with our old friend Pulverbatch at the Yard, and that is precisely what we will do.'

'You ain't finishing that then?' Quint turned from the window and gestured at the breakfast plate.

'No, I think not.' Adam pushed back his chair. 'I have no idea where you bought the rashers of bacon, but they would be better employed as razor strops than as foodstuffs. They are very nearly inedible.' Adam stood up gingerly and moved away from the table. As Quint removed the plate with the offending bacon on it and returned it to the kitchen, the young man crossed to the davenport desk in the far corner of the room and sat down. He lifted the inclined top and pulled out a sheet of notepaper. Reaching for his pen and ink, he began to compose a letter to Inspector Pulverbatch.

Adam had met this officer the previous year when he had discovered the body of the blackmailer, Samuel Creech; Pulverbatch had been in charge of the official investigation into the man's murder. Adam had not seen eye to eye with the inspector's methods, which had nearly resulted in the conviction of an innocent man, but he had been curiously impressed by Pulverbatch's poise and self-assurance. For his part, the Scotland Yard man had seemed to view Adam's interventions in the case with tolerant benevolence. They had parted friends.

The young man could see no reason why Pulverbatch would refuse to help him in this case; particularly since, as he now recalled, the inspector had been made aware the year before of Adam's connections with senior officials in the Foreign Office.

Quint had now returned to the room. He took up a position by the table and stared at the gas lamp on its top. Adam signed his name with a flourish and returned his pen to its stand. 'That should do the trick,' he said. 'I have told the inspector of your sister's concerns for her daughter. I am certain that we can trust him to assist us in the search for her.'

Quint continued to glare fixedly at the lamp as if he were attempting to mesmerize it. He said nothing.

'There is a postbox in the Gray's Inn Road, is there not?' Adam folded the sheet of paper and sealed it in an envelope. He lifted the desk top again and took out a red penny stamp. He moistened it and affixed it. 'If you take it there, it should be at the Yard within a couple of hours.'

Quint snatched the letter from his master's hand with a look that suggested he would be happier to eat it than post it, and left the room, banging the door behind him.

* * * * *

'Inspector Pulverbatch speaks very highly of you, sir,' Sampson said. 'He's only sorry he can't be here to greet you himself. He asked to be remembered to you, mind.'

'You must return my compliments to the inspector, sergeant,'

Adam replied. 'It is "sergeant", is it not?'

The man opposite him, a burly individual squeezed into a blue uniform that looked to be one size too small for him to be comfortable, nodded.

They were both sitting at a wooden desk in a darkly panelled room. The letter to Inspector Pulverbatch had triggered an immediate response. By return of post a message had reached Doughty Street inviting Adam to present himself whenever he wished at Room 241 in the vast building in Great Scotland Yard, which housed the headquarters of the Metropolitan Police. The young man had been obliged to walk what had seemed like miles along dimly lit corridors in order to reach it, but he had been welcomed there like a visiting dignitary. Now, three large volumes bound in black leather were piled on the desk in front of him.

The sergeant patted the top of one of them. 'Here they are, sir,' he said. 'All the pictures of women in their dishabills as we've confiscated in the last three months. Just like the inspector said you wanted.' The expression on Sergeant Sampson's face indicated that he was desperately curious to know what reason Adam had, other than prurience, for looking through the books, but that he was far too deferential and too impressed by the young man's familiarity with the great Inspector Pulverbatch to ask.

Adam had no intention of enlightening him. He pulled the nearest volume towards him and opened it. 'I am very grateful to you and to Mr Pulverbatch,' he said. 'You have given generously of your time.' He paused briefly. 'But there is no necessity for you to remain while I look through these photographs.'

Sampson flushed slightly and tugged at his collar. He looked as if he would be only too happy to leave. 'I'm afraid that won't be possible, Mr Carver, sir. Mr Pulverbatch was very particular about me keeping an eye on the books.'

'Does he suspect that I might otherwise purloin some of the pictures?' Adam was amused, but the sergeant was puce with embarrassment. He flushed even deeper.

'No, of course not, sir, but these books is police property, sir, and

'. . . and . . .' Sampson's voice trailed away.

'You need say no more, sergeant. I understand.'

Adam began to leaf through the pages of the first book. Mounted on each page were photographs of women in varying stages of undress. Sampson sat back on his chair, gazing with every appearance of fascination at a cobweb on the ceiling, as the young man began to examine them.

The book contained women of all kinds. There were blondes and brunettes, slender girls and fat girls, white girls and a surprising number of black ones. They adopted a variety of poses, some significantly more indecent than others, as they faced the camera. After turning a dozen pages, Adam began to find the acres of bare flesh curiously unstimulating. All the bodies blurred into one and he concentrated on the women's faces. The sergeant shifted restlessly in his chair. Time passed.

Adam finished one volume and moved on to the next. Forty minutes after he had begun his task, he stopped and pointed to the top of one of the pages. 'This is she,' he said, as much to himself as to Sampson.

It was recognizably the same girl who had posed for the photograph Sunman had given him.

'She's a neat bit of muslin, ain't she?' the policeman said, leaning forward. He seemed unaware of the story Adam had told of his servant's supposed kinship with the young woman he was seeking – Adam doubted if he would have spoken so familiarly had he known it. Pulverbatch, he assumed, had told his subordinate very little. 'Not that she's wearing any muslin there. She ain't wearing very much of anything, is she?'

It was true. Dolly was naked. She was sitting on a dining chair, one leg crossed over the other, smiling somewhat desperately into the camera. A dark drape hung behind her. There was nothing to indicate where or when the daguerreotype had been taken.

'And you say that these are not all that the police have found?'

'Lord, sir, we've got thousands and thousands of them.' The sergeant pointed at the books on the desk. 'These is just the recent ones.' He pointed at the books on the desk. 'Bit of a stroke of luck chancing on this particular filly so soon.' He leaned further across the desk and peered at the photograph. 'Not many as pretty as her, though, is there?'

'Who might have taken it? Have you any notion of where she was when she posed?'

Sampson shook his head. 'Could be almost anywhere, Mr Carver. Somewhere in town, obviously. But there's dozens of photographers within a mile of here who might have taken it. "Artistic studies", they calls 'em.' The sergeant's voice was full of contempt. 'It's not what I'd call 'em.'

'What would you call them, sergeant?'

'Filthy pictures.'

'But you've no notion of who might have taken these "filthy pictures"?'

'As I say, Mr Carver, there's no way of telling. They all look much the same. Pretty girl. No clothes. Dark backdrop. Sometimes the girl's pretending to be an angel or a goddess from olden times, but that ain't enough to tell us who the photographer is.'

'Such a pity,' Adam said. 'I had hoped I might be able to speak to him.' He took the photograph from its mounts and turned it over. As he did so, he noticed something on the reverse side of the picture. Pushing back his chair, Adam moved closer to the window to catch the light, angling the photograph towards it. 'There *is* something here,' he said. 'There's a letter embossed on it. Or stamped in some way. It looks like a "P".'

'Ah yes, sir, I was coming to that.' Sampson spoke with a self-satisfied air. 'We may not know much about the wretches who take these photos, but we know a bit about them as sells 'em. Some of 'em likes to mark their stock when it comes in. Keep a track of it, you might say.'

'And this "P" indicates who sold this one?'

'Pennethorne. He's a gentleman with an interest in what you might call unusual literature, Mr Carver.'

'And where would I find Mr Pennethorne?'

'In Wych Street, with half the other buggers as sells this stuff. If you'll pardon my language, sir.'

* * * * *

Pennethorne's shop stood halfway along Wych Street, in one of the ancient buildings that characterized the thoroughfare. Adam looked at the overhanging wooden jetties above that jutted into the street and wondered when the houses had first been built. In the days of Queen Elizabeth, perhaps. The street must have escaped the devastation of the Great Fire, and still stood as a relic of London's Tudor architecture. He must, he thought, bring his camera here to record the buildings. But, for the moment, he turned his attention to the shop which had brought him there.

In its window there was an array of photographs of young ladies. The photographer had apparently chanced upon his subjects while they were engaged in the act of dressing themselves. Several were trying on crinoline petticoats; others, lacing up their Balmoral boots, were exhibiting more of their ankles than young ladies usually displayed in public. None of the women was Dolly.

Adam pushed the door open; a bell above it sounded as he walked into the shop. At the back, a face appeared momentarily, peering through an opening half hidden by billowing red drapes. Seconds later, the man was at Adam's side. He was tall and lean and was gazing sideways at his potential customer with the look of a fox eyeing up a hen.

'Am I speaking to the proprietor?' Adam enquired. 'Are you Mr Jacob Pennethorne?'

'I am, sir,' the lean man said.

'My name is Carver. Adam Carver. I am looking for a young woman.'

Pennethorne emitted a strange, high-pitched giggle like that of a small boy caught out in some embarrassing misdemeanour. It was such an unlikely noise to issue from a grown man that Adam almost turned around to see who else had entered the shop.

'That's what so many of my clients are doing, sir,' Pennethorne said. 'Looking for a young woman. We've plenty of them here, sir, plenty indeed.' He gestured towards the shelves behind him, then walked over to a wooden counter at the side of the shop. Wiping first one palm and then the other on the sleeves of his jacket, he picked up a magazine and handed it to Adam. 'Any of these young women serve your purpose, Mr Carver?'

Adam looked at the cover of the periodical. Most of the page was taken up by an engraving of what seemed to be a scene in a music hall bar. A gentleman in a top hat was surrounded by several ballet girls in short skirts and high-heeled boots. One of the girls was embracing the top-hatted gent; another, her leg on a bar stool, was adjusting her garter.

'Ain't she a corker, sir?' the shopkeeper said, a long finger snaking across the page and indicating the most buxom of the ballet girls. 'I've got the photograph that was engraved from, if you was interested.'

'She is indeed very fetching. Particularly in that costume. But she is not the woman for whom I am searching. The young lady I seek is called Dolly. Dolly Delaney.'

Pennethorne's demeanour changed immediately. His unctuous desire to ingratiate himself disappeared, and he snatched the magazine from Adam's hands, turning to replace it on the counter. 'Don't think I know anyone of that name,' he said over his shoulder.

'Oh, but I think you do, Mr Pennethorne. I was very reliably informed that you have had dealings with the young lady in question.'

'I see lots of women in my job, Mr Carver.' The shopkeeper, his back still to Adam, was now tidying the piles of magazines on his counter. 'Some of 'em are ladies. More of 'em ain't. I tell you, I don't know one called Dolly.'

'My informant was really quite adamant not only that you knew the lady, but that you had employed her.'

'He's mistaken then, ain't he?'

'I doubt that very much. He's a very well-informed gentleman. Gentlemen who work at Scotland Yard so often are.'

Pennethorne spun round to face Adam again.

'Aha, I see I have caught your attention. Yes, Sergeant Sampson asked to be remembered to you. He has not seen you for some time,' he said.'

'He ain't 'ad no cause to see me.'

'However, he went on to say that, should my enquiries about the whereabouts of Dolly Delaney prove unfruitful, he would be obliged to undertake some of his own.' Adam smiled blandly at the shopkeeper.

Pennethorne stood for a moment, clenching and unclenching one fist, and then he surrendered. 'Ain't no call for Sampson to come poking his nose round my shop,' he said surlily. 'He's right. I know Dolly.'

'I knew we could reach a happy agreement on the subject, Mr Pennethorne.'

'She's a dancer at one of the theatres in Drury Lane, ain't she?' Adam nodded.

'She come to me about three months ago,' the shopkeeper went on. 'Said she needed some extra rhino. I arranged for her to see a friend of mine. He took some photographs of her.'

'Photographs such as the ones in your window?'

'A little more *interesting* than those,' Pennethorne admitted. 'A little more the kind I keep in my back room.'

'Did you see her again?'

'She returned a few times. Seemed to want the money.'

'So she posed for your friend again?' Adam caught the eye of the shopkeeper who looked away.

'Maybe four times in all.'

'Has she been here recently?'

Pennethorne shook his head.

'What about this friend of yours? The one who took the photographs. Where would I find him?'

Pennethorne stepped back. He raised both hands, palms outwards, as if fending off an attack. 'Discretion, Mr Carver,' he said. 'Discretion is the watchword in this business. I can't go around giving you names, now, can I?'

'Oh, I think you can, Mr Pennethorne. One name, at least. Either to me – or to Sergeant Sampson.'

The shopkeeper lowered his arms and stared balefully at Adam. He was clearly trying to decide just how well acquainted the young man was with the police.

Adam smiled sweetly at him. 'It's one or the other of us, Mr Pennethorne,' he said. 'You can be sure of that.'

'Patch,' the shopkeeper said, after a brief pause, spitting the word out like a pip from an orange. 'His name's Walter Patch.'

'And where would I find Mr Patch?'

Pennethorne glared at Adam as if in hopes that his gaze might prove as terrible as Medusa's. 'Off Fleet Street. Bride Lane, round the back of the church.'

'He has his home there?'

'A shop. Sells cameras and other such stuff.'

'And the photographs?'

'He's got a room upstairs. Nice and private. The girls go there.'

'Thank you, Mr Pennethorne. You've been most helpful. If you think of anything more, you must let me know.'

Adam handed Pennethorne his card and was turning to leave, but the shopkeeper had not yet said all he wanted to say. He took a step or two closer to the young man and thrust his head forward belligerently. 'What exactly do you think you're doing, Mr Carver? Coming here and looking down on the likes of me and Wally Patch when all *we're* doing is providing a service for coves just like yourself. Who do you think buys these photographs, eh? Working men? They're too pricey. It's gents as buys 'em. Just remember that when you're sneering down your nose at us.'

'I shall endeavour to do so.' Adam was taken aback by the sudden vehemence of the man's words.

But Pennethorne had not finished. 'And what about the girls?' he asked. 'You think we force 'em to shed their petticoats? Better than goin' on the streets, ain't it? Girl bares her body – where's the harm in that? Like as not, this Dolly bint enjoyed it.'

'Perhaps she did, Mr Pennethorne,' Adam said, taking a step

backwards, 'perhaps she did. But it would have been all one and the same to you and Mr Walter Patch had she not done so, would it not?' And, politely doffing his hat, Adam turned and left the shop.

* * * * *

'So, Quint, Dolly was supplementing her income by exposing her charms to Pennethorne's photographer.' The two men were standing opposite the entrance to the Prince Albert and watching the people who went in and out of the theatre.

'Bit of a come-down, ain't it? Dancing for the gentry one night and waggling her chest and bedding at a camera the next.'

'That's true. *Facilis descensus Averno.*'

'If you says so.' Quint looked wary at the sound of Latin, as if the words of the ancient language might be some malign spell purposely directed against his well-being.

'"Easy is the descent into hell," Quint. Virgil, *Aeneid*, Book Six. One minute Dolly's tripping the light fantastic in one of London's best-known theatres; the next she's working in a penny gaff out east – although we never did find out which one. And the next she's so desperate for cash, she's baring her body for a vendor of indecent pictures.' Adam shook his head. 'It doesn't seem to make sense. Why did she need the money so very badly? We can surely assume that her admirer from the Foreign Office was generous enough with his gifts.'

'Maybe summ'un was rooking 'er. And she didn't want 'er friend to know.'

'Perhaps she wanted to get away from her friend and needed the money to do so.' Adam pondered the possibilities. Blackmail was not beyond the bounds of credibility, he supposed, although any blackmailer would have been more likely, surely, to direct his attention to Dolly's paramour. And, if she wanted to escape from her liaison, there must have been methods of doing so that did not involve her taking off her clothes.

'You goin' to see this Patch cove in Bride Lane?' Quint asked.

Adam nodded. 'I shall do so. Although I am not sure how profitable such a visit will prove. In all likelihood, he will have no more to tell me than Mr Pennethorne.'

'Who will 'ave tipped 'im the wink you're on the way to see 'im.'

'Indubitably. So he will be well prepared with lies and equivocations. Perhaps I should have visited him as soon as I left Pennethorne. But, as I say, I doubt he will have more to tell us than that gentleman. In the meantime, I think we need to speak to this young lady, Quint.' Adam nodded in the direction of the tall, dark-haired chorus girl to whom he had spoken several days earlier. She had emerged from the theatre and was making her way towards New Oxford Street.

'The one with the feather boa and the red hat?'

'The very one.'

'We could speak with 'er now.'

'No.' Adam shook his head decisively. 'I am of the opinion that we should speak to her in her own home. She is more likely to tell us what we want to know. On the street or in the theatre, she will have the opportunity to evade our questioning.'

'Where's she live, then?'

'That is what you are about to find out. Follow her.'

The two men were already walking in the woman's wake as she strode purposefully along Drury Lane.

'Me?' Quint spoke indignantly. 'Ain't you following 'er as well?'

'She has met me at the theatre. She will recognize me, but she has never seen you. Track the lady to her lair, Quint.'

'What if she gets on a bus? Or a tram?'

'She will hardly do the latter,' Adam said, exasperated by his servant's determination to place obstacles in the path of doing almost any task that was asked of him. 'The nearest tramways are miles away. If she takes a bus, then so will you.'

'That might be a bit of a poser,' Quint said warily.

'In God's name, why?'

'I ain't exackly got a pocketful of jingles for the fare.'

'What of the money I gave you last Friday?'

'It's gorn.'

'Oh, for goodness' sake.' Adam took several coins from his jacket

71

pocket and thrust them into his manservant's hands. 'Here is more. Just keep the girl in sight.'

* * * * *

In the event, the young woman did not take a bus or a tram, as Quint had feared. She walked along New Oxford Street and then turned into Tottenham Court Road. With Quint grumbling in her wake, she took a turn to her left into Goodge Street. There she stopped to talk to a flower girl who was selling wilted blooms from a doorway. She obviously knew the girl and they chatted for what seemed to Quint, impatiently stamping his feet on the opposite side of the road, like hours. Eventually, with a wave, she left the flower girl and continued on her way. Goodge Street ran into Mortimer Street, and still the woman walked on.

'Where the 'ell's she going?' Quint muttered as his quarry crossed the north side of Cavendish Square and then veered right into Wimpole Street. She was now heading towards the Marylebone Road. In this street of elegant houses from the previous century, the young woman with a tattered feather boa looked out of place; Quint himself was beginning to feel a little conspicuous. He watched from a distance as she approached the main door of one of the houses and rapped firmly on it. 'What's she about?' he said to himself. 'They'll send her on her way faster than a dog'll lick a dish.'

He was wrong. The door was opened by a maidservant and the dancer from the theatre was immediately admitted. It was a brief visit. With Quint still puzzling over the question of why she would be a welcome visitor at such an address, the young woman emerged. She was followed onto the pavement by a plump gentleman in a grey morning coat and darker trousers. They turned to face one another and the man began to speak. He continued to do so for some time, his hand reaching out to rest occasionally on the girl's arm. She made several attempts to interrupt the man but he waved them away. Just as Quint was wondering whether or not to approach a little closer in the hopes of hearing what was being said, the girl shouted, 'I ain't 'aving it, I tell you!' and turned away from the gentleman in the morning coat. With a flourish she threw her tatty boa over her shoulder and set off towards Regent's Park.

The man watched her go and then, visibly annoyed, retreated into his house.

Shaking his head, Quint followed the girl. When she reached the Marylebone Road, she paused briefly before negotiating the traffic and crossing to the other side. She turned towards Baker Street. Quint nearly lost her amid the crowds. He reached the park side of the thoroughfare himself and then caught sight of her red hat bobbing along amongst less colourful headgear. He increased his pace as the hat disappeared in the direction of the Baker Street station.

The girl, it seemed, was intent on taking the new underground railway which ran between Paddington and Farringdon Street. In the eight years it had been running, Quint had been an irregular traveller on it. Out of curiosity he had used it a few times in its inaugural year, but he had been unimpressed. In his heart of hearts, he did not truly like trusting himself to any means of getting from A to B more sophisticated than his own two legs. And rattling along in an open truck beneath the city streets, as third-class passengers were obliged to do, had not appealed to him. However, now it seemed he had no choice.

The girl entered the station and bought a threepenny ticket. Quint did the same. Descending into the gloom of the underground station at Baker Street, he felt the chill in the air increase. 'Colder than the bleedin' grave down 'ere,' he muttered to himself, confirmed in his belief that this was an unnatural mode of transport. The smell of the steam from the railway engine drifted up the stairs and grew stronger as Quint approached the subterranean platform. The large numbers of people gathered on it and the swirling fog left by the train that had departed a few minutes before made it difficult for him to keep his eye on the girl, but he could still just see her. The bright red of her hat was a beacon which he could follow as she made her way along the platform until she was nearly at the point where the black maw of the tunnel gaped. Quint trailed in her wake, pushing unceremoniously past his fellow travellers. Several of them voiced their discontent as he shouldered them aside, but he ignored them all. He took up a position some dozen yards short of where the girl was standing, watching as she reached up and adjusted her hat.

When the next underground train pulled into the station, the young woman stepped into a second-class carriage. She found a seat and, carefully arranging her dress, settled into it. She took no notice of Quint who, together with a crowd of other passengers, had followed her onto the train. The train set off into the tunnel and Quint swayed from side to side, trying to maintain his balance. He stumbled, cursed and regained his footing. Why couldn't the bleedin' dollymop just walk home, he thought, as engine and carriages headed noisily through the dark towards Portland Road, the next station on the line. She'd walked everywhere else.

CHAPTER SEVEN

'She got off at King's Cross, didn't she?'

Quint was leading his master into the maze of streets behind the station. All of them looked alike to Adam: dismal terraces of grey brick. The only landmark he knew in this part of London, apart from the station itself, was the German Gymnasium, and that was some distance to the west. Quint, however, moved with confidence as if he knew the area of old. Not for the first time, the young man was impressed by his servant's knowledge of the city.

They turned a corner into a street that, to Adam, was indistinguishable from a dozen others but which seemed familiar to Quint. Ahead of them an old woman in a battered bonnet and a coarse shawl was crossing the road. She was carrying a basket over one arm, and a grubby bundle tucked under the other. She passed a bill-sticker, halfway up his ladder, who was struggling to affix a large poster to a wall already entirely covered with them. 'Every Disease of the Eye . . .' said one that caught Adam's attention with its huge lettering, '. . . Cured by Ede's Patent American Eye Liquid.' To the left of that, another was proclaiming the virtues of Crosby's Balsamic Cough Elixir. Quack potions both, Adam thought.

Quint followed the old woman across the road, beckoning to his master to do the same. The two men walked fifty yards along the terraced street. The old woman, labouring under her load, turned into another street.

Quint came to a halt at one of the houses. ''Er rooms are there,' he said, pointing downwards. 'It's a thousand quid to a bit of dirt that she knows where the Delaney girl is.'

Looking over the area railings, Adam could see a faint light shining in the basement. A short flight of stone steps, narrow and very steep, led down to a tiny square yard. 'You stay here, Quint. She won't wish to entertain two strangers appearing on her doorstep.'

'Might not want to entertain one.'

'True, but I am a presentable enough visitor. And she knows me from my visit to the theatre.'

Adam descended gingerly. Once in the yard, he was confronted by a red door, so low that anyone of his height would have to stoop to enter through it. He could hear the sound of someone playing a piano in the basement room. He tapped lightly on the door and the music stopped immediately. There was a pause, and then the door was abruptly pulled open. The girl from the chorus looked out and eyed him up and down.

'Oh, it's you,' she said. She didn't sound surprised to see him. 'I thought you might find me. You'd best come in.' She stepped back to allow Adam to enter. 'I don't want no bleedin' hanky-panky, mind. I'm not the girl you want for that. Not tonight, anyways.'

Adam held out his hands as if to reassure her that hanky-panky was similarly absent from his own plans for the evening. He ducked his head and walked into the basement flat the girl called home.

A cottage piano stood against the left-hand wall, looking oversized within the narrow confines of the room. On top of it, several slim volumes of sheet music rested. Glancing quickly at the illustrated covers, Adam saw one that was entitled *Marriott's Cremorne Quadrilles* and another that appeared to be the piano accompaniment to a song called 'The Belle of Belgravia'. Above the piano were two coloured and framed prints: one of the queen and the late Prince Albert, and the other of a flock of sheep grazing on some grassy meadow. Both queen and consort, Adam noted, looked cross-eyed, while the sheep were a shape no living sheep had ever been.

'They ain't mine,' the girl said, noting the direction in which Adam's eyes had strayed. 'They come with the room. I ain't got no taste for sheep.'

'What about Her Majesty?'

'I can take 'er or leave 'er.'

Adam smiled. 'I do not think we were properly introduced,' he said. 'My name is Adam Carver.' He bowed his head in a formal acknowledgement.

'And mine's Hetty. Hetty Gallant.' The girl laughed. 'Ain't you the real gent?'

Adam bowed again. 'I strive to be so,' he replied.

'And what's a real gent like you wanting with a girl like me?' Her voice was flirtatious. 'Followed me all the way from the theatre, have you? I was half expecting to see you the other night. You're the one who was looking for Dolly.'

'I am still looking for Dolly.'

'Well, I ain't so sure as I can 'elp you.'

'Can't help me or won't help me, Miss Gallant?'

The girl shrugged, reaching out her left hand and playing a swift trill of notes on the piano. 'Bit of both, maybe,' she said.

'Your dancing master was of the opinion that Miss Delaney might have gone off with one of her admirers. Could that be true, do you think?'

'You ain't going to get much out of McIlwraith in the way of the truth. He'll lie and look at you. And there you were' – Hetty was scornful – 'believing any old taradiddle he cared to tell you.'

'I am too trusting, perhaps.'

'Ain't you just!'

'Why would Mr McIlwraith "lie and look at me" about Miss Delaney?'

Hetty laughed again. 'Cos he makes some extra readies by letting the likes of that octerpus Wyndham come backstage and make a bleeding nuisance of 'imself. He prob'ly thought *you* was after Dolly.'

'So he exaggerates the extent of her interest in this man Wyndham.' Adam was beginning to understand.

'And he reckons you'll be all worked up worrying about him. So you'll pay Mac the Toad a bit more to see her.'

'Privileged access, as it were.'

'You've got it now.' Hetty spoke like a schoolmaster recognizing that a particularly dim pupil had made a sudden intellectual breakthrough. 'He'll 'ave been disappointed you didn't go back to 'im with your tongue 'anging out and 'arf a sov in your 'and.'

'And is this Wyndham the paragon of male beauty that Mr McIlwraith claims?' Adam knew from his own encounter with Adolphus Wyndham that he was a very undistinguished-looking gentleman, but he was curious to know what the girl might say.

'If you mean, is 'e a looker, no, 'e ain't. All right, I s'pose, if you like that kind.'

'And what kind is he?'

'Young,' Hetty said, in a voice that suggested she had little time for those of tender years. 'Bum-fluff on his cheeks. You could smear it with butter and get the cat to lick it off. But' – now the young woman spoke in tones of disgust – 'he's just another one that's up your petticoats before you've chance to tell 'im your name.'

'So your friend had no particular interest in Mr Wyndham?'

'As I said at the theatre, Dolly ain't got no time for 'im. Whatever McIlwraith might say.'

'So if Mr McIlwraith hasn't told me the truth about Dolly, maybe you can. Do you know where she is?'

'Why're you after 'er?' Hetty smoothed invisible creases from her dress before shooting a shrewd look in Adam's direction. 'Dolly's been a good friend to me. I ain't going to be the one to land 'er in 'ot water.'

'I'm beginning to suspect that she may already be in hot water, Miss Gallant. She has disappeared from her home and from her place of employment. Before she did so, she was earning extra money by – what shall I say? – "unconventional means".'

'What d'you mean by that?' Hetty's hands were on her hips, her chin thrust aggressively forward. ''Ave you seen those pictures of 'er peeled to the buff—?' She clearly had more to say but she was interrupted by a sudden noise from outside. 'What the 'ell was that?'

Adam moved quickly to the window and looked up. Quint

was silhouetted against the late afternoon sky. He was reaching towards the cobblestones in order to pick up something that he had dropped.

'It's only my man,' Adam said. 'He's waiting for me in the street.'

'Your man?'

'My servant. His name is Quint.'

'Might as well arsk 'im down, then,' Hetty said sarcastically. 'The more the merrier.'

Quint had now retrieved whatever it was he had dropped, so Adam beckoned to him through the window. The sounds of Quint descending the stairs were swiftly followed by his appearance in the doorway.

'Bleedin' thing jumped out of my hand,' he remarked, holding up a length of iron bar.

'What the devil was it doing in your hand in the first place?' Adam asked.

''Ad it in this pocket, first off,' the manservant said, hauling at the cloth of his jacket to show where he meant. 'I was shifting it to the other 'un but the bugger's got a life of its own. Always 'andy to 'ave, mind. Never know when you might need to wallop summ'un.'

Hetty, who had been eyeing Quint with poorly concealed distaste, began to back into the corner of her room. 'No need for any wallopin' 'ere. You'd best know I can scream like a bloody cockatoo, if I want to. And there's always a copper standing near the railway arches.'

'There will be no walloping of any kind, Miss Gallant.' Adam raised his hands soothingly for the second time in ten minutes. 'For God's sake, Quint, put that wretched thing away. Have you no idea how to behave in the home of a young lady?'

Grumbling to himself, the manservant thrust the iron bar back into the depths of his jacket.

'These daguerreotypes of Dolly as nature intended,' Adam said, trying to return the conversation to its earlier subject.

'What of 'em?' Hetty, still staring suspiciously at Quint, was on her guard.

79

'Dolly must have been very much in need of money to agree to pose for them.'

The young woman nodded. 'She wanted ready gilt so's she could leave town. Desp'rate, that's what she was. Desp'rate to get away.'

'To get away where?'

The young woman shrugged. 'Anywheres,' she said. 'As long as it was out of London. She got the coins for dropping her petticoats, but those went. Don't ask me 'ow. In the end, she even spoke to that interfering old cow what pesters all the girls.'

'And who might she be?'

'Bascombe, her name is. She runs some charity. I've got a card for it somewhere. She give all the girls one.' Hetty pulled open the drawer of a battered bureau, rummaging around in it for a few seconds before pulling out a small square of card. She handed the card to Adam, who held it up to the light from the basement window. 'The National Society for Returning Young Women to their Friends in the Country', the lettering on it read, followed by an address in the city.

'She wants to get us girls out of the theatres and into the country,' Hetty said. 'Christ alone knows what we'd all do in the country. Stop our sinning, Bascombe says. Start our starving is what I says.'

'But Dolly spoke to Mrs Bascombe?'

'Miss Bascombe.' Hetty corrected him. 'She said to me she was going to see her.'

'What did you say?'

'Laughed in her face.' The young woman looked a little embarrassed. 'I didn't think she was serious. I thought she was 'aving me on.'

'You have little time for Miss Bascombe and her ideas, I see.'

'She's a fool,' Hetty said vehemently. 'There's worse ways to earn your money than dancing on the stage. Much worse ways. Look at my Aunt Loo. She died of the matches.'

'Of the matches?'

'The phossy got into her bones. I wasn't going to have that happen to me.'

Adam was still looking puzzled. Quint stepped in to explain. 'Woman must have worked at one of the match factories down Bow way. The fumes from the matches get to 'em. Gets to the bones in the jaw.' He gestured towards his own jaw. 'Rots 'em away.'

The young dancer was nodding in energetic agreement as Quint spoke. 'Right old sight she was at the end. Couldn't bear to look at 'er. So I'm not going to have some 'oity-toity old prune telling me I'm 'eading for the fires of 'ell if I do a few jigs on stage.' Hetty stared belligerently at Adam and Quint as if they were about to second Miss Bascombe's notions of female propriety. 'I'm not going to listen to some old trout as always dresses like she's off to see a body planted in the churchyard, am I?'

'I don't suppose you are, Miss Gallant.'

Hetty's anger with Miss Bascombe seemed to have spent itself. She laughed. 'She's a sight, that one. As ugly as bull-beef. And you wouldn't believe what she 'as on 'er head.' The girl laughed again. 'I wouldn't wear a hat like 'ers if it was given away free with a pound of tea.'

Entertained as Adam was by Hetty's energetic contempt for Miss Bascombe's dress sense, he was eager to return to the subject of the girl for whom he was searching. 'Your friend Dolly,' he said. 'Her fee for her modelling had gone, you say. Would she have had any other money?'

Hetty shrugged. 'Maybe, maybe not. She had a necklace or two. And rings. One of 'em that twerp Wyndham give her. Nice, that was. She could have took 'em to the swinging dumplings.'

Adam leaned towards his servant.

'Down the pawn shop,' Quint muttered in his ear.

'I don't see as how she could have done that, mind,' Hetty continued. 'If her pockets was jingling, she wouldn't have gone to see Bascombe.'

Although she was still keeping her distance from Quint, the young woman had clearly lost any fear of her visitors she might have once had; she had moved back to her battered piano and was tapping out a simple melody on its keys. 'Be lovely to have some real gilt,' she said longingly. 'Some that was your own, and no fancy man could kiss or kick it out of you.'

'Perhaps some day you will, Miss Gallant,' Adam said.

Hetty continued to move her fingers across the keyboard and looked coquettishly at him. 'Maybe I will at that, Mr Carver, or whatever yer name is,' she said. 'As for the rest of it, if you want to find Dolly, you'd best go and see that old cow Bascombe.'

'I think I shall, Miss Gallant,' Adam said, raising his hat and turning to leave. 'Come, Quint, we shall leave the young lady to her music.'

The two men were halfway up the short flight of stone steps that led up to the street when Hetty, deserting the piano, appeared at her door. ''Ere, 'andsome,' she called. 'I got something else you might want to 'ear about.'

Adam looked down at her shapely figure silhouetted against the light. 'Go ahead, Quint,' he said. 'I shall catch you up in but a moment.' He returned to the small basement area.

Hetty moved very close to him and rested her hand on his arm. 'Tonight ain't a good night for me to be entertaining you,' she said. 'I've got what you might call other commitments.'

'You have been very helpful, Miss Gallant.'

'Hetty,' the girl said, stroking her fingers across the young man's forearm.

'You have been very helpful, Hetty.'

'Another night, when I ain't got these other commitments,' she went on, 'I could be even more 'elpful. If you was to be passing by, say the night after tomorrow, I could be very 'elpful indeed.' She leaned in to him and kissed him on the mouth. He responded and their tongues briefly touched before she pulled away. 'Night after tomorrow,' she said, and moved back into her room.

* * * * *

'Which way to the King's Cross station, Quint?' Adam asked as he strode up to join his manservant, who was loitering on the street corner a hundred yards from Hetty's flat.

Quint pointed to the right and they began to retrace their steps through the grey streets behind the Pentonville Road. Neither of them spoke.

Adam, the taste of Hetty Gallant's mouth and lips still on his, forced his thoughts to Dolly Delaney. There were so many questions about her disappearance that needed answering. Why was the girl so eager to leave town? And what had happened to the money she had earned from her modelling? Pennethorne had said that she had posed naked on several occasions. Surely this must have earned her more than a few pennies? How had she spent it so quickly that she was obliged to think of taking charity? And what of the Bascombe woman? Had Dolly been to visit her? He took out the card and looked again at the address. There was no help for it. He would have to visit the National Society for Returning Young Women to their Friends in the Country.

While Adam had been asking himself these questions, his servant had been leading the way like a military scout pushing forward into enemy territory. As they turned into the Pentonville Road, Quint began to whistle. He whistled as if he was well aware that he was producing no tune but was confident that, if he just kept whistling, he would eventually hit upon one by chance.

'What the deuce was all that business with the iron bar?' Adam asked, as they approached the Great Northern Railway's London station.

'Like I said, guv. A cosh is always 'andy to 'ave.'

'In one of the dens of iniquity you frequent, possibly it is. It was scarcely likely to be needed in the living room of a young *danseuse*.'

The older man made no reply but continued to whistle. Even amidst the noise of the traffic that now swirled about them, the sound was exceptionally piercing.

'And I wish you would refrain from that, as well, Quint.'

'What?' the servant asked in an aggrieved voice.

'Whistling like some damned butcher's boy.'

'Ain't my fault if I've got a taste for music. That 'Etty bint banging on her piano has set me off.'

'Well, do stop it. It's jangling my nerves. And I'm hungry. Let us find something to eat.'

Quint pointed to where a hot-potato stall stood on the other side of the street. Dodging a cab which came thundering past, its driver flicking his whip at his horse, they crossed the street.

'Warm your 'ands and fill your belly,' the owner of the stall said, as they approached. 'And all for only 'arf a penny.'

To both of them he dispensed a large potato, glistening with salt.

'I suppose this spot of yellow grease is butter, is it?' Adam said, prodding doubtfully at what he had been given. Quint, who was already attacking his potato like a wolf tearing at a lamb, made no reply. Tentatively the young man bit into his own food. He took one mouthful and then another. 'This is rather good,' he said, after several more mouthfuls. 'I am surprised I have never dined *al fresco* here before. I must recommend it to Cosmo.'

There was silence as the two men finished their potatoes.

'I do declare I am still hungry,' Adam said. 'Could you force yourself to eat another, Quint?'

His servant indicated that he undoubtedly could.

'We'll have another of those apiece, my good man.'

The potato man stared at Adam, clearly unused to the idea of a gentleman wanting to sample his wares. Then he took two more potatoes from the brightly polished can in which he kept them and handed them over. Adam and Quint began to eat again.

'Why would Dolly be earning all this money and yet never have any?' Adam asked after a few moments had passed. Quint, his mouth full of potato, made a series of inarticulate noises. 'Where is she spending it?' Adam was addressing his questions as much to himself as to his servant.

Quint swallowed what he had been chewing and blew noisily on the potato in his hand to cool it. 'Maybe she ain't been spending it,' he said.

His master looked enquiringly at him.

'Maybe she's bin giving it to somebody else.'

Adam thought for a moment. 'You are still of the opinion that the

84

girl is being blackmailed? That she is handing her earnings over to an extortioner?'

Quint shrugged. 'Could be,' he said.

'But it need not be so.' Adam was glimpsing other possibilities. 'She might be supporting a relative who has fallen on hard times.'

'Her dear old ma,' Quint suggested, blowing once again on his potato.

'Or a father. A brother.'

'A beau what's in danger of ending in the workhouse.'

'You are showing an unexpectedly romantic side to your imagination, Quint. But you are right. There could be another lover whom Dolly is supporting.' Adam thought for a moment or two. 'And yet, if that is the case, why is she so eager to leave London?'

Quint, who had just taken another huge bite from his hot potato and thereby rendered himself speechless once more, shook his head to indicate that he had no answer to the question.

'Hetty said her friend wanted to shake the dust of the city from her feet,' Adam continued. '"Desperate" was the word she used. Why would she be so desperate?'

CHAPTER EIGHT

The National Society for Returning Young Women to their Friends in the Country had its headquarters in one of the narrow streets adjacent to St Paul's. As Adam approached the building – a tumbledown relic of the previous century that seemed an unlikely home for any organization calling itself a 'national society' – he was aware of the great dome looming over him and over the rest of the people hurrying and scurrying through the streets. A brass plaque advertised the Society's presence, and Adam lifted a lion's head knocker and let it rap twice on the shabbily painted door. Shuffling footsteps could be heard behind the door, and it creaked open. The bald head of an elderly man gradually emerged, like a slow-motion jack-in-the box.

'If you're delivering the coal,' the old man said, 'you need to go round the back.'

'I have no coal, sir,' Adam said. 'I am looking for Miss Bascombe.'

The bald head withdrew behind the door. Adam waited some moments and was about to try the knocker once more when the head reappeared. The old man had found a pair of armless glasses, which he had propped on the bridge of his nose.

'You don't look much like the coalman,' he admitted. 'Miss Bascombe, you say?'

'If she is here. I understand this is the office of her Society.'

'Oh, she's here, all right,' the old man said, sounding as if he rather wished she wasn't. 'You'd best come in.' He opened the door wider, and Adam was able to walk into a cold and dark vestibule. The decrepit doorman, his frame bent almost double at the waist, peered up at the visitor. 'She's up there,' he said, jerking his thumb towards the ceiling. 'You'll make your own way.'

This was clearly a statement rather than a question and Adam, nodding briefly, looked towards the crooked wooden staircase at the end of the hallway.

The elderly concierge shambled into what was either a small room or a large cupboard to the left. He settled himself with difficulty on a high stool, and appeared to go to sleep.

Adam began to climb the stairs. As he did so, he caught the briefest glimpse of rooftops and St Paul's dome through the filthy glass of a tiny window that provided what little light there was. At the top of the staircase there was a landing, with two doors opening off it. One was ajar, and Adam could just see in the room the shapes of chairs and a table, all covered with sheets. He tapped on the other door. In the quiet of the building it sounded, he thought, like the knocking that rouses the porter in *Macbeth*.

It proved as nothing compared with the thunderous bellow that came from inside the room. 'Enter!'

Adam could scarcely believe that the voice belonged to anything human, let alone female. It seemed to rattle the door frame and agitate the dust in the air. He hastened to follow its instruction.

Miss Bascombe was sitting behind a large desk, silhouetted against the light from a bay window. The only other objects in the room were two chairs and a vast cabinet of Gothic design, which looked more like a scale model of a cathedral in northern France than a piece of furniture. A portrait of a mournful-looking man with a long beard hung on one wall.

'My late and very much lamented father, the Reverend Septimus Bascombe,' Miss Bascombe bellowed, noting Adam's eyes straying in the direction of the picture.

'A fine-looking man indeed,' the young man said weakly, feeling some comment, however banal, was required.

Miss Bascombe made a noise that could have been either an indication of assent or a snort of contempt and waved him towards one of the chairs.

She was a woman of enormous presence and imposing bust, reminding Adam very much of Mrs Gaffery, his landlady in Doughty Street. The founder and life president of the National Society for Returning Young Women to their Friends in the Country was evidently one of those formidable spinster ladies from the upper-middle classes who had decided to devote their energies to the improvement of those less fortunate than themselves, uncaring of whether or not the less fortunate wished to be improved. She gave the immediate impression that most members of the human race were profound disappointments to her. None the less, she was prepared to continue her generous, if possibly unavailing, efforts to better them.

As he explained the reason for his visit, Adam was conscious that she was examining him, rather like an entomologist peering down a microscope at a particularly unprepossessing species of beetle. He tried to retain his self-confidence, but he felt himself wilting under her pitiless gaze. When he came to an end, there was an ominous silence.

'Young man, I am unconvinced that it would be to the Society's benefit to tell you what I know of Miss Delaney.' Miss Bascombe continued to roar as if she was addressing a large congregation in the nearby cathedral. 'Or, indeed, to the benefit of the foolish girl herself.'

'I wish simply to speak with Miss Delaney. Her friends are anxious to know that she is well.' Adam spread his hands and smiled what he hoped was his most engaging smile. 'I can assure you that I am entirely respectable and so, too, are my motives in making my request of you.'

'You may well be as respectable as the Bank of England, Mr Carver,' Miss Bascombe boomed, looking as if she believed the exact opposite, 'but I am none the less disinclined to give you the information you want. The Society can only thrive and flourish and continue its valuable work if I, and others engaged in that work, behave with the utmost discretion. The poor, misguided young women who come to us must be able to trust us implicitly.'

Even at top volume, Miss Bascombe managed to speak in reverential tones. Her voice suggested that the activities of the National Society for Returning Young Women to their Friends in the Country were significantly more important than, say, any trifling business Mr Gladstone and his colleagues in government might currently be conducting in Westminster. 'For all I know to the contrary, you might have *designs* upon Miss Delaney.'

'Only designs for her safety and well-being, ma'am.'

Miss Bascombe made a sound somewhere between a loud snort and a horse-like neigh. It didn't give Adam the impression that the lady was warming to him, or growing more likely to accede to his request. Silence fell as he wondered what to say next, interrupted only by stertorous breathing from the other side of the table.

'Such a noble cause your Society serves,' he said eventually.

Miss Bascombe, who clearly thought his statement self-evident, said nothing.

Adam stumbled on with his flattery. 'So many young women who have been rescued from the dangers of an improvident – and, dare I say it, immoral – life in the city and re-introduced to the simpler virtues of the country. I can only congratulate you on your achievements, ma'am.' Looking around the Society's shabby office, he was suddenly struck with inspiration. 'The fine work you do cries out for the support of all decent people. The moral support and, of course, the financial.'

Miss Bascombe, who had been looking distinctly bored by his words of praise, was immediately more attentive. She sat forward in her chair, her bust coming gently to rest on the table top. 'As you say, Mr Carver, the Society proves the saviour of many a young girl whose fate would otherwise be too terrible to contemplate.' She gazed briefly into space as if she was doing exactly that. Then she turned to stare pointedly at the young man. 'And to save souls from the sins of the city demands the outlay of pounds, shillings and pence. For myself, the joy of setting trembling footsteps once more on the path to virtue is reward enough, but there are so many other expenses involved.'

Adam reached into his pocket. 'Perhaps I might be allowed to make a small donation to so worthy a cause,' he said.

Miss Bascombe bowed her head regally to indicate that he would, indeed, be so allowed.

'A cheque drawn on my bank in Fleet Street. Would that be acceptable?'

'Ah, Child's of Fleet Street.' The woman's voice dropped to what was, by her standards, a mere whisper. She spoke as if she was naming a place of religious pilgrimage. 'Most acceptable, most acceptable.'

'I was thinking five guineas might be of some assistance to your Society.' In truth, Adam was also thinking that he must be mad to offer so substantial a sum to an organization of such dubious benefit to society. Was finding Dolly Delaney so important a task to him? Was there any honourable way in which he could suggest to Sunman that the Foreign Office might reimburse him? He pushed these thoughts to the back of his mind and continued to smile amiably at the large lady on the other side of the table. 'Or six, perhaps.'

'Most kind, most kind.' Miss Bascombe pushed a silver pen in Adam's direction.

He picked it up and began to fill out one of the cheques in the book that the bank had sent him only recently. 'I understand perfectly that you cannot divulge information about your young women to casual enquirers, ma'am. I regret that I obliged you to spell out to me what should have been immediately apparent. It was a failure of both taste and intelligence on my part.'

Miss Bascombe passed him a sheet of blotting paper. 'You are too harsh on yourself, Mr Carver. I was, perhaps, a little hasty in my earlier remarks.'

Adam handed over the cheque.

'It is only reasonable that the true friends of a young lady in unfortunate circumstances should be eager to hear good tidings of her,' Miss Bascombe acknowledged.

'They are *good* tidings, are they?'

'Oh, excellent, Mr Carver, excellent.' The cheque disappeared swiftly into a drawer in the desk. 'The young lady in question was, as perhaps you know, eager to leave the city.'

'I had heard as much,' Adam admitted.

'The Society was able to advance her the monies to achieve her ambition. I advised her to travel northwards. To York. We have an office in the capital of the north. I told her to present herself there. I wrote to our representative there, a Mr Ridgewell, to notify him of her impending arrival. He was to find employment for her with a good family, and to provide her with another ten shillings to help her in settling into her new home.'

* * * * *

As Adam emerged from the ramshackle building into the sunlight, he breathed a sigh of relief. Conversation with Miss Bascombe was a demanding activity. He felt he could congratulate himself on his success in persuading her to part with the information about Dolly Delaney, although he wondered what his banker would make of his sudden charitable interest in young women returning to their friends in the country.

Across the narrow street a man was leaning against the wall of a baker's shop. He was dressed in a dirty grey jacket and crumpled trousers. A battered bowler hat, several sizes too small for him, was perched unsteadily on his head. He was chewing on the unlit stub of a cigar and staring balefully at the baker's customers as they passed him and entered the shop.

Adam began to walk towards Cheapside. As he approached, the man spat out the cigar stub, pushing himself away from the wall and moving into Adam's path. 'You're the son of Carver the railway builder, ain't you?' he said.

Adam, forced to halt, looked at the man in surprise. He did not much like what he saw.

'My father was engaged in the financing of railway companies, yes.'

'I thought you were. When I saw you come out of that door over there, I said to myself, "That's Carver's boy, that is. Bit older than when I last saw him, but definitely Carver's boy. Who'd have thought I'd run across him again?"'

91

'I make no secret of the identity of my father. My late father. Although I am struggling to understand what business it can be of yours.' Adam smiled in an attempt to blunt the brusqueness of his words. He did not wish to antagonize the stranger unduly, but nor did he wish to prolong the conversation.

'Been dead a few years now, ain't he?' The man showed no sign of moving out of Adam's way.

'Again you are correct, sir, but again I am at a loss as to know how it concerns you.' The persistence of this belligerent loafer was beginning to annoy him.

'You don't recognize me, do you, *Mister* Carver?' The man placed a hissing emphasis on the word 'Mister' as if there were some doubt as to Adam's claim to the title. 'No surprise in that. You weren't much more than a young pup straight out of school when last we met. And I'm not the man I was. You'd scarcely believe the changes a few years living in the gutter will make.'

'You are correct, sir. I do not recognize you. Now, if you would oblige me by standing aside, I will leave you.'

'My name is Benskin. Job Benskin.'

Adam, who was moving to the left to evade the man and proceed on his way, stopped abruptly.

'Ah, that's caught your attention, ain't it?' Benskin said. 'Not quite so high and mighty now, eh?'

'I remember you. I remember your name. And your face.' It was true. Looking again at this dishevelled and unshaven man, Adam could indeed recall him. On his occasional visits to his father's offices in Cheapside, he had seen Benskin there. Lurking obsequiously in the background, always ready to dart forward and offer papers to sign or an appointment book to consult. Then he had been smartly dressed and well-trimmed. Charles Carver had thought highly of him, but Adam, when he had considered him at all, had disliked him. He was too oily, too insincere. 'You were a clerk at one of my father's companies.'

'I was. And much good it did me.'

'I am sorry if you have found yourself fallen on hard times, Mr

Benskin. But there is little I can do to help you. My father passed away several years ago and I have resigned any interest I might have had in his businesses.'

'Don't you go pussyfooting around with me, you young imp. "My father passed away."' The man mimicked Adam's voice with bitter intensity. 'Because Job Benskin knows. Why don't you go ahead and say it? Charles Carver killed himself. That's what the rumour is, isn't it? He couldn't face the disgrace. Another week and your precious father would have been in the *Gazette*, wouldn't he? He would have been bankrupt. Or, even worse, he would have been in the courts. As he should have been. Damned rogue that he was.'

Adam flushed with anger. 'You are impertinent, Mr Benskin. I will not listen to these slanders and calumnies. I must ask you again to step aside and allow me to pass.'

The man turned his head and spat into the gutter. 'I ain't stopping you, you arrogant young devil. But you'd do well to remember what I says. Job Benskin knows. He ain't going to be fooled by all the fol-de-rol your father's fancy friends put about. Charles Carver didn't *pass away*. And he didn't kill himself, neither.'

Adam had been staring past Benskin but, at these words, he started. He looked down and caught the man's bloodshot eye. 'What in heaven's name do you mean by that?'

'That would be telling. And I ain't telling for nothing.'

'If you are angling for money, I have none about my person to give you.'

The man moved back a step or two, a sneer on his face. Adam considered whether or not he should pursue the conversation. Could this broken-down scarecrow truly have important information about his father's death? It was unlikely, he decided. Benskin would probably say anything that he thought might seize the attention. Gathering together all the dignity he could muster, Adam stepped past the man, continuing on his way towards Cheapside. But, after he had taken only a dozen paces, he heard once more the bitter voice behind him.

'Job Benskin knows.'

*   *   *   *   *

Walter Patch's place of business was tucked away behind St Bride's Church. Although Adam had been told by Miss Bascombe that she had despatched Dolly to York, he had not yet decided for certain whether or not he believed the girl had actually gone. For the time being, he saw no harm in pursuing any other lines of enquiry he had. The photographer was one of these. As Adam examined the window of Patch's premises, in which two wood and brass cameras stood on their tripods, Sir Christopher Wren's famous steeple soared above him. Little light could reach the front of the shop, and he wondered how on earth Patch managed to take photographs there. It was not for nothing that they were often called 'sun' pictures. He took a step back and looked upwards. The building had three storeys and its neighbours only two; its top floor rose beyond the shadows cast by the church and had large windows facing east. Ah, he thought, that explains it.

Adam pushed open the door of the shop and entered its gloomy interior. There was a tall, well-dressed customer already in the shop. He was standing at a wooden counter, talking to a shorter man with a tobacco-stained moustache, whom Adam assumed was Walter Patch. As the customer continued to speak, Patch's eyes drifted away from him and focused on his new visitor. Adam nodded at the photographer, who stared at him unblinkingly for a moment before returning his attention to the man in front of him.

The customer was talking of the glass plates that he needed for his camera. Patch picked up a notepad and began scribbling in it with a pencil.

'If you could have them delivered, Patch,' the tall man said. 'The usual address.' Then he turned and left the shop, raising his hat briefly to Adam as he passed him.

Patch watched him go and then turned to the young man. 'You're that nosey bugger Pennethorne warned me about, ain't you?' He spoke cheerfully enough. It seemed the photographer was likely to be less troubled by the young man's questions than his confederate.

'Almost certainly I am,' Adam acknowledged.

'The one who's asking all the questions about the girls.'

'One particular girl.'

'Well, I ain't going to be much help to you even if I wanted to be. Which I don't. They come here, they drop their drawers, I point the camera at 'em and they goes. Simple as that. I don't bother much with names. Most of 'em wouldn't tip me their real moniker anyway. Who's this one you're interested in?'

'Dolly Delaney.'

'Blonde bint?'

Adam agreed that Dolly was fair-haired.

'I remember her. Pennethorne sent her round from Wych Street. She come 'ere three or four times.'

'And?'

Patch laughed. It wasn't a very pleasant laugh. 'What d'you think? We goes upstairs. She casts off 'er clobber. I set up my camera on its tripod, disappear under the cover and take pictures of 'er.'

'Did she speak to you at all? Have you any notion why she chose to have these pictures taken?'

The photographer snorted briefly and contemptuously. 'Why? Why d'you think? Money, of course.' He rubbed his thumb and forefinger together. 'And she didn't do much in the way of talking. Some of 'em tend to gab a lot beforehand and some don't. She didn't.'

'And you wouldn't want your models talking while the pictures were being taken. For fear of spoiling them.'

'Exactly. It's hard enough to get most of them to sit still without encouraging them to start flapping their mouths and ruining the plates that way. They ain't cheap, you know.'

Adam did know. His own experiments in the art of the daguerreotype had been surprisingly expensive. He made to speak again, but, before he could properly begin, Patch had interrupted him.

'Don't go doing what you did with Pennethorne, if that was what you was planning. Trying to cod me with talk of the police. They may scare Pennethorne, but they don't set my teeth a-trembling. I got friends who could put the fear of God up that berk Sampson fast enough.'

Adam said nothing and Patch leaned forward, baring his yellowing teeth. 'You know who that gent is who just left?'

'I have no notion.'

''E's a magistrate, ain't he? And I got other customers just as nobby as him. And they're all very pally with Walter Patch. He supplies 'em with what they need in the photographic line, does Walter Patch, and they ain't going to take too kindly to anybody who tries to stop him doing so.'

'I am not trying to stop you dealing with your customers, Mr Patch. I am merely seeking information about one girl who visited you.'

'I've told you as much as I know.'

'Which seems to be very little.'

'Well, maybe I know something and maybe I know nothing but, either way, I ain't telling you any more.'

Adam was wondering how to proceed with his questioning when there was the sound of the door opening, and another customer entered the shop.

With a twist of his face, half-scowl and half-grin, in the young man's direction, Patch crossed the room to serve him.

Adam was left to pick up and examine some of the advertising leaflets, scattered over a glass-topped cabinet, that the camera companies issued to extol their wares.

'You know 'ow much I can charge for an ordinary portrait?' the photographer asked, when he returned. 'About a bob a go.' He looked up at Adam. 'And 'ow much do you reckon I can charge for a picture of a nice-looking woman in the buff? Go on, have a guess.'

'I have no notion.'

'About three times as much.'

'A profitable business, then.'

'Very profitable, and I ain't going to let a smooth young gent like yourself or an interfering buzzard like Sampson get in the way of it.'

'And what of the young women who sit for you?'

Patch flapped his hand in exasperation. 'Nobody's twisting these dollymops' arms to get 'em in front of the camera,' he said. 'We pay 'em and they're glad to get the gelt. We ain't such villains, you know.'

'Your friend Mr Pennethorne said much the same.'

'He ain't my friend. He's a business associate. But no doubt he's right in what he said. We both are. We ain't doing no harm. And most of the time Sampson and the other miserable bluebottles who come pestering us can't prove we're breaking the law.' Here, Patch walked away from Adam to return to a position behind his wooden counter. He took a piece of cloth from underneath it and began to wipe its surface carefully. 'So why don't you just bugger off and leave us alone?'

* * * * *

Adam waved his hand at the waiter in the Marco Polo and indicated, by an assortment of elaborate gestures, that he would welcome another Scotch and soda. He was sitting in the club's smoking room, a place which now always reminded him of poor Mr Moorhouse, but today he was thinking of Charles Carver.

The meeting with Benskin the previous day had unsettled Adam. He had, he realized, seen so little of his father for so many years before his death that it seemed as if it was only when he was a boy that he had known him. And in truth, even then he had seen his father infrequently; when he was not at school, he was largely entrusted to the care of servants.

The waiter returned with his drink and Adam continued to think about his father. He remembered that the old man had taken him once to Wyld's Great Globe in Leicester Square. And they had seen a panorama of the Siege of Sebastopol later in the day. Adam thought he must have been about ten years old at the time. Further pictures from the past flashed into his mind. The two of them had been to the Zoological Gardens that same summer – the summer before they had left the house in North Moulton Street. He had liked the hippopotamus, and his father had told him that it was a gift from the Pasha of Egypt. What was the creature's name? Obaysch, that was it. Obaysch the hippo. He was there still, as Adam remembered reading an article on the Zoo recently in *The Illustrated London News*. Indeed, he had been curiously moved to hear that, during all the years that he had been growing up, boarding in Shrewsbury, studying in Cambridge, travelling in Greece, the animal that had lodged in his memory had continued to live in Regent's Park, visited by thousands of other children as delighted by the sight of it as he had been.

Adam raised his glass to his lips and considered what he had always been told of his father's death. Charles Carver had hanged himself in a room in the Langham Hotel. Faced with the final disappearance of the fortune he had built up over decades and with the exposure of the fraudulent means he had, for years, been employing to sustain it, the railway baron had taken his own life.

The consequences for Adam himself had been enormous: the scandal had been largely hushed up but the money to support him at Cambridge was gone. He had been obliged to leave. That first expedition to European Turkey with the late Professor Fields had saved him from the idle indigence into which he might so easily have fallen, but it had also distanced him from the investigations into Charles Carver's affairs. When he had returned, the executors of the railway baron's will had rescued what little could be salvaged from the wreckage of his businesses, and Adam had an income of sorts. But was there more to learn now about his father's death, nearly five years later?

The young man drank the last of his Scotch and soda and sighed so loudly that another club member, dozing in a leather armchair a dozen feet away, awoke and glared at him.

'My apologies for disturbing you, sir,' Adam said, standing and leaving the smoking room at a swift pace. Surely, he thought as he left, that wretched man Benskin could not know something that he did not?

CHAPTER NINE

As he emerged from the doors of the German Gymnasium, after another exhilarating hour with the épée, Adam looked up at the sky. Although it was only just approaching half-past six in the evening, it was growing dark.

He stepped onto the cobbled walkway which led to Pancras Road. It was a warm evening and he unbuttoned his jacket. As he took a few strides away from the building, out of the twilight a figure came swiftly towards him. Instinctively, Adam took a pace back and the movement saved him. The man had a knife which flashed across Adam's chest, ripping through the fabric of his jacket.

Off balance, the assailant stumbled. Adam seized him and they both fell, struggling, to the ground. The man from the shadows again swung the knife in Adam's direction and the young man grabbed wildly at his attacker's arms, succeeding in holding him by the wrists. Adam was now on his back, the cobbles pressing into him as his adversary twisted and turned in his grasp, trying to force the knife down into his face.

The unknown attacker was strong and, despite Adam's straining efforts to hold him off, he began to press the blade in his right hand ever closer to the young man's left eye. In desperation, Adam released his hold on his opponent's other hand and punched his right fist into the man's stomach.

There was a wheezing gasp and the man fell to one side. Adam was able to sit up but he remained half stunned by the suddenness of the assault. He was still in danger, he realized, and he willed himself to his feet. His attacker had also pulled himself upright.

Both men stood on the cobbles, a yard apart, breathing heavily as they stared at one another. The assailant still held the knife in his hand. Adam could feel blood trickling down his fingers from a cut in the palm of his hand.

The man lunged towards him once more, but the punch to the stomach had winded him and his aim was poor. Adam was able to grasp his wrist again and force the knife backwards. The man directed a punch at his head with his other hand and Adam ducked, the movement allowing him to grasp the man's fist in his fingers. Swaying back and forth, the two of them began a bizarre wrestling match as each tried to force the other backwards. Adam was squeezing his attacker's right wrist in a desperate bid to force him into dropping his weapon; the man was unable to do more than cling determinedly to it.

Grunting with effort, Adam's attacker slowly forced him backwards until the young man felt his heel catch on one of the cobbles. He staggered and was obliged to release his hold on the other man in order to maintain his balance. The attacker tumbled forward, carried by his momentum, but righted himself before he fell. His knife hand was now free again. He took a swift step towards Adam but was stopped in his tracks by a shout from the entrance to the Gymnasium.

'Enough!'

Another figure appeared. He was holding a long, thin sword which he was pointing menacingly at the throat of Adam's opponent.

The attacker took one look at the newcomer and turned and fled.

The thin blade glinted briefly in the evening light before the man from the Gymnasium slipped it swiftly back into its casing. Fencing sword became Malacca cane. Its owner reached out his hand and helped Adam to his feet.

'You are a lucky fellow, Señor Carver,' Juan Alvarado said. 'That rogue intended to kill you.'

Adam was leaning forward slightly, brushing dirt from his trousers and struggling to regain both breath and composure. He picked up his hat, which had fallen to the ground in the first moments of the fight, and held out his unwounded hand. 'I do believe he did,' he said. 'I owe you my deepest gratitude, Alvarado. If you had not arrived when you did, I think he might have succeeded.'

'I am happy to have been of service.' The Argentine swordsman shook his pupil's outstretched hand. He looked at Adam with undisguised curiosity. 'You have some dangerous enemies, my friend.'

'He was just a ruffian out to rob me.' Adam did not believe this but he had no desire to offer Alvarado a lengthy explanation of why he did not. He pulled a silk handkerchief from his pocket and wrapped it carefully around the cut on his other hand. 'A more violent ruffian than usually roams the street, but a ruffian none the less.'

A small crowd, some of whom had either seen or half seen what had happened, was beginning to gather around the two men. Somebody suggested in a loud voice that the police should be summoned.

'I do not wish to speak to the police,' Adam said and began to push his way through the press of people. The Argentine followed.

No one made any attempt to stop them and, as they walked into Pancras Road, the crowd behind them began to disperse.

'In my city, in Buenos Aires, an attempted killing would not be so unusual. During the years of civil war there were many such assassinations. But in London, in the capital of the great empire . . . ' Alvarado left his sentence to drift unfinished between them.

'Murders are, perhaps, more common in London than you imagine,' Adam said. 'And, as I say, this was no deliberate attempt to kill me. The robber simply grew more violent the more I resisted. He did not set out to do away with me.'

'If you say so, my friend.' Alvarado made little attempt to hide the fact that he remained unconvinced. 'But, should you need any assistance in the future, I am at your service.'

The two men had stopped as they emerged onto the Euston Road. The Argentine turned to Adam and made the briefest of bows, at the same time raising his swordstick in a swift salute. Adam raised his hat, scuffed and battered from the fight, in acknowledgement and Alvarado walked briskly away in the direction of the new St Pancras railway station.

* * * * *

It was close to eight in the evening when Adam returned to Doughty Street. As he opened the door from the street, he could hear what sounded like voices raised in disputation on the staircase leading to his rooms. Closing the door behind him, he realized that it was but one voice and the voice belonged to Mrs Gaffery.

Suppressing a weary sigh, Adam began to climb the stairs. When he reached the small landing outside his flat, he found his landlady haranguing Quint.

'Vagabonds accosting me on my very doorstep,' she was saying, loudly. 'Without so much as a "By your leave" or an "If you please". Thrusting notes into my hand as if I was the common postman. It will not do, Quint. You can inform your master of that from me.'

Quint, who was staring past Mrs Gaffery, apparently entranced by the flowery wallpaper with which the stairwell was decorated, caught sight of Adam approaching. 'You can tell him yerself,' he said.

As swiftly as her considerable bulk would allow her, Mrs Gaffery spun on her heel and confronted the new arrival. 'Mr Carver,' she said, 'I have been explaining to your man Quint here. I cannot become the go-between for any ill-kempt mendicant who wishes to communicate with you.'

'No one would want you to do so, Mrs Gaffery,' Adam said soothingly, wondering what had happened to ruffle his landlady's feathers so comprehensively.

'Well, you must tell that to the bearded lout who stood between me and my own home this afternoon. "Here, missis," he says, "give this to that man Carver." The impertinence of the fellow! "Madam to you," says I. And then he pushed *this* into my hand.' Mrs Gaffery waved a grubby-looking piece of paper in Adam's direction. 'It's filthy. I had a good mind to throw it away immediately. But a letter is

102

a letter. However disgusting, it should reach the person to whom it is addressed.'

Adam could now see that Mrs Gaffery was holding an envelope between the forefinger and thumb of her right hand. With a look of sour distaste, she delivered it to her tenant. Then she moved majestically past him and began to descend the stairs.

'Thank you, Mrs Gaffery,' Adam called after her. 'This will not happen again.'

'See that it does not, sir,' the landlady replied, and retired into her own sanctum on the ground floor.

Quint, relieved of any need to remain on the landing, had already disappeared into the flat. Adam was left alone, looking at the letter he had been given. The envelope was, indeed, soiled. It was covered in grubby fingerprints and looked unpleasantly as if it had shared a pocket, at least temporarily, with a used handkerchief. Adam held it as gingerly as Mrs Gaffery had. He looked at the address, curious as to the identity of his correspondent.

'To Charles Carver's Young Pup, Doughty Street,' he read. He sighed inwardly. This must be Benskin again, he thought. How had the wretched man discovered where he lived? Trying to touch as little of the envelope as he could, Adam opened it and extracted the paper inside. It looked like a sheet torn from a notebook. The copperplate handwriting on it, however, although in cheap ink which had smudged in places, was surprisingly neat.

'*You arrogant young rogue,*' the letter began without any further ado. '*You may think yourself very high and mighty, strutting around Bloomsbury like a peacock, but you don't fool Job Benskin. Job Benskin knows things about the Carver family that you don't. There's truths about your precious father and his precious goings-on that you'll maybe want to hear. And about why he died. And how. But it's going to cost you. For proofs of what Job Benskin knows it's going to cost you fifty guineas. If you come to the Three Pigs in Whitechapel tomorrow night with that sum about your person, then you'll hear the gospel from Job Benskin. If you don't, you'll continue to preen yourself in ignorance.*' Adam turned over the paper in search of more but there was only the signature: '*Yours in eternal contempt, Job Benskin,*' it read.

He folded the paper and placed it back in the envelope, which he thrust into his pocket. What, he wondered, was he to make of this? In their meeting in the street near St Paul's, Benskin had more than hinted that Charles Carver had died as a result of foul play. This was surely unlikely. His father had not been murdered; he had destroyed himself. And, assuming that to be the case, what other 'secrets' could the man reveal? He might know something of the circumstances of the railway baron's death which Adam himself did not, but could that something possibly be worth fifty guineas? Almost certainly not.

And yet the young man was once again reminded of how little he himself really knew about his father's last days. As events had pushed Charles Carver closer and closer to the awful decision to take his own life, his son had been idling away his time at college. He had seen little of his father during those final few months. Perhaps Benskin, the clerk who had been ever-present in the London offices of the railway company, had been privy to secrets to which Adam had not.

There was, Adam decided, only one way to find out. He followed his servant into his rooms.

'What do you know of the Three Pigs in Whitechapel, Quint?' he called.

The older man's head emerged from the small boxroom which was his own domain. 'It's a boozing-ken off the high street,' he replied.

Not for the first time Adam was quietly impressed by Quint's encyclopaedic knowledge of all the many thousands of establishments in the city that offered drink for sale. 'A rough and ready sort of place, I suppose?'

'Some might call it that.'

'What would you call it?'

'An 'ell-'ole.'

'Not the sort of place I should venture to visit alone?'

'Not unless you want your pockets emptying.' The manservant paused, as if bringing the Three Pigs and its ambience to mind. 'Or your jaw broke.'

'Neither of those eventualities sounds an attractive one. You must accompany me there. Two will be safer than one.'

Quint looked as if he doubted the proposition. 'Ain't no call to go sticking our 'eads where they ain't wanted,' he said.

'But our heads *are* wanted there, Quint. At least, mine is. A gentleman named Benskin makes it very clear that he is expecting to see me at the establishment in question.'

Adam took off his jacket and hung it on the coat-stand in the corner of the room, then threw himself into the easy chair by the fire. 'Come, do you not wish to discover what the wretched man wants?'

'If we go down the Pigs, causing trouble, our necks won't be worth a jigger,' Quint said. 'In fact, they won't be worth 'arf a jigger.'

* * * * *

Adam stood by the area railings and looked down at Hetty Gallant's flat. It was nine o'clock in the evening and the street was dark save for the light coming from the windows of the surrounding houses. He wondered if he was acting sensibly by returning to see the young dancer. There was no doubt that the invitation to do so had been given when he and Quint had called upon Hetty two days before. And there was no question that she was an attractive woman. Long of leg and lovely of feature, just as Cosmo had said ladies of the chorus should be. He remembered with pleasure the kiss she had bestowed upon him. But perhaps it would be unwise to involve himself with Dolly's friend? To question her was one thing; to try to bed her quite another.

He was still debating what he should do when his eye caught a movement above him. He looked up. A thin-faced woman had twitched back the curtain on a first-floor window and was staring down at the street, a melancholy ghost watching with envy as the living went about their business outside. He raised his hat politely, uncertain whether or not she could see him. It appeared she could. The curtain fell back into place and the woman's face disappeared.

Adam returned his attention to the basement flat. He could now hear raised voices coming from below. Hetty, it seemed, already had a visitor. He took several steps back into the darkness of the street as the door of Hetty's flat opened suddenly and a man stepped into the tiny basement yard. From where he was standing, Adam could not see his face but he could hear his voice. It was educated, upper-class and, at that moment, whining and petulant.

'I will not be treated in this fashion,' it said.

'You ain't being treated in any bleedin' fashion, you silly bugger.'

Taking a step forward, Adam could just see Hetty's figure, framed in the doorway to her rooms. She was standing with her hands on her hips like an Irish washerwoman in a *Punch* cartoon.

'I will not be teased and vexed by some little madam who earns her living by exposing herself to the public gaze.'

'Ain't nobody doing any vexin' but you.'

'I have travelled all the way out to this godforsaken part of town and now you are proposing to send me away. That is surely enough to try the temperament of a saint.'

'I ain't sendin' you away, sweetheart.' Hetty's voice suggested that she was struggling to sound soothing, when her urge was to lose her temper. 'Jest sayin' it ain't a good idea for us to be together right now.'

'Precisely. You are sending me away.'

Adam watched as Hetty flung out an arm in exasperation. He still could not make out more of the man than a shape in the darkness. ''Ave it your own way, then,' she said. 'I'm sending you away. We shouldn't be seen together. Remember what 'is nibs said the other day? No consorting until after it's all over.'

'Damn and blast the man!' The voice from the dark sounded bitter. 'He doesn't understand how I feel. I want to be with you.'

'And I want to be with you, my love.' Hetty spoke more gently than she had before. 'But it ain't possible.'

The man now took several steps forward and his face was illuminated in the yellow glow from Hetty's window. Adam recognized him immediately. It was Harry Vernon – Sunman's colleague from the Foreign Office who had involved himself so indiscreetly with Dolly Delaney. He looked tired and woebegone. His shoulders drooped and his face was frozen in misery. Hetty came closer to him and kissed him on the cheek. Vernon seized her like a shipwrecked sailor clutching at passing flotsam and pulled her into his embrace. Hetty allowed him to do so for a moment and then pushed him away. 'After it's all over, eh, love?'

Vernon nodded. The anger that had been driving him a few minutes before was now entirely gone. 'I shall return to my club,' he said in a dull monotone.

'That's the ticket, sweetheart.' Hetty patted his hand with hers. 'And we'll set the sparks flyin' when we can.'

Vernon turned without any farewell and began to climb the stone steps. Behind him, Adam heard the door to Hetty's flat close with a bang. There was no time for Adam to do more than retreat more deeply into the darkness of the unlit street and hope that he could not be seen. However, the Foreign Office man was clearly not taking much notice of his surroundings. He trudged past, oblivious of the presence of Adam, who watched as his hunched shadow reached the one gas lamp in the street and headed off towards the Pentonville Road.

Adam smiled ruefully to himself. Hopes of a romantic encounter with the dancer would have to be postponed. This did not seem like the time for a social call. But the visit had not been uninteresting, he thought. So it was not just Dolly Delaney with whom Harry Vernon had been conducting a liaison. Vernon must have been the plump gentleman in Wimpole Street whom Quint had seen Hetty visiting. The man was an unexpected Lothario, but it would seem that he was involved with not one chorus girl but two. Adam smiled again. He wondered what Sunman would make of this news.

The young man was still debating with himself whether or not he would do so when he heard the door to Hetty's rooms open again.

'You coming to visit, 'andsome?' The young woman's voice

sounded from the darkness. 'Or you planning to jest stand out there all night and catch your death of cold?'

Adam smiled to himself. 'Am I welcome?' he asked.

'You was invited, wasn't you?'

'I do believe I was.'

'Well, then, you're welcome.'

Feeling an exhilarating mix of desire and anticipation, Adam made his way down the steps to where Hetty was waiting.

CHAPTER TEN

'**H**ere, you've got to call off this bleeding peeler you've set on me.'

As Adam left the gates at the end of Doughty Street and turned down Guilford Street towards the Gray's Inn Road, a man approached him and seized him by the forearm. It was Jacob Pennethorne, the shopkeeper from Wych Street.

Adam had been reflecting with a mixture of pleasure and puzzlement on his night with Hetty. What a curious and delightful girl she was. He was not sure he had ever met anyone quite like her. Although she had bestowed her favours so generously, he still had little idea what she truly thought of him. When he had left her rooms as dawn was breaking, she had been almost brusque in her farewell. Many men in his position – Cosmo Jardine, for example – would not have concerned themselves with what a chorus girl might or might not think, but Adam found he could not be so blasé. He could not help but ponder on what had occurred. Pennethorne's interruption of his thoughts was therefore both irritating and impertinent. He shook off the man's hand and spoke curtly to him. 'I have no notion of what you are talking about.'

'This bugger Sampson,' Pennethorne said irately. 'He's been round three times since you came a-visiting. He's taken away half my stock. You've got to have a word with him.'

Adam looked at the shopkeeper. The man did not look well. His hair was greasy and unwashed, his face pale. Although it was a warm spring morning, he was sweating profusely. Adam considered ignoring him and walking away, but decided against it. 'We cannot talk about this in the street,' he said. 'There is a tavern around the corner in the Gray's Inn Road. Let us go there.'

Once settled in the saloon bar of the Goat and Compasses with a brandy and water in front of him, Pennethorne seemed less angry and more depressed. He sat on a three-legged stool and stared mournfully at the patterned oilcloth which covered the bar floor.

'Now,' Adam said, 'perhaps you will tell me what you mean by harassing me in the public highway.'

'I told you already,' the shopkeeper said, still looking downwards. 'It's your pal Sampson. Ever since you come to Wych Street asking about that Delaney girl, he's never left me in peace. Badgering me the livelong day. Stealing my goods. I want you to tell him to stop it.'

'I have no power to prevent a policeman from doing what he believes to be his duty.'

'I ain't so green as a cabbage, you know,' Pennethorne said, looking up from his examination of the oilcloth. 'You want me to think it's a bleeding coincidence that Sampson's round my shop five minutes after you've gone. You set him on to me. You can set him off.'

Adam thought for a moment. As he did, the door from the street opened and three young men, in high spirits, entered the pub and called for the barman. Pennethorne watched them morosely.

'I assure you that I had nothing to do with Sergeant Sampson's visits to Wych Street,' Adam said. He held up his hand to quieten his companion, who seemed still in the mood to argue the point. 'As you know, I spoke to him before I came calling upon you but I had no influence on any decision he may have made to mount a raid upon your shop.'

'Sez you,' Pennethorne remarked bitterly.

'Says I,' Adam agreed. 'But I am willing to speak to the sergeant and suggest that no further purpose will be served by turning up so regularly on your doorstep.'

The shopkeeper eyed him suspiciously. 'And who's to say he'll pay any regard to you? If you ain't the one who's told him to badger me.'

'There can be no guarantee, I admit. But I have reason to believe that Sampson will heed what I say.'

Pennethorne tipped back his head and downed the last of his brandy and water like a heron swallowing a fish.

'However,' Adam continued, 'there is a quid pro quo.'

'A quid! I ain't paying you any bleeding money,' Pennethorne hastened to say.

'Not that kind of a quid. More a kind of reciprocal arrangement.' The haggard shopkeeper still looked baffled. 'I scratch your back and you scratch mine. I speak to Sampson, and you give me more information than you did the other day.'

Pennethorne stared at the young drinkers on the far side of the bar who were now cheerfully swapping insults and mock punches.

'I do declare, Barrington,' one shouted, 'you're nothing but a forty-faced liar!'

A red-faced youth with bristling sideburns, presumably Barrington, was waving his pot of ale in the air, sloshing quantities of liquid over the side. 'Every word the truth,' he roared. 'I swear it on the grave of my sainted mother.'

'Your mother's alive and well and living in Pimlico,' his friend said. 'I've met her myself.'

'So you have,' Barrington said, and slapped him heartily on the back. All three young men laughed as if this remark was the funniest they had heard in days and retired with their drinks to a table in the far corner of the saloon.

Pennethorne watched them go, with a look on his face that suggested he was cursing the lot of them to hell and back.

'I've told you all I can tell,' he said eventually, turning his attention back to Adam.

'I don't believe you have. And, until you do, I won't be hurrying to have a word with Sergeant Sampson.'

Pennethorne gazed at Adam as if he hoped that sheer fury might shrivel the young man in his seat. He stood abruptly and walked to the bar, beckoning angrily to the barman. Returning with another brandy and water, he slumped onto his seat.

'There was another man asking after that Dolly girl,' he said after another pause. 'A few days before you were.'

'Why did you not tell me of this when I visited you before?'

Pennethorne said nothing.

'Did you know him?'

The shopkeeper threw back half his drink.

'Did you know him?' Adam repeated.

'Yes, I knew him.'

'And his name is?'

Pennethorne twisted on the three-legged stool as if trying to propel it into motion across the bar-room floor and out of the door into the Gray's Inn Road.

'He's been a customer of yours in the past, has he not?'

The man stopped turning in his seat and nodded miserably.

'Well, I appreciate your loyalty to your clientele, Mr Pennethorne, but I need a name. What is the name of this man?'

'And, if I give it to you, you'll get this swine Sampson off my back?'

'I will do my very best.'

'Wyndham. His name's Adolphus Wyndham.'

* * * * *

As Quint had said, the Three Pigs was not a salubrious tavern. It was located in a filth-strewn courtyard off Leman Street, not far from where they had visited the penny gaff. Adam noticed that the smell of horse dung, so commonplace in its assault on the nostrils throughout the city, was stronger here than on the main thorough-fare. There must be a stable close by. The pub was a building that appeared to be falling in on itself. The roof bowed in the middle and a battered chimney looked as if it were about to slide down it. Windows on the upper floors were broken and a sign, creaking in the slight breeze that was blowing, seemed in imminent danger of falling onto the head of an unwary passer-by. It would have been difficult to find a greater contrast to the brightly lit and inviting gin palaces that lined Whitechapel High Street only a few minutes' walk away.

'It ain't exackly nobby, is it?' Quint said.

'It lacks a certain *je ne sais quoi*,' his master agreed.

'Place like this,' Quint went on, 'you'd best let me do the gabbing. If you open *your* ivory box in the Pigs, talking like you do, Gawd knows what'll 'appen.'

'I shall be as quiet as a statue,' Adam said, pushing open a door that might once have been green but was now the colour of mud.

They entered a hubbub of noise. Drunken shouting echoed around a room that was small but packed with people. The shrill sound of a penny whistle came from one corner and, from another, the cracked notes of someone trying to sing. No one paid much attention to the new arrivals. There was one stained wooden table to the left of the door with nobody sitting at it. Quint, tugging at his master's sleeve, nodded in its direction. They pushed through the crowd of amiably inebriated drinkers, several of whom stared at Adam, and settled on two three-legged stools beside it.

'We had better partake of some refreshment now we are here,' the young man said, pushing a sixpence across the grubby tabletop. 'Go and buy us pale ales, Quint.'

His servant pocketed the sixpence, stood and then looked towards the bar. 'Oh, Gawd,' he said. 'That's all we bleedin' well need. Jem Baines.'

'What is the difficulty, Quint? Who is Jem Baines?'

Quint gestured vaguely in the direction of the bar.

'A vicious bastard,' he said. 'I'd 'eard 'e was in Coldbath Fields for knockin' 'is tart about. Best place for 'im.'

Adam looked across the room, struggling to see past swaying drinkers. Three men were leaning against the counter, each with an arm around a blowsy, bosomy woman. As he looked, one of them pushed himself away from the counter and, still attached to his female companion, moved towards the table where the two visitors were sitting. People stood back swiftly to let him pass.

'It seems as if Mr Baines has seen you as well, Quint,' Adam said.

Baines pushed aside a thin, gangling man who had been slow to get out of his way and came to a halt in front of them.

'Well, if it ain't my old pal, Quint Devlin,' he said, grinning like a devil welcoming a newly deceased sinner to hell. 'You remember Quintus, don't you, Kate?'

The woman with him, red-haired and large-busted, looked much the worse for drink. Her eyes were glazed as she stared dully at the newcomers. She made a vague grunt of assent.

''Ow you doing, Quint?' her friend asked.

'Not much better for seein' you, Baines.'

'Now, that ain't friendly, cully, is it? Not friendly at all. When you ain't seen your old pal Baines since Julius Caesar was a pup.' The man was squat and barrel-chested, with a face that looked like a constipated pug dog. 'Years since I seen old Quintus 'ere,' he confided to Adam. 'Tell you 'ow long it is. Last time I seen 'im, 'e 'ad a full 'ead of 'air. Now look at 'im. Damn near bald as a bladder of lard.'

'What d'you want, Baines?' Quint snarled.

'Ain't so much what I want. More a case of what *you* want. Coming in the Pigs after all these years.' Baines leant forward, his hands on the table, and thrust his face towards Quint's. 'You come looking for a bit of tail?' he asked. 'Is that it? Maybe you fancy a go at Carroty Kate 'ere, eh?'

'Piss off, Baines. I ain't got the time to be bothered with you. Or your draggle-tail tart.'

'You always was a bit of a dismal Jimmy, wasn't you, Quint?' The man, pushing himself upright again, didn't seem in the least put out by Quint's rudeness. 'What about your chum? Reckon 'e wants to take 'er outside? Do a perpendickler up against the wall? Kate'd be happy with that, wouldn't you, dear? Nice, 'andsome chap with flash whiskers. Rather than an old goat like Quintus.'

Although he and Quint had agreed that he would leave the talking to his servant, Adam was growing weary of keeping silent.

'Charming though your lady friend undoubtedly is,' he said, raising his hat to Carroty Kate, who sniggered briefly, 'we are not here to avail ourselves of her services. We are here to meet a gentleman named Benskin. Perhaps you are acquainted with him?'

Baines stared at Adam as if he was a rare beast escaped from

114

the Zoological Gardens. He swivelled his head in the direction of Quint, clearly searching for some kind of explanation for the arrival of this strange creature in the Three Pigs.

None was forthcoming.

Baines turned back to Adam. He seemed to be debating how to respond to him. The atmosphere, already tense, grew more so. Quint had his hand in his pocket, his fingers clasped around the metal bar he carried there. The barrel-chested man stared thoughtfully at Adam for a moment and then laughed.

'You've got a tongue as runs on wheels, ain't you, cully? *Avail? Acquainted?* We ain't used to such fancy words in the Pigs.' He laughed again. 'But, if you don't want a turn with Kate, I ain't goin' to force you. Run along, girl.' He slapped the redhead on her rear and she turned back to the bar, swaying from side to side as she returned to the other girls. 'You looking for Benskin, you say?'

'The gentleman delivered a note to my rooms, requesting my presence here this evening.' Adam smiled at Baines. 'So, of course, I hastened to fulfil the engagement.'

The man shook his head as if he could scarcely believe what he was hearing. 'A tongue as runs on wheels,' he repeated.

'Do you know the gentleman in question, Mr Baines?'

'Ah, now that would be telling, cully, wouldn't it?' Baines turned and beckoned to a short, wiry man, his face pitted by smallpox, who was standing by a door at the rear of the bar. The man hastened across the room towards them. Baines leant into the man's ear and whispered a few words into it. The pockmarked man listened, nodding repeatedly, and then retraced his steps. Opening the door, he disappeared through it.

Baines returned his attention to Adam and Quint. 'On account of always wantin' to 'elp a flash gent like yourself,' he said, picking at a front tooth, 'I've sent that runty cove Williams to see if there's anybody calling 'isself Benskin out the back.'

'That is very good of you, Mr Baines. And do you think there will be?'

Baines shrugged. ''Oo can tell?'

The door at the back of the bar opened and Williams reappeared. He made his way to the table where they were sitting and there was another whispered conference between him and Baines. After a short exchange, Williams was dismissed and retreated to his post by the door.

'Seems there *is* a cove by the name of Job Benskin out the back.' Baines was grinning cheerfully, displaying a set of discoloured and mangled teeth as he spoke. He sounded as if this was exactly the eventuality for which he had been hoping. ''Oo'd 'ave thought it?'

'And may I speak to him?'

'Seems the cove wants to speak to you. Ain't that 'andy?'

'Very gratifying for all parties. Should I wait here for Mr Benskin?'

'Jest walk through and see 'im.' Baines waved his hand towards the door.

Adam stood and his servant followed suit. The young man shook his head slightly. 'You will remain here, Quint,' he said. 'There is no need for you to accompany me.'

'Ain't no telling who's through that door. Might be this Benskin cove. Might be 'alf a dozen bruisers breathing on their knuckles.'

'It will be Benskin, I have no doubt. He asked me to visit him here. Why should it not be he?' Adam began to walk towards the door. 'Have a drink, Quint,' he called over his shoulder. 'Exchange reminiscences with Mr Baines here. I am sure the two of you have much to tell one another.'

Quint looked with distaste at the pug-faced man. Baines grinned back at him.

As Adam reached the door, Williams opened it for him and the young man walked into the rear room.

* * * * *

'I've give you the chance once, Quint Devlin,' Baines said. 'If you wants to join paunches with Kate over there, she's yours for the taking. Can't say fairer than that.'

'I ain't int'rested in trulls like 'er.'

'Now, that ain't kind, Quint, that ain't kind. You 'ear that, Kate?'

Baines called over to the bar, where the red-haired woman was pouring a large tumbler of gin down her throat. 'Quint 'ere's calling you a trull.'

The woman turned unfocused eyes towards the two men. She was clearly unable to hear what Baines was saying above the noise in the bar.

'See,' Baines said. 'She's very partickler about who she lets get 'is 'ands on 'er, is Kate.'

Quint had decided that the best way to deal with the annoyance of the other man was to ignore him. He was staring fixedly at one of the dirt-encrusted windows of the pub, as if counting the motes of dust that floated in the dim light filtering into the room from the street.

But Baines was not to be ignored. 'Is this the way to treat an old pal, cully?' he said in a wheedling voice. 'One as you ain't seen for so many years?'

Quint snorted with contempt. 'Last time I see you, Jem Baines,' he said, 'you was so drunk you'd 'ave opened your shirt-collar to take a piss. And, if we was ever pals, then I must've blinked and missed it.'

Baines, who seemed determined not to take offence, cackled cheerfully.

'And there ain't no cause I can see for you to stand there looking as pleased as a dog with two choppers,' Quint said.

At this, Baines held his arms wide, the palms of his hands out-spread, as if to suggest that there was no dealing with some people. 'Why'n't you do as my shirt does and kiss my arse?' he remarked.

Baines was about to make his way back to the bar when there were sounds from the back room. Raised voices could be heard. One of them was clearly Adam's. Quint stood, knocking over the stool on which he had been squatting, and began to move towards the door. Baines swivelled to face him and thrust his hand forcefully into his chest. Quint swung his fist at the other man, who ducked. Just as Quint prepared a further punch, the door opened and Adam strode out, his face red with fury. He was followed by Job Benskin,

117

who stopped in the doorway, a smirk on his face.

'Come, Quint,' Adam shouted. 'We have heard enough nonsense here. We are leaving.'

Within seconds the two visitors were out of the Three Pigs, its door swinging shut behind them with a crash.

Adam strode through the wretched courtyard at such a pace that Quint had difficulty keeping up with him. 'You plannin' on telling me what Benskin said to you?' he asked as they continued to march down Leman Street.

'Not now, Quint.' Adam was breathing deeply, clenching and unclenching his fists. His servant could not remember seeing him in such a rage since the night in Thessaly nearly a year ago when he had discovered that Quint, on the instructions of Professor Fields, had stolen a manuscript from a monastery library in far distant Meteora.

'You plannin' on ever telling me?'

'The man Benskin is a fool and a rogue. I do not wish to talk of him.'

CHAPTER ELEVEN

'Now, you ain't going to talk about what happened at the Pigs.'

'That's correct.'

'And we ain't goin' to do a blame thing about whatever it is that cove Benskin told you which you ain't going to tell me.'

'Equally correct.'

'So, what in 'ell *are* we going to do?' Quint tipped much of his pint of half-and-half down his throat, banged his tankard onto the table and stared truculently at his master.

The two men were sitting in the same tavern in the Gray's Inn Road where Adam had previously spoken with Jacob Pennethorne. It was the morning following their visit to the Three Pigs.

Adam, who was drinking a glass of negus wine, leaned back in his chair. 'The contemptible lies that rogue Benskin told me . . .'

'Which you ain't plannin' to tell me.'

'Which I am not planning to tell you. These pretended proofs of what happened to my father which he offered to sell me. These we shall ignore.'

'Easy enough,' Quint said. 'I ain't got no bleedin' idea what they are.'

'These lies, I repeat, we shall ignore. We shall instead concentrate our attention on the matter of the missing Dolly.'

Quint was quiet for a moment. His pained face suggested he was struggling to reconcile several different trains of thought. 'What about this barney you was in the other night?' he asked eventually. 'Outside the gymnasium. You reckon that 'ad something to do with the bint?'

'It seems most likely. I think it was one of the same men who attacked me when I was returning from Whitechapel. And *they* made it abundantly clear that their threats were a consequence of our interest in Dolly.'

'And 'e 'ad a chiv?'

'He had a knife on the occasion of our first meeting. He held it rather closer to my windpipe than I cared for.'

'But this time 'e was going to use it?'

'He made every effort to do so.'

Quint took another draught of his ale. 'We got to do something,' he said. 'The bloke was out to croak you.'

'What are you suggesting we do? Go to the police?'

Quint winced. 'I ain't that big a noddy,' he said. 'The bluebottles're always more trouble than they're worth.'

There was a silence. Adam, lost in thought, seemed almost to have forgotten Quint's presence. His servant, his ale finished, was wondering whether his master might be prepared to pay for another.

'You sure we ain't going to do anything about this Benskin cove?' Quint asked eventually. 'I could pay 'im a little visit with my cosh.'

Adam continued to say nothing. He ran over in his mind what the down-at-heel ex-clerk had said at the Three Pigs, the allegations he had made. Could there be any truth in them? The man had claimed that his father had not killed himself. That he had not been alone in the hotel room at the time of his death, but in the company of a lady of the night. That he had been murdered by another man who had enjoyed the courtesan's favours. Benskin had then asked for fifty guineas.

Hearing this version of events in the back room of a squalid drinking den had so enraged Adam that he had stormed out. The story could not conceivably be true, he'd thought. Now . . . he was not so sure, and acknowledged to himself that he had been remiss in choosing not to look more closely into what had happened to his father.

'That man Baines. You said you knew him.'

Adam's manservant grunted agreement.

'What does he do?'

'Do?' Quint sounded contemptuous. 'When he ain't in the Pigs shunting booze down 'is neck, you mean? 'E's an 'ooker.'

'A hooker?'

The manservant waggled his fingers in the air. 'Puts his mitts into other people's pockets. Or cracks 'em on the nut and eases 'em of their purses that way. 'E's bleedin' useless at it, mind. 'E's spent half his life in clink.'

'Could he be allied with Benskin in some plot to extract money from me?'

Quint thought for a moment and then shrugged. 'If 'e is, 'e ain't sucked it out of 'is own thumb. 'E ain't bright enough.'

'And neither does Benskin seem a man of much genius. There must be someone else behind it.'

An old man in dirty corduroy trousers and jacket and a battered wideawake hat, who was the pub's only other customer, stood and tottered towards the bar. Adam watched him go.

'Could this fellow Wyndham, the stage-door lurker, have anything to do with all this?' he mused. 'His name keeps cropping up in our enquiries.' Adam took another sip of his negus. 'He seems an unlikely candidate for the role of Dolly's kidnapper. If, indeed, she has been kidnapped rather than, as seems most likely, made her way to York. But could he be involved in blackmailing me?' Adam considered the matter. 'Why on earth would he be? I had never met him or heard of him until a few days ago. In any case, he comes of good blood.'

'So does black pudding,' Quint said.

'You are right, of course.' Adam nodded in appreciation of his servant's curt common sense. 'A man could come from the finest family in the land and yet be a deep-dyed villain.' He swirled the dregs of his wine in his glass and peered at them, as if half expecting that they would have transmuted into another, more satisfying drink. He set the glass down with a sigh. 'He didn't seem a man of any great intelligence, but I suppose I should speak to him again. At the very least, I could prove to my own satisfaction that he wishes neither Miss Delaney nor myself any harm.'

* * * * *

'Dolphie, old boy, this gentleman is asking for you.'

Adolphus Wyndham looked up in surprise from the depths of the large leather armchair in which he was slumped. 'Oh, it's you again,' he said. 'Carter, isn't it?'

'Carver,' Adam said. He nodded his thanks to the genial, sandy-haired man who had led him to the dimly lit bar where Wyndham was sitting, staring into space and clutching a glass of whisky.

Adam had arrived at the Corinthian Club in the early afternoon. The same drunken attendant who had been present on his first visit had been on duty in the wood and glass cubicle at its entrance, fast asleep and emitting a sequence of whistles, grunts and snores. Adam had rapped on the glass window of the cubicle several times but the only result had been to increase the volume of the noises issuing from within. He had been about to set off alone into the club in search of his quarry when a passing member had volunteered his services as guide. This gentleman now retired, leaving Adam with Adolphus Wyndham, whose expression did not suggest open-armed welcome.

'Seems quiet,' Adam said, looking around the room. Its only other occupants were two men in uniform, junior officers in the Royal Artillery as far as he could tell, who were engaged in an intense conversation in a distant corner. One of them looked up, caught Adam's eye briefly and immediately returned to his discussion with his friend.

'Always like a graveyard at this time of day,' Wyndham said. 'Livens up a bit once we head towards the dinner gong.'

'But you enjoy a little peace here? Far from the madding crowd, as one might say.'

'Don't know about that, old boy,' Wyndham said doubtfully. 'Just nice to get a chance to have a bit of a think about things from time to time.'

'Exactly,' Adam said. Wyndham had not invited him to take a seat but he did so anyway.

'Can I help you, old man?' Dolly's one-time admirer looked irritated by his visitor's arrival, but not unduly concerned by it. 'Thought we'd said all we had to say to one another that night I was playing billiards with Smithy.'

'I think perhaps you may have a little more to add.'

'Not sure that I do, old boy.'

'I think perhaps there was something about yourself and Miss Delaney that you did not tell me.'

Wyndham now seemed distinctly uncomfortable. He was pulling at his collar and turning in his chair to look towards the door. 'I've told you all I know.'

'No, I don't believe you have.'

'I say, that's rather bad form, ain't it?' Wyndham tried to sound offended but succeeded only in sounding plaintive. 'Doubting a chap's word and all that.'

'It is somewhat ungentlemanly of me, I agree,' Adam said. 'But circumstances force me to it. I do have the strongest reasons for believing that you were not entirely truthful with me when last we spoke. I have had a conversation with Mr Pennethorne.'

Wyndham sighed and reached up to scratch his throat. 'I suppose I did tell you a fib or two,' he said. 'No double-thumpers, but not exactly the plain unvarnished, either.'

'Suppose you tell me the plain unvarnished now.'

'I'd rather not, old boy. Bit embarrassing, to be perfectly honest.'

'I think I must insist.'

Wyndham continued to wriggle in his seat and peer over his shoulder at the exit from the bar, like a penniless diner contemplating escape from a restaurant before the bill's arrival.

'If you've seen Pennethorne, he's probably told you everything,' he said eventually.

'I would much prefer to hear it from your own lips.'

'Well, not much to tell.' Wyndham was now staring miserably at a point just over Adam's shoulder. 'I wander along to old Penny's shop from time to time. Buy a few pictures from him. You know the kind of thing I mean.'

'I do.'

'Purely for artistic reasons.'

'Of course.'

'The female form divine and all that.'

'I understand entirely.'

'And I was looking through his wares one day when I saw a familiar face. Don't always look too closely at the faces, to be honest, but I did with this one, for some reason.'

'It was Dolly's, I presume.'

'Well, that was the odd thing. It was Dolly, I'm sure. But it wasn't her name written on the photograph. It was another name entirely. Esther, or something similar.'

'The pseudonym she had adopted when she posed for the camera. I would imagine many of the women protect their identity by doing so.'

'Ah, I hadn't thought of that.' Wyndham sounded genuinely surprised.

He was not, Adam reflected, a very clever man. There was surely no possibility he could be behind Dolly's disappearance. And Adam's fleeting thought that he might be in collusion with Job Benskin to extort money from him was obviously misplaced.

'So you saw a photograph of Dolly. What did you do next?'

'It was quite a shock, seeing her. Not the sort of situation in which you expect to come across an acquaintance.'

'No, I suppose not.'

'Pleasant kind of shock, though.' Wyndham looked furtive and a little ashamed. 'Maybe I told you I'd been pursuing the girl for some time. With no luck at all, I might add. Very much "Hands off, Dolphie, what sort of a girl do you take me for?" You know the routine, I imagine.'

Adam indicated that he did.

'Well, there I'd been, dreaming of Dolly's charms and getting nowhere, and here I was, suddenly getting an eyeful of said charms.

So I did what any chap would do in the circs.'

'And that was?'

'I asked old Penny if he'd got any more photographs of her.'

Adam continued to ask questions for another five minutes, but it was clear enough that he would get no more information. Wyndham was exactly what he seemed to be: a dim moocher who wasted his days in his club and at the race track, and his nights at the theatre in pursuit of women who weren't much interested in him. Pennethorne had been right about the man wanting to know more about Dolly, but his interest was not in any way sinister. It was merely idle prurience. There was nothing Wyndham could tell him that would lead him to the missing girl. It seemed as if his best informant remained Miss Bascombe, and that Dolly must indeed have left the city. Thoughts of Dolly, he found, led almost immediately to thoughts of Hetty. He had not seen her since they had spent the night together. He could not decide whether he wanted to see her again very much, or not at all. He was still debating the question as he walked into Piccadilly and hailed a cab to take him back to Doughty Street.

CHAPTER TWELVE

'Y ou are an admirer of Browning?'

Adam looked up from the volume of poems he was reading. He was standing outside a bookshop near the British Museum. He had picked up a rather battered copy of *Men and Women* from a trestle table under the shop's window and was glancing through the lines of 'A Toccata of Galuppi's'. It was a work he had read several times before but he was still uncertain exactly what thoughts and emotions the poet wished to convey. The sense of melancholy and questioning doubt in the poem, however, was clear enough. Adam was surprised when he heard the man speak by his side, as he had not noticed his approach. Gilbert Waterton was standing at his shoulder. Adam returned the Browning volume to the table and the two men shook hands.

'His verse is an acquired taste, Mr Waterton, but I enjoy his tangled lines and twisted metaphors.'

'I have always found him a poet of almost wilful obscurity, but perhaps I have been missing hidden delights. Hidden from me, at least.' As if by mutual agreement, they had both begun to walk away from the bookshop in the direction of New Oxford Street. 'How are you, Carver?' Waterton asked. 'Are you any nearer a solution to the mystery of this girl's disappearance?'

Adam described what had happened recently: the visit to the Whitechapel penny gaff; his conversations with Pennethorne and Patch; his visit to Miss Bascombe and the National Society for Returning Young Women to their Friends in the Country.

'So the girl has travelled north?' Waterton spoke as if he had visions of the *danseuse* hauling a sledge across a frozen snowscape.

'It would seem most probable.'

They crossed New Oxford Street in silence and continued along Museum Street.

'You have family connections in York, do you not, Carver?' Waterton said suddenly.

'My father was born in the city, if that is what you mean,' Adam acknowledged, slightly taken aback. How had Waterton known this? he wondered. Could Sunman have told him? Did Sunman even know? Adam thought it unlikely that he had himself ever told very many people about his family origins. Although he was not ashamed of the fact that his father had been born in humble circumstances, the son of an ostler at a coaching inn, it was not something of which he frequently spoke. 'But I have no other connection with the place. I have not been there since I was a child.'

'None the less, you are familiar with the town—?'

'I would not say that. As I say, I have not visited it for more than ten years.'

Waterton made a gesture of irritation, as if to suggest that Adam was being pedantic. 'You must go to York,' he said, in a tone of voice that suggested there could be no debate about the matter. 'You must locate this wretched girl and bring her back to town.'

The two men walked side by side in silence for a while.

'Perhaps it would be as well if I left town temporarily,' Adam said eventually, nodding to himself.

Waterton raised an eyebrow in query, and Adam described what had happened when he had left the German Gymnasium two days previously.

'This man attacked you?' Waterton stopped in the street, his hand on Adam's arm. He looked shocked.

'Yes. As I say, he had a knife. I suppose I was lucky to escape injury.'

'And this murderous assault could only have been a consequence of your enquiries into Miss Delaney's whereabouts?'

'What other reason could there be for it? I lead an otherwise

127

blameless life, Mr Waterton.' Adam smiled. 'In any case, I had been knocked to the ground a few days earlier – possibly by the same rogue, although I cannot be sure – and told in no uncertain terms that I should put an end to my interest in Dolly.'

'But you chose to ignore the threats?'

'I object rather strongly to ruffians informing me of what I can and cannot do. Their blusterings made me only more committed to finding the girl.'

'So you will go north in pursuit of her.'

'I think I probably will.'

'And you will go on as if this attack upon you had never taken place?'

'What would you have me do, Mr Waterton? Retire ignominiously from the fray? I owe it to my honour as a gentleman to continue the search for poor Dolly.'

'I suppose you do,' Waterton said, 'although preservation of one's honour is sometimes an over-rated virtue. Preservation of one's life should surely take precedence. If you do journey to York, you must take the greatest care. Sunman and I would never forgive ourselves if something were to happen to you.'

They had stopped at the corner of Museum Street. Waterton pointed his cane in the direction of High Holborn. 'I am going this way,' he said.

'And I am making towards the Strand,' Adam said, but he did not move. 'There is one other complication,' he continued after a pause.

Waterton looked at him enquiringly. Adam stepped to one side to allow a young mother and her sailor-suited child to pass by and then, rather to his surprise, found himself telling the older man the story of Benskin and his father.

Waterton listened carefully, nodding from time to time in encouragement. 'Let me ask you but one question, Carver. Did this man Benskin want money?'

Adam hesitated slightly before he replied: 'He asked me for fifty guineas. In exchange for further proofs.'

Waterton raised his arms like a clergyman about to bless his congregation. 'Well, there you are. He is no more than a commonplace extortioner out to fleece you with his lies. You did not give this bloodsucker what he asked, did you?'

'I am not such a fool as all that, Mr Waterton.' The young man smiled ruefully. 'Besides, I have not it to give him. I am not so well off that I can throw away that amount of money. I told Benskin as much.'

'And what did he say in reply?'

'He cursed me several times. Told me that I would get no more information from him unless I paid him what he asked.'

'And where did you say this encounter took place?'

'In a pot-house in Whitechapel.'

'Not a very salubrious locality.'

'No, indeed.'

'If you wish for my advice, Mr Carver – and I assume that your reason for telling me this is to solicit my opinion – I would ignore what the man said. It sounds like a cheap and grubby story told in a cheap and grubby location. It is unlikely to be true. And now, I must take my leave of you.' Waterton raised his hat and made an almost imperceptible little bow. 'Remember what I have said. If you travel north in search of Harry's tawdry mistress, you must be prudent and vigilant.'

Adam watched Waterton's tall, dark figure as it strode away. Then he turned and took his own path through the crowded London streets.

* * * * *

'And that, I believe, is mate.' Cosmo Jardine took his hand from the bishop he had just moved and smiled triumphantly at his companion.

He and Adam were sitting at a table in the chess room at the cigar divan in the Strand. The place had been one of their regular haunts when they had both first arrived in London from Cambridge. They had not visited it for more than a year but had kept up their subscriptions – 'What is a mere two guineas?' Cosmo had asked with the kind of insouciance that led him so permanently into debt – and this afternoon it had suddenly seemed to both men the ideal place at which to rendezvous.

Adam looked down at the pieces arrayed on the chess board for a little while and then raised his palms in submission. 'Mate it is,' he said. 'You are a positive Staunton.'

Cosmo waved a hand at the waiter who was circumnavigating the room and then pointed to the two cups in front of them. The waiter nodded and scurried away. Clearly pleased with himself, the painter surveyed the other tables in the room, where a dozen pairs of players were hunched over their boards. 'I saw him here once, you know,' he said.

'Staunton?'

'Yes, it was the year you were in northern Greece, I think. Your first visit. He was playing against another old timer. George Walker, was it? Lord, the amount of fawning and flattery he received! It was sickening to behold. It was as if Zeus had descended from Olympus.'

'He was a great player.'

'It is more than likely that he still is. I read his chess articles in the *Illustrated London News* occasionally and they are most illuminating. I did not object to the man himself, but to the obsequiousness of his admirers.'

The waiter had returned and, crouching deferentially, placed two more cups of hot coffee on the table.

'How goes the search for the missing Dolly?' Jardine asked, beginning to set up the pieces for another game.

Adam considered the question for a moment, holding his cup and staring at the black liquid within it as if he were unsure what it might be. 'I have yet to find her,' he said. 'I am of the opinion that she has left London. I think maybe the answers to all the questions lie up north.'

As Cosmo sipped his coffee, his friend spoke of the dancer's probable flight to York and the proposal by Waterton that he should follow her there.

'But you do not wish to go? You would prefer to stay in town?'

The painter had caught a note of ambivalence in Adam's voice as he spoke.

'No, I shall go,' the young man said. 'But the truth is that I have had much to trouble my mind recently. I have not been able fully to concentrate on the matter of Dolly's disappearance.'

'Pray tell, dear boy,' Jardine drawled. 'An affair of the heart, perhaps?'

'Nothing to arouse your prurient interest, Cosmo. An odd man who approached me in the street some days ago.'

'The streets are full of odd men, old chap. Sometimes I think that half of London should be on the omnibus to Bedlam. Without a return ticket.'

'This particular one said something that has provided me with much food for thought.'

'An Ancient Mariner, a grey-beard loon who held you with his skinny hand and had a strange tale to unfold?'

Adam laughed uncomfortably. The painter, he thought, was curiously close to the truth. 'In a manner of speaking, yes. This man – his name is Benskin – was once a clerk who worked for my father. He has very obviously gone down in the world since the death of my father and the loss of his fortune.'

'A smaller ship sinking in the wake of the larger vessel.'

'Something like that. Later in the week, he called at Doughty Street and left a note asking me to meet him in a dingy public house in Whitechapel.'

'And you *went*?' Jardine was aghast at the thought. Adam nodded. He doubted whether his friend had ever set foot east of Aldgate.

'I was curious to know more of what he had to say.'

'It is easy enough to guess what the general tenor of his remarks would have been.' Jardine tasted his drink once more. 'Mendacity mixed with mendicity. A series of lies about the bitter blows fate has dealt him, followed swiftly by a begging request for financial assistance. There was no need to venture into darkest Whitechapel to be certain of what he wanted.'

Adam said nothing.

'Am I not correct?' Jardine persisted. 'He proposed transferring monies from your pocket into his?'

'He wished for imbursement, yes.' Adam hesitated. Should he confide in the painter? Cosmo was not renowned for his discretion. And yet he was his oldest friend. He should surely trust him. 'He said he had something to tell me about my father . . .'

'What could he tell you that you did not already know?'

'This must go no further than ourselves, Cosmo.'

'I swear a solemn oath to that effect.' The painter held up his hand in mocking parody of a witness in court.

'I am serious, Cosmo. This is not a matter for jest.'

Jardine, noticing the anxiety in his friend's eyes, lowered his hand. 'In that case, old man, I shall jest no more.'

'When Quint and I went to the tavern in Whitechapel, Benskin was in a room at the back. I left Quint in the bar with some grubby acquaintance from his past and spoke alone to Benskin.'

'And what did the fellow have to say for himself?'

'He told me that my father was murdered.'

Jardine raised his eyes in surprise and leaned back in his chair. 'That is absurd, Adam,' he said, after a moment's silence. 'The man has spent too much of his newfound leisure in reading *The Mysteries of London*. Or other penny dreadfuls.'

'That is more or less what Waterton said.'

'Waterton?'

'Gilbert Waterton. He works with Sunman at the FO.' Adam thought it unwise to volunteer more details about the man. 'I met him earlier today.'

'And you told Waterton of Benskin's claims?'

Adam nodded. 'Benskin had more to say for himself. Something I did not tell Waterton.' Adam hesitated again and then continued. 'He told me that my father was with a tart when he died.'

'Perhaps he was,' Jardine said warily. He did not wish to offend Adam, but the idea of an older, wealthier man entertaining a younger woman in a hotel bedroom did not strike him as entirely improbable.

'That may have been the case,' Adam acknowledged. 'It is not a subject on which I wish to dwell. What is more important is that Benskin claimed my father was killed by another of the woman's admirers who surprised them together. A man of wealth and influence.'

'And the police were not informed?'

'The murderer had the power to keep everything quiet.'

'That is not very likely, is it? In England no one has that power. Not even the royal family. Not even Mr Gladstone.'

The waiter was approaching their table once again. Jardine noticed him out of the corner of his eye and waved him impatiently away. The man retreated. Adam was staring miserably into the middle distance.

'What am I to do?' he asked. 'If the man is right, I should not be wasting time in York – I should be exerting myself to the utmost in discovering the identity of the woman's other admirer and bringing him to justice for the murder of my father.'

'He cannot be right.'

'He might be.'

'He is not. Think no more of it, Adam,' Jardine said. 'It is a cock-and-bull story he has invented while he has been brooding over his beer in some backstreet tavern.'

'He said he had proof of what he alleged. If I handed over the money he wanted, he would provide me with it.'

'And you gave him the money?'

'The man was asking for fifty guineas, Cosmo. Even if I had such an amount of ready cash, I would not be such a fool as to give it immediately to a rogue like Benskin.'

'No, of course not.' Cosmo had lit one of the cigars the divan provided for its customers. He leant back and blew a series of smoke rings into the air. The two young men watched them spiral upwards and then disintegrate one by one.

'But I do need to find out whether or not he was telling the truth,' Adam said. 'In all likelihood, as you say, he is spinning me an improbable yarn in an attempt to extort money from me.'

'Almost certainly.'

'But there is the smallest chance that he is not.'

Jardine sighed and reached out to tap ash into the brass ashtray on the table. 'This is what I would do if I was in your position, old man,' he said. 'Absent yourself from the hurly-burly of the city for a while. Follow Dolly's trail northwards. Finding her seems to have become a matter of importance to you. I am not sure I understand why, but I do not think you will be able to concentrate on other aspects of your life until you have located the girl.'

'You are right. I have begun to think it a matter of honour to do as I said I would do.'

'But before that, I would seek your revenge on the chessboard.' Jardine waved his hand towards the pieces between them. 'And then I would join an old friend in a trip to the Grecian.'

'I am not certain that I am dressed for the theatre.'

'I am not talking of Her Majesty's, you know,' Jardine said. 'This is the City Road, not the West End. There will be no requirement for evening dress. No ban on frock coat and coloured trousers.'

Adam took a cigar himself and allowed his mood to brighten. 'You are right, Cosmo,' he said, moving a pawn forward. 'I will now trounce you on the black-and-white squares. Tonight I shall accompany you to the Grecian. I shall forget Benskin and his ridiculous tale. And then, tomorrow morning, I will arrange to travel to York and find this girl.'

PART TWO

YORK

CHAPTER THIRTEEN

Adam emerged from York's railway station into weak and watery spring sunshine. Quint followed him, carrying their luggage. To their left ran the city's walls, a modern arch breaching the ancient fortifications to allow access for the railway engines. As they turned towards the city, the twin towers of the Minster's western front met Adam's eyes.

'What a magnificent sight, eh, Quint?' he said, 'One that makes the petty discomforts of the journey pale into insignificance.'

His servant, who was still suffering the not so petty discomforts of hauling his master's handmade leather suitcases out of the station entrance, merely grunted.

Little more than forty-eight hours had passed since Adam had told Cosmo Jardine of his decision to travel north. The following day a telegram had been despatched to a hotel in Coney Street, York, to book rooms for himself and Quint. The day after that, the two men had climbed aboard a Great Northern Railway train leaving King's Cross station at 10 a.m. They had been lucky, and had managed to find a compartment to themselves. At Grantham, they had been joined by an elderly clergyman with a wispy grey moustache and a look of amiable vacuity. After raising his hat politely to them, he had taken out a book in which he had been lost for the rest of the journey. Adam had been amused to notice that the book was not the Bible nor a work of theology, but one of Routledge's Railway Novels. By twisting his head slightly Adam had been able to see that it was Bulwer-Lytton's *The Last Days of Pompeii*.

The train had made good time. The clergyman had been so absorbed by his tale of Roman death and destruction that he had not noticed their arrival in York. Adam had touched him gently on the shoulder to return him to the nineteenth century.

'Ah, we are here so soon,' the old clergyman had said, struggling to his feet and reaching up to the luggage rack for his shabby leather valise. 'The hectic rush of modern life.'

As he and Adam stepped onto the platform, he had nodded his head in farewell and shuffled off, his valise in one hand and his novel in the other.

'Get our bags, Quint,' Adam had ordered, watching the old man depart. With a muttered curse, Quint had hauled their cases from the luggage rack.

Now both man and master were outside the railway station, looking across the River Ouse to the heart of the ancient capital of the North.

'How fine a day it is!' Adam inhaled and exhaled with exaggerated delight. 'Is the air not purer outside London? We shall walk to our hotel and relish every breath of it we take.'

'What about these bleedin' cases?' Quint asked.

'Tell one of the porters to arrange for their delivery to the hotel.'

Their luggage entrusted to a beefy porter who guaranteed its arrival at the hotel within the hour, Adam and Quint paid the halfpenny toll to cross the new bridge that spanned the Ouse and took them from the railway towards the Minster and the centre of the city.

Halfway across, Adam paused and leant against the bridge's ironwork. He looked down at the waters of the river swirling beneath them. 'I do hope that we can find this young woman for whom we seek.'

Quint joined him at the parapet, releasing a long stream of tobacco-stained spit which dropped into the Ouse. 'Ain't no reason to worrit,' he said. 'She's jest jumped at the gelt that Bascombe woman give her and come up 'ere to spend it.'

'I pray you are correct, but I have real fears for her safety. There was her eagerness to leave London, for one thing.'

Quint had himself only ever left the capital reluctantly. He thought back to his own departure from the city several years before, when he had joined Professor Fields's first expedition to escape a particularly persistent creditor. 'Mebbe someone's got 'is claws into 'er for rhino,' he said.

'That is a possibility you have suggested more than once, Quint. I am coming to the conclusion that you are, in all likelihood, correct.'

The two men stared down at the Ouse. A boat passed under the bridge, filled with passengers. One of them called up to them and waved his hand. Adam raised his hat to him and smiled. 'Come,' he said to Quint, 'our hotel awaits our arrival.'

* * * * *

The following day, Adam set out to find the northern offices of the National Society for Returning Young Women to their Friends in the Country. The address he had been given was not, at first, easy to locate. In York's twisting medieval streets it was all too possible to lose one's way. Only the vast, looming towers of the Minster, which were visible – or so it seemed – from every point in the city, allowed him to orientate himself.

Eventually, Adam found the place for which he was looking. It was a narrow alleyway which led off one of the main streets. This opened into a paved courtyard in which a stunted tree, starved of sunlight, was struggling to put forth a few green leaves. The court was surrounded by small houses built, Adam guessed, in the middle of the previous century. None of them was used any longer as a private residence. All were now offices of one kind or another. He could see the nameplate of a solicitor's firm, and another that advertised the presence of a corn merchant.

The house he wanted stood immediately opposite the exit from the alleyway. The Phoenix and Sun Fire Insurance Company occupied its ground floor. Up above were the offices of the National Society for Returning Young Women to their Friends in the Country.

Adam climbed the stairs and knocked on the green door that immediately confronted him.

'Come,' said a reedy voice from within.

The young man walked into a dark, wood-panelled room. Two small windows on the far wall allowed little sunshine to enter and Adam found it difficult at first to make out more than looming shadows in the gloom. As his eyes grew swiftly more accustomed to the half-light, he could see a large sideboard to the left with what appeared to be two blue Chinese vases sitting on them. On the right was a tall chest of drawers. In the middle, sitting behind a vast table that was the only other large piece of furniture in the room, his head silhouetted against one of the windows, was a man with a face as long as an undertaker's, fronted by prominent teeth. From what Adam could see of his expression, it was not welcoming.

The man put down a sheaf of papers he had been examining, then stood and gestured impatiently to a chair by the huge table. 'Pray, take a seat. I shall be able to give you my undivided attention in but a moment.'

As Adam lowered himself onto the uncomfortable, high-backed chair, the buck-toothed man re-seated himself and began to leaf through the pile of papers on the table once more. It was only too obvious that he was doing this more to impress upon his visitor the degree to which he was a busy man than to take note of what was in them. A minute passed. Adam felt himself growing irritated and was about to cough pointedly when the man finally put down the papers and spoke to him. 'My name is Ridgewell. I am the secretary for the Society in the North of England. How may I help you?'

Adam's story of his search for Dolly Delaney was listened to in silence. Ridgewell's face suggested that he was having difficulty believing that any of it was true. When Adam finished, the secretary sniffed loudly and turned to stare at the Chinese vases as if he had just noticed them and found them to be aesthetically offensive.

'I will be blunt, Mr Carver,' he said. 'If the decision were mine to make, I should not divulge the information you require.' Ridgewell now twisted his head to look coldly at Adam. 'However, Miss Bascombe has written to me. You seem to have made a favourable impression on her.' The man's tone of voice indicated that he could think of no good reason why this should be so.

Looking back on his meeting with Miss Bascombe, Adam reflected that the founder of the National Society for Returning Young Women to their Friends in the Country had given little hint at the time that he had met with her approval. Although his cheque certainly had.

'She wishes me to offer you any assistance I can. I will therefore endeavour to answer any questions you may wish to ask me.' Ridgewell settled back in his seat with the air of a man preparing to endure an unpleasant but necessary ordeal.

'Dolly came to see you, did she not?'

Ridgewell nodded briefly.

'On which day was this?'

'Perhaps a week ago.' The man reached for a large morocco-bound ledger on the tabletop and pulled it towards him. He took a pince-nez from the top pocket of his jacket and placed it precariously on his nose. Turning the pages of the ledger, he came eventually to the one he required and peered at it. 'Yes, I wrote a note of it. I record all the visits made to this office in here. It was last Tuesday. Eight days ago.'

'She asked for help?'

'She demanded it. She wanted money. However, I had already decided that the best action the Society could take for the girl was to find her work. Not to hand her further monies to squander in self-indulgence.' Ridgewell closed the ledger with a sudden bang and pushed it away from him. He settled back in his chair, his pince-nez still perched on the bridge of his nose.

'Were you successful in finding her employment?' Adam asked, struggling to keep his distaste for this self-righteous pedant from his voice.

'I had arranged for Miss Delaney to take up a position as a maid in a very respectable household in a village not ten miles from the city.'

'Let me hazard a guess. She did not take it.'

'She did not.' Ridgewell pursed his lips in disapproval. 'A most ungrateful young woman she proved herself to be. She told me, in the most unmannerly terms, what she thought of the post.'

'And what did she think of it?'

'She thought it was beneath her dignity. Although what dignity a young chit who has cavorted on a public stage can be said to possess, I do not know.'

'So she refused the job of maid. Did you offer her any other assistance?'

'Even supposing that I had felt inclined to offer her further help – which I did not – I had no opportunity to do so. When she realized that I was unprepared to give her money, as she requested, she swore at me and left.'

'Where do you suppose she went after she had left you? Back to London?'

'She had not the wherewithal to return to the city. I formed the very definite impression that she had come to our offices here in York with the sole intention of cozening more money from the Society.'

'Surely Miss Bascombe had requested that she be given more money?'

'I am made of sterner stuff than Miss Bascombe. I am less easily taken in by the stories young women like Miss Delaney invent to account for troubles which, in truth, their own sins have brought upon them.'

'So she had such a story?'

Ridgewell waved his hand in the air as if to disparage anything Dolly might or might not have told him. 'I scarcely listen to these tales, Mr Carver. I have heard so many of them in my time with the Society, and so few of them are true.'

'But she did tell you something of her circumstances,' Adam persisted.

Ridgewell sighed. It was clear that he was growing weary of the conversation. 'She had some cock-and-bull story about a gentleman of high standing who wished her dead. Who might have followed her to York in order to do away with her. It was so obviously fantastical that I paid it very little heed.'

'You did not think it might have contained any truth at all?'

Ridgewell laughed. It was not a pleasant laugh nor, indeed, one that indicated much in the way of genuine mirth. 'It was nonsense, Mr Carver. Smoke and gammon, to employ a vulgarism. The girl was desperate to gull us out of further monies. She was inventing some fairy tale based on her reading of cheap novelettes.'

'I do not think the girl can read, Mr Ridgewell,' Adam said, remembering what McIlwraith had told him.

'It scarcely matters from where she took her story. She was foolish enough to believe that I would be foolish enough to believe her. That is all.'

* * * * *

'The girl has no money. So it is unlikely that she has left the city. To do that, she needs cash. How will she get it?'

'Spread her legs,' Quint said shortly.

'Crudely expressed but that is a possibility. I think, however, that Dolly would have to be very desperate before she sold herself on the streets.'

'If she's out of blunt, she has to do something to get it,' Quint said, with the air of someone pointing out an obvious truth. 'And I ain't sure 'ow she's going to crack an 'onest crust.'

'True enough. She might, I suppose, look for a photographer to take the kind of pictures of her that the seedy Mr Pennethorne did, but I think that such men might be hard to find outside London. It is much more likely that she would try to gain employment on the stage once more.'

'Ain't so many places in a town like this to flash her pins.'

'Exactly, Quint. As so often, you hit the nail on the head. In London, as we discovered to our cost, there are hundreds of theatres, great and small, where an actress or a dancer can ply her trade. Here in York, there are but few in comparison. We can visit them all in the course of a single day.'

The two men were sitting in a chop house in Davygate. They had just finished a midday meal. Quint had also finished the pint of ale which had accompanied the food. Adam had drunk only half of his. He picked up the pewter tankard and tilted it towards what little light succeeded in struggling through the place's grimy windows. The liquid in the tankard glowed amber and briefly looked more appetizing than it was.

'Ain't exackly cheery here, is it?' Quint remarked. 'It's like a boneyard on a wet Sunday.'

'I have eaten in livelier establishments,' Adam agreed.

They were very nearly alone in the place apart from a surly waiter. Across the room was the only other customer, a tall, melancholy man in a greatcoat and muffler. He was dressed to suggest that, even though spring had arrived, he had every reason to believe that winter was about to make a comeback. He was sitting at a table on his own, eating a plate of bacon, sausage and black pudding as if his life depended on finishing it as quickly as possible.

'He's a heavy grubber, ain't he?' Quint said, watching with some fascination as the man pushed meat unrelentingly into his mouth.

'Never mind our fellow diner,' Adam said. 'Concentrate your thoughts upon the fair Delaney. The story she told the egregious Mr Ridgewell is a curious one.'

'What?' Quint tore himself away from his examination of the over-dressed man. 'That some nob wanted her dead?'

'Why should she believe that her life was in danger?'

'Mebbe she got wind we were on 'er tail. And reckoned *we* were out to make cold meat of 'er.'

'Perhaps she did learn that we were in search of her. But, suppose she did, why should she assume the worst?'

'It's a licker to me,' Quint said, shaking his head. He gave the impression he was losing interest in the subject. His master took another taste of his ale and then pushed the tankard to one side. He had drunk enough of it, he decided.

The man dressed as if for the depths of winter, having now finished his meal in double-quick time, was making his way out. Adam nodded at him as he passed their table. With courtesy and a look of infinite sadness, the man raised his hat and then made his way into the street.

''E's left 'is paper,' Quint said. He stood and walked over to the table where their fellow diner had been bolting his meal. He picked up a copy of the *York Herald*. ''E ain't even cut the pages.'

'Bring it over here, Quint.' Adam took a small, folding paperknife from his pocket. His servant handed him the *Herald* and he carefully slit open the pages. 'The theatres will all advertise in here, I am sure. Yes, here we are.' Adam gave a small smile of satisfaction. 'A whole column of dramatic and musical delights. There is, of course, the Theatre Royal. It is the oldest and most distinguished theatre in the city.'

'Likely she went there, then.' Quint was leaning back in his chair and picking his teeth.

'No, I think not.' Adam ran his eyes down the page of advertisements in the newspaper. 'I think she would avoid the best-known establishment. She needs a job but she also needs to remain anonymous. She could not do so at the Theatre Royal. And she would have a better prospect of employment in one of the smaller companies.' The young man stabbed his finger at the page. 'Here we are. The Grand Theatre, Goodramgate. Alfred Skeffington presents his world-renowned company of players in *The Skeleton in the Cave, or, The Bloody Crime of Eugene Aram*. This is the one we shall try first.'

* * * * *

On entering the Grand, the first person Adam saw was an elderly, grey-whiskered man who was pushing a broom half-heartedly across the faded tiles in the theatre lobby. Bent almost double, he seemed to be tracing some elaborate pattern on the floor rather than cleaning it. When Adam spoke to him, he was so lost in his private task he had not heard the young man approach. He straightened up in surprise.

'If it's Mr Skeffington you're wanting,' the man said, after he had recovered his composure and returned to pushing his broom. 'He's backstage somewhere.' He pointed along a narrow and dusty corridor that circled the Grand's auditorium and led further into the building.

'How shall I know him?'

'Oh, you'll know him all right. There's no mistaking Mr Skeffington. Just follow the sound of his voice.' There was a pause and Adam could hear, at the other end of the passage, a distant booming, like a bittern calling for its mate across the reedbeds of East Anglia. 'There it goes now. He'll be reciting what he calls "the Swan of Avon" to himself. That's bloody Shakespeare to you and me. I reckon he's outside one of the dressing rooms. Down there to the end and then bear right.'

Adam did as the doorman suggested and walked along the passageway. The rumbling sounds of blank verse grew louder as he did so. The words were those of Othello telling how Desdemona had come to love him. As he turned a corner, his boots clicking on the wooden floor, Othello's speech came to an abrupt end.

From the shadows of a doorway, a figure emerged and approached Adam. It spoke in the same reverberant tones in which the Moor of Venice had just described the winning of his wife. 'You have travelled, young sir, from that vast and ever-proliferating metropolis to which William Cobbett once attached the epithet, "The Great Wen"?'

The man who addressed Adam with these words presented a strange spectacle. His body was small and compact and cloaked in a billowing dressing gown of purple serge. His head, out of all proportion to the rest of him, was huge and surrounded by a straggling mane of hair and beard. His voice thundered resonantly as if its owner was always projecting it in the direction of the Gods. Adam could not easily tell the man's age. Alfred Skeffington – for this must surely be the man for whom he was searching – could have been a slightly decrepit fifty-five or a sprightly seventy-five.

'I have come from London, sir, that is true. I am not certain how you could have known that so instantly.'

'You have the look of a denizen of the Wen, my boy. You do reside there, do you not?'

'I do.'

'Then, my dear young fellow, you have my deepest sympathies.' Mr Skeffington held out his hand. 'I have lived there myself,' the actor-manager said, shaking Adam's hand vigorously. 'Several *lustra* have passed since last I was obliged to trudge its chartered streets but I have never forgotten the horrors' – here he dropped the young man's hand but continued to stare intently at him – 'the horrors, I repeat, of existence within its confines.'

'Horrors, Mr Skeffington?'

'Ask me no more, young sir. I implore you, ask me no more. Memories too painful to contemplate begin to burst the tombs in which I have long succeeded in burying them.' The old actor took a small white cambric handkerchief from the pocket of his purple gown and began to dab at his left eye.

'I am sorry that I have aroused unhappy recollections of your past, sir.'

Skeffington raised his hand, waving it slightly in Adam's direction. 'It is no matter, my boy, no matter. "I would forget it fain, but, O, it presses to my memory" – *Romeo and Juliet*, Act 3, Scene 2.' He returned the handkerchief to his pocket and seemed almost immediately more cheerful. 'But how can I help you? Your name, young Londoner, your name.'

'My name is Carver, sir, Adam Carver. I have come to York in search of a runaway.' Adam had decided already on the story he would tell to explain his interest in Dolly. 'A girl who has deserted her family to flee to the city. I have been commissioned by them to find her. It is thought that she might have attempted to join a company such as yours.'

He held out Dolly's now much-thumbed cabinet card. Skeffington showed no interest in it. Instead, he turned to open a door to one of the dressing rooms behind him. 'Follow me, Mr Carver.'

A desk in the corner of the room was piled high with papers and manuscripts. Others were heaped about it. Skeffington strode through them all. When he reached the desk, he swept his arm across it, knocking further small hills of paper to the floor. 'Take a seat, sir, take a seat.'

Adam looked about him. Parts of a small wing-backed chair could be glimpsed beneath another miniature mountain of paper. He hesitated, wondering whether or not to perch on it.

'Throw them to the ground, young man,' Skeffington said airily, 'throw them to the ground. Let them find their rightful level.'

'What, may I ask, *are* all these piles of paper, sir?' Adam picked one sheet out of the many on the chair and looked at it. He could make little sense of the words on it.

'Plays, Mr Carver, plays. Wretchedly written plays. Plays of pitiably poor quality. Plays that no theatre company will ever perform.' The actor gestured at the manuscripts with all the contempt of Coriolanus scorning the plebeians of Rome. 'You can have no conception of the number of would-be dramatists Yorkshire holds. And every one of them feels it incumbent upon himself – or herself, for the fair sex is as likely to feel the promptings of the muse as the other – to despatch his – or her – theatrical lucubrations to Alfred Skeffington. I am a man beset by bad drama.'

'Are there not works amongst them that might interest you?' Adam had removed the piles of paper from the chair and lowered himself gingerly into it.

'Not a one! None that shows any understanding of the art of the theatre.' Skeffington seized a handful of the nearest manuscript, waved it in Adam's direction and then hurled it over his own shoulder. 'There's no mileage in a play that has nothing but words. That is what they do not comprehend. Sensation, Mr Carver, sensation! That is what is required. Scenic effect and mechanical effect must thrill the eye. Words, alas, come a very poor second. Sometimes I wish that this were not so, but it is.'

There was a pause as the actor took a turn about his paper-strewn office. He picked up a couple of pages from one of the many manuscripts he had been sent, glanced at them, snorted with disdain and cast them away with a gesture of impatience.

Adam watched as they settled on a different pile of papers from the one on which Skeffington had found them. 'A melodrama, perhaps, is what theatregoers most enjoy,' the young man observed after a further moment's silence.

'A *sensational* melodrama, sir, a sensational one.'

'Such as *The Skeleton in the Cave*,' Adam suggested.

'Indeed, indeed,' the actor said complacently. 'Our own production is sensational indeed. And it has the added bonus that it is a story set in Yorkshire. Even in matters of murder, I find that the average Yorkshireman believes the best is only to be found within the bounds of his own county.'

'For my own part,' Adam ventured, 'I do not always find myself in agreement with the majority. I have not often found such theatrical works very convincing.'

'You are right yet again, Mr Carver, they are not. What stories they tell us!' Skeffington beamed at Adam. 'Rich and poor babies exchanged, with surprising frequency, by conniving nursemaids. Innocence and loveliness perpetually pursued by vice and debauchery. Wicked squires wearing tail coats and waxed moustaches. Not, I suspect, a very accurate portrayal of life in our villages and country houses. Even in Yorkshire. But audiences lap it up, sir, lap it up.' The actor suddenly clutched his stomach. Turning away from Adam, he fumbled in the drawer of a baize-covered desk, piled high with more papers. Pulling a small brown bottle from it and uncorking it, he raised it to his mouth.

'Are you well, Mr Skeffington? Should I call for assistance?'

The actor shook his head, still imbibing from the bottle. Eventually, with a smack of his lips that suggested deep satisfaction with what he had just drunk, he lowered it.

'Dr Collis Browne's Chlorodyne,' he said, holding up the small flask for Adam's inspection. 'A miraculous concoction. Twenty drops of the good doctor's medicine and the inner man is wonderfully soothed. For years, I suffered most dreadfully from the gripes. "All goodness is poison to thy stomach" – *Henry VIII*, Act 3, Scene 2. I owe my new well-being to Dr Collis Browne. He is one of the great benefactors of the age. If ever your inner man should turn upon you, I recommend this elixir unreservedly.' He returned the bottle to the desk drawer.

'I shall certainly bear your recommendation in mind, sir.'

'Do, my dear boy, do. What is it, Jesmond?'

A figure had appeared at the door to Skeffington's room. It was that of a man in middle age, with greasy and thinning fair hair and a protuberant paunch. He scowled at the actor before replying to him. 'You ain't forgot you're visiting the Townswomen's Guild this afternoon, have you?'

Skeffington clapped his hand to his brow and let out a long moan. 'I *had* forgotten, Jesmond, I had. The merciful waters of Lethe had washed over the memory of that particular appointment. But here you come with your cruel reminder of it. Have you no pity, Jesmond, no compassion for your suffering fellow man?'

'All I know is they're expecting Shakespeare's Tragic Heroes at three o'clock.' Jesmond turned on his heel and left the dressing room as abruptly as he had arrived in it. Skeffington shook his huge head like a lion worrying its prey. He stared mournfully at Adam. 'You can have no idea, sir, of the humiliations heaped upon us poor players,' he said, suddenly plunged into apparent despair. 'As if it was not enough to parade oneself before the swinish multitude in some witless comedy, to listen to the cachinnation of fools as one struts and frets one's hour upon the stage, I am also required to hold forth on Lear, Othello and the Dane to an audience of portly matrons and twittering maiden aunts.' The actor sighed deeply. 'It is no profession for any man of real distinction.'

'And yet you perform an undoubted service, Mr Skeffington.' Adam felt obliged to offer some consolation, so miserable the man now seemed. 'Think of the pleasure you give to thousands.'

Skeffington brightened immediately. 'You are right, sir, of course. Your sturdy common sense recalls me to myself. There are many in this hurly-burly world of ours who suffer from what Mr Carlyle calls, in his inimitable way, "asphyxia of the soul". And there are *plenty* of souls here in York that are well and truly asphyxiated. It is our job to help these poor, stifled souls to breathe again. To inspire them with a love of art and beauty and the finest things in this life.' Skeffington gestured grandly in the direction of the poster advertising *The Skeleton in the Cave*. 'And now, like Milton's uncouth swain, I must away to fresh woods and pastures new. It has been a delight and a privilege to talk to you, young man.'

'Before you go, sir, may I ask you again to look at the girl's photograph?' Adam held out the card and this time the actor, taking a monocle from his pocket, condescended to squint in its direction.

'A pretty girl,' he acknowledged. 'There are so many pretty girls who wish to take to the stage. They come to visit me, bedizened with their tattered finery. I always advise them against it.'

'But have you seen this particular pretty girl, sir? Has she asked to join your company recently?'

'You must speak to Mr Timble, sir. The estimable Mr Timble. Not a sparrow falls, metaphorically speaking, in this great theatre but Timble knows of it.' Skeffington cast off the purple dressing gown, revealing a dark jacket and trousers beneath. He took a huge black cape, seemingly several sizes too large for him, from a peg on the door, swirling it about his tiny body and all but disappearing within it. Only his leonine head remained within view. 'As for myself, I have an appointment. In Bottom's immortal words – the *Dream*, Act 4, Scene 1 – "I must to the barber's, monsieur, for methinks I am marvellous hairy about the face".'

'I had hoped, Mr Skeffington, that you would be able—'

The actor thrust his right arm out of the enormous cloak and held it aloft. 'No more, Mr Carver. The barber's chair awaits me. I cannot visit the fairest ladies of this fair city with my locks untrimmed. Timble, sir, Timble is the man for you.' With one last flourish of the giant's cape, he turned and stalked out of the room.

* * * * *

'Skeffington's all right,' Timble said grudgingly.

After the actor's abrupt departure for the barber's shop, Adam had returned once more to the lobby where the elderly cleaner was still busy with his broom. The man had seemed unsurprised to see him again and had cheerfully pointed him in the direction of his new quarry.

Adam had found Timble sitting at a desk in a small room tucked away behind the dressing rooms. He was methodically making his way through what looked like a large pile of bills.

'Gets some strange ideas in his head, that's all. If I told you what he wanted for the show last Christmas, you wouldn't believe me.' The theatre manager, a mournful-looking man in late middle age, with straggly grey hair and a beard, gazed at Adam.

After a brief silence, the young man realized that he was waiting for him to ask the obvious question. 'What did he want, Mr Timble?'

'Animals. Wild animals. A bear and a camel. For the pantomime.'

'I suppose it must have been difficult to obtain them.'

'We got the camel from Jamrach's in the Ratcliffe Highway. Had it sent up here on the train. Caused quite a stir, I can tell you.'

'I imagine it did.'

'Ever had any dealings with camels?'

Adam confessed that he had not.

'Nasty brutes. They spit everywhere. The pit was awash.' Timble picked up one of the bills from the desk, examined it, sighed and placed it back on the pile. 'It only lasted two nights. The orchestra was up in arms. We had to send the beast back to Jamrach's. Cost us a bloody fortune.'

'What about the bear?'

'Oh, the bear was no trouble. He's still here somewhere.'

Adam looked hurriedly over his shoulder.

'In York, I mean. We sold him to a street performer. I saw him in Petergate the other day.' Timble now had two large pieces of paper, one in his left hand and one in his right. He looked from one to the other, then stood up and moved across his office to a small stove in the corner. He opened the grate on its front and thrust both papers into the stove's fire. Slamming the grate shut, he walked back to his chair. 'I don't suppose you've come to talk about camels and bears, though. You say the old man told you to see me?'

Adam nodded. 'Mr Skeffington thought that you might know a woman for whom I am searching.' The young man gave the theatre manager the photo of Dolly.

Timble was in no hurry to give judgement. He held the cabinet card first in his right hand and then in his left. He moved it nearer to his face and then further away. He tilted it slightly to one side and, shifting his head to the same angle, peered myopically at the girl. 'Yes, I've seen her,' he said eventually. 'She come here a few days ago. Calling herself Jessie Smith. Not her real name, of course. Never thought it was. Said she could sing and dance and wanted a job. She'd talked to Skeffington and he sent her to me.'

'And did you find a job for her?'

'Nothing going,' Timble said. 'No vacancies at present. No call for dancers in a murder story. We might need some for a show Skeffington's thinking of for the summer. I told her to come back in a month.'

'And she left the theatre immediately once you had told her this?'

The theatre manager nodded.

'Did she give any indication of where she was staying? Or of her future plans?'

'She just went. I've no notion where.'

Adam sighed with disappointment. He was wasting his time in pursuit of this girl. He began to think that his best option was simply to take the train back to London and tell Sunman that he couldn't find her. And then he could return to his old life, to his photography and his writing, and forget that there was such a young woman as Dolly Delaney.

And he could shake the truth about his father out of that wretch Job Benskin.

Yet did he want to return to London with his tail between his legs? To admit to Sunman and Waterton that he had failed them? He did not. For the present, he would continue to look for Miss Delaney. He tipped his hat politely to Timble. 'Thank you for your time, sir. I am sorry to have troubled you.'

'Think nothing of it. I wish I could be of more help. She seemed a nice young thing.'

Adam had turned and opened the door to Timble's ramshackle office and was halfway through it when the theatre manager spoke again.

'There was one thing. She said she knew Cyril Montague. From London.'

The young man came back into the room.

'Aye,' Timble said. 'She'd worked with him at the Gaiety, according to her account. She must have thought it would change my mind for me. But when there's no dancing job to be had, it don't matter a fig who you know or don't know. There's just no job.'

'Cyril Montague? The name sounds familiar. Who is Cyril Montague?'

'Maybe you saw him in London yourself, sir. Quite the nob in his day, Cyril. A few years ago. Name in the papers, crowds of admirers at the stage door. But his habits got the better of him. Or the worst.' Timble mimed a man smoking furiously.

'Tobacco?' Adam asked, puzzled.

'Opium,' Timble said. 'It's the very devil for making a man forget. Poor Cyril kept forgetting on the stage of the Gaiety. So now he's up in York, forgetting his lines every night on stage here and driving Skeffington to distraction. Standing there like a dying duck in a thunderstorm, trying to remember what he's supposed to be saying. Some nights the only time he shows any spark of interest is when the play ends. He'd elbow the Devil himself out of the way to take a curtain. The old man'll lose patience with him soon, but Cyril's still hanging on by his eyelashes.'

'Is Mr Montague in the theatre at present?'

Timble began to wheeze and shake his head. It took Adam several moments to realize that the mournful-looking theatre manager was laughing. 'Cyril in the house?' he said through the wheezes and gasps. 'At this hour? We're lucky if he arrives for curtain up. In any case, tonight is the one night in the week he isn't on stage.'

CHAPTER FOURTEEN

'There is one question which I failed to ask Timble when I saw him.'

Quint, who had just finished hanging his master's frock coat in the hotel room's solid mahogany wardrobe, turned as he heard his voice.

Adam was sprawled on a long sofa beneath the window, smoking a cigarette. 'I forgot to inquire whether or not Dolly had said she would return to the theatre.'

'Ain't very likely, is it?' Quint closed the wardrobe door with a crash. 'Didn't you say this Timble cove told 'er there was no work to be had?'

'Ah, but that is not exactly the case. He told her there was no work to be had *at present*. However, he also claimed that he had mentioned the company would need dancers in the summer. He advised her to come back in a month's time. But did she say anything that suggested she would take his advice? I omitted to ask him.'

Quint's bored grunt said as eloquently as any words might have that he couldn't see that this mattered very much.

'But it *is* of significance,' Adam said, in reply to the grunt. 'If she said she would return, then she was planning to stay in York. We are not wasting our time in looking for her. I should have asked him.'

'Go round the Grand and ask 'im in the morning.'

'It would be better to put the question to him more immediately.'

'Go round the Grand this evening, then.'

'I cannot. I am determined this evening to speak to Cyril Montague. Tonight, I am told, is the only night in the week when he is not on stage. I have no time to go in search of Timble. You must find him, Quint.'

'And 'ow the devil am I supposed to do that? You're forgetting I ain't ever clapped eyes on 'im.'

'Everybody at the theatre knows him. Someone will point him out to you.'

'And if he ain't at the theatre, I jest go round asking every cully in York if 'is name's Timble, I suppose?' Quint spoke with heavy sarcasm.

'If he isn't in the Grand, he will be somewhere close. Montague may be having a night off, but the play goes on. Timble will want to be on hand. Try the local alehouses. You will enjoy that.'

* * * * *

Quint entered the bar and peered about him.

He had been to the Grand but his quarry had not been there. Luckily, the man in the box office had seen Timble leave and had known where he would be going. He would, the man had said, be in the Punchbowl in Stonegate.

The pub had only a handful of customers and only one of them fitted the description Quint had been given. He was sitting at a corner table, reading a copy of the *York Herald*, a half-empty bottle and a glass in front of him. He looked up as Quint approached and stood by the table, eyeing him like a funeral director measuring a corpse for its coffin.

'Can I help you, sir?' Timble asked, peering over the top of his newspaper.

'The name's Quint Devlin,' the manservant said. 'You've already spoke to the cove I works for. Gent called Carver. There was a question 'e was going to ask you and never did. 'E's told me to come along and ask it for 'im.'

Timble looked Quint up and down. He seemed slightly surprised but not perturbed by his appearance in the pub. 'Well, good evening to you, Mr Devlin,' he said eventually. 'I'm sure I'm happy

156

to oblige your master if I can.' He gestured to the other chair pulled up at the table. 'Would you like to join me in a drop of the gin?'

Quint nodded and sat down. The theatre manager beckoned to the barman and another small glass was brought to the table. Timble filled it with gin. Quint raised the glass in a half-toast and then upended its contents swiftly into his mouth. He banged it back on the table top, making the gin bottle wobble slightly, and let out a whistle of appreciation.

'Nice drop of the lightning,' he said.

'Would you like to wet the other eye, Mr Devlin?' Timble asked, making as if to pour a second glass from the gin bottle.

With a grunt and nod, Quint indicated that, on consideration, he would.

'So, what is the question your master wishes to put to me?'

Quint retailed in his own particular way Adam's request for further information and the theatre manager paused for thought.

'Yes,' he said, after a few moments, 'yes, now I think of it, the girl did say she was coming back. I should have said as much to your master. She seemed very eager to do so. Yes, I think we'll be seeing her again before too long.'

Quint leaned back on his stool and stared at his boots, muddy from the York streets. That had been easy, then, he thought. His task was done. His master's additional question had been answered. It seemed as if the dollymop might still be in the city. He could say his farewells to this Timble cove and be on his way. But he was comfortable in the Punchbowl and the weather outside was not pleasant. He looked at the half-bottle of gin, which was close to empty.

Timble noted the direction in which his new companion's eyes had strayed. 'Time for another modest quencher, Mr Devlin?'

Quint, who rarely turned down the offer of alcohol, nodded. 'That bottle's a dead 'un, mind,' he said.

The theatre manager stood and walked to the bar. After a brief colloquy with the barman, he returned with another half-bottle.

'A fine-looking gent your master,' Timble said, as he settled back into his seat. 'Couldn't help but notice his bearing when he come to visit. An ornament to any company, he'd be.'

Quint, who was more interested in the gin than the conversation, said nothing, but looked meaningfully at the bottle.

The theatre manager poured another glass. 'The fact is, Mr Devlin, we're in a bit of a pickle at the Grand at present. Skeffington don't know it yet, but one of our young men has run off with one of our young women.'

Quint picked up his glass and rolled the gin around it before throwing the liquid down his throat with one sudden movement. He still said nothing.

'Yes,' Timble went on, not, it seemed, discouraged by his fellow drinker's silence. 'Mr Bellingham and Miss Devonshire have both gone. Last seen heading for the railway station with a couple of portmanteaus and an engagement ring.'

Quint slammed his glass down on the table with unexpected force. In the quiet of the pub even the barman was surprised and looked across at him. Timble did not blink.

'That's about the gauge of it,' the theatre manager said. 'All very well for them, and who would want to stand in the way of young love? Well, youngish love. Not Horatio Timble. But it leaves us in the lurch. Last night of *The Skeleton in the Cave* soon. We can manage somehow, get through a few performances without them. But we open *The Spectre Bridegroom* in less than a week, and now we've got no bride and no bridegroom.'

There was a silence for a moment.

'Skeffington will be in a fearful wax. Ranting and yelling like we're all as deaf as posts. And he's been in such a good mood of late. As merry as a mouse in malt.'

There was another pause as Quint shuffled in his seat and Timble toyed with his glass.

Eventually, the theatre manager leaned across the table. 'Your Mr Carver's a genteel-looking chap,' he said. 'I don't suppose he's ever taken to the stage, has he?'

* * * * *

Cyril Montague's rooms were very close to the theatre, in a ramshackle building in a courtyard off Goodramgate, almost opposite the east front of the Minster. The door was already open when Adam climbed the rickety staircase to the attics and found them. He called out Montague's name and heard a faint, inarticulate response from inside. Assuming it to be an invitation to enter, he did so.

The room was in half-darkness. Curtains of crimson damask had been hastily and incompletely pulled across the only window, and a thin shaft of light from a gas lamp outside shone through the gap that had been left. Dust danced in this light. There was little furniture in view, and even less ornament.

Montague was sitting on a black horsehair sofa pushed against one of the walls, a long-stemmed pipe in his mouth. An opium lamp stood on a small table beside him. The sickly smell of the drug hung in the air. It was potent but not, Adam noted, unpleasant. Montague took a long pull on the pipe and sent the smoke furling from his nostrils with a deep sigh of satisfaction, watching it drift across the room.

'Have a whiff, my dear,' he suggested companionably, offering the pipe. 'There's paradise in these plumes.'

Adam shook his head, taking stock of the man he had come to ask about Dolly.

The actor was wearing a blue smoking jacket and a red smoking cap in the shape of a Turkish fez – a tassel on the top flicked back and forth as he moved his head. Montague's lips, Adam noticed, were rouged and his face was lightly powdered. He did not seem particularly surprised to see his visitor, nor did he seem troubled by Adam's unheralded arrival.

'A thousand and one apologies for the austerity of my humble lodgings, my dear,' the actor drawled. 'The grumpy old thing who owns them took away most of the furnishings last week. I do declare I haven't a *seat* to offer you.' He smiled beatifically and put the pipe to his lips once more.

'It is of no account, Mr Montague,' Adam said, 'and I am sorry to intrude. Mr Timble suggested that I should call upon you.'

'Ah, the worthy Timble.'

'He thought that you might be able to help me with some enquiries I am pursuing.'

'I would be *deliriously* happy to help, of course.' The actor had turned to the opium lamp on the table and was making some adjustment to it. He was clearly more interested in that than in his visitor. 'But what do I know of *enquiries*? Absolutely nothing, I would venture to say.'

'I am looking for this young lady.' Adam held out the cabinet card which showed Dolly beneath her parasol.

Montague turned and squinted at the photograph. He held it up to what light there was. He seemed to be having difficulty focusing on it. '*Delightful* creature,' he said eventually. 'A friend of yours?'

'According to Mr Timble, she claimed to be a friend of yours.'

'Never seen her in my life, my dear.' Montague returned to fumbling with the paraphernalia of his drug.

'Her name is Dolly Delaney. She told Mr Timble that she knew you from London. That she danced in the chorus at the Gaiety.'

'Ah, the chorus!' Montague said, now abandoning both pipe and bowl and turning bleary eyes towards his visitor. He spoke as if this explained all. 'So many pretty little poppets, forever shaking their curls at a man. No use to me, of course. They all blur into one after a while. Perhaps dear Dolly *was* among the dancers at the Gaiety . . . or the Princess's? Could it have been the Princess's? But I don't remember her.'

'She has not been to see you here in York?'

'In York?'

For just a moment, Adam glimpsed a hint of something other than amiable stupor in Montague's expression, but it was gone as swiftly as it had appeared.

'*Nobody* comes to see me in York, my dear. Neither here nor when I tread the boards. Have you *seen* the houses Skeffington gets? Not enough to pay for milk for the theatre cat. "What's the crowd like tonight, Timble?" I ask each evening. "Bad, Cyril, bad," he says every time. I should never have left the smoke.' His voice was full of self-pity. For one moment, Adam feared that Montague was about to cry. Indeed, the actor made a show of wiping a furtive tear from the corner of his eye. Then he clasped his hand to his brow like the wronged husband in a melodrama of adulterous love. 'That an artist like myself should have to work with such poor players as strut and fret their hour upon the stage here,' he said, now looking around for his pipe and then falling upon it. 'You wouldn't *credit* the people old Skeffington has working for him,' he went on. 'There's Kitty Devonshire takes the ingénue roles and I *swear* she's forty if she's a day. As for Bellingham, the man's *shameless*. He pads his calves, you know.' Montague patted one of his own lower limbs. 'The wretch will do *anything* to make his legs look better in tights.'

'And what of Mr Skeffington himself?'

Montague said nothing but puffed furiously at his opium. His eyes closed and Adam began to suspect that the actor, his outburst over, was drifting off to sleep. He was about to speak again when Montague opened first one eye and then the other. The tassels from his red smoking cap were hanging over his face and he pushed them to one side.

'Skeffington?' he said. 'He's a regular barnstormer, ain't he?'

There was another silence. Montague's eyes closed and again Adam wondered if he had fallen asleep. Again, the actor came slowly to life.

'Alfred ain't a bad sort, I suppose. Although he brought me here under false pretences.' Montague now sounded petulant. 'According to him, I was to play Romeo, Hamlet, the great Shakespearean roles. And, once I *exile* myself to this uncouth city, what do I find?'

Adam made a gesture to indicate that he had no idea what had awaited Montague in York.

'*The Miller of Mansfield and His Maid.*' The actor, who had briefly put aside his pipe, spat out the words as if they were curses.

'I do not think I am familiar with the work,' Adam said.

'Then you are a lucky man, sir. Thank the Lord that *we* are now finished with it. Such a teacup-and-saucer sort of a play.' Montague twisted his face into a moue of distaste. '*Frightfully* respectable. If we can't have the Bard, I prefer something with a little more blood and thunder.'

'Like *The Skeleton in the Cave*?'

'Well,' the actor conceded, 'our present production is at least a little more *lively* than that *wretched* miller and his *sickly* maid.'

'You are playing Eugene Aram, of course.'

'Of course,' the actor said, with some complacency. 'Who else in this raggle-taggle band that Skeffington has gathered together could do justice to the role? That man Bellingham and his padded legs? I think not.'

'I am sure that you are magnificent in the role, sir.'

Montague bowed his head in acknowledgement of Adam's outrageous flattery, as if to concede that, yes, on consideration, 'magnificent' was exactly the word to describe his performance.

'But I wonder if I could ask you, as a favour, to look again at the photograph of Miss Delaney. She has gone missing and her family is eager to find the girl.'

Adam held out the cabinet card once more. Montague had returned to his opium pipe and was blowing spirals of scented smoke across the small room. He reached out a beringed hand and took the photograph. He stared at it for a few moments. For a second time, Adam thought he saw a gleam of something more than drugged indifference in the actor's eyes but it was almost immediately gone again.

Montague gave back Dolly's picture. 'The *poor* poppet,' he said. 'Do you suppose something *awful* has happened to her?'

'I do not know, Mr Montague. What do you think?'

The actor shrugged. 'I'm sure I don't know, my dear. As I say, I have never met the girl. But awful things do happen to such creatures all too often.' He took another, final pull on his pipe and blew the smoke upwards. His eyelids began to droop. 'And now I am beginning to feel most *devilishly* tired.'

Cyril Montague, with the precision of a man who had undertaken the task in all kinds of states and conditions, began to dismantle his opium kit. He dowsed the lamp and laid his pipe, which had ceased to smoke, carefully on the table. Adam watched him. Once the actor had finished the job to his satisfaction, he took off his tasselled cap and curled up on the horsehair sofa. Within seconds he was asleep.

The room was so full of opium fumes that Adam had begun to feel light-headed himself. With one last glance to ensure that, this time, Montague really was asleep, he made his way down the rickety staircase and back to the fresh air of the city streets.

CHAPTER FIFTEEN

'I am certain that Montague knew more than he was telling me.'

'Thought you told me he was so sillyfied with the pipe that 'e didn't know how many days make a week.'

'He was. But he was still crafty enough to keep something from me. I would swear on a stack of bibles that he has seen Dolly recently. But why was he reluctant to admit that he even knew her? Did he think that I intended her harm?'

'Maybe he thought you was 'er sweetheart. Come to take 'er back to the smoke. And 'e doesn't want you to know where she is 'cos 'e's after 'er 'imself?'

'An interesting theory, but Cyril Montague is, I think, more likely to be "after" the gentlemen of the cast rather than the ladies.'

Quint said nothing. Adam looked over to where his servant was standing. The older man had pulled back the curtain on the hotel window and was peering into the street below.

'I hope I do not shock you with that suggestion, Quint.'

The manservant turned back into the room and shrugged his shoulders. 'It ain't no concern of mine,' he said tolerantly. 'If a molly boy fancies other molly boys, what's it to me? More judies for them as does like them.'

'A very wise remark. Live and let live, say I.' Adam reclined further in his chair and, clasping his hands behind his head, stared up at the ceiling stucco. 'Cyril Montague is a man whose path in life is heading relentlessly downhill,' he said after a pause. 'Once he was the toast of Drury Lane, a star shining in the dramatic firmament. Now he's playing to empty rows of seats in a small provincial theatre.'

'Ain't that always the way,' Quint remarked mournfully. 'Rooster one day, feather duster the next.'

'You're quite the philosopher today, Quint, are you not?'

The manservant made a sound in acknowledgement that was halfway between a wheeze and a snarl.

'So Timble believes that we should audition to tread the boards, does he?' his master said after a pause.

'That's what he sez to me in the Punchbowl. Job for you and job for me.'

'Was the man drunk when he made this suggestion?'

'He'd been pushing the bottle about a bit. But 'e weren't that far gone.'

'So it was not the drink talking.'

''E sez they need a new man for the company. On account of this Bellingham cove 'aving legged it with a tart. And they could always find something for a cully like me.'

Adam stretched out his legs in his chair and examined his shoes as if he was debating whether or not to summon the hotel boots to polish them. 'Could we join Skeffington's motley crew, do you think?' he asked. 'What are your accomplishments, Quint? Can you sing? Can you dance? Can you strike a theatrical pose?'

Quint looked doubtful. 'I knows "Villikins and his Dinah",' he said after a pause.

'Well, then, we must prepare our audition pieces. Yours can be a verse or two of that moving tribute to doomed love.'

'It ain't me as Timble's chiefly int'rested in. I told you. 'E wants summ'un to take Bellingham's place. 'E reckons you'll fill the bill.' The manservant paused and looked at his master. 'What you goin' to do? Ain't no point you doin' "Villikins and his Dinah" as well.'

Quint sounded distinctly possessive of his chosen audition piece.

'I couldn't hope to compete with you, Quint. But I have strings to my own bow. Perhaps a speech from the Bard? Skeffington is clearly a great Shakespearean. A soliloquy by the gloomy Dane would probably be just the ticket.' Adam sprang from his chair and stepped into the centre of the room. Tugging briefly at the collar of his shirt, he cleared his throat and began to declaim:

'O, that this too too solid flesh would melt
Thaw and resolve itself into a dew!
Or that the Everlasting had not fix'd
His canon 'gainst self-slaughter! O God! God!
How weary, stale, flat and unprofitable,
Seem to me all the uses of this world!'

Adam's face went blank and he ceased speaking. 'I am afraid I have forgotten the rest. Something about an unweeded garden and things rank and gross, but the exact phrasing escapes me.' He looked at his servant. 'What do you make of brother Hamlet's words, Quint?'

Quint merely grunted. 'Dull as a sermon,' he said. 'Ain't a patch on "Villikins".'

* * * * *

In the event, neither Adam nor Quint were required to perform an audition. The following morning found the company at the Grand so desperate to fill the gap left by the departing lovers that, when the two men arrived to volunteer their services, they were greeted with open arms.

'Fate must have sent you,' Timble said, as all three men stood in the dingy lobby. 'I said to my friend Mr Devlin here, I said a genteel-looking man like yourself, Mr Carver, was just what was required in the circumstances. Did I not say exactly that, Mr Devlin?'

Quint agreed that he had.

'I regret that I have very little experience of the stage, Mr Timble,' Adam said. 'I worry that I may not prove so welcome an addition to your number as you imagine.'

Timble waved away his concerns. 'If you can remember your

lines and not fall over the scenery,' he said, 'you will be doing as well as most of your fellow thespians. Rather better than some, if truth be told.'

'I shall do my best, sir.'

'I am convinced you will.'

'The play will open next week?'

'In five days. But there is time enough to prepare you for your role.' Timble paused and looked at Adam. 'The young lady you were looking for,' he said. 'Miss Delaney? I suppose it would be too much to hope that you have found her?'

'I regret to say that Dolly is still missing.'

'Pity, she was a pretty thing. She could have taken Kitty Devonshire's place. And she would have been an improvement. In terms of looks, anyway.'

'Perhaps she will come calling upon you again.' Adam could only hope that this might be the case. One of the reasons he was happy to join the Grand's company was his belief that Dolly might make another attempt to gain employment there. Another was his conviction that Cyril Montague, opium-addled though he was, knew more than he was telling.

'Perhaps.' The theatre manager seemed to have lost interest in the subject of Dolly once he realized that she would not be available to play in *The Spectre Bridegroom*. 'Perhaps she is no longer even in York.'

'That is true,' Adam admitted. 'We cannot be certain that she has stayed in the city.' He was, however, more or less sure that the girl *was* still in York. Where else could she have gone? Back to London? She had been so eager to leave the metropolis that it seemed unlikely she would have returned there so swiftly. And, when she had sought a job at the Grand, Timble had at least held out the possibility of future employment. No, Adam was convinced that the dancer was somewhere close at hand. Working at the theatre himself would give him the ideal opportunity to track her down.

'What of Quint here?' he asked Timble.

The two men turned their attention to the manservant, who had wandered over to the open door to the street and was scowling at passers-by.

'There is always room for another pair of hands to build sets and move props,' the theatre manager said. 'If Mr Devlin were prepared to pitch in and help.'

'Oh, Quint will be happy to do his bit,' Adam replied.

'Ain't I wanted to sing "Villikins", then?' Quint had heard his name and come back to join them.

Adam shook his head. 'There is a job backstage for you,' he said. 'Although, if you wish to entertain your fellow workers with "Villikins", you must feel free to do so.'

'I spent 'alf the night recallin' two more verses to mind,' Quint said indignantly. 'You telling me that was all a waste of time?'

'Alas, I fear so.'

'Don't you go fretting yourself, Mr Devlin,' Timble said. 'There'll be plenty of chance for your talents to shine in the future. Everyone at the Grand gets their turn eventually. Why, I've even been in front of the lights myself once. Back in '68. Porter in the Scottish play, I was. Nobody else to do it so on I go. Forgot most of my lines and had to make them up as I went along.'

Still chatting, the theatre manager took a grumpy Quint by the arm and guided him in the direction of the props room. Adam was left to smoke a cigarette in the lobby, but he was not alone for very long: Alfred Skeffington soon bustled through the door. He hailed Adam as if he was a conquering hero returned from battle.

'So, Timble tells me you are coming to join us!' How did the old actor know he had said yes to the proposal? Adam wondered. There was no time to ponder the question at length. Skeffington was in full flow. 'We few, we happy few, we band of brothers,' the actor said, leading Adam into the maze of narrow passageways and criss-crossing corridors that were hidden backstage at the Grand. 'And sisters, of course. May it never be said that I would forget the ladies.'

'Timble was pointing out your difficulties since Mr Bellingham left and—'

'Ah, the wretch,' Skeffington interrupted, briefly furious, 'and, to think that I plucked him from the obscurity of a penny gaff in Bradford and allowed him to bestride the stage here in York. Ingratitude is indeed, as the Bard says in *Lear*, sharper than a serpent's tooth.'

'I shall endeavour to fill the gap in your ranks that his departure has created, Mr Skeffington.'

'I am sure you will, my boy, I am sure you will.' The actor-manager made an effort to slap Adam on the shoulders but he was too short. Instead, he gave the young man a painful blow in the small of the back. Adam winced but Skeffington, not noticing his discomfort, continued to discourse cheerfully as they ventured ever further into the theatrical labyrinth. 'Timble informs me you are a Varsity man, sir. But that you did not take your degree. Some difficulty with the authorities, perhaps?' Adam peered down at the actor whose expression was now that of a tolerant uncle prepared to overlook the minor indiscretions of a youthful nephew. 'Some undergraduate scrape which landed you in hot water and required your relocation to another town?'

'Not exactly, Mr Skeffington.' Adam could not decide whether he was annoyed by this obvious curiosity or amused by it. 'I was not sent down from Cambridge, if that is what you mean. If anything, I rusticated myself. Let us say that, in the aftermath of my father's death, it was not possible to maintain the position to which I aspired.'

Skeffington nodded as if this made everything clear. The two men sidestepped a large drum and a pile of discarded clothing that were blocking the way and continued to walk.

'Look out, Mr Carver!' the actor shouted suddenly.

Adam had been close to colliding with a huge sheet of copper which was suspended on ropes hanging down from the upper reaches of the theatre. He jumped nimbly to one side.

'For thunder,' Skeffington said, in answer to the young man's unspoken question. 'It's a rare piece that does not benefit from a good thunderstorm. "Blow, winds, and crack your cheeks! Rage! Blow! You cataracts and hurricanes, spout till you have drench'd our steeples, drown'd the cocks." *Lear* again, Act 3, Scene 2.'

The diminutive actor had launched himself so loudly into his Shakespearean quotation that he had attracted the attention of a stagehand, who appeared from behind a piece of scenery with a querying look on his face. Skeffington waved him away imperiously and guided Adam out of the surrounding confusion. A few steps further, and Skeffington suddenly darted forward, pulling back a red curtain. To Adam's surprise, the two of them emerged onto the stage of the Grand. He realized that he had completely lost his sense of direction during the meanderings backstage.

'I understand from Mr Timble that you have never donned the buskin before,' the old actor remarked. 'You are taking your first, faltering steps to the green room.'

Adam admitted that this was so.

'Do not for a moment imagine that you are setting out on a path of flowers,' Skeffington said sternly, as if Adam had just claimed that appearing on stage was something anyone could do with ease. 'No – it can be a briery way, my boy, and thorns of misery can spring up beneath the feet of the unsuspecting wanderer.'

Adam endeavoured to look as serious-minded a prospective student of acting as he could.

'However, the fundamentals of our noble art are easily learned,' the actor went on. 'Excellence is the product of experience, but competence can be achieved through the exercise of a little intelligence. I shall demonstrate a few of the simplest expressions.'

Skeffington walked towards the footlights and swung round to look at Adam. He adopted the stance of a man about to confront an audience. 'Head down, shoulders rounded, face cupped in hands.' The actor followed his own instructions. 'Raise shoulders up and down thus.' His face still covered, he began to shrug his shoulders vigorously. After a few moments, he dropped his hands and beamed at Adam. 'Emotion conveyed . . . grief!'

'Very affecting, Mr Skeffington,' Adam said.

'It is, it is,' the actor agreed. 'But here is another. See if you can put a name to it.' He opened his eyes wide, made his mouth into as nearly circular an 'O' as he could and placed both hands, fingers extended, on his cheeks.

'Fear?' Adam ventured.

'Horror,' Skeffington said, sounding slightly disappointed by the young man's obtuseness. 'I suppose the two are close relations of one another. However, enough of the tired tricks of an old trouper. It is time for you to demonstrate what thespian skills you possess. Perhaps we have another Garrick in our midst, about to make his debut at Goodman's Fields, hmm?'

'I very much doubt it, Mr Skeffington.'

'We shall not know until you step before an audience. But what attitude should you strike now?' The actor put his finger to his chin like a man in a caricature of thoughtfulness. 'I have it. Joy! Give me joy, Mr Carver, joy unbounded!'

Adam, feeling intensely uncomfortable and hoping that no one was close to witness this audition, twisted his face into the best simulacrum of ecstatic happiness he could manage. It was, he feared, perhaps closer to idiocy than joy.

Skeffington made a grunting noise that suggested he was of much the same opinion.

'Ah . . . interesting, interesting,' he said. 'Perhaps we should try another emotion. Anger. Show me *anger*, my boy.'

This was easier. Adam was surprised by the facility with which he could pretend to rage.

So too was his mentor. 'Very good, sir, very good,' Skeffington enthused, as the young man snarled and grimaced on the dimly lit stage. 'Eyes rolling, breast heaving, teeth gnashing. Excellent! I can see that we shall not miss Mr Bellingham in the least.' Adam continued to glare into the stalls. 'Although perhaps we shall have to find you roles a little more *farouche* than those our decamping friend undertook. You may relax now, my boy.'

As Adam returned his features to their normal state, Skeffington began to circumambulate the stage at a slow pace. It was surprising, the young man thought, how much kingly dignity so short a figure could project. The actor looked like a conqueror awaiting the submission of those he had conquered.

'The theatre is a noble calling, Mr Carver. Let no one persuade you otherwise.' Skeffington wagged an admonitory finger as if Adam had just been arguing for the essential depravity of the stage and those who worked on it. 'A general prejudice exists in the breasts of parents and preceptors alike against our profession. We are rogues and vagabonds, they say.' Skeffington paused in his pacing and shook his shaggy head mournfully. 'It is true that many unhappy players have drowned their souls in fermented liquors or expired before their time in workhouse dormitories. But others have rolled along Piccadilly in their own carriages and conversed intimately with the finest in the land.' Skeffington resumed his circling of the stage. 'We humble followers of Thespis must seek for the greatest amount of instruction,' he went on, apparently addressing an audience situated in the upper reaches of the theatre, 'combined with the largest amount of amusement, the highest utility blended with the highest refinement and . . .' Here, Skeffington waved his hand vaguely in the air, inspiration briefly deserting him. 'But you take my meaning, I am sure.'

'I do indeed, sir, and I shall strive to be worthy of your finest aspirations.' Skeffington's speech was temporarily uplifting. For a moment or two Adam fully believed what he had just said.

The feeling did not last, however. His idealistic glow was already beginning to fade a little when a swarthy man with long, greasy black locks poked his head around the curtain at the back of the stage and spoke to Skeffington.

'The costumes for the wedding guests are here. Timble told me to let you know.'

The actor waved his hand airily and the head disappeared as suddenly as it had materialized.

'For *The Spectre Bridegroom*,' Skeffington explained. 'Our next production culminates in a wedding feast. A scene of lavish ostentation and tumultuous activity. York will rarely have seen its like.'

'I do not believe that I have met that gentleman as yet,' Adam remarked, nodding towards the curtain. It would be a good idea, he thought, to put as many names to faces at the Grand as he could.

Skeffington struck his hand to his brow. 'A thousand pardons, my boy. I did not have the grace to introduce you.'

'You did not have the time.'

'No, that is true. Like Puck in the *Dream*, he was here and gone "swifter than arrow from the Tartar's bow". His name is Venables. He plays the secondary villains.'

'I believe there may be others in your company I am still to meet?'

'There is my wife, of course. Mrs Frances Eleanor Skeffington. Nell to her multitudes of admirers, and my noble helpmeet. There's Kitty Devonshire. A delightful young woman but shoulders like a champagne bottle. All droop and slope. Wardrobe has a terrible time with her.' Adam was about to remind Skeffington that Kitty had gone but the old actor remembered himself. 'Of course, the wretched girl's gone, hasn't she? Embarked upon connubial bliss with that rogue Bellingham.' He continued to count off the members of his company. 'Then there is Miss Delgado, a lady of Spanish origins. She is still with us, I hope. She takes the breeches parts. Her lower limbs look lovely in the trousers, although I must confess her enunciation of her lines is not always understood by every member of the audience.' Mr Skeffington paused. 'Nor indeed by every one of her fellow actors. But we are working on the problem.'

'And what of Mr Montague?'

'Ah, poor Cyril.' Mr Skeffington said. 'A man of uncommon talents but never able to keep his hands on the pounds, shillings and pence that his genius earns him. The bailiff and the broker's man are as familiar to him as the butcher and the baker are to those of us who lead better-regulated lives.'

'You have known the gentleman in question for some time?'

For a moment, Adam thought the actor might not answer his question. Skeffington gave the young man an appraising glance, clearly curious as to the reasons for it. Did he think that Adam shared Cyril Montague's sexual tastes? If he did, it seemed to be of no great concern to him.

'Let me see now. I first saw poor Cyril in a pantomime in Rich-

173

mond many years ago,' Skeffington said. '*The Enchanted Fairy of the Island of Abracadabra*, if I recollect correctly, was the title of the entertainment. He was the second clown and did little but steal sausages and fall over. None the less, even in that tawdry role, he showed a spark of genius.'

'So you hired him for your company?'

'Ah, no. Not then. I am talking about the early fifties. I had no company at the time. I was merely a toiler in the vineyard of Drury Lane. But I followed his career with interest. I watched his spark blaze forth in triumph. I watched it fizzle like a firework and die. When I learned that he was anxious to leave the Great Wen, I wrote to offer him employment here in the north.'

'And he came, of course.'

'Like "a reeking post, stew'd in his haste, half breathless." *Lear* once more, Act 2, Scene 4.'

'He was anxious to claim the job—?'

'The years have not been kind to Cyril. Rewarding roles were beginning to elude his grasp. He had been given a glorious opportunity to play the Dane and he had been very nearly hooted off the stage. He could barely remember a line.'

'You knew of his problems?' The actor inclined his head in stately agreement. 'And yet you were prepared to put him on the stage here?'

'As I have said, young man, Cyril Montague was once possessed of a spark of genius. He has it still, although he has made every effort to extinguish it.'

Adam wondered what Skeffington's true motives were in inviting Montague northwards. Kindness towards a fellow actor fallen on hard times? Perhaps, although the old man was running a business as much as an artistic venture. He could not afford to be sentimental. And Timble had made it clear that Cyril was a liability. Adam's own conversation with him had shown that the man would be a difficult colleague with whom to work.

'When did he arrive in York?'

Skeffington shrugged shoulders that seemed too narrow to support the weight of his mighty head. He was growing bored with the conversation. 'He came for *The Miller of Mansfield*. So . . . just over a month ago,' he said. 'But no more of poor Cyril. Let us return to our exercises in the emotions. Show me your jealousy.'

* * * * *

After a draining hour miming a variety of emotions for Skeffington, Adam had decided on a walk to clear his head. His mind now hard at work turning over recent events, he had not noticed that he had turned into one of the city's market areas. On either side of him were fruit and vegetable stalls, their holders bellowing their wares. It was late in the day, the crowds had thinned out and the market men were eager to dispose of their final goods. One waved a cabbage at him and made it clear that it was an unbeatable bargain; another invited him to inspect his rhubarb and assured him that he would find it impossible to locate its like anywhere else in Yorkshire.

Adam nodded and strolled on. His eye was caught by a ragged urchin who was idling ahead of him. Half a dozen radishes had fallen from one of the stalls and were lying on the cobblestones. None looked very appetizing but the boy, first stooping to pick them up, thrust one of them into his mouth with greedy relish. The stallholder saw him and shouted at the child, who ran off, clutching the remaining radishes to his chest as if they were rare and costly delicacies.

Adam moved on, still thinking of the chorus dancer and what might have happened to her. At the corner, where a narrow, cobbled alleyway joined the market, a man was playing a tin whistle with more enthusiasm than skill. His cap, lying flat on the pavement, contained three small coins and what looked to Adam like a brass button.

'Penny for a tune, sir,' the man said as Adam approached.

Adam reached into his pocket and took out the only coin that came to hand. 'I have but a halfpenny,' he said. 'You need only play me half a tune.' He threw the halfpenny into the man's cap and continued to walk.

He had now emerged from the market altogether. Looking to his right, he could see a narrow street of medieval buildings. Most seemed to contain butchers' shops – the cobbles were stained with blood, and the smell of meat and offal wafted along it. He turned to the left and began to make his way towards the Minster, which he could see rising above the city like some fortress over its fiefdom.

Walking the streets of York, Adam struggled to make sense of what he had learned since he had arrived in the city. What did he know for certain? One indisputable fact was that Dolly had made her way there and had spurned the employment offered to her by the unsympathetic Ridgewell. She had attempted instead to find the kind of work to which she was accustomed. She had approached Mr Timble at the Grand, but he had been unable to help her. Where had the young woman gone after that? She might have stayed in York; she might have returned to London.

Adam would, he thought, put money on her staying. Why should she return to London when she had been so eager to leave? And what of Cyril Montague? When Adam had called upon him, the dissipated actor had been in an opium-induced world of his own, but the young man was sure that Montague had recognized the girl in the photograph he had shown him.

Perhaps he did not know her as Dolly Delaney, but he knew her. And he had seen her in York, Adam was sure of it.

CHAPTER SIXTEEN

With a flourish of his cape, Adam strode into the wings. He had, he knew, forty minutes before his presence was next required. During all that time, Cyril Montague would be on stage.

Several days had passed since he and Quint had joined the company. Although Adam had found no trace of Dolly Delaney, they had been eventful days. He had found a ready acceptance in the company at the Grand: Mrs Skeffington, a kindly woman twice her husband's size, had taken an almost motherly interest in him; Miss Delgado had flirted incomprehensibly with him in what he had originally assumed was her native tongue but turned out to be her own idiosyncratic version of English; and Cyril Montague, on being formally introduced, had looked at him as if he was sure he knew him but couldn't quite place where they had met before. The other male actors had initially viewed him with suspicion but they were all good-natured, effervescent young men and had been unable to maintain their antagonism for more than twenty-four hours.

Adam's debut in *The Spectre Bridegroom* was soon upon him, filling him with nervousness, but he found that Timble had been largely correct. As long as he could remember his lines, which, since he was a spirit returned from the grave, were few in number, and could avoid bumping into the props, he could play his part. And he found the applause that greeted him when he took his bow before the curtains at the end of the evening surprisingly rewarding. He had always thought that he was someone who would not enjoy public acclaim, but it appeared he had been mistaken.

Tonight was the third performance of *The Spectre Bridegroom*. Adam had decided to use the time when he was offstage to search Cyril Montague's rooms.

Adam strode through the stage door and out into the street. A respectably dressed man and his wife gazed at him in astonishment as he marched past them. For a moment, he was puzzled. He did not usually attract such surprised attention from passers-by. Then he recalled that he was dressed in his stage clothes and daubed with greasepaint applied by the enthusiastic hand of Skeffington's make-up man. As he was, after all, supposed to be a spectral bridegroom, he could expect curious stares, at the very least, from any citizens he might encounter. Luckily, few seemed to be about on Goodram-gate and, walking swiftly, he soon turned into the courtyard he had visited a few days earlier.

Once again, Adam found the building in which Montague had his lodgings. As he had expected, its main door was open: the place was home to a score of people other than the actor and all would need access day and night. Adam climbed up to the attic room, stumbling twice on the creaking stairs. On both occasions he cursed under his breath and paused, waiting for someone to emerge from the rooms he had just passed, although no one did. There was the sound of a child crying from one of them and the voice of a man calling for beer from another, but their doors remained closed. Everyone in the building, Adam guessed, was so used to the sounds of their fellow lodgers coming and going that he would have to do far more than merely trip on a stair to attract attention.

He reached Cyril Montague's door. Unlike the one downstairs, it was locked. Adam crouched to peer at the lock. He saw immediately that it was so ancient it would present no barrier even to a housebreaker as inexperienced as he was. He took his penknife from his pocket, opened the blade and inserted it in the lock. After pushing the knife up and down a few times, with a click the door opened.

The sweet, sickly smell of opium rolled out of the room as Adam pushed the door open and entered. He looked around. The place was as he remembered it. It would not take long to search. Other than the horsehair sofa and the table on which the actor's opium lamp stood, it contained only one other piece of furniture: a battered chest of drawers. There was nowhere very much to hide anything.

Quickly, Adam crossed to the sofa and felt down the back of it. Nothing but dust, two toothpicks and a bent farthing came to hand. He picked up the lamp briefly and turned it over in his hands, wanting to see how it worked. His curiosity satisfied, he replaced it on the table and turned his attention to the chest of drawers. He pulled out the first drawer, full of clothes, and rummaged through it. There was nothing else there. The second drawer was the same. The bottom drawer was empty save for a large scrapbook.

Adam took it out and carried it to the window, where the faint evening light allowed him to see what was in it. Rather touchingly, the book contained newspaper cuttings of the reviews Montague had received in the days of his glory. Adam read a few of them, noting how someone, presumably the actor himself, had circled in red ink certain words and phrases such as 'brilliancy', 'animation of spirit' and 'striking display of thespian genius'. He closed the scrapbook and walked across the room to put it back in the drawer.

Turning, Adam surveyed the shabby garret in which Montague now spent his days, lost in opium dreams of former triumphs. Was there anywhere else where he could be hiding anything of interest? He looked down at the ragged carpet which half covered the floor. One of its corners was curled up. Adam bent down and pulled it further back. Underneath, lying flat on the floorboards, was a brown envelope. It had clearly been placed there recently – after his visit to the actor's rooms, perhaps?

The young man reached his fingers into the envelope and drew out a large, folded sheet of paper. He unfolded it and spread it out on the floor. It was a playbill, advertising performances of *The Bohemians of Paris* at the Gaiety Theatre the previous year. In large red letters, towards the top of the bill, the name of Cyril Montague was prominent. At the bottom, in much smaller black letters, were the words: 'Featuring the rest of the Gaiety's very own company of pulchritudinous Terpsichoreans: Miss Bella Tremayne, Miss Marie La Touche and Miss Dolly Delaney'.

* * * * *

'There is some clue to Dolly's whereabouts in Montague's dressing room. I am convinced of it.'

Quint emitted one of his repertoire of expressive grunts. It was the one that signified doubts about the validity of what the previous speaker had said.

'Montague knows the girl,' Adam insisted. 'He has denied it but he could scarcely have appeared in the same play as her last year without knowing her well enough to recognize her when she arrived in York. Why else would he be hiding the playbill from the Gaiety? And he knows that she is still in the city.'

'Well, what we goin' to do about it, if he does? Follow 'im round town? 'E never goes anywhere 'cept the Grand and those poky lodgings around the corner. If 'e ain't on stage, 'e's at 'ome with a pipe in his chaffer.'

'And I have ransacked his rooms without finding anything that would help us in our search beyond that playbill. *Ergo* I need to look in the theatre. After it has closed and everyone has left. How am I to do that?'

'A key might be 'andy,' Quint said.

'A key would be very handy,' Adam agreed. 'But I am scarcely in a position to take possession of one.'

'Who 'as 'em?'

'Well, Skeffington has one, of course. However, it is Timble who takes responsibility of the others that exist. And, as much goodwill as that gentleman bears me for stepping into the breach after Bellingham's abrupt departure, I doubt if it would extend to giving me a key so that I can roam through the Grand on my own in the early hours of the morning.'

'Mebbe 'e could give you one without knowing it,' Quint said.

Adam looked at his servant, who tapped the side of his nose with his forefinger.

Quint peered through the glass frontage of the barber's shop. Its floor was strewn with red sand. Two chairs were standing in the centre of the room. Around their legs, entangled in the red sand, were clumps of hair. One chair was empty; in the other was Timble, his face lathered with shaving cream. He had removed his jacket – it was hanging from a large wooden coat-stand at the back of the room – and the barber was poised above him, razor in hand. There could be no doubt that Timble would be otherwise engaged for the next twenty minutes at least. Quint had more than enough time to make his way back to the Grand and go through the drawers and cupboards in the manager's office. He stepped back from the barber's window and retraced his steps to the theatre.

At this time in the morning, there were few people in the Grand. Bunn, the aged and decrepit doorman, recognized Quint and nodded briefly as he passed. The manservant, who had soon made himself as familiar with the labyrinth backstage as he was with the more unsavoury streets of London, walked swiftly to Timble's office. At the door, he looked right and left. There was no one in sight. He turned the handle and found, to his relief, that it opened. He stepped into the room, closing the door behind him.

In sharp contrast to Skeffington, Timble kept his office tidy and organized. On one wall was a row of pigeonholes, each filled with correspondence. The manservant was tempted, from mere curiosity, to examine the contents of one or two of these but decided against it. Where would Timble keep his keys? Quint scanned the room. There was a table in the middle with a heavy, fringed cloth hanging over it. There was nothing else in the office apart from a wooden coat-stand, a battered secretaire which looked twice as old as he was, and a chair that was even more ancient. The front of the secretaire was open to reveal the writing desk within and a small stack of paper sitting on it. Beside the paper was an inkpot and pen. Quint glanced at the top sheet on the pile. It seemed to be the draft of a letter to a theatrical costumier in Leeds. Further inside the secretaire was a row of little compartments. Each had a key in it.

Quint bared his teeth in a grin. Timble had made it easy for him. Not only was the front of the secretaire unlocked and open, but in his obsession with order and organization, the theatre manager had labelled each of the keys. Quint took out the one marked 'Stage Door' and felt in his pocket for the wax mould he had brought with him. He placed the mould on the writing desk and pressed the key firmly into it. After a few moments, he prised the key out and stared with satisfaction at the shape it had left. He put the key back into the small compartment and thrust the mould deep into the pocket of his fustian jacket.

He was about to leave when he heard footsteps in the passageway. They stopped outside Timble's office. Quint just had time to throw himself under the table and its fringed drapery before the door opened.

Someone entered the room. It was not Timble. From his position on the floor Quint could see the man's legs, and the well-tailored black trousers and polished boots did not belong to the rather down-at-heel theatre manager. The legs moved across the room. The man, Quint judged, was now standing by the secretaire. Several minutes passed. From the slight sounds he could hear, he guessed the new intruder was leafing through the pile of papers on the writing desk. Quint was just starting to feel the first twinges of cramp when he heard a brief curse, then the legs passed once more across his field of vision and exited the room. The door closed. Quint waited a little while before hauling himself from under the table. He groaned slightly as he stood and straightened his back. He was getting too old for this game.

* * * * *

'I didn't see anything but 'is legs, did I?' Quint was indignant. ''Ow am I s'posed to reckernize a pair of bleeding legs?'

'You say they were clad in black cloth. Were they long legs? Short legs? Fat legs?'

'They was just legs.'

'But you think they were attached to someone who had no more business being in Timble's office than you had?'

''E was after something, same as me,' Quint opined. 'Not one of the keys, mind. I could 'ear paper rustling. 'E was scrabbling through the papers on the desk.'

'And what were they? Were they letters? Invoices? Business papers?'

Quint shrugged. 'Didn't look at 'em,' he said. 'I was after getting this.' He held up the wax mould.

Adam peered at it with interest. 'And that will be sufficient to enable you to produce a key to open the stage door after the theatre has been locked for the night?' His servant nodded. The young man took the mould and turned it over in his hands.

'Watch it,' Quint said. 'You don't want to spoil the pressing.'

Adam handed it back.

'And how does the process work?' he asked.

Quint once again tapped the side of his nose. 'Ask me no questions and I'll tell you no fibs,' he said.

'Ah, well, like any great craftsman, you must have your secrets, Quint, and I shall enquire of you no further. But you will present me with the key before tonight's performance?'

'You'll 'ave it by seven,' his servant promised. 'And it'll fit the lock like a finger in mud.'

CHAPTER SEVENTEEN

dam ran his fingers across the key in the pocket of his coat. Not for the first time, he marvelled at the varied skills of his manservant. Few of Quint's talents were those which society chose to admire or reward, but several of them had proved invaluable in recent weeks. Exactly how he had been able to produce this copy of the key to the stage door, Adam did not know. He had seen the wax mould with the shape of the key impressed into it; he was now clutching the finished object in his pocket. The precise steps that had led from one to the other were unclear to him. His servant had simply left the hotel room at five in the evening with the wax impression he had made in Timble's office and returned two hours later with a key he said would open the door to the theatre.

It was now well gone one in the morning and Quint's claim was about to be put to the test. Adam took the key from his pocket and fitted it into the lock. He smiled to himself as he felt it turn. Quint had been right.

The stage door opened and Adam entered the Grand. Closing the door behind him, he used a safety match to light the dark lantern he had brought with him. The now familiar corridors and passageways of the Grand's backstage area loomed out of the darkness. A staircase to the left led up to dressing rooms, and Adam was just about to put his foot on its first step when something made him freeze into immobility. There had been what sounded like a cry in the distance. Surely there could be no one else in the theatre, could there? At this hour? The performance had finished soon after 11.30 p.m.; the audience would have left by midnight; the players and the theatre staff within another half-hour. Who could still be here?

Adam strained his ears to catch any further sounds. There was nothing. He was about to dismiss what he thought he had heard as no more than the result of an overactive imagination and climb the stairs when there was the unmistakeable noise of someone moving around further in the building. He stopped again.

The noises had come, he decided, from the auditorium. Adam slid the screen across the dark lantern, covering its light. In the resulting blackness, moving gingerly along the passage that led towards the stalls, it felt as if a pit might open beneath his feet at any moment. Adam took step after exaggerated step, like an actor miming extreme stealth, until, reaching one hand ahead of him, the other still holding the lantern, he touched the velvet of a curtain. It was the one, he realised, which hung across the doorway to the stalls. Groping his hand around in the fabric, he could sense that the double doors were open, each one pushed back against the wall as they would be before a performance. He slipped through the curtain and entered the auditorium.

The faintest of lights was illuminating the theatre. From where was it coming? Adam was puzzled at first but, peering through the darkness, he noticed that the main drapes on the stage appeared to be up. The glimmer of light was in the wings. He began to make his way down the central aisle of the stalls, feeling his way from one row of seats to the next. As he reached the tenth row, he stumbled and the lantern clattered against the back of a seat.

Immediately, there was a sound from the stage and the weak light disappeared completely.

Adam remained where he was. There could be no doubt that someone else was in the theatre, and he wondered whether or not to call out and make himself known to his fellow intruder. He stood in the middle of the aisle, debating what was best to do, for a minute or more. The darkness was complete.

Once again, he strained to hear any sounds of movement but

there was nothing. This is ridiculous, he thought. He could not stand there, frozen in Cimmerian blackness, until the morning. With a decisive gesture he pushed back the screening panel on his lantern, and its light shone forth.

Its beam travelled down the aisle towards the stage and lit up the shape of a tall man dressed in black. Adam was startled, and the man reacted more quickly than he did. He ran swiftly and directly towards Adam, who had no time to move before the figure crashed into him. The lantern went flying and darkness returned as Adam was propelled backwards, the other man falling heavily on top of him. He gasped beneath the weight, catching the smell of meat and wine on the breath of his attacker as he tried to hold onto him, but the man twisted and turned in his grasp and was up on his feet before Adam had fully recovered from the shock of their collision. He disappeared into the dark, leaving his victim still stretched, wheezing, on the carpet. Moments later, Adam heard the sound of the curtain on the stalls entrance being torn aside and footsteps walking rapidly down the corridor outside. A door slammed and his assailant was gone.

He must, Adam thought, have eyes like a cat to move with such speed in the enveloping blackness. He hauled himself into a sitting position and rubbed his back. Nothing, he decided, had been broken in the fall. He reached out his hand and felt for the lantern. His groping fingers grasped it thankfully when it came to hand. Its flame had been extinguished when it had crashed to the floor. He took his silver match safe from his pocket and lit it again. Holding onto the back of a seat, he pulled himself to his feet and held out the lantern at arm's length.

The light flashed across the rows of the stalls. Adam was just wondering whether or not he should follow the man in black, now doubtless long departed from the building, when it fell on what looked like a pile of clothing on the stage. He moved further along the aisle. There was definitely something there. He reached the end of the rows of seats and walked swiftly to the short flight of stairs on the right that gave access from the auditorium to the stage. He climbed up them and onto the projecting apron.

Somebody was spread-eagled on the boards, apparently staring up at the elaborate plaster decoration of the Grand's ceiling. He walked across the stage and directed the light from his lantern onto the face of the sprawled figure.

There was no doubt about it. It was the girl in the photograph that Sunman had given him. He had finally found Dolly Delaney.

Adam set down the lantern and knelt by her side. Picking up her arm, he felt for a pulse. There was none. He moved his hand cautiously across her body, thinking as he did so that, even though the girl was clearly dead, this seemed like an unpardonable liberty. As he reached her left side he could feel a damp stickiness. Holding up his hand, he could see that the palm was covered in dark, viscous blood. More blood had pooled on the boards beneath her. The girl had been stabbed, and her life had leaked away on the stage of this shabby provincial theatre. The noise he had heard ten minutes before had been her cry of pain as the knife had entered her heart.

Adam took a handkerchief from his pocket and tried to wipe away the blood. He could not do so. It seemed to be everywhere. He then realized that he was kneeling in it and, with a shudder of distaste, stood up. As he stared down at the red patches soaking into his trousers, there was a loud call from the auditorium.

'You there! Stay exactly where you are.'

Adam held out the lantern at arm's length, peering into the gloom it only half illuminated. Two men were approaching, moving down one of the side aisles at a swift pace. The one who had shouted out to him, tall and well-built, was dressed in a brown tweed suit that had seen better days. A brown bowler was perched on his head. His companion, a stout figure in navy blue, was a police constable.

'We need to have a word with you.'

* * * * *

'So, you say the girl was already dead when you found her.' The man in tweed, who had introduced himself to Adam as Inspector Moughton of the York Police, was gazing mournfully at Dolly's body. He looked like a preacher about to remind his congregation of the brevity of human life.

'She was, Inspector. The man who bowled me over – he must have stabbed her while I was in the passageway outside. I heard a cry but it took me some time to get to the stalls. When I did so, this wretch came at me before I knew what was happening. By the time I recovered myself, he was gone and poor Dolly was lying in her own blood.'

'Ah yes, the fellow who knocked you down. The man in black.' Moughton beckoned to the constable to approach him. 'Could that have been who spoke to you, Thirlwell? Told you there was a disturbance in the theatre. A man in black.'

'Might have been, sir.' The constable spoke slowly, as if pondering his superior's question from a number of philosophical standpoints. 'The gent that spoke to me had on a black cape of sorts.'

'He was a gent, though, was he?'

'He spoke very genteel-like, sir. He said he'd seen a light in the Grand and heard noises. He thought I should go and see what was going on.'

'So you alerted our fellow guardian of the law, Bassett, who's now outside.' Moughton gestured in the direction of the exit. 'And you and Bassett go beetling along Goodramgate until you bump into me on my way back to the station. And all three of us come to the Grand. So here we all are, no more than two minutes after the gent first spoke to you.'

'That's about the size of it, sir.'

'And you never thought to ask this gentleman in the black cape to accompany you to the theatre?'

'No, sir.'

'You just let him waltz off into the night?'

'Yes, sir.' Thirlwell spoke stolidly in a Yorkshire accent. He seemed unaware of any implied criticism in Inspector Moughton's words. 'As I say, sir, he was very genteel-like.'

Moughton turned back to Adam and raised his eyebrows very

slightly, as if to suggest something about the calibre of the men he was obliged to employ. 'So you see, Mr—?'

'Carver.'

'You see, Mr Carver, we don't have too much in the way of corroborating evidence for the man in black who knocked you down. Constable Thirlwell saw a gent in a black cape. But half the gents in York have black capes. And we don't know that this particular gent was ever inside the theatre. He might have been doing exactly what he said he was – just passing by the Grand when he heard a disturbance. So he does the public-spirited thing and tells Thirlwell here.'

'He *must* have been the man who struck me to the floor.'

'We find the stage door open. We come in and we find you.' Moughton was ignoring the young man's remark. Instead, he nodded in the direction of the handkerchief Adam was still holding. 'Red-handed, you might say.'

'You have it all wrong, Inspector.'

'Do I, now? That would be your argument, of course, but I ain't so sure. I'm inclining more to the idea that I've got it all right.'

'I have spent much of the past fortnight looking for this poor woman. Her name is – was – Dolly Delaney. I wanted to speak to her, not kill her.'

The inspector had moved away from the girl's body and was standing centre stage, his eyes moving restlessly across the boards. 'What's this?' he asked suddenly.

Another handkerchief was lying several feet away from the body. In his shock at finding Dolly, Adam had not seen it. Moughton picked it up. 'There's something on it.' He sniffed the handkerchief cautiously. 'Chloroform,' he said. 'Somebody drugged the girl first. Maybe she was carried onto the stage.'

'She was most definitely stabbed here.' Adam pointed to the blood stains.

Still holding the white handkerchief, the police inspector returned to the body and gazed down at it once again. 'Aye, you're right there,' he said.

'Can we not remove the poor girl to a better place than this?'

'She'll have to go to the morgue.' Moughton beckoned to his constable. 'Go and find a doctor, Thirlwell.'

'They'll all be abed, sir.'

'Well, get one out of bed, man! We need someone to look at the body here before it can be moved.'

Constable Thirlwell looked as if he might have more to say but, noting the expression on his superior's face, decided against it. He turned and headed towards the exit. The inspector watched him depart before addressing Adam again.

'You had been looking for this Delaney woman, you say?' Moughton was clearly intrigued. He seemed to be reassessing his original judgement of the situation.

Adam wondered how much more to tell him. Sunman had warned him against speaking to the police but this was probably a situation in which he had no choice. The man from the Foreign Office would surely not expect him to remain silent under suspicion of murder. 'There are people in London who wished to speak to her.'

'Are there indeed?' Moughton sounded as unimpressed as it was possible to be by the thought of people in London. 'Not much chance of speaking to her now, is there?'

There was no time for Adam to reply. Another constable was approaching from the back of the stalls. Trailing behind him was Quint. The pair climbed the steps to the stage.

'Found this one skulking about t'stage door,' the policeman said. 'He give me lip when I asked him what he were doing.'

'Oh, he did, did he?' Moughton eyed Adam's servant suspiciously before addressing him directly. 'And who might you be? Loitering around the theatre in the early hours of the morning when all respectable folk are tucked into their cotton sheets?'

Quint said nothing, staring stonily into the wings.

'The man is my servant, Inspector.'

Moughton spun on his heel as if he had forgotten Adam's presence and was startled to hear a voice from behind him. 'Your man, is he? Any idea why he's doing all this loitering?'

'None whatsoever, Inspector. Perhaps he was unable to sleep.'

Moughton said nothing in reply but beckoned the newly arrived constable to his side. The two policemen moved across the stage, the inspector guiding his junior colleague with a hand on his arm. By now, some of the gas lights in the auditorium had been lit. Other officers, Adam could see, were standing phlegmatically in the stalls, awaiting the orders of their superior.

'What the devil are you doing here, Quint?' he hissed. 'I thought I told you to stay at the hotel.'

Quint shrugged. 'Thought it was a better idea to follow you.'

'Well, it wasn't. Now we're both being treated as suspicious characters.'

There was silence as Adam glared at his manservant and Quint unconcernedly scratched his ear. On the other side of the stage, Moughton and his constable were still deep in whispered conversation.

'Found out one thing, mind,' Quint said eventually.

'And that is?'

'Not just me following you. Summ'un else was as well.'

'Are you certain?' Adam sounded surprised. 'Who was this mysterious person stalking me?'

'Couldn't tell. It was black as Satan's boots out there. I could just see a shadow. Stopping when you stopped. Moving when you moved.'

'What happened to the shadow when I reached the theatre?'

'Disappeared. Round about the time you was fumbling with that key I got you.'

'Perhaps it was simply some honest burgher of York making his way home through the city streets, unaware that you were misinterpreting his actions as those of a felon dogging my tracks. When he disappeared, it was because he had left the theatre behind him and was well on the way to his bed.'

'No, it was 'cos 'e was up a drainpipe.'

'I thought you said just this moment that he had disappeared.'

''E 'ad,' Quint said, 'but 'e come back. Leastways, I saw 'im again.

You'd just got in the door. He was shinning up a pipe at the side of the theatre. On the side by the alleyway. Then 'e 'auled 'imself in through one of the winders.'

'The dressing rooms are on that side, are they not?'

Quint nodded.

'Timble tours the theatre after everyone has departed for the night. He makes certain all the doors and windows are locked.'

'Well, 'e must 'ave missed one.'

'The man up the pipe had no difficulty getting himself into the building?'

''E just slipped right through.' Quint made an odd, undulating movement with his upper body. 'Wriggling like an eel in a basket.'

Adam glanced across the stage. 'Hush now. We will talk of this later. The constabulary is returning.'

* * * * *

There were voices outside and the door of the cell opened. A burly constable, his face like a slab of raw meat, appeared in the entrance. Adam recognized him as one of those who had been present in the theatre.

'Inspector Moughton wants to see you,' the man said, pointing upwards, as if his superior officer might be floating somewhere near the ceiling.

In the corridor outside was another policeman, tall and silver-haired, whom Adam had not seen before. The two constables escorted him past a row of barred doors and up a flight of stone steps. At the top of these was another corridor, but the doors on this one clearly did not lead to cells. One of them was half open and the silver-haired constable pushed at it. It swung back against the wall and he gestured to Adam to enter. The room was empty save for a wooden desk and two chairs, on one of which Quint was sitting. He looked tired and disgruntled.

'I've seen better 'orse boxes than those bleedin' cells,' he remarked. 'And most of *them* smelled better.'

Before Adam could make any comment of his own, there were

the sounds of steps outside and Inspector Moughton appeared in the doorway. 'You're a lucky man, Mr Carver,' he said.

'Am I, Inspector? I am not certain that I feel particularly lucky this morning.'

'You have friends who are men of influence,' Moughton said, sounding less than delighted to acknowledge the fact. 'We did as you asked and telegraphed the Honourable Richard Sunman at the Foreign Office. Eight o'clock this morning, back comes a message, quick as a flash – "Release the prisoner immediately or face the consequences," it says. Or words to that effect. I was all for facing the consequences, seeing as how we're talking about a murder case. But my superintendent, he's more of a cautious man, more of a diplomatic man.'

'So, I'm free to leave?'

'Yes, you're free to leave. You and your . . . confederate.' Moughton nodded in the direction of Quint, who was scratching the crotch of his trousers and looking bored.

'I had nothing to do with the death of that girl, Inspector,' Adam said, taking his hat and coat from the silver-haired constable.

'So you said last night.'

'However, I assure you I shall find the person who *did* kill poor Dolly.'

'Aye, and we shall all of us catch larks when the sky falls,' Moughton said wearily.

* * * * *

Quint brought his master a drink.

'Brandy and water. Now there's a reviver for the spirits,' Adam said, as he sank into a chair by the fire of his hotel room. 'Pour yourself one, Quint. We both need reviving after a night like that.'

'I ain't feeling too bad,' Quint said. 'I spent a month in Coldbath Fields back in '58. Grindin' the wind on one of them bleedin' treadmills.'

'So a night in York Gaol is unlikely to discompose you?'

Quint shook his head disdainfully, as if to suggest that only a

193

milksop would worry about an overnight stay in a cell. Despite his claim that he was none the worse for his experience, he was nonetheless pouring himself a generous measure of brandy. 'You look bleedin' awful, though,' he said now, to Adam, downing the drink in one gulp. 'Eyes like burnt holes in a blanket.'

Ignoring his servant's comment, Adam continued to sip his brandy and water. In his mind, he re-ran the events of the last few hours. He tried to picture what had happened in the Grand. Dolly must have been standing on the stage, peering into the darkness of the auditorium. Her assailant had moved out of the wings and approached her. Before she had had time to register that there was someone behind her, the chloroform-soaked handkerchief would have been clamped over her mouth. Within moments she would have been unconscious. So the noise he had heard could not have been made by Dolly – he had assumed initially that he had heard her cry of pain as she had been stabbed, but he had clearly been wrong. The chloroform would have rendered her insensible. So if it had not been Dolly, was it her killer who had called out? But that was surely an absurd idea. Why should he? Killers did not usually wish to draw attention to themselves. And so, if the noise had not been Dolly and it was not her attacker, then there was only one other conclusion: there had been someone else in the Grand in the early hours of the morning. The person Quint had seen climbing through the open window? Or had that been the murderer? But would the intruder have had time to reach the stage and stab Dolly? The answer was probably yes. There had been more than enough time between Adam opening the stage door and his entering the auditorium through the curtains for the person to have made his way down from the dressing rooms and attack Dolly. But what about Dolly herself? What had she been doing in the theatre? She must surely have arranged to meet someone there. Her assailant? Or somebody else? The person who had called out?

Adam moved to the window of the hotel room and looked down into the street below. Two riders passed beneath him, the sound of their horses' hooves ringing against the cobbles. A lone woman, her head covered by a grey shawl, was walking down Coney Street towards the Mansion House. He thought again about the cry in the dark of the theatre. The murderer must have heard it as well. He would have been standing on the stage, the young girl bleeding at his feet. He would, doubtless, have frozen in position, desperately struggling to decide the direction from which the sound had come. And then he would have become aware of Adam himself, stumbling along the aisle of the stalls. He would naturally have assumed that it was Adam who had called earlier. He had struck the young man down and made his escape.

Unlike Adam, he would still be unaware that there had been a fourth person in the theatre. 'I must find that fourth person,' Adam said to himself. Other questions continued to course through his mind, however. Why had the girl gone to the theatre at all, so long after the final curtain call of the night? How had she been able to get into the building? Adam had entered without trouble, but he had been in possession of the key Quint had filched from Timble and copied. Dolly would not have had that advantage. Was it not more likely that she had been in the Grand during the performance? She might have simply stayed behind when the show was over. Hidden herself, perhaps, in one of the dressing rooms and emerged when everybody else had left. If that was the case, Adam could think of only two explanations for her behaviour: she had wished, as he had, to search the theatre during the few hours when it was quiet and deserted; or she had arranged to meet someone she trusted. If she had indeed known Cyril Montague from London, as Adam was near certain she had, it might have been him. Or a lover, perhaps? Could it even have been Vernon, her middle-aged Lochinvar from the Foreign Office, who had travelled up to York? At the very least, her rendezvous would have been with someone she knew, and knew well. And, in all likelihood, that someone had betrayed her trust and killed her.

As Adam explained some of his reasoning to his servant, Quint poured them both further generous measures of brandy.

'The important question is who else was in the theatre.'

'Must have been Timble,' Quint said. 'Maybe he was taking longer to shut up the place than usual.'

'I doubt it. Timble is a man of habit and routine.' Adam put down his drink. He leaned back in his chair, stretching the muscles in his arms. What, he wondered, was his own best course of action now? He could stay in York and try to identify the fourth person who had been in the theatre – perhaps that person had even been a witness to Dolly's demise and could point an accusing finger at her killer. But the real question, he began to think, was why Dolly had been done to death. Find the motive and find the murderer. In order to do that, he decided, he had to know more of the girl and her involvement with Vernon. There was too much about that affair which he had not been told. Sunman, Adam now realized, had entrusted him with only a little of the story. He must confront his devious friend and demand to know more of what was going on.

'Our northern adventure is finished, Quint,' he said with sudden decisiveness. 'We must return to town.'

'About bleedin' time,' Quint said.

PART THREE

LONDON

CHAPTER EIGHTEEN

'This Delaney chit has been nothing but a nuisance from the first moment Harry Vernon set eyes upon her.'

'For God's sake, Sunman, the girl is dead! She was murdered. Conveniently for Vernon – and for yourselves, some might say.'

'You cannot believe that we were responsible for her unfortunate end.' The young aristocrat sounded genuinely shocked at Adam's words. Sunman turned to Gilbert Waterton as if to appeal for his moral support as the two men and Adam stood in one of the smaller rooms on the second floor of the new Foreign Office, which had been completed only a few years earlier. Despite its modernity, the weight of centuries of power and grandeur already seemed to permeate the building.

Two days had passed since Adam and his servant had spent their uncomfortable night in York Gaol. On the afternoon following their release, the young man had gone to the Grand to inform Skeffington that urgent business demanded his immediate return to London. *The Spectre Bridegroom* would once again be missing its bridegroom.

The old actor had taken the news with surprising equanimity. True, he had ranted briefly about ingratitude and the inconstancy of modern youth, yet he had been swiftly reconciled to the idea of Adam's departure. At their final parting, he had even embraced him, his heavy head resting briefly and uncomfortably on Adam's chest as he had told him that there would always be a place for him in Alfred Skeffington's company: 'If you ever return to this fair city, look us up, and we shall "carouse together like friends long lost". *Antony and Cleopatra*, Act 4 Scene 12.'

The actor's relative calm had been explained when Adam had spoken to Timble.

'We had a visitor,' the theatre manager had said. 'Just this morning. An old pal of Skeffington's, name of Brass. They did the Moor together in Portsmouth in '63. Brass is looking for a job.'

'And Skeffington told him he could take the role of the bridegroom,' Adam had guessed.

Timble had nodded.

'He had another part lined up for you. He wasn't looking forward to breaking the news.'

'Not a role in which I might have shone, then?'

'It's what you might call a thinking part,' Timble had said. 'It would have given you plenty of time to think.'

'So, not very much in the way of lines?'

'Not a single one, in point of fact.'

Adam had laughed. 'It seems I have saved Skeffington the trouble of an awkward conversation. And still he berates me for my disloyalty.'

'He doesn't mean it, Mr Carver.' Timble had held out his hand. 'You going on the last few nights saved our bacon.'

Adam had shaken the hand that was offered him. On the next day, he and Quint had taken the train to London. By early evening, they were back in Doughty Street.

Now Adam was bringing the men in the Foreign Office up to date with what had happened. 'The police in York assumed that I had killed Miss Delaney,' he said. 'They may yet be of that opinion.' Sunman waved his hand dismissively. The opinions of the police, or indeed anyone in York, he managed to suggest, were of no interest to him. 'My dear chap, there is no possibility that you will be arraigned on a charge of murder,' he said. 'Put that contingency far from your mind.'

'I shall endeavour to do so,' Adam said drily. 'But the fact remains that Quint and I were committed to a police cell, however briefly.

You will forgive me if I continue to worry that we may be returned there.'

'You will not be.'

'So you say, but I cannot help but believe that the best way to ensure that is to find the person who did kill the poor girl. And my only chance of doing that lies in your telling me more about how a dancer in a Drury Lane theatre came to the attention of the Foreign Office in the first instance.'

Sunman pulled one of the high-backed chairs in the room away from the table, as if to sit down, and then, apparently changing his mind, stayed on his feet. 'As I have said to you from the beginning, Adam,' he said, 'from the time of our meeting at Kensal Green when poor Moorhouse was interred, it is not possible for me to tell you everything about the girl. I can only reiterate that it was of vital import that she should be traced. Now that she is dead, we must reassess the circumstances. She was a danger to herself and others. We must decide whether or not the danger still exists.'

Adam turned away in exasperation, looking at Waterton, who said nothing. He took several paces around the room before returning to face his friend. 'I am sorry, Sunman, but I cannot be stonewalled like this. You must answer some of my questions.'

The young man from the Foreign Office stared blankly at the wall behind Adam, as if mesmerized by the portrait of a huge man in eighteenth-century wig and breeches that hung there. He sighed once or twice and, in turn, glanced at Waterton.

'It is only fair that Carver should know more than we have hitherto told him,' the older man said.

'Very well.' Sunman turned to Adam with the air of a man who had made an unpleasant decision and felt the better for it. 'What do you wish to ask me? As far as it is within my powers to do so, I will endeavour to answer your questions.'

'This poor girl Dolly,' Adam said. 'I think the phrase you used of her was that she was "in possession of information".'

Sunman inclined his head slightly to acknowledge that this could, indeed, have been the way he had expressed it.

'What information did she possess?'

'The gentleman who became so enamoured of the young lady ...'

'Yes, Harry Vernon,' Adam interrupted. 'There is no need for such periphrasis. You forget I have met the man. You mentioned his name not two minutes ago. You must tell me more of the relations between them.'

Sunman looked sharply at his friend, as if he were about to tick him off for impertinence. Instead, he frowned and continued. 'Vernon wrote Miss Delaney a series of letters. Indiscreet letters. *Very* indiscreet letters. It is of paramount importance that we have them. I cannot emphasize too strongly the need to locate these letters and destroy them.' The Foreign Office man paused to weigh his words. 'In fact, I do not think it is too much of an exaggeration to suggest that the future direction of our foreign policy rests on the recovery of those letters.'

Adam looked at his friend in surprise. Sunman's face was now fixed in so self-conscious an expression of seriousness that he felt horribly tempted to laugh. He looked across at Waterton, but his demeanour was also that of a man attending the funeral of a deeply loved parent.

'This is the stuff of melodrama, old man,' Adam said after a brief pause. 'Compromising letters? A nation's fate in the hands of a dancing girl?'

'None the less, it happens to be true. Vernon knew a great deal about our intentions towards the new German Reich. And the *fool*' – Sunman spat out the word with unexpected venom – 'the fool entrusted vital details of them to paper. And, what is worse, in an epistle addressed to some wretched trollop from Drury Lane. If that information reached the ears of people in Berlin, or even people in the other capitals of Europe, it is difficult to predict the consequences. Suffice it to say, they would be enormous.'

'Surely, if so much is at stake, you can call upon the services of the police ... the army.' Adam was puzzled. 'Why on earth did you approach me? Why did *I* end up travelling north in pursuit of the girl?' There was silence in the room. Adam could hear the ticking of the large brass clock on the mantelpiece behind him. And he realized suddenly why Sunman had commissioned him to find Dolly. 'Your superiors haven't been told about this, have they? Only you and Vernon know about it.'

'And Waterton here.' The young aristocrat, usually so self-possessed, looked acutely uncomfortable. 'Harry had already told him about it.'

'Harry is a distant cousin of mine,' the older man said. 'He trusts me. We have few secrets between one another.'

'But why have you kept so important a matter to yourselves?'

'Harry may have behaved irresponsibly but he is a good friend. His career would be finished, ruined, if it emerged that he had been so . . .' Sunman searched for the exact word he wanted.

'Stupid?' Adam suggested.

'Imprudent. We – that is, Waterton and I – believed that the entire imbroglio could be resolved without the need for others to know of his imprudence. We believe that still.'

Sunman fell silent. Carriages passed in the street below. Somewhere, further along the corridor outside, a door slammed.

Adam took his silver cigar case from his jacket pocket. He offered it to Sunman and Waterton who both shook their heads. Adam extracted one of the small cigars he kept in it and, after preparation, lit the end. He blew a plume of smoke in the direction of the window. Waterton watched it drift in the air as if he was following the movements of a fly he intended to kill.

'The Delaney girl must have kept the letters,' the older man said eventually.

'Why should she not?' Adam asked. 'To her they would be love letters, not state secrets.'

'If she had thought of them only as *billets-doux*, we would not face the potential disaster we do. Or not as great a disaster.' Waterton sighed. 'The girl,' he continued, 'must have realized something of the importance of what Vernon had written. On one of their trysts, she suggested that he might like to buy back the letters in question.'

'She was blackmailing him?' Adam asked.

Sunman turned from the window. 'In effect.'

'It was at this point,' Waterton said, 'that poor Harry, realising the trouble he was in, approached me.'

The room was silent as Adam absorbed what he had been told.

'Am I to look for these letters?'

'Of course. With the girl dead, their importance only increases.'

'How am I to know them if I do find them?'

Waterton looked at Sunman, who made his way to a desk in a corner of the room and opened a drawer. He pulled out a sheet of paper, which he handed to Adam. 'That is in Harry's handwriting. You may keep it.'

Adam looked briefly at the document, which seemed to be the agenda for some Foreign Office meeting, and then folded it in two and slipped it inside his jacket pocket.

Sunman now walked over to a rosewood chiffonier on which stood a decanter of whisky and glasses. He raised the decanter enquiringly. Adam shook his head. The young aristocrat poured two drinks. He gave one to Waterton and moved to the windows with his own. He stood there, taking sips from his tumbler and looking down into King Charles Street.

Adam looked at Waterton. 'And you went to Sunman, after Vernon approached you?'

Waterton made no reply. It was Sunman himself who answered Adam's question. 'No, Harry also spoke to me. The day after he had spoken to Waterton here.' He set his whisky glass down on the desk in the centre of the room. 'In truth, I did not think that you were best pleased, Gilbert, when I became involved.'

Waterton waved his hand to indicate that no such thoughts had ever passed through his mind.

'However, Harry must have been in the mood for confession,' Sunman went on, 'and I was an obvious person in whom to confide.'

'Why so?'

'I am a friend. And I know something of our relations with the Germans without being too closely connected to them.'

'Surely,' Adam asked, 'from Vernon's point of view, there was a danger that you would simply tell your superiors what he had told you?'

Sunman looked offended. 'Harry spoke to me in the strictest confidence. It would not have been the act of a gentleman to betray that confidence. In any case, it seemed clear to me, and to Waterton, that the whole unfortunate affair could be resolved without anyone else knowing of it. The girl merely had to be found and the letters taken from her. That is why I spoke to you.'

'But the problem has not resolved itself quite as easily as you anticipated.'

'No, it most certainly has not. The murder of the girl has added complications we could not have foreseen.'

The three men glumly contemplated those same complications.

'I suppose she might have attempted to blackmail Vernon earlier in their association?' Adam said after a moment.

Sunman looked puzzled. 'Earlier?'

'I take it he had been playing the libertine with the young lady for some time?'

'A year, I believe.'

'She could have threatened to write to his wife at any time then. He is married, I assume?'

'He is, although he is not happy in the marriage. In his case, the angel in the house has long been more of a devil.'

'Why so?'

'The woman drinks.' Sunman spoke as if he could scarcely credit that a female should have any taste for alcohol at all, let alone an immoderate one. 'Although she comes from one of the best families in Buckinghamshire. Harry was thought to have landed quite a catch when first he wed her. Experience has taught him that the day he joined his fortune to hers was one of the worst of his life.'

'None the less, Dolly could have seriously upset Vernon's apple cart by revealing their affair to his wife months ago.' Sunman nodded.

'And she had made no attempt to extort money from him previously?'

'No,' Sunman said. 'And yet I fail to see the relevance of that.'

'It suggests to me one of two things. Either there was a quarrel between the lovers, which prompted her to take advantage of the information that had come her way. Or she had a confederate who urged her to do so.'

Sunman nodded thoughtfully. 'That is true,' he said. 'It is unlikely that the girl could have appreciated the significance of what she had been told herself. She must have shown the letters to a third person.'

'Another dancer?' Adam asked.

'Yet why would that other dancer be any more likely to understand the importance of the information in the letters than Dolly?'

'That too is true,' Adam admitted.

'What of this man McIlwraith whose name you mentioned?' Sunman asked abruptly.

Adam waved his hand dismissively. 'If I am any judge of character, he is not the kind of man to involve himself in blackmail,' he said. 'Persuading a lovelorn stage-door Johnny to cross his palm with silver, perhaps. But not blackmail.'

Waterton moved to the centre of the room. He began to run his fingers across the surface of the desk, as if testing to see how much dust had accumulated there. 'And the actor Montague?' he asked finally. 'You say he lied to you about not knowing the girl—?'

'His name and hers were on the same playbill. Which he was hiding beneath the carpet in his lodgings. He must have known her.'

'Might he be her confederate?'

'He might have been, but I doubt it.'

Waterton continued to brush his fingers along the grain of the wood on the table. 'He is not likely to be the killer, is he?' he said eventually. 'A man so in thrall to opium that he cannot live his life without regular recourse to it?'

'Cyril has no obvious motive for the murder,' Adam said.

'Unless he was her fellow blackmailer.'

'As I say, I doubt very much that he was. He may have needed money but the man cares only for his pipes and an audience's applause.'

There was a pause. Waterton had ceased stroking the table and was now staring intently at an elaborately carved wooden inkstand which was sitting on it. Sunman, too, had fallen silent, returning to his contemplation of the bewigged gentleman in the portrait.

'There is one suspect we have not mentioned,' Adam remarked.

Waterton looked up and raised his eyebrows in enquiry.

'In any case where blackmail ends with the murder of the blackmailer, the person who most directly benefits from the death is the one being blackmailed.'

'Harry?' Waterton sounded incredulous. 'A murderer? Impossible!'

'You forget,' Adam said, 'that only a few months ago you would have been equally surprised if someone had told you he was conducting an illicit affair with a *danseuse*.'

'Perhaps, but I refuse to believe that Harry is the killer!'

'How can you be so certain?'

'Would a murderer look anything like Harry Vernon?' Sunman asked, suddenly returning to the conversation.

'I do not know. How would a murderer look?'

'His depravity would surely be written on his face.'

Adam caught his friend's eye and shook his head slightly. 'I would recommend a trip to Madame Tussauds and its Chamber of Horrors, old man,' he said. 'Go down to the Baker Street Bazaar and gaze upon those wax models of murderers and torturers. The greatest horror is that the majority of them look little different to you and me.'

CHAPTER NINETEEN

A dam sat in a chop house in a street near Trafalgar Square and toyed idly with the rump-steak pudding he had ordered. It was delicious but he was not, he decided, as hungry as he had thought. Taking a few last mouthfuls, he laid down his knife and fork and leaned back onto the wooden panelling of the booth in which he was sitting. The panels of each booth came up to a point just below the neck of the averagely sized man. Looking across the room, he could see the apparently disembodied heads of his fellow diners arranged in rows. It was just after noon and the chop house was full. The noise of several dozen conversations swirled around the room. Harried waiters scurried back and forth between the kitchens and the booths. One materialized by Adam's side and looked enquiringly at the half-eaten rump-steak pudding.

'Leave it,' the young man said. 'I may gain a gastronomical second wind.'

The waiter, touching his forefinger to his head, retreated and left Adam to his thoughts. What was the truth, he wondered, about the letters? The *very* indiscreet letters? Adam had assumed that the Foreign Office was concerned because Harry Vernon had given hostages to fortune by addressing Dolly in overly affectionate terms, thereby making himself vulnerable to blackmail. It was a commonplace enough story. Most of the blackmailers in London would be out of business if all married men and women paid strict attention to their wedding vows. Other versions of events had occurred to Adam, including the possibility that Vernon had told Dolly secrets he shouldn't have told her; but he had been imagining minor snippets of gossip or small hints of government policy that another European power might have found interesting – might even have paid money to receive. Nothing on the scale which Sunman and Waterton were suggesting, however. Could it be true? Surely no man in a position of high responsibility would divulge such important information to a dancer in a Drury Lane chorus line?

It was unlikely, Adam decided, but not impossible. As Ovid had remarked so long ago, *Credula res amor est*. Men in love are likely to believe anything. Vernon might have thought that Dolly was so enamoured of him that she could be safely told whatever he chose. He could not have imagined that she would betray him, as she appeared to have done. All he had probably wanted, Adam thought, was to show how powerful and important a man he was, how far he was trusted with the nation's secrets.

Adam looked down at the gravy oozing from his pudding and congealing on the plate. His food seemed less and less appealing by the minute. What, he wondered, was he to do next? Could he just walk away from this whole business? He decided he could not. The men at the Foreign Office were expecting him to help them and he had a responsibility to do so. In a strange way, he felt that he owed it to the girl – to poor, dead Dolly – to find out what had happened to her.

A copy of the *Daily News* was lying on the table in the next booth. Adam left his seat and went to pick it up before returning to his meal. He opened the pages and began idly to scan them. The marriage of the Queen's daughter Louise to the son of the Duke of Argyll seemed still to be holding the nation's attention. A new concert hall named after the late Prince Consort had just opened. Otto von Bismarck had been appointed chancellor of the new German Reich. The headline to a small story at the bottom of the newspaper's fifth page jumped out at him: 'The People's Roscius Returns in Triumph from the Provinces.' Here was coincidence indeed, he thought, as he read the paragraph. He had just been talking of Cyril Montague to the men in the Foreign Office and here was news that the actor was forsaking his old friend Skeffington and coming back to London to play Romeo at a theatre in Holborn.

The waiter returned, and this time Adam signed to him to remove his plate. The man retreated with the remains of the pudding, but Adam made no move to leave the booth, continuing to sit on the poorly padded wooden bench and stare across the chop house. He would go and see Cyril Montague now that he had returned to the city, he decided. But something else was nagging in the back of his mind, something about Dolly and the letters. What was it? Something somebody had said to him. Was it Cyril? No, Montague had steadfastly denied knowing her. Somebody had said something, however. Who had it been . . .?

Suddenly, Adam snapped his fingers. A waiter stopped at his booth. Adam irritatedly waved the man away. He needed no more service. He had recalled what had been lurking in his memory. When he had been at the theatre only a day or two after his meeting with Sunman at Kensal Green, he had asked whether or not it was possible to deliver a note to the young dancer. And how had the dancing master McIlwraith replied? Of course. 'Dolly can't read letters, sir,' he had said. 'She can't read anything at all.'

If Dolly had been illiterate, her lover would surely not have been sending her letters of any kind, indiscreet or otherwise. Why send missives that someone else would have to read to her?

Either Sunman and Waterton were lying to him, or they knew even less about her than Adam did.

Adam sighed. As ever, thoughts of Dolly led inevitably to thoughts of Hetty Gallant. He had seen nothing of her since his return to London; indeed, he had seen nothing of her since the one night they had spent together before he had travelled to York. He was obliged to admit to himself that the pleasures he had enjoyed then seemed unlikely to be repeated, and he was not certain how he felt about that. Hetty was a lovely, lively girl but it was perhaps best that they should not meet again. Yet he could not so easily forget her. Her face and figure haunted him. And besides, had he not seen her in company with Harry Vernon?

He could not quite rid himself of the thought that she was in some way intimately connected to the mystery of Dolly Delaney and her murder.

* * * * *

In the event, Adam had no need to visit Holborn to see the 'People's Roscius'. The following day, he was reading in his rooms in Doughty Street when there was a knock on the door. A long knock, which began as a series of timid taps and then developed quickly into a succession of noisier and more determined thumps on the woodwork.

'I'm coming,' Adam called. 'No need to break down the door,' he muttered beneath his breath as he replaced the book on the shelf and walked through his sitting room and into the hall. Who could this be? he wondered. Surely there was no reason why Mrs Gaffery should be calling upon him, was there?

He reached the door and pulled it open. Standing on the threshold, his hand raised to deliver another blow, was Cyril Montague. 'Ah, there you are, you wretch,' he said. 'I was beginning to think you were out on the town. I *swear* I have been knocking and knocking these five minutes past.'

'So I heard, Mr Montague. How can I help you?'

'Are you not going to ask me in, my dear? So *vulgar* to hold important conversations in a stairwell.'

Adam stepped to one side and, with a gesture of half-hearted welcome, invited his visitor to enter. Montague walked through the door as if he was expecting an audience to applaud him for doing so.

Adam followed and pointed him in the direction of the sitting room. 'Please sit down, Mr Montague. This is an unanticipated pleasure. I have only just heard that you were in town.'

The actor looked at the two wing chairs in the room and chose to seat himself in the one nearest the fire. Adam took the other.

'Such a *rush*, my dear. One minute I was treading the provincial boards with darling old Skeffington; the next, I'm summoned to the Royal Pantheon to give my Romeo to the eager multitudes of the great metropolis. I do declare I haven't had a *moment's* rest in days. If I'm not careful, I shall be falling asleep before your humble hearth.'

Montague, Adam could not help but notice, did not look well: his eyes were bloodshot, and the make-up which he seemed to wear both on-and off-stage was streaked with dirt. His body slumped in the chair like a puppet which had just had its strings cut. Only his voice, which remained determinedly jaunty, suggested a man who was anything other than at the end of his tether.

'Who is that *ogress* downstairs?' Montague continued. 'She came roaring out of her den like a lion in search of its prey. I had the utmost difficulty in persuading her that we were old friends and that you would be simply *overjoyed* to see me.'

'Mrs Gaffery can come as a shock to those who have not encountered her before,' Adam acknowledged. 'She owns the house. She is, I suppose, my landlady.'

'She must feast upon raw meat in that lair on the ground floor! I do declare I am *trembling* at the very prospect of passing her door again. Are there no other means of departing your rooms?'

Adam shook his head and the actor sighed. He was indeed trembling, although Adam doubted it was through fear of meeting Mrs Gaffery again. Montague looked in immediate need of his drug of choice. In its absence, Adam suggested a drink, which his visitor accepted eagerly. He then sat, hunched in the chair, sipping the brandy Adam provided. He looked thoroughly miserable. Silence descended on the room.

'I am pleased to renew our acquaintance, Mr Montague,' Adam said eventually, 'but I have an appointment in town in a short while.' This was not entirely true, but the young man wondered if saying so might nudge his visitor into speech. 'Can I help you in any way, or is this merely a social call?'

'Ah, forgive me, my dear.' The actor made a visible effort to recover his vitality. '*Transported* by delight as I am to see you once again, I am entirely forgetting the other reason for my visit.' He wiped his hand across his brow, sending tiny clouds of face powder floating into the air. 'I was mortified, simply *mortified*, to discover that I might have led you astray in York.'

'Astray, Mr Montague?'

'On the question of Dolly Delaney.'

'The girl you had never met?'

Montague laughed nervously. 'The girl in the photograph you showed me,' he said. 'I may have been hasty in saying that she was unknown to me.'

'So Dolly *was* in the chorus at the Gaiety.' Adam had seen the hidden playbill. He knew this to be the case but he wanted Montague to acknowledge it.

The actor nodded.

'And she came to see you in York?'

There was a pause and then Montague nodded again. 'A girl calling herself Dolly Delaney turned up in my dressing room at the Grand one night. *What* a state the poor little thing was in! All of a quiver from the moment she arrived to the moment she left.'

'What had happened to distress her?'

'My dear, she was in fear for her *life*. She was convinced that some gentleman she knew here in town wished her dead. It was the reason she had fled to York.'

'And you were able to offer her assistance?'

The actor looked shame-faced. 'To be *brutally* frank, my dear, I didn't believe her. Chorus girls often have the most *florid* imaginations. I thought she was telling me a story to encourage me to give her money.'

'And did you?'

'A little. But it was clearly not enough. She was back at the stage door a couple of days later.'

'And you gave her more money.'

'I had none to give, my dear. I was *absolutely* stony myself.'

'And you never saw her again?'

Montague took a long sip of his brandy. He said nothing.

'You *did* see her again,' Adam persisted.

'Not *exactly*, my dear. I *arranged* to see her again.'

'Ah, I think I see.' Light was beginning to dawn. 'You agreed to meet in the Grand after the show was finished.'

'I didn't want her to know where my lodgings were. So I said that she should come to my dressing room at one in the morning. I knew I would be the only person left in the theatre at that hour. I told her I would leave a side door open.'

'Why so late? Why not meet her in York during the day?'

'My dear, I was embarrassed to be seen with her. She was positively *hysterical* at the stage door. I attract *quite* enough attention amongst *hoi polloi* without the companionship of a screaming woman. And, as I say, I didn't want her at my rooms.'

'Why see her at all? Why not send her away?'

'I felt sorry for the poor mite. I thought I could borrow a sovereign or two from Timble to give her and then she would disappear from York entirely. My conscience would be clear, and I could forget about her.'

'What happened on the night she was to come to your dressing room?'

'I fell asleep.'

'Asleep?'

'My dear, you can have no idea how *exhausting* it can be, giving oneself to the crowd.' Still crumpled in the chair, his make-up disintegrating and running down his cheeks, Cyril Montague was a picture of exhaustion. Adam filled the actor's glass with another shot of brandy.

'If I understand you correctly then, Mr Montague, you were still asleep when Dolly entered the Grand. Did you awake at any time? Did you see her before she was killed?'

The actor shook his head. 'My dear, I had no idea she *had* been killed. Not until the following afternoon. I awoke in the early hours in my chair in my dressing room. I had the most *blisteringly* bad headache. There was no sign of Dolly so I let myself out of the stage door and went back to my lodgings. It was only when I dragged my poor, *suffering* carcase to the theatre at about five the next day that

Timble told me the girl was dead.'

'But, if that is so, you must have been in the theatre at the same time as the murderer! The same time as myself and the police! Did you not hear or see anything of anyone else when you left?'

Montague gave a half-embarrassed shrug. 'I was not at my most observant, Mr Carver.'

'And we all failed to see you.' Adam spoke almost to himself. He had another thought. 'Do you have the habit of calling out in your sleep, Mr Montague?'

'Calling out, my dear?'

'Some people do, you know. Involuntary cries when they are comfortably resting in the arms of Morpheus.'

'Well, since you mention it, and I think it *most* impolite that you should, dear boy, one or two of my *closest* friends have told me that I can be quite the little chatterbox in the early hours. Awake or asleep. But it is *very* rude of you to speak of it. What *possible* interest can you have in my bedroom habits?'

'It is of no consequence, Mr Montague. Forget I said it.'

So that, Adam thought, was the explanation of the cry in the theatre that had disturbed both him and Dolly's murderer. The actor, he assumed, must have smoked a pipe or two more that evening than he usually did. Overcome by exhaustion and his drug, he had slept. And he had called out in his sleep. When he had awoken, he had still been half-befuddled and had thought only of getting to his bed. But how had he evaded the attention of Moughton and his men? He must have left during the short period, immediately after Quint had been apprehended, when all of them were in the auditorium.

Adam looked at Montague directly. 'But you must tell all this to the police.'

'My *dear*!' Montague squealed with horror at the idea. 'How *can* I? They will think that I murdered the girl myself! I will be *flung* into some dark dungeon and left to *rot*.'

'I am sure that Inspector Moughton will do no such thing, but he must be told that you were there.'

'No, it is out of the question.' The actor had folded his arms and twisted his body so that he was half turned away from Adam. He looked and sounded like a sulky child. 'I will *not* go back to York.' As he spoke, there was a sudden noise from the hall. 'What is that?' Montague asked in alarm, rising from the chair and spilling some of the brandy from his glass.

'There is no cause for concern. It will only be Quint, returning from whatever den of vice he has been haunting this afternoon.'

Montague was not to be soothed. He had already emptied the last of the brandy down his throat and was ready to depart. 'I must love you and leave you, my dear. Thank you for listening to my tale. Here I have been positively *pouring* my heart out to you, and the time has simply *raced* away. But I owe the audience in Holborn a Romeo tonight, and I must fly.'

'You cannot go without promising me you will speak to someone else about this, Montague.' Adam had risen to his feet himself.

The actor's mask dropped for a moment. 'I cannot, Carver. I am frightened. I am certain that someone is following me.' Montague looked over his shoulder as if he believed his pursuer might have followed him into Adam's rooms. 'I do not know what to do. I am entirely at the end of my rope.'

'Speak to the police.'

'I cannot,' Montague repeated.

'You have spoken to me.'

'That is a very different matter.'

'Speaking to me might be worse than speaking to the police. How do you know it was not I who murdered the girl?'

'*My dear!* Perish the thought.' Montague gave a short, half-hysterical laugh. It was clear that he had not heard that Adam had been arrested, however briefly, in York.

'I was asking about Dolly's whereabouts. Might I not have been in pursuit of her in order to kill her?'

'I may not be the man I was, my dear, but I have not *completely* lost my powers of judgement. You're no more a killer than I am. No, it's someone else and I *swear* he's following me.' Again, Montague looked wildly around the room as if his possible pursuer might even now be hiding behind the furniture. 'I have only spoken to you,' he said, 'because I needed to unburden my conscience. The girl was a sweet girl in her own way, and it was because of me that she was in the theatre to meet her death.'

There was a clatter from outside. The actor made a sudden high-pitched, whinnying noise, something between a laugh and a cry of fear. He jumped to his feet and almost ran out of the door. As he did so, he nearly collided with Quint, who was entering the room from the hall.

'Where's the bleedin' fire?' the manservant asked indignantly, but Montague had already left the flat and his steps could be heard on the staircase.

CHAPTER TWENTY

'**W**hat do you think you're doing round 'ere?' Quint spoke quietly to himself as he watched the man he had been following for two hours. The object of his attentions was standing at the corner of Piccadilly Circus and the Quadrant, outside one of the entrances to Swan & Edgar's. 'This ain't your beat, is it? You're a long way from home.'

The man Quint was eyeing so suspiciously was Job Benskin. Before he had left him to make further enquiries into Dolly Delaney's past history, Adam had set his servant a task: 'Now we are back in town,' he said, 'I cannot have the sword of Damocles hanging over my head in the shape of this wretched man Benskin and his wild stories. I must know more about him. Where does he live? What does he do with his days? My time is still taken up by this Dolly Delaney affair, so I am trusting you to find answers to these questions, Quint.'

''Ow the 'ell am I supposed to do that? I don't even know what the cove looks like.'

'You saw him at the Three Pigs. When I emerged from the back room, he followed me.'

'I ain't sure I'd know 'im again. We was out the door into the street like scalded cats through a back window, remember.'

'I have faith in your powers of recall, Quint. Go back to the Three Pigs. Try to avoid that lout Baines but make enquiries about Benskin. I must know if he truly does have the knowledge of my father's last days, as he claims. And the only way to discover that is through knowing more of Benskin himself.'

So, very reluctantly, Quint had returned to the pothouse in Whitechapel where they had last seen the down-and-out clerk. By a stroke of luck, there was no sign of Jem Baines when he arrived. One of his associates was there, propping up the bar with a pint pot clasped in his ham-like fist, but he did no more than snarl in Quint's direction and turn back to his drink. It was only just after one o'clock, and perhaps too early in the day for fisticuffs.

Quint had ordered himself a pint of half-and-half and settled into a seat as far away from the man at the bar as he could. There was no need to be deliberately provocative. He had not had long to wait: he had been there no more than ten minutes when the door to the Pigs opened and Benskin walked in. Although he had caught only a glimpse of him on his previous visit, Quint knew him immediately. He did not look a happy man. 'Face as long as a fiddle,' Quint had said to himself.

Benskin had ordered a brandy and water which he nursed to his chest as he stared morosely around the bar, his eyes passing over Quint with no sign that he recognized him. For a minute or two, he continued to clutch the brandy, like a mother nursing her sleeping child, before abruptly lifting it to his lips and swallowing it in one gulp. He had banged the shot glass on the counter and marched out of the alehouse.

Quint had waited the briefest of moments and then followed, anxious that he should not lose his prey so soon after finding him. The thug at the bar watched him go, hurling a half-hearted insult at him as he left.

Outside, Benskin had still been in sight, heading up Leman Street towards the high street at a surprising pace. Quint set off in pursuit and was twenty yards behind him as the former clerk turned towards the city. Despite the crowds, he was able to keep his man in sight without too much difficulty. Through Aldgate and Leadenhall Street, Cornhill and Cheapside, Benskin passed, unaware of the figure tracking him. Along Newgate Street and on into High Holborn, his pace had showed no sign of slacking. After reaching Oxford Street, he turned abruptly to the left and Quint had nearly lost him in the warren of Soho streets and alleyways – he had been forced to move forwards until he was scarcely more than a few steps behind his quarry. On several occasions he was sure that the man would turn and realize that he was being followed, but Benskin had seemed oblivious to his surroundings. He had a destination in mind and he was determined to reach it.

And now he was standing in front of one of the West End's largest shops, scratching his backside and attracting disapproving looks from several of the customers who entered it.

'You'll be getting yourself moved on, if you keep loitering there with your fingers 'alfway up your arse,' Quint said to himself, as he watched from a vantage point further along the Quadrant.

Indeed, one of the shop's doormen was already eyeing Benskin with suspicion. It was only a matter of time before the shabby vagrant was told to be on his way. 'Any minute now,' Quint whispered, and then noted with surprise that one of the gentlemen exiting Swan & Edgar's had stopped to talk to Benskin. What was he doing? Was he a charitable soul who was handing him a few coins? Did he want Benskin to carry his goods to a waiting carriage? No, he had nothing with him apart from a walking cane. Quint moved nearer to the pair.

The gentleman was dressed in a light-coloured paletot and dark trousers. He was tall with a black beard that looked too luxuriant for his thin face. He was talking to Benskin, who was listening intently and nodding from time to time. The man in the paletot raised his cane and pointed up Regent Street, and the two unlikely companions began to walk towards Oxford Circus. 'This is a turn-up, ain't it?' Quint remarked to himself and proceeded to follow them.

* * * * *

The bells of a nearby church were striking six as Adam let himself into the house in Doughty Street and peered cautiously along its entrance hall. The first door which opened off it, he noticed to his relief, was closed. He had no wish to encounter his landlady at present. He had spent the day in extensive and entirely fruitless enquiries into Dolly Delaney's life in London and he was a frustrated man. The very last thing he wanted was a conversation with Mrs Gaffery.

He began to tiptoe carefully up the stairs. He had almost reached the top when he came to a sudden halt. The door to his rooms was ajar. Was Quint at home? Adam imagined that his servant would still be in pursuit of Job Benskin. The young man mounted the last two stairs even more quietly than he had done the rest and approached the entrance to his rooms. He pushed open the outer door.

The door to the living room was also half-open and Adam could hear the sounds of someone moving about inside. He pushed open the second door and was faced with a scene of chaos. Chairs were overturned. The table had been moved and the carpet beneath it had been rolled back. His books had been pulled from the shelves and flung to the floor.

So intent was he on his task, the man responsible did not see Adam. He crossed the room from the bookshelves and now crouched by a small cabinet under one of the windows. He pulled out the cabinet's bottom drawer and began examining its contents.

The man was not Quint. He was dressed in a black corduroy suit that had seen better days, and a battered billycock hat. A dirty black muffler was wrapped around his face. Adam recognized him immediately. He did not know the man's name but it was undoubtedly the same man who had attacked him with a knife when he was leaving the German Gymnasium. The man was muttering beneath his breath as he pulled reams of paper from the cabinet. The paper, Adam realized, was his manuscript for *Travels in Ancient Macedon* which he had stored there two years since and forgotten. The intruder was clearly uninterested in it. Cursing, he cast the sheets of paper to one aside. He was looking for something else.

Adam was suddenly outraged by this invasion of his home. 'What the devil d'you think you're doing?' he shouted.

The man, taken utterly by surprise, started as if he had glimpsed a ghost. Before he could turn to see who had entered the room,

Adam was upon him, the young man's left arm curling around the trespasser's neck.

The man in corduroy twisted as best he could in Adam's grip, making choking noises as he did so. His hat fell off. He threw back his arms and pushed Adam off-balance. Both men tumbled backwards but the young man continued to cling to him. The pair rolled around the room, Adam still with his arm clamped firmly around the other man's neck but the intruder's weight fully upon him. His uninvited guest struggled furiously to be free, lashing out his arms and legs in all directions. His elbows caught Adam several blows in the ribs and, winded, the young man was eventually obliged to release his captive. The man immediately jumped to his feet and ran from the room.

After a moment's delay to recover his breath, Adam followed him. Taking the stairs three at a time, he reached the street and looked wildly one way and then the other. A figure in black was disappearing down Doughty Street in the direction of the Foundling Hospital. Adam began to chase after him, but soon realized that the man had too great a head start. The young man saw the figure run past the street gate and its porter and turn into Guilford Street. When he reached the corner himself, the intruder had vanished into the London crowds. There was little point in continuing the pursuit. He looked at the porter, an elderly Crimean veteran called Knibbs, with a bristling beard and a wooden leg.

'Did you know that man?' Adam asked.

'Know 'im, sir? 'E sez you did. That's why I lets him through the gate. Mr Carver's expectin' me, 'e sez.'

'Did he have the appearance of someone with whom I might be acquainted?' Adam, exasperated, raised his voice. 'A villainous-looking rogue dressed in corduroy?'

'Beggin' your pardon, Mr Carver, but you has some odd sorts visitin'.' The porter was offended. ''E didn't seem any worse nor better than some you've told me to let pass.'

'You are right, Knibbs.' Adam, still looking down Guilford Street in vain hopes of catching a glimpse of his intruder, recovered his temper. 'My apologies. I did not mean to cast aspersions on your judgement.'

The old soldier was perched on a three-legged stool by the street gate, his false leg outstretched and an unlit pipe clamped in his mouth. 'I'd 'ave stopped 'im jest now, when he comes runnin' past me,' he said, 'if it weren't for this.' He tapped on the wood of his lower right limb. 'If it weren't for the fact that me leg lies buried in a pit afore Sebastopol, where I left it for me queen and country, I'd 'ave stopped 'im.'

'I am sure you would,' Adam said, wondering, not for the first time, what the point was in employing a one-legged man as a gate porter. However, Knibbs was not someone worth antagonizing. For all kinds of reasons, the young man thought, it was more useful to have him look on you with favour rather disfavour. He pressed a coin into the porter's hand and returned to the house.

Inevitably, Mrs Gaffery was standing at the door to her rooms. She must have heard the commotion as Adam pursued the intruder into Doughty Street. She was in a state of voluble outrage and it took the young man several minutes to soothe her. Eventually, with a last suggestion that he could find new accommodation if he did not wish to live like a respectable person, Mrs Gaffery retired and slammed shut her door.

Adam trudged back up the stairs and entered his own rooms. He looked about the ruin of his sitting room. He noticed a black object lying amidst the pages of his manuscript and he reached to pick it up. It was the man's billycock hat. He turned it over in his hands. It had lost much of its shape and hardness but there was a dirty white band running around the inside of its brim. Letters, now very faded, had long ago been inscribed on the band in black ink. The letters were 'JB'.

CHAPTER TWENTY-ONE

'He's in the room at the back, sir. It ain't up to much but it's the best dressing room in the house.' He followed the stolid man in an ancient cutaway coat as he made his way further into the depths of the Royal Pantheon Theatre, Holborn. The man was clutching a cheap cigar in his right hand and plumes of rancid-smelling smoke surrounded him. His name was Albert Danvers and he was the manager of the theatre in which Cyril Montague was scheduled to perform.

Adam had decided that he needed to talk to Montague once more. The man knew more of Dolly Delaney than he was telling, and he must be made to speak. Adam was not sure how he was going to force the truth from him but was determined to do so.

The two men reached a green door and Danvers grabbed at its handle. The door was locked. The theatre manager knocked loudly. 'Montague!' he called, 'there's a gentleman to see you. Name of Carver. Says he needs to see you before you go on.'

He knocked again, even more noisily than before. 'I was warned about this, Mr Carver. I was warned. He'll let you down, they said. He'll get himself so hazed with the smoke that he won't know where he is.' The manager continued to bang on the door and shout Montague's name. 'But I decided to take a chance on him. He's a fine actor, Cyril, an artist in his own way. Looks like he's let me down, though. Just like they said. He's dead to the world, if you ask me. We'll never get him coherent by curtain up.'

'He's definitely in there, is he?' Adam asked.

'Saw him go in to put on his slap about forty-five minutes ago. He was a bit bleary but I thought he'd liven up when he saw the house. Nothing like a good audience to get Cyril going. Now he's out cold, I reckon.' Danvers fell to his knees and peered through the keyhole. 'Oh God, he is! He's flat out on his dressing table. I can see his back. Cyril! Cyril! Wake up, you bastard! I've got half of Holborn sitting in the stalls and waiting for you to play a star-crossed bloody lover!'

The manager struggled to his feet, still cursing. 'We'll have to break it down,' he said with sudden decision. 'Give it a bloody good kick, sir. The doors in the theatre are all as thin as paper. One blow from an athletic young man such as yourself and it'll be matchwood on the floor.'

Adam raised an eyebrow. He wasn't so sure. The door to Montague's dressing room looked solid enough. However, Danvers was gesturing impatiently for him to do as he had been asked. Lifting his leg, he struck the panel just beneath the lock with the heel of his boot. Nothing happened.

'Again, sir,' the manager urged him. 'And harder. It is about to splinter.'

Adam kicked at the door once more. This time the wood did give way slightly, a small gap appearing between the door and its frame.

Danvers, excited by the success, began to shout further insults at the comatose actor inside. 'Wake up, damn you, you posturing sot! You powder-faced ninny! You'll pay for the damage to this bloody door, Cyril. It's coming out of your cut of the box, I can tell you. One more go, sir, and we're through to him.'

This last remark was addressed to Adam, who leaned back slightly to add more thrust to his kick. As his foot hit the woodwork, the door collapsed inwards, falling to the floor with a tremendous crash.

Montague, slumped over the table in front of a mirror, still made no move. The contents of his make-up kit were strewn around him.

'He's about as lively as a boiled owl, ain't he?' Danvers said, stepping over the shattered remains of the door. He looked thoroughly disgusted with his star performer. 'I can't recall ever seeing him in a state as bad as this. Usually he can crawl on stage no matter how many pipes he's had, but we're not going to get a Romeo from him tonight, that's for certain.' The manager moved across the room and stubbed out his foul-smelling cigar in a bowl of pigment on the dressing table. He grabbed the actor roughly by the shoulder. 'Come on, Cyril. For the last bloody time, look lively.'

Still standing by the broken door, Adam could see Montague's body move as Danvers shook it. There was no sign of life.

'Is it only the opium that has felled him?' he asked.

'What else could it be, sir?'

'Drink?'

'He ain't much of a drinker. Not for an actor.'

Adam followed the manager into the dressing room, kicking aside a panel of wood that had broken off the door. He walked up to the actor, who was still sprawled, head down, on his dressing table. Adam reached out his hand and pulled back one of Montague's eyelids. He lifted his wrist and felt for a pulse.

'I do believe, Mr Danvers,' he said after a few moments, 'that the poor man is not drugged but dead.'

'Dead?' The manager seized hold of Montague's other wrist. 'He can't be dead! I've got three hundred people out there, waiting for the balcony scene.'

'You will have to find yourself another Romeo, sir. Cyril Montague has most definitely played his last role on life's stage.'

* * * * *

'Heart failure, of course.' Dr Nethersole was a shrivelled, elderly man with a disproportionately large beard and booming voice. 'It happens all the time to those possessed of intemperate habits. As, I believe, the late gentleman was. One minute you are, to all appearances, as fit as a fiddle; the next you are resting on the shoulders of six strong men as you are carried to the grave.'

The doctor, summoned from his home in Red Lion Square, had arrived at the theatre in a grumpy mood, but examination of Montague's body seemed to have had a cheering effect upon him. As

226

he pronounced his verdict on the late actor, he looked positively delighted.

It was as if, Adam reflected, Cyril Montague's demise had been nothing more than an exhilarating confirmation of a theory Nethersole had long held. 'So his final indulgence in his habit was fatal, was it, Doctor?' the young man asked. 'There can be no doubt about that?'

'No doubt at all, sir,' Nethersole roared. 'No doubt at all.' He sounded offended that Adam could even suggest otherwise. 'The slow accumulation of poison in the body. The swift nemesis striking the overburdened heart. There could not be a clearer case.'

Adam remembered the fear that Cyril Montague had displayed during his visit to Doughty Street. The belief that he was being followed. He looked at the actor's body, which was now covered by a sheet and stretched on a trestle table in the Royal Pantheon's props room. 'There is no possibility, Dr Nethersole, that there might be some other cause of death? Some other poison that has been introduced into his body?'

'Other poison, sir?' The physician spoke as if Adam was deliberately striving to anger him. 'What other poison?'

'Arsenic, perhaps?' The young man racked his brains for the name of toxic substances. 'Strychnine?'

Nethersole snorted with derision. 'You are not, I take it, a medical man?'

Adam acknowledged that he was not.

'I thought as much. If you were, you would not make such extraordinary suggestions. The ingestion of strychnine is followed by severe convulsions. Do you not remember the case of William Palmer, sir, who killed poor Cook?'

Adam was obliged to confess that he did not.

'It was back in '56,' Nethersole said sternly, as if the young man's ignorance of this fifteen-year-old murder was a sure sign of an inadequate education. 'Palmer administered strychnine to his victim and Cook was racked by seizures. Are there any indications that this man' – he nodded in the direction of Cyril Montague's shrouded body – 'suffered in such a way before he died?'

Adam shook his head.

'As for arsenic poisoning, one of the nearly immediate consequences of swallowing it in quantity is extreme bodily effusion. Not to mince words, sir, the individual's bowels open uncontrollably. We would certainly be aware of the fact, if this poor devil had been administered arsenic. No, there is no doubt about the cause of death. Mr Montague died from heart failure brought about by his own indulgence in opium.'

Dr Nethersole closed his medical bag with a flourish and stared balefully at Adam. 'And now, gentlemen, my dinner – although doubtless cold and congealed by this hour – still awaits me at home. My bill will be with you tomorrow, Mr Danvers.'

* * * * *

'Well, that went off better than we could have hoped,' Danvers said. He and Adam were sitting in a private box at the Royal Pantheon. Its ormolu decoration, now filthy with age, showed that the theatre had once been a more prestigious venue than it now was.

The two men were looking down on the audience leaving the auditorium after a performance that, with the loss of its leading man, had very nearly not taken place. The manager had considered cancelling it after the discovery of Cyril Montague's body but had decided that, with the audience already in their seats, he was risking a riot. 'They'd turn savage,' he had said. 'There'd be blood in the aisles.'

And so, with catcalls beginning to echo around the theatre, the curtain had risen on *Romeo and Juliet* as, backstage, Dr Nethersole made his post-mortem examination of its leading actor. When it was over and the doctor had returned to his interrupted dinner, Danvers had invited Adam to stay and watch the last two acts of the drama. The young man had seen no good reason to refuse.

Montague's understudy, an eager recruit to the company named Arthur Bellows, had jumped at the chance of playing Romeo. Belying his name, Bellows had proved almost inaudible in his speeches.

'He's speakin' like a mouse in cheese,' Danvers had said at one point in exasperation. 'The audience aren't catching a ruddy word of it.'

The understudy had made up for the weakness of his voice with the frenetic energy of his movements. He had raced from one side of the stage to the other like a rabbit pursued by a fox, waving his sword in the direction of his fellow performers at both appropriate and inappropriate moments. During the balcony scene, he seemed as likely to throw his lover over his shoulder and run offstage with her as exchange brief kisses. Even after Romeo had taken the poison and fallen to the floor of the Capulet crypt, Bellows had continued to writhe convulsively for several minutes as the awakened Juliet bewailed his death. The audience, to Adam's surprise, seemed to enjoy his performance. When he took his bow, still apparently twitching in his death throes, they roared with approval.

'Better than we could have hoped,' Danvers repeated, as the crowds trooped out of the Pantheon. 'I think I should give that understudy another chance tomorrow night.'

'Mr Bellows certainly gave an interesting interpretation of the role,' Adam remarked cautiously.

'He was livelier dead than poor Cyril sometimes was when he was alive,' Danvers said. 'We'll have to find a way for him to be heard beyond the first rows, mind.'

The two men left the box and made their way down the curving staircase that led to the theatre lobby. The last stragglers from the audience were leaving. A doorman was bowing obsequiously to them.

'Well,' said Danvers, holding out his hand, 'this has been a night and a half, ain't it? Who'd have thought, when you came knocking at the door of my office earlier this evening, that we'd find poor Cyril dead as a doornail in his own dressing room?'

'Who indeed?' Adam said. The two men shook hands. 'Did anyone else visit Montague whilst he was here in the Pantheon?'

Danvers shook his head. 'Not to my knowledge,' he said. 'He ain't been such a popular man of late.'

'What about the other actors? Would any of them have visited his dressing room?'

'Can't think of any reason why they should. Anyways, if they had, they'd have found him with his toes turned up, wouldn't they?'

'I suppose they would have done.' There was doubt in Adam's voice and Danvers took note of it.

'Here, you've not still got it in your head that he was poisoned, have you? You heard what the doctor said. It was his intemperate habits as did for him. The only poison was that filth he smoked.'

'Of course, you are right.' Adam decided he had no wish to enter any further debate with the manager in the lobby of his theatre. 'Nethersole is right. It was opium that proved poor Montague's undoing.'

'Exackly. He was hocused most of the hours God sent. No wonder it did for him. Well, I've got to go and take a look at tonight's box.' Danvers held out a sweating hand and Adam took it once more. It rested in his own briefly, like a fish on a slab, and then the manager was gone, walking swiftly back into his own domain.

As Adam turned to leave, he noticed a small figure standing by a door that led through to the stalls. It was the dwarf, Billy Bantam, whom he had met briefly at the Prince Albert. He had been watching them.

Bantam stared venomously at him, then approached to within a few feet and spoke. 'You ain't the only gent what's been looking for him tonight, you know.'

'Looking for whom? For Cyril Montague?'

''Oo d'you think?' the little man sneered.

Adam was eager to ask more questions but the tiny man immediately spun on his heel and retreated further into the theatre. He moved at a surprising pace, and was lost to view within moments. Adam made as if to follow him, and then decided the questions could wait. He stopped and turned to the magnificently attired doorman. 'That was Billy Bantam, was it not?'

'Was it, sir?' The doorman spoke in a deep, booming baritone. He sounded, Adam decided, as if he had once trodden the boards himself. 'It might have been. He's in and out of half the theatres in London. Mr Danvers knows him of old. We all of us know him of old.'

'And Mr Danvers allows him to come and go in the theatre as he pleases?'

'Pretty much, sir. He's harmless, is Bantam. Miserable little bugger, if you'll pardon my language, sir, but harmless.'

CHAPTER TWENTY-TWO

'I have no evidence to prove this, Quint, but I do not share the doctor's opinion. I do not believe that Cyril Montague died of heart failure. I think he was murdered.'

'Who'd want to kill 'im? Another Miss Nancy like 'isself?'

'I doubt it. Do you not think it odd that Montague should cross the Styx so soon after he had called upon me here?'

'You mean, 'ow come 'e pays a visit 'ere and next day 'e's as stiff as a board?'

'A peculiar coincidence, is it not?'

'Mebbe 'e knew something someone didn't want him to know.'

'And poor Cyril was sent to join the great majority to prevent him speaking further to me?'

'Could be,' Quint said.

'But how could the murderer – if there were one – be certain that Montague had not already told me the vital information?'

'Mebbe you're next on his list.'

'Thank you, Quint. That is a cheering idea, indeed.'

Master and servant were sitting in a tavern in the Gray's Inn Road. Each had reported to the other the events of the previous day. Adam had told Quint of the death of the actor, and the intruder in Doughty Street. Quint had told his master of the meeting between Benskin and the mysterious gentleman in the paletot. Adam had been just as puzzled by it as Quint. Eventually, he had decided that it was of no immediate relevance and should be dismissed in favour of more obviously important matters.

Both men now had pints of India Pale Ale in front of them. Adam had taken a few small sips from his; Quint's pint pot was almost drained to the dregs. He picked it up and peered into it, as if he thought the mere act of doing so might miraculously refill it. Adam pushed a silver threepenny bit across the table.

'Go and buy yourself another drink, Quint. I cannot bear to see you looking so melancholy.'

The manservant hauled himself to his feet and lumbered across the room towards the bar. Adam crossed his hands behind his head and leaned back in his seat. The more he thought about it, the more convinced he was that Cyril Montague had been murdered. Dr Nethersole had dismissed the idea of strychnine or arsenic, but there were other poisons, were there not? The effects of which the doctor might not recognize. Perhaps the murderer knew more about poisons than did the elderly medic. But who could he be? Bantam, the tiny man with the face of a depraved child, had been in the Royal Pantheon immediately after the discovery of Montague's body. Surely he could not have been the killer, could he? It seemed improbable. Yet what had he been doing there? And who was the other gentleman of whom Bantam had spoken? Had he really existed?

There were too many questions that could not be immediately answered. Adam unclasped his hands from the back of his head and rested them on the tavern table. Idly, he traced the line of the grain in its wood with his forefinger and then picked up his drink, taking a swift sip of the ale. He had to think logically of the matter, he decided. Suppose Montague had not died of heart failure brought about by his opium habit. Suppose he had been killed. What was the unknown murderer's motive for despatching him? It could only be that the actor had known something which would incriminate the person who, as Adam still suspected, had poisoned him. Incriminate that person in the earlier murder of Dolly Delaney. If Montague had indeed been killed, his death must be linked with what had happened in York.

But what could the actor have known that proved so fatal? He had been in a show with Dolly, of course, so he might have then learned something from her. But *The Bohemians of Paris* had been staged at the Gaiety nearly a year ago. Why would whatever he knew have only recently become dangerous? Because, Adam speculated, the opium-addicted actor had spoken to him in Doughty Street. What exactly had the man said? He tried to re-run the conversation in his head. Had there been anything out of the ordinary in it? Yes, he thought, there had. He remembered the strange phrasing that poor Montague had used when describing the girl's visit to him. 'A girl *calling* herself Dolly Delaney,' the actor had said. At the time, Adam had thought it an odd way for Montague to express himself. Cyril knew Dolly. The playbill from the Gaiety proved that. But, in York, the girl was only 'calling herself' Dolly Delaney. What had Cyril meant?

Suddenly Adam could see an explanation. It was a moment of revelation, and he slapped the table with his hand. Quint, who was just returning to his seat, clutching a fresh pint of pale ale, looked at him in surprise.

'The girl on the cabinet card,' Adam said. 'The one we were pursuing. The one who was killed in York.' He paused and once again ran through the possibilities in his head. Yes, he was certain he was right. 'She wasn't Dolly Delaney. In all likelihood, Dolly is still alive.'

'She looked ready enough for the boneyard to me,' Quint said. He raised his pint pot to his lips and took a long pull on his drink. 'Dead as a herring.'

'No, do you not see, Quint?'

The manservant, his face a blank, clearly did not.

'She exchanged identities. In the weeks before the *carte de visite* was created, Dolly became someone else. It was that someone else who posed for the assorted photographs we have seen. Who worked at the Prince Albert. Who caught Adolphus Wyndham's eye.' He waved his hand like a magician drawing attention to the outcome of a particularly ingenious trick. 'And it was that someone else who was murdered in York.'

Quint stared at the tavern window behind his master.

'You are endeavouring to remain sphinx-like and inscrutable, Quint, but the task is beyond you. Your eyebrows betray you. You still do not understand.'

'Dolly ain't dead because the Dolly we followed to York wasn't the real Dolly. What sort of a gammon yarn is that?'

'No gammon. I am certain it is the truth. Let us consider the hypothesis. Dolly decides, for reasons that we do not yet know, that she wishes to become someone else. She persuades a friend to exchange identities with her. Dolly becomes Miss X. Miss X becomes Dolly. What follows from this, Quint?'

Quint, rubbing the stubble on his cheek, looked as if he still could not imagine what followed.

'Why, if Dolly became Miss X, then it was Miss X who visited Miss Bascombe and received the money to travel to York. If it was Miss X who travelled to York, then it was that same Miss X who was cornered in the theatre and killed.'

'And if my aunt had been my uncle, she'd have had a pair of balls beneath her arse,' Quint said with some contempt. 'What proof have we got that the tart ain't the tart we thought?'

'None at all, but I am convinced I am correct.'

'And who's this Miss X you keep gabbing on about?'

'As always, Quint, you ask the pertinent question. Who indeed?' Adam tapped his fingers on the table. 'But I am sure that Cyril Montague knew that the dancer who came to see him in York wasn't Dolly. Why else would he describe her as "a girl *calling* herself Dolly Delaney"?'

'So why didn't sissy Cyril tell anyone the girl wasn't 'oo she said she was?'

'I am not certain.' Adam sipped again at his drink. 'Perhaps he knew Miss X as well as the real Dolly. There must have been some connection between them, otherwise why would she have gone to see him? Perhaps he felt sorry for her and did not wish to cause her any further trouble.'

'Why in 'ell is the girl pretending to be someone else in the first place?'

'As I say, I do not know. That is for us to find out.'

'And one more thing,' Quint said. 'This toff with his trousers down. Didn't he know 'oo 'e was doing the blanket hornpipe with? He thought she was Dolly, didn't 'e? I know some of these Champagne Charlies are so dumb they'd lose their arses if they were loose, but 'e'd 'ave some idea 'oo 'e was riding, wouldn't 'e?'

Adam sighed. His manservant had expressed it crudely, but he was right, of course. What of Harry Vernon? He had given the cabinet card to Sunman. But if Adam was correct, that photograph was taken after someone else had adopted Dolly's identity. Surely Vernon would be unlikely to be unaware who the woman he had been bedding for some time really was. *Ergo*, he must know that the cabinet card did not portray the real Dolly. And so he must have been deliberately trying to deceive his colleague. And, if he was, that raised further questions. Adam thought back to the night he had enjoyed Hetty Gallant's company. Who had he seen in earnest conversation with the girl? Who had she been entertaining before she welcomed Adam into her bed? None other than Harry Vernon. At the time, he had thought only that the plump man from the Foreign Office had a surprisingly complicated love life. Now other possibilities arose in Adam's mind, few of which were either agreeable or comforting.

* * * * *

'When we spoke of Dolly before, you said that she had been with the company only a few weeks. Can you recall the exact date on which she began work here?'

Adam was once again in one of the props rooms at the back of the Prince Albert, watching Cosmo Jardine applying paint to a vast theatrical flat which was hanging vertically from the ceiling. This one appeared to represent a burning building: lurid red flames leapt across it; tiny black figures scampered through them. Perhaps, on second thoughts, Adam decided, it was meant to depict the fiery furnaces of Hell. What production at the Albert could possibly require such scenery? Was some strange version of *Faust* being planned?

'I am not certain that I can,' his friend said. Giant brush still in hand, he began to climb a stepladder to reach the upper area of the flat. 'Do the civil, will you, old man, and hold this wretched ladder so it doesn't tumble down?'

Adam moved forward and seized either side of the steps as Cosmo climbed higher.

'I noticed her almost immediately, of course,' the painter continued. 'Which man would not? But I do not think I could tell you the very day and the very week. It was about the same time the other girl showed up in the chorus line.'

'Which other girl?' Arms outstretched, Adam tipped back his head to see what his friend was doing.

'Best not to look up, old chap. Liable to get paint in the eye.' Jardine was making sweeping movements with the brush across the top of the flat, adding further red to the flames. 'The dark one. The one with the opinions. No sooner had she arrived than she was ticking off poor McIlwraith for the way he treated the dancers. The man was a positive slave-driver, if you were to believe what she said. The wonder is that McIlwraith has kept her on. I think he must have a secret yearning to be bullied and nagged. Some chaps do, you know.' Jardine paused to shout instructions to a stagehand who was staggering out of the wings under the weight of what looked like a large bush. 'Myself, I prefer the quiet and the demure to the noisy and the scolding but . . .'

'For God's sake, Cosmo, what is the girl's name?' Adam knew the answer already but he wanted his friend to confirm it.

'Hattie?' Half the painter's attention was still on the stagehand, who had come to an abrupt halt and was peering through the foliage he was carrying. Jardine waved him in the direction he wanted him to go before returning to the question of the chorus girl. 'No, *Hetty*. That is it. Hetty something or other.'

'Gallant.'

'That is she. We talked of her before, I recall. She may well be

237

here, should you wish to speak to her.'

Hetty was not in the theatre. A brief conversation with McIlwraith, who winced visibly at the mention of her name, was enough for Adam to ascertain that she had left after the afternoon rehearsal and was not expected back until the evening performance.

* * * * *

His servant was waiting for Adam when the young man emerged from the stage door. Quint was leaning against a gas lamp and chewing morosely on a quid of tobacco. As his master approached, he turned and spat the tobacco into the gutter.

'We know anythin' more about the girl?' he asked, wiping his mouth on his sleeve.

'That is a foul habit,' Adam remarked. 'Can you not restrict yourself to the smoking of the weed?'

'They're both good for a man,' Quint replied. 'Chewing *and* smoking. They get the circ'lation going.'

'Well, I am not so sure that a doctor, should you ever visit one, would agree with you. But perhaps he would be wrong. Perhaps you are in the forefront of medical thought, Quint, and it is tobacco that keeps you in the pink.'

''Course it is,' said Quint, as if there was no doubt in the matter. 'That, and beer.'

'Ah, I had forgotten beer.' The two men had emerged from the side street into Drury Lane and were making their way towards High Holborn. 'And, in answer to your question, we know a lot more about the girl.'

'If we knew where she lived, it'd be a start.'

'We know exactly where Dolly lives, Quint. We have done so for some time.'

'Oh, we 'ave, 'ave we?' The manservant's face was fixed in an expression that suggested he was, because of the goodness of his heart, tolerating what was exceptional idiocy on his master's part.

'We have even been to her humble abode ourselves.'

This was too much even for Quint to endure. 'Well, why in

'ell didn't we jest tell 'er that 'er toff boyfriend wanted to see her? 'Stead of chasing off to bleedin' York and stumblin' over a stiff in the theatre!'

'At the time we met Dolly, she was living in basement rooms north of King's Cross.' Quint was silent. Adam watched the light begin to dawn in his servant's eyes. 'She was living there under an assumed name,' he went on. 'She was calling herself—'

'Hetty,' Quint interrupted. 'She was calling 'erself Hetty. That judy I followed on the underground.'

'Exactly, you have it at last. Hetty Gallant *is* Dolly Delaney.'

CHAPTER TWENTY-THREE

Adam pushed his way through the crowds emerging from the entrance to King's Cross station. As he moved on and turned left towards the Caledonian Road, the streams of people began to thin out. When he took another left turning, heading in the direction of Hetty's lodgings, they became no more than a trickle.

A watercress girl just ahead of him was dolefully calling, 'Four bunches a penny, four bunches a penny!' over and over again but there were few to take notice of her. He wondered idly why the girl had strayed away from the busier streets. There would be little business for her here. The thought clearly occurred to the girl herself and she turned to make her way back to the main road. Her wicker basket hanging over her right arm, she nearly bumped into him.

'Cress, sir?' she asked. 'Four bunches a penny.'

'No, thank you.'

'Fresh this morning, sir.'

Adam looked at the pinched little face and the bedraggled black hair. He reached into his pocket and found a penny. The girl took it and solemnly handed him four wilting green bunches. They did not look fresh this week, never mind this morning. The watercress seller continued on her way back to the crowds of potential customers, once again crying her wares. Adam stared at his impulse purchase and could not think what to do with it. Eventually he knelt and propped the cress against the doorstep of one of the houses. Perhaps its occupants would welcome the gift.

The young man made his way around the next corner and realized he was in the street where the young woman who was calling herself Hetty Gallant lived. On his previous call, he had thought the terraces hereabouts indistinguishable one from another; now, looking about him, he could see that this street was slightly more distinguished than its neighbours. The houses were a little bigger, a little more ambitious in their architecture. Perhaps the street was the work of a builder who had hoped to attract more middle-class residents to the area. If it was, Adam suspected that he had hoped in vain.

As he approached the house in which Hetty had her rooms, his heart began to thump within his chest. He could not decide whether the prospect of seeing her again was delightful or discomfiting. Their night together had been one of pleasure but they had not met since he had said farewell to her the following dawn. And now he was arriving with accusations which, although he was certain they were true, could only cause her embarrassment and distress. No, it was more than that, he reminded himself. It was entirely possible that the girl in whose arms he had enjoyed himself so much knew more than she should about the murder of her friend.

Adam stopped in front of the house itself and looked over the railings into the entry to the basement. A dishevelled slavey, hands red raw, was kneeling there. She was scrubbing the step that led into Hetty's rooms. Seeming to feel Adam's presence above her, she glanced up. Blushing, her face now the colour of her hands, she struggled to her feet and moved quickly inside. The young man made his way down the narrow steps to the tiny area yard. The girl was standing just inside Hetty's lodgings. She looked scared.

'I am sorry, miss,' Adam said. 'I did not mean to disturb you, but I am in search of the lady who lives here.'

'She's gorn, sir,' the servant said. She was trembling and could scarcely speak.

'I intend you no harm, Miss.' Adam strove to sound reassuring. He peered beyond the girl and into the rooms. They were so dark that he could see little. 'I wish simply to speak with Miss Gallant.'

'She's gorn, sir,' the slavey repeated.

'What is it, Nan?' A harsh voice emerged from inside the basement lodgings. 'Who's that with you?'

A thin and angular woman came into the area yard, brandishing a sweeping brush as if it was a weapon of war. It was the woman who had looked down from the upstairs window on the evening he had seen Hetty – or Dolly, as he reluctantly believed he must now think of her – with Harry Vernon.

''E wants to see 'Etty, Mrs Threave.'

'I'd like to see her myself,' the new arrival said. 'And there'd be hell to pay if I did. Not to mention the ten bob in back rent she owes.'

'I am sorry that Miss Gallant has proved such a difficult tenant, ma'am,' Adam said, raising his hat. 'May I ask when she first took the rooms?'

'Don't know as I can say exactly.' The landlady was eyeing Adam with obvious suspicion. 'What's it to you, anyways?'

'I am a friend of the young lady. I am interested in her whereabouts and her well-being.'

Mrs Threave snorted. 'I know the sorts of friends *that* woman had,' she said. 'I seen plenty of 'em coming in and out of my house. Kicking up the devil's delight at all hours of the day and night.' She turned to the slavey, who was still standing in the yard, clutching her scrubbing brush and staring blankly at Adam. 'Nan, get up them steps and clean the hallway upstairs. I'll deal with this gent.'

The girl, still eyeing Adam as if she had never before seen anyone quite like him, backed up the steps and disappeared into the house above them.

The landlady watched her go and then turned to the young man again. 'I don't know as I can tell you anything about Hetty,' she said. 'She was here and now she's gone. And she's took my ten bob with her.'

'Perhaps a florin towards the payment of her debts might help you remember something about her,' Adam suggested.

'It might,' Mrs Threave agreed. 'Half a crown might help me even more.'

Adam smiled and took the larger silver coin from his pocket. The landlady extended a bony hand and snatched it from him, like a buzzard swooping on its prey. Adam smiled again. 'How long had Miss Gallant been lodging with you?' he asked.

'She arrived here at the beginning of the year. Maybe the third week in January. And she was trouble from the beginning.'

'Trouble?'

'Noisy. Playing on the piano morning, noon and night. Gentlemen callers. Although I ain't sure it's all that gentlemanly to come a-calling on single ladies after nightfall.'

'Gentlemen in the plural?'

'Well, two at least.'

'What did the gentlemen look like?'

'Gentlemen. Dressed in the kind of suits you don't see round here too often. One of them, the one that come visiting several times, he had a round, red face like a big, silly baby.'

Mrs Threave, it was clear, didn't have much time for gentlemen of any description but, Adam noted, she must have been talking about the plump and clean-shaven Harry Vernon.

'What about the other one?'

The landlady shrugged. 'Thinner,' she said. 'Taller as well. Bearded. I only saw him the once. It was babyface who was round all the time.'

It could have been anyone, Adam thought. Probably a stage-door admirer she had invited to visit her. 'Perhaps I could be allowed to look around the rooms before you re-let them?'

'You ain't planning to take 'em yourself, I suppose?' The note of sarcasm in Mrs Threave's voice suggested that she was under no illusion that her lodgings might appeal to Adam.

'Alas, no. I have no need of accommodation at present.'

'Well, if you ain't wanting 'em, you ain't looking at 'em.'

'Suppose I was to advance another half a crown towards paying off the arrears in rent Miss Gallant has so thoughtlessly accumulated?' Adam reached into his jacket pocket and extracted another silver coin. He held it up to the sunlight. Mrs Threave moved towards it like a compass point heading northwards. 'Would that make a difference to your thoughts on the matter?'

'I reckon it might.'

The young man flicked the coin in the air. The landlady shot out a hand and neatly snatched it before it had travelled more than a few inches. She thrust the half-crown deep into the folds of the large apron she was wearing. 'Look all you like,' she said, standing aside and waving towards the dark interior of the basement lodgings.

Adam raised his hat again and stepped into the room. Mrs Threave followed him, treading close on his heels. The prints of the royal couple and the grazing sheep, which he had noted on his previous visit, were still there. The young man's eyes were now drawn to the mantelpiece where two china figures stood. One was recognizably an elephant. The other was less recognizably the Duke of Wellington.

'That's Jumbo,' Mrs Threave explained, still standing at his elbow. 'Me and the old man went to see him. At the zoo.'

Adam took another few steps into the room and so did the landlady. He could feel her presence behind him and her eyes boring into his back. He turned to confront her. She glared at him, a Gorgon in a cotton apron. 'I was rather hoping, ma'am,' he said as politely as he could, 'that my last half a crown would buy me a little privacy.'

Mrs Threave glared suspiciously at Adam before swivelling on her heel without another word and leaving. He could hear her climbing the steps out of the area yard and then calling for the girl Nan.

Adam began to move about the room. He was unsure for what he was searching; he didn't even know that there was anything to find. Although it was a bright morning, little light seemed to filter down into the basement. A brass oil lamp was sitting on a table and Adam lit it. It flickered as if its fuel was running low but its flame was strong enough to illuminate the darker corners of the room.

At first glance, the place seemed almost exactly as he remembered it from his visit a few weeks earlier. Either Hetty had left in a hurry, leaving her possessions behind her, or she had had none to leave and the furniture and ornaments, like Jumbo the elephant, all belonged to Mrs Threave. The piano was there as before. But surely the piano had been Hetty's, Adam thought. He had just heard the landlady's complaints about it being played, so she would scarcely have provided her tenant with the instrument herself. But why would Hetty leave it behind? A piano, even one as dilapidated as this one was, was an expensive purchase for a young woman of irregular income. If Mrs Threave was concerned about rent money Hetty owed her, she need only sell it and she would cover the debt several times over.

Adam lifted the lid and tapped out a short melody on the keyboard. There was still a pile of sheet music on the piano stool, he noticed. He picked up the song on the top. '"Walking in the Zoo",' he read. '"As Sung with Distinguished Applause by the Great Vance".' The picture on the front of the song-sheet showed a frock-coated and moustachioed gentleman sauntering past a row of cages in the Zoological Gardens. Behind him, another man, presumably a keeper, was poking a large steak in the general direction of a sad-looking lion imprisoned in one of them.

As Adam looked at the coloured lithograph, a piece of paper fell from the song-sheet and fluttered to the floor. He thought at first that it was one of the pages of music but, bending to pick it up, he realized that it was something else. It was a page torn from a notebook. Fine quality paper, he noticed, rather to his surprise. At the top was a date. Yesterday's date. Underneath a time of day was written on it in a rather delicate hand: a quarter after seven. This was followed by a capital P and another number, this time 3. He turned the page over. There was nothing on the other side. Adam looked again at the writing. What, he wondered, could it mean? A rendezvous time, perhaps? He peered more closely at the figure seven of the noted time. It was written in the European style with a bar through the upright of the number. He pocketed the note and continued his search, but found nothing else that shed any light on the girl's whereabouts.

After ten minutes, Adam left the rooms, shutting the door behind him. He climbed the steps to the street level and looked up. Mrs Threave was standing at the upstairs window and watched him as he turned and made his way towards King's Cross.

CHAPTER TWENTY-FOUR

'There is a man watching us.'

'Don't be so bleedin' silly, Harry. 'Oo'd be watchin' us, fer Gawd's sake?'

'That man over there. By the Smith's kiosk.' Harry Vernon was shifting from foot to foot with anxiety.

Hetty Gallant turned to look across the crowded station concourse towards the bookstall.

'Don't let him see that we have noticed him.'

'If you mean the bloke as was reading the paper, he's bought it and gone orf to catch 'is train. There ain't nobody watching us.'

Vernon allowed himself to peer gingerly in the direction of the kiosk. To his relief there was no one in front of it save two schoolboys from Christ's Hospital in their distinctive blue coats, knee breeches and yellow socks. 'Well, perhaps I was mistaken,' he conceded.

''Course you was.'

'I was certain that it was a man from the FO.'

'From your office? Don't the buggers ever let you go on 'oliday? They ain't always got to keep an eye on you, 'ave they?'

'No, of course not.' Vernon took off his hat and ran his hand through what little remained of his hair. His face was red and he was perspiring freely. 'But I am not, strictly speaking, "on holiday", as you put it. My friends in the FO are unaware of our excursion to the Continent.'

'So, we're on the scoot, are we?' Hetty laughed and put her arm through her companion's. 'We'd better 'ave some fun and frolics, then. Where're we going? We going to Paris? I've always fancied going to Paris.'

The girl continued to chatter cheerfully as, arm in arm, she and Harry Vernon were carried along by the throng of passengers making their way to the boat train. Vernon said nothing but kept twisting his neck to look behind them, as if still half convinced that someone would be following. Suddenly, he came to a halt. A gentleman in a black frock coat walking a few steps to his rear nearly collided with him. Muttering imprecations under his breath, the gentleman sidestepped and moved on. Vernon remained rooted to the spot, the crowds flowing around him like water around a rock.

'What is it, 'Arry?' Hetty Gallant tugged at her companion's sleeve. 'What the 'ell's the matter?'

'My bag!' Vernon was distraught, looking frantically about him. 'Someone's stolen my bag!'

'What bleedin' bag? Ain't the bags all gone to the luggage van? You paid that porter to take 'em twenty minutes back.'

'No, my brown leather case! I had it with me a few moments ago. Now it's gone.' Vernon was in a state of near panic, so vociferously distressed that other travellers were beginning to stare at him as they passed.

'You 'ad it when you was worriting about the cove with the paper.' Hetty spoke gently, as if to a child. 'You must've put it down and left it there.'

'Oh, my God, my God! We must go back at once and find it.' Vernon was close to hysteria, and more and more people were taking notice of his agitated behaviour.

'For Gawd's sake, 'Arry. Stop making such a bleedin' 'ullaballoo. We'll go back and get it.'

'Is this yours, sir?' A uniformed porter emerged from the crowd, holding out the missing case. 'I thought I saw you leave it behind when you and the lady was chatting together back there.'

With an inarticulate cry of joy, Vernon seized the leather case. 'Thank the Lord!' he said. 'Thank the Lord! I thought it was gone.' He now seemed as overwhelmed by relief as he had previously been plunged into despair. It was left to Hetty to find a sixpence from her own bag and press it into the hand of the porter, who touched his finger to his forehead and left. Passers-by were still staring curiously at them. Vernon was clutching the case to his chest like a mother holding a child rescued from a blazing building. He was making odd, gulping noises, as if he might be about to burst into floods of tears.

'What the 'ell you got in there, 'Arry? The Crown bloody Jewels?'

Vernon shook his head, still unable, it seemed, to speak. 'Papers,' he gasped eventually. 'Important papers.'

'Important? They must be. You was dancing around like you'd eaten a live chicken.' Hetty looked at her companion with concern. 'You feelin' better now?'

Vernon nodded.

'You certain sure about that?'

'Yes, I am recovered.' Vernon made a noticeable effort to regain the self-control he had lost. 'I must apologize, my dear, for my outburst. My work has been a burden to me of late. My nerves are not what they should be. But, as I say, I am now myself again.'

Hetty looked at him as if she was uncertain whether or not to believe him. 'Well,' she said with slightly forced jollity, 'we'd best be off.'

After presenting their tickets to a guard positioned at the gate leading to the platform, Harry Vernon and Hetty Gallant made their way to the train for the Continent.

* * * * *

'Harry Vernon has disappeared.'

Adam had returned from his visit to Mrs Threave to find that he had been summoned once again to the Honourable Richard Sunman's room at the Foreign Office.

'Disappeared?'

'He has not been here for three days. His wife has not seen him since Saturday.' Sunman was striving hard to maintain his sangfroid, but it was only too clear that he was agitated. He could not sit still and his fingers drummed on the baize of the desk. 'If only I could speak to Waterton.'

'He is not in town?'

'He has taken leave and is travelling in Switzerland, I believe. This business with Harry has upset him greatly.'

Judging by his appearance, it had also upset Sunman.

'Actually, I think I may be able to throw some light on Vernon's recent whereabouts,' Adam said. He held out the torn page from the notebook which he had found in the basement rooms near Waterloo.

Sunman reached out a slim, white hand to take it. He glanced briefly at the writing on it and then put the paper on the desk. 'A time of day,' he said, clearly unimpressed. 'How the devil does this help us to locate Harry?'

'I'm fairly certain Vernon wrote it.'

Sunman snatched up the paper once more and peered closely at it. 'By Jove, I think you're right. The seven is in the German style he used.' He looked across at Adam, puzzlement in his eyes. 'But how could you recognize Harry's handwriting?'

'I have seen a document he wrote. You gave it to me. Do you not remember?'

'Of course.' Sunman sighed. 'I had forgotten. With all the worry of this business, I sometimes think I am losing my mind.'

'The document included numerals. I noticed at the time that he put a small horizontal line through the upright stroke of a seven. It struck me as unusual. Not many Englishmen do, but it is common in Europe.' Adam stared up at the ersatz rococo plastering on the ceiling. 'Does he have connections on the Continent? I think the time might refer to the departure of the boat train. In fact, I am sure of it. I have looked at Bradshaw's Continental. And the P followed by a three indicates the platform from which it departs.'

'Harry's mother was German. He was born in Berlin. He has hordes of cousins scattered across Prussia.' Sunman was still looking at the page from the notebook. 'Where did you get this?'

'I found it tucked away in the pages of a song-sheet. In the room of a girl calling herself Hetty Gallant.' Adam, still gazing upwards, paused briefly. 'I believe her real name is Dolly Delaney.'

There was sudden silence in the room. Adam looked across the table. He was, he realized, rather enjoying the revelation of what he now knew or strongly suspected.

His friend, sitting behind his desk, looked stunned. His face was pale and he held one hand to his head like a barrister checking his wig was still in place.

'Have you lost your senses?' Sunman said eventually. 'The Delaney girl is dead. You found her body yourself.'

'No, Dolly is very much alive. The girl in York was someone else. Probably the real Hetty Gallant. I think the two girls exchanged identities some time before they were both employed at the theatre.'

'But why should they do so?' Sunman stared again at the paper with the train time on it, as if it might offer a solution to the mystery. 'And what of Harry? Did he not even know the true name of his own mistress?'

'Oh, I am pretty sure he did. I think he was even instrumental in persuading Hetty to call herself Dolly and vice versa.'

'But why, Adam?' Sunman sounded plaintive, as if the swapping of names had been an elaborate charade designed solely to make a fool of him. 'In God's name, why?'

'I cannot be certain. Although I do have my suspicions. Whatever happened, I do not think it looks very promising for Harry.'

'No, it does not.' The young aristocrat had dropped the page from the notebook. 'It most certainly does not.'

Adam watched his friend, and was once again half-guiltily aware that he was relishing his discomfiture. 'There is yet more to this, Sunman, is there not? This is nothing to do with compromising letters. There is something major that you are not telling me.'

The baron's son, whose air of effortless superiority had long-since deserted him when he spoke on the subject of Harry Vernon, threw his hands in the air. 'Oh, very well, Adam, you may as well know everything. Any letters Harry may or may not have written to his doxy now fade into insignificance.'

'And yet you told me that they were of signal importance. "The future direction of our foreign policy rests on the recovery of those letters." Those, I think, were your exact words.'

'Oh, God, Adam, I no longer know.' Sunman rested his head in his hands. 'I was basing my remarks on what Harry had told me was in the letters. But I now find that he has been lying to me from the beginning. Perhaps there never *were* any letters. But this time there can be no doubt of the trouble we face.' He paused. 'Harry has disappeared and he has taken documents with him.'

'Documents?'

There was another pause as Sunman raised his head from his hands and stared miserably at Adam. 'They are plans – naval plans.'

'And they are of great importance?'

Sunman nodded.

'What plans are they?'

At first Adam thought that his friend had not heard him. He was about to speak again when Sunman looked up and said, 'A submarine. They are plans for a submarine.'

'An underwater craft?'

'Precisely. There have been various attempts in the last ten years to create a craft that can travel beneath the waters under its own power. The Americans on both sides in the recent conflict tried to do so. So have the French. The results have not been encouraging.'

'But we have been successful where the French and the Americans have failed?'

Sunman did not answer Adam's question. Indeed, his next remark seemed at first to have strayed from the subject in hand: 'I do not suppose that you have heard of a gentleman named Narcís Monturiol?' he asked.

'I cannot say that I have.'

'There is no reason why you should have done. He is a Spaniard. Resident, I believe, in Barcelona. Six years ago, he built a craft which he named the *Ictineo*.'

'From the Greek word for "fish", I presume.'

Sunman nodded. 'Yes,' he said, 'combined with some strange,

Spanish version of "*naus*" for boat.'

'And his fish-boat was a success?'

'Up to a point.'

'What point?'

The baronet's son sighed, as if he could barely contemplate continuing the conversation, raising a hand to his brow like a man suffering from a hangover. 'I do not pretend to understand these matters, Adam,' he said. 'Our education in Homer and Horace scarcely prepared us to fathom the miracles of modern science. Suffice it to say that the Spaniard's craft was still not fully seaworthy.'

'But we now have the plans for a submarine that is? Is that what you are saying?'

Sunman held out his hand, now a parent soothing a fretful child. 'I am about to tell you, Adam,' he said. 'Happily for us, Señor Monturiol is something of an Anglophile. He was more than willing to entertain an English engineer we sent to his homeland to engage him in long conversations about his craft. The details of what was discussed are beyond the comprehension of those of us who are not engineers. However, our man returned from Barcelona with new insights into the problems facing him. He set about creating blueprints for a vessel which, unlike all such previous vessels, would actually work. Harry was the man here in the FO who was given the task of liaising with the engineer and with senior officers in the navy. He was one of a handful of people in the country who had access to the plans. And now he has vanished, and so have the plans from his office.'

'How inconvenient.'

'*Inconvenient?*' Sunman snapped. 'If these plans get into the wrong hands, the consequences will be far more than "inconvenient".'

'And German hands are the wrong hands?'

'Very much so. Any hands other than British ones are wrong hands at present.' Sunman had adopted the manner of a schoolmaster instructing one of his dimmer pupils. 'Think of it, Adam. Prussia has just defeated France and her King Wilhelm has become the emperor of the unified German states. Everything now changes in Europe and the very last thing we want is for such, ah' – Sunman paused for the briefest instant – 'such *sensitive* plans to go astray. If there are to be craft developed capable of remaining underwater and eluding detection, then they must be British boats, not German. Or, indeed, French.'

Adam thought himself at least reasonably acquainted with recent events on the Continent and he was content to accept Sunman's analysis. 'In that case,' he suggested, 'you must inform someone else of what has happened. Granville himself, perhaps.'

The name of the Foreign Secretary made Sunman blanch. 'I cannot involve my superiors at this late stage,' he said. 'How the devil am I to break the news to them that Harry has, in all likelihood, fled the country and intends to sell our secrets to the Prussians? No, we must bring the matter to a conclusion ourselves.'

'We?'

'You and I. I will authorize funds to be advanced to you so that you may travel to Berlin. He has clearly gone there, and he must be found.'

Adam understood that it was now not only Harry Vernon's career that was at stake. The future reputation and career of the Honourable Richard Sunman were also at risk.

'I will telegraph a friend at the embassy there,' Sunman continued. 'His name is George Etherege. He will help you.'

'What will you tell him about me? And about my interest in Harry Vernon? You cannot vouchsafe to him the real reasons for my visit.'

'No, of course not.' The Foreign Office man spoke impatiently, as if Adam was being deliberately foolish and obstructive. 'I shall concoct some story to explain your desire to find Vernon. But you must waste no time. Go and pack your bags for Berlin.'

PART FOUR

BERLIN

CHAPTER TWENTY-FIVE

A dam sauntered into the room the hotel had given to Quint. It was darker and much more cramped than the one he was occupying himself. The two men had travelled across the Channel to Calais by steamer the previous day and then on to Paris by train. In the French capital they had changed trains and made their way to Berlin. They had registered at the Deutscher Hof as man and servant and been shown to their rooms. Adam's was on the first floor and looked out over the tree-lined boulevard known as Unter den Linden. Quint's was in the rear of the basement and looked out over a stable yard.

'There's a strong scent of horse in here,' Adam remarked, as he pushed back the faded curtain which hung crookedly across the room's one window. He peered out. 'Ah, that would explain it – I thought, for one terrible moment, it might be you, Quint. The hotel management does not seem to have given you the most comfortable of berths.'

'I've slept in worse dosses,' Quint said shortly.

'So have we both. In Turkish Greece we dreamed of accommodation such as this.' Adam let the curtain fall and turned back to the room. He began to prowl restlessly around it, picking up objects at random and examining them. A small round pot was sitting on the dressing table, its lid beside it. Adam sniffed at its contents. 'Bear's grease?' he said. 'What do you need bear's grease for, Quint? Your thatch has almost disappeared. You've been balding as long as I've known you.'

Quint looked almost sheepish. He grabbed the pot from Adam's hand and replaced it on the table. 'Well, I got Bayley's Bear's Grease to thank that I've still got *some* left, then, ain't I?'

Adam held out his hands, palm outwards, in a placatory gesture. 'I had no intention of giving offence, Quint,' he said. 'Apply what unguents you like to whatever part of your anatomy you wish. We have other matters to consider. The purpose of our visit to Berlin for one.'

'This toff that's legged it, you mean?' The manservant opened a drawer in the dressing table and pushed the pot of bear's grease into it. ''E's a pretty poor article, ain't 'e? Lettin' 'isself get bled by a dollymop? Then scarperin' when word gets out.'

'That may not be exactly what has happened. It seems that the gentleman in question – Mr Harry Vernon – may have been looking one way and rowing another,' Adam said.

Quint closed the drawer and considered this for a moment. 'You mean, 'e's not so green as 'e says? 'E's fooled ev'rybody?'

Adam nodded. 'He's been pretending to be the victim in the whole affair . . .'

'But 'e's been pulling everybody's strings?'

'Precisely.' Adam rubbed his chin, as if checking on the effectiveness of his last shave. 'There was something curiously theatrical about his extravagant expressions of regret on the one occasion that I met him. He sounded much more like Alfred Skeffington pretending to be a remorseful man than he did a man who was genuinely full of remorse.'

* * * * *

The Honourable Richard Sunman's friend at the British Embassy had left his card at the hotel that morning and, after an appropriate interval, had followed it with a message that Mr George Calverley Etherege hoped to meet Mr Adam Carver in the Café Beethoven on Friedrichstrasse at 4 p.m.

Adam had wondered how he was to recognize his guide to the city, but one glance at the man who entered the main door of the café on the stroke of four o'clock was enough to dispel any concern.

With his perfectly tailored suit, silk waistcoat and top hat, George Calverley Etherege could have been nothing but what he was. To complete the picture of the upper middle-class Englishman, he even had a copy of *The Times* tucked under his arm.

'Last week's, I'm sorry to say,' he said as he sat down, noticing Adam's glance at the newspaper. 'Nothing you won't have read back in London. I thought it might assist in our recognizing one another.' He removed his gloves and reached across the café table to shake hands. 'My name, as I'm sure you've surmised, is Etherege. Welcome to Berlin. Your first visit, I believe?'

'It is. I have long wished to travel here but I have not found the opportunity to do so until now.'

'You could not have chosen a more auspicious time to arrive in the city,' the diplomat said, waving his arm negligently in the direction of one of the white-aproned waiters. '1871 has so far been an extraordinary year for the Prussians. And for Germans in general. They now have an emperor, as I'm sure you know.'

The waiter approached the table and stood by it, bowing as he did so.

'What will you have, Carver?'

'Oh, coffee will be sufficient. Without milk.'

'*Zwei Tassen Kaffee, bitte. Schwarz.*'

The waiter, nodding his head repeatedly, left them.

'In other circumstances, I would relish the prospect of witnessing the birth of a new Germany,' Adam said. 'But, as Sunman must have told you, I have a very particular reason for coming here to Berlin.'

'Ah, yes, the friend who has gone missing. The friend with family connections with the city.'

'Have you learned anything about Vernon?' Adam asked.

'A little, but I am not certain that what we have learned will be of any value to you. *Nihil ad rem*, as the lawyers might say.'

'Perhaps you should allow me to be the judge of whether or not your information is of relevance to the affair.' Adam smiled, hoping to remove any hint of impoliteness from his remark.

'Ah, the affair.' Etherege returned the smile. 'And just what is the affair? That is a question which I cannot help but ask myself. Sunman told me of your visit, but he was a little unforthcoming about the reasons behind it. And behind your interest in Harry Vernon.'

The return of the deferential waiter with their coffee allowed Adam a moment before he needed to answer. He wondered how much, if anything to tell, the elegant man from the embassy. Sunman had trusted the man enough to enlist his aid but had advised caution in revealing too much of his mission: 'The less Etherege or anyone knows, Adam, the better.'

'Vernon is an old friend. As you know, he works at the FO. He has been subject to severe pressure of late. His closest colleagues, Sunman among them, have grown concerned about his state of mind.'

'He is suffering from neurasthenia?'

'I would not go as far as to call it that, but he has become a little erratic, shall we say, in recent months.'

'Erratic enough to disappear from London without trace.'

'Not entirely without trace.' Adam tasted his coffee. It was strong and bitter. 'There were signs that he had taken the boat train to the Continent. We assumed that he would come here, where he has connections.'

'You were correct in your assumptions. He has indeed arrived in Berlin. After Sunman telegraphed me, I sent a man to the Potsdamer Bahnhof to watch for Vernon.'

'And he turned up?'

'On the train from Paris. With a young woman. Our chap followed them for a while.'

'So you know where they are?' Adam could scarcely believe his luck.

'Alas, no.' Etherege looked mildly embarrassed, as if he had been caught out in some insignificant but undoubted faux pas. 'Vernon gave our chap the slip. He lost them near the Gendarmenmarkt.'

'Harry realized he was being followed?'

'Probably. Although it is a busy area of the city. Our chap may simply have lost sight of the cab in which he and his companion were travelling.'

Adam sighed. 'So we have no notion of where Harry is. He could be anywhere.'

'*Nil desperandum*, old chap. I've told the man who lost him to damn well find him again.'

'In a city the size of Berlin?'

'There is a limit to the number of places he could be. He is a gentleman, is he not?' Etherege picked up his coffee cup and peered at it as if fearing it had been somehow contaminated in the journey from the bar to their table. 'He will not be lodging with some working man's family in Moabit or patronizing some low haunt in Wedding. He will be in a hotel within a stone's throw of Unter den Linden, I'll warrant.' He set down his cup without drinking from it. 'And there are other means of tracing his whereabouts than simply traipsing the streets of the city.'

'There are?'

'But of course. One can ask discreet questions in the right places.'

'I am far from certain that I know where the right places are in Berlin.'

'Ah, but you have the inestimable advantage of my local knowledge upon which to draw.' Adam looked at the man from the embassy, who was now smiling ironically, all trace of his earlier embarrassment gone. 'You must come to Frau Kestelmann's tomorrow evening,' Etherege said with the air of a man bringing a long debate to its conclusion. 'If your friend Vernon is still in Berlin, one of her guests will know of it.'

'Frau Kestelmann's?'

'A lady of much charm and intelligence. Her origins are a trifle mysterious, although rumour has it that she was once an actress in Munich. She came to Berlin in the aftermath of the '48 revolutions. Somehow she has manoeuvred herself into a position of great influence in the city's society.' The diplomat smiled again, as if in enjoyment of a private joke. 'Nobody quite knows how. Her Thursday evening gatherings are attended by all the best and the brightest in Berlin. One would almost say that she presides over a *salon* if the word were not so damnably French.'

'And you can contrive to get me an invitation?'

'Oh, the lady is quite the Anglophile. There will be no difficulty. Sunman mentioned your literary success to me. I will tell her that you are a writer whose book on his travels in European Turkey was the sensation of the season in London. She will be falling over herself to meet you. And I will not be stretching the truth by too much.'

Adam laughed. 'I think perhaps you will,' he said. 'My Macedonia book has not been much talked about in the last few years. And, if I believe my publisher, it has long since ceased to sell.'

Etherege waved his hand briefly, dismissing the young man's remarks. He picked up his cup again and this time sipped the strong coffee. 'A little exaggeration will do no harm,' he said.

* * * * *

Arthur Bury looked across the Alexanderplatz. He had located his quarry once more. His superior, Mr Etherege, would be pleased, just as he had definitely not been pleased when Arthur had been obliged to report that the man and woman he had followed from the Potsdamer Bahnhof had disappeared. He had told Arthur in no uncertain terms that they must be found again and found quickly. The young British embassy official had set about doing so immediately. It was not the kind of work he had expected to be undertaking on his first posting abroad, but he was eager to please.

He had trailed around the most expensive hotels on Unter den Linden, asking questions of porters and describing Harry Vernon and his companion to bellboys. Eventually, at one of the hotels closest to the Brandenburger Tor, he had struck lucky. A doorman named Karl, dressed in a uniform more resplendent than that worn by any member of the new emperor's army, remembered them. They had booked into the Deutscher Hof the previous day, although not under the name of Vernon. No, they were not in the hotel now. The lady – if, indeed, she was a lady, and Karl was not at all sure she was – had gone shopping. The gentleman had left separately. Arthur had missed him by no more than five minutes. However, by a stroke of good fortune, Karl had heard what instructions that same gentleman had given to the cab that had picked him up outside the hotel. For the payment of a small gratuity, the doorman was prepared to share the information he had overheard. Vernon had told the cabman to take him to the Alexanderplatz. After thanking Karl in his not entirely correct German, Arthur had hailed another cab outside the Deutscher Hof and headed off down Unter den Linden.

When he had arrived at the Alexanderplatz and paid off his driver, Arthur had had another piece of luck. The square was as busy as it always was, thronged with people and horses and carriages; on one side, a troop of soldiers was marching through Alexanderplatz towards the red tower and frontage of the recently built city hall, the Rotes Rathaus. Arthur's eyes had been drawn to the marching men – and he had immediately noticed his quarry standing on the pavement to their left. He had been no more than fifty yards away from him.

Vernon was not watching the soldiers, but nor was he looking in Arthur's direction. He had been staring up at the sign of a *Photographisches Atelier*, his hat in his right hand as he brushed his left through his thinning hair.

And now, even as the soldiers moved into the distance and out of the square, Vernon still continued to gaze vacantly at the sign.

Just as Arthur was beginning to think that his fellow Englishman must have decided, for unfathomable reasons of his own, to have his photograph taken, he was approached by another man. This man was most definitely German. He was tall and thin and had, Arthur thought, the air of a man accustomed to the exercise of authority. The newcomer raised his hat to Vernon, who waved his own, still held in his hand, in a vague greeting. The two men moved away from the entrance to the photographic studios, the German's hand in the small of the Englishman's back as if he was guiding him in the direction he wished him to go. It was he who was doing most of the talking, although Vernon made the occasional remark and, at one point, seemed to be gesturing in the direction the soldiers had just disappeared.

Arthur decided that he needed to be close enough to hear what was being said. He set off along the pavement, eyes fixed on the two men, and almost immediately careered into a large gentleman in black, who turned furiously to confront him. '*Entschuldigen sie mich*,' Arthur said, raising his hat and stepping swiftly to one side. He quickened his pace, leaving the large gentleman behind. For a moment, he thought he had lost sight of those he was following, but he spotted them again approaching the corner of the square where it joined Spandauer Strasse.

As they reached it, the distinguished-looking German raised his arm in what Arthur initially thought was some kind of salute. Seconds later, he realized his mistake. A barouche drawn by two elegant greys detached itself from a group of carriages on the far side of the street and made its way towards them. The man had been beckoning it to him. The driver of the barouche dismounted and opened its door. The German stood back and indicated that his companion should climb into the carriage. Vernon hesitated briefly and then did so. The German followed him, speaking briefly to the driver, who climbed back to his seat, flicked his whip in the air above the horses' heads and guided the barouche into the traffic.

Arthur, who had broken into a run when he saw what was happening, arrived at the pavement edge just in time to watch the vehicle disappearing into the distance. 'Damn, damn, *damn*,' he muttered to himself. He sighed deeply and wondered what he should do. He had lost the man Vernon again. Mr Etherege would be furious.

CHAPTER TWENTY-SIX

rau Kestelmann owned a large and imposing villa on the edge of the Tiergarten. After presenting their cards, Adam and Etherege were ushered into a room on the first floor which seemed to have been transported into modern Berlin from the previous century. Sweeping scrolls and curlicues of stucco decorated its walls and ceiling; paintings of classical ruins hung either side of the door through which they had entered, and a full-length portrait of a bewigged gentleman in court dress could be glimpsed at the far end of the room. Meissen porcelain stood on a series of occasional tables placed at regular intervals around the walls. On one, Adam noticed figurines of characters from the *commedia dell'arte* – Arlecchino, Pantalone, Colombina – arranged in a richly coloured dance; on another was a vast bowl with porcelain putti perched uncomfortably on its perimeter as if about to dive into the depths of whatever liquid it might hold. There was, however, no chance to admire more of the room's decoration as their hostess was gliding across an elaborately patterned Persian carpet to greet them.

'Ah, you must be the English traveller whose praises Mr Etherege sang,' she said, holding out a white-gloved hand for Adam to take. Like her salon, Frau Kestelmann looked to be a refugee from a more elegant world than the workaday Berlin in which her visitors lived. She spoke English as if it were her native language but one which she had nonetheless decided, for obscure reasons of her own, to pronounce with a thick, Teutonic accent. 'Welcome to my home. I have asked my bookseller to despatch *Travels in Ancient Macedon* to me. It sounds perfectly fascinating. I must read it as soon as I possibly can.'

'I hope your bookseller will be able to locate a copy of it, Frau Kestelmann. It has become almost as rare as a Shakespeare First Folio.'

'Oh, he will find it,' she said with careless confidence. 'I have paid him to do so. But, come, you are a stranger here in Berlin. I must introduce you to some of my other guests.'

Frau Kestelmann took Adam by the arm and swept him past Etherege into the middle of the room. It was already filled with people in groups of three and four, sipping drinks and conversing in the exaggeratedly bright voices peculiar to such gatherings. For the next twenty minutes Adam was paraded around the party by his hostess like a racehorse led through the paddock before the start of the Derby. He shook hands and exchanged pleasantries with several dozen people whose names, dutifully delivered to him by Frau Kestelmann, he knew he would not remember the following morning. A general, festooned with medals, was eager to hear Adam's opinion of recent events in Paris, of his own army's siege of the city and the chaos which apparently reigned now the French had been left to their own devices. The general's wife wished to know what ladies in London were wearing that season – Adam was hard-pressed to formulate an answer. An author who had, Adam was informed, written a novel about marital infidelity in Brandenburg that was much admired, took his hand and scowled ferociously at him. After lecturing him briefly on the merits and demerits of modern European fiction, he stalked off, demonstrating every indication of being mortally offended, although quite why, Adam had not the slightest idea. Before he had any time to ponder greatly on the novelist's rudeness, Frau Kestelmann led him briskly on to his next encounter – this one with a jolly, moustachioed man who had, according to his hostess, once been Prussia's minister of justice.

It was all thoroughly exhausting and Adam was delighted when the social carousel finally ceased to swirl so rapidly around him and he was left alone. Frau Kestelmann had deserted him, floating away to envelop another guest in her overpowering social embrace. He was able to stand and contemplate the huge portrait he had seen when he had first entered. Who was its subject? he wondered. A prince or a duke, perhaps? The Germans of the last century had had so many. His speculations were soon interrupted.

'Carver, may I present the Graf von Ravelstein.' Etherege appeared suddenly at Adam's shoulder, accompanied by a tall, ramrod-backed man in his fifties. The newcomer's hawk-like face was marked by a duelling scar on his left cheek. Clearly, in his youth, he had been a member of one of the student fencing societies in which such a scar was a badge of honour. 'Ravelstein, this is a countryman of mine, Mr Adam Carver.'

The German inclined his head in acknowledgement but made no attempt to shake hands. Adam, who had been preparing to do just that, was obliged to change his mind and bow slightly in response.

'I have heard of Mr Carver, of course,' Ravelstein said. 'He is the gentleman who travelled in Macedonia and Thessaly and wrote of his most interesting experiences there. It is a pity that his book has not been translated. He would have many readers here in Berlin and in the new Germany.'

The *Graf* spoke fluent English and, unlike Frau Kestelmann, with only the faintest hint of an accent.

'Perhaps you could recommend a Berlin publisher to our young friend,' Etherege suggested, a hint of mischief in his voice.

'*Ach*, publishers,' the count said, 'they are a villainous crew. I know nothing of them. But I am surprised Herr Brauer was unable to assist you.'

'Herr Brauer?' Adam was puzzled.

'The writer with whom you were conversing. The gentleman who invents adulteries among the Brandenburger bourgeoisie.' Ravelstein's contempt for the ill-tempered novelist could not have been clearer.

'We did not find the opportunity to talk of publishers,' Adam said.

'Of course not. I do not believe that you can have come all the way from London and taken up residence in the Deutscher Hof to exchange the gossip of authors with that fellow.'

'No, indeed. I had not met him before today.'

'But then, I think to myself, why *has* Mr Carver arrived in our city? Does he have some particular purpose in mind?'

'I am here only to see the new Germany of which you spoke a moment ago.'

The count nodded several times, as if pondering an exceptionally difficult philosophical problem, and then stroked the scar on his face. 'And Mr Etherege here is to be your guide. Does he, I wonder, perform that service for all Britons who travel to Berlin? Surely not.'

Adam had no immediate reply and was still trying to formulate one when Etherege himself came to his rescue. 'I knew Mr Carver's father many years ago. It seemed but an act of politeness to offer to show his son around the city in which I have made my home for the last ten years.'

'So you were a familiar of the late railway builder.' Ravelstein turned his eyes to the diplomat and then back to Adam, like a fox trying to decide which of the chickens in the roost was the plumpest. He seemed briefly inclined to pursue the topic but changed his mind. 'Mr Carver, it has been a great pleasure to meet you,' he said abruptly, 'but I see my old friend General von Friedberg is in the room and I must hurry to speak to him. You English gentlemen will, I am sure, excuse me.' The count clicked his heels together and, with another slight inclination of his head, left them.

'Who exactly is that man?' Adam asked.

'Ravelstein?' Etherege took his companion's elbow and guided him towards a corner of the room where there was no one to overhear them. 'He is a puzzle, is he not?'

'He seems remarkably well informed. He knew I've been staying at the Deutscher Hof. He knew my father's profession.' Adam smiled. 'Damn it, he knew of *Travels in Ancient Macedon*. And even its author has almost forgotten that particular volume.'

'Ravelstein makes it his business to be well informed.'

'But who is he?'

'He has no official position in the new German government.' The diplomat nodded briefly at two gentlemen in military uniform who passed by, and watched as other guests drifted towards them. Once again he steered his companion away from the crowds. 'However, he has one inestimable advantage over many who do have such positions.'

'And that is?'

'He has the trust of Otto von Bismarck. He has known the chancellor for nearly forty years. Since they were both law students at Göttingen.'

'So Ravelstein is a lawyer?'

Etherege laughed. 'As much, or should I say as little, of one as Bismarck. Ravelstein is a keeper of secrets.'

Adam turned to look at his companion. 'What kind of secrets?' he asked.

'Oh, all kinds. His work is very familiar to us at the embassy.'

'He is a clandestine agent for Bismarck's government?'

Etherege raised his fingers briefly to his lips. 'We do not like to advertise our knowledge of the fact. But, yes, that is as good a description of his position as any.'

The two men had reached the long windows at one end of the room, which opened onto a terrace. They stood there, looking out at the late afternoon light. Etherege rested his hand briefly on Adam's arm. 'There is something else about the *Graf* that perhaps you should know,' he said.

Adam raised his eyebrows enquiringly.

'When Bismarck and Ravelstein were young men together in Göttingen, they were also friendly with two foreigners who had come to Germany to study.' Here, Etherege smiled briefly, opened the door onto the terrace and stepped outside. Adam followed him. The diplomat clearly had something more to say but, equally clearly, he was determined to say it in his own way and his own time. 'One of them was Motley, the American historian. You will have heard of him, of course. He was ambassador to the Court of St James's and was recalled suddenly at the end of last year. You will remember the story from the newspapers—? Perhaps you have even read his work. It takes the history of the Dutch Republic as its subject, I believe.'

'And the other?'

Etherege paused for effect. There was no doubt that he was enjoying the slow revelation of his information. 'His name was Vernon,' he said eventually. 'James Henry Vernon.'

'Harry Vernon's father?'

'The very same.'

'That *is* interesting.'

'I thought you would find it so. What is even more interesting is that one of my informants tells me that your Mr Vernon met with another man, a German, in the Alexanderplatz this afternoon. From the description, it was almost certainly Ravelstein.'

'And why would Ravelstein wish to meet with Harry Vernon?'

'Mr Vernon is your friend, is he not? I was rather hoping you might be able to tell me that.'

'I am as much at a loss as you are, Etherege, to answer that question.'

'Ah, well, perhaps we could both hazard a guess.' The diplomat caught Adam's eye and smiled shrewdly. 'And there is one last fact about the *Graf* that I should tell you.' They had reached the terrace's stone balustrade and were looking down on a lawn surrounded by plane trees. A man, presumably a gardener, was wheeling a barrow across it. 'He is a very ruthless man, Mr Carver, and a very dangerous one. You would be well advised to take great care in any dealings you might have with him. And now I think it is time we went back inside and took our leave of our hostess.'

CHAPTER TWENTY-SEVEN

Quint passed through the lobby of the hotel, happily unaware of the disdainful looks bestowed upon him by guests and staff alike. Servants were expected to enter their rooms via a door from the stable yard behind the building, but nobody had yet dared to tell Quint that. As he crossed the black-and-white marble floor in the direction of the stairs to the basement, he nearly collided with a young woman who was heading towards the main door onto Unter Den Linden. Both parties took a step back. Quint made a sound that might have been an apology. He looked at the woman and recognized her immediately. 'You're the judy we saw at the back of King's Cross,' he said.

'I'm the lady you was privileged to visit in 'er rooms in north London,' the young woman replied.

'We've been a-lookin' for you.'

'Well, ain't that plummy? But I ain't been looking for you. So, if you'll be so good as to shift your carcase, I'll be on my way.'

With that, the woman took a step to one side, ostentatiously adjusted the white fur stole that hung around her shoulders, and strode out of the hotel. Quint watched her go.

From the reception desk, one of the hotel's assistant managers, a timid man, watched him. He knew he should already have told this fierce manservant that the lobby was not a place for him, but, hampered by the fact that he had only a limited command of the English language, he had balked at the task. Now he screwed his courage to the sticking place and began to make his way towards Quint. '*Geehrter Herr*,' he began. 'Dear sir.' But he was too late.

Quint had abandoned any idea of descending to his own room. He needed to tell his master of his encounter. With no notion that one of the hotel's employees was waving half-heartedly in his direction, he set off at pace towards the ornate, curving staircase that led to the first floor. Behind him, the assistant manager dropped his hand and sighed.

Quint took the stairs two at a time, barrelled purposefully along the corridor and burst, unannounced, into Adam's room. 'I've just seen 'er, guv,' he said.

Adam was sitting in a chair by the window, smoking a cigarette and trying to understand what he could of the headlines in the *Norddeutsche Allgemeine Zeitung*. He looked up in surprise as his servant tumbled into the room. 'Who have you seen?'

'*Er*,' Quint repeated impatiently and with added emphasis. 'The tart we've followed from London. She's 'ere in the same 'otel.'

'Are you certain it was she?'

'She was got up to the nines but it was 'er all right.'

'We need to speak to her. Did you not stop her and engage her in conversation?'

'I couldn't, guv.' Quint gestured in annoyance. 'She was out of the 'otel in a flea's leap. I couldn't stop 'er.'

* * * * *

'My dear Etherege, I did not know that you were a visitor to Café Beethoven. I have not seen you here before.'

George Etherege was sitting at a table by the window which looked out onto the passing throng in Friedrichstrasse. He was not watching the crowds but reading a novel. A cup of black coffee was on the table in front of him. He looked up as he heard his name.

'Good morning, *Graf*,' he said. 'I could say much the same of you. I am here most mornings and I have not seen you before.' He placed a silver bookmark carefully between the pages of his novel and closed it. He put the book down close to his coffee cup.

Ravelstein picked it up and scrutinized the lettering on its spine. '*Lothair*. A novel by your prime minister, is it not?'

'Our former prime minister. Mr Disraeli was in office three years ago. Mr Gladstone is prime minister at present.'

'Ah, of course, I had forgotten.'

Etherege allowed himself a brief, inward smile at the absurd notion that Ravelstein might be unaware, even temporarily, of the identity of the current British prime minister.

'A curious occupation for a man of power,' the *Graf* went on. 'Scribbling stories for the reading public. I cannot imagine my old friend Bismarck indulging in such a pointless activity.'

Etherege smiled to himself again. 'No,' he agreed, 'it is hard to picture the Iron Chancellor as a writer of fiction.'

'He has far better things to do with his days.'

'I have no doubt he does.'

Ravelstein placed the book back on the table and beckoned to one of the white-aproned waiters. 'Would it be an imposition if I joined you?' he asked, sitting down before Etherege had a chance to indicate whether it would or would not be.

A young waiter, barely of an age to shave, appeared at Ravelstein's shoulder.

'*Einen schwarzen Kaffee, bitte.*'

'*Jawohl, Herr Graf.*' The boy scurried off as if his life depended on the speed with which he returned with the black coffee.

'I hope you will not think me impertinent, Mr Etherege—?' Ravelstein looked enquiringly at Etherege.

'I am sure I will not, *Graf.*'

'But I feel I must say something to you – warn you, perhaps – about the gentleman with whom you attended Frau Kestelmann's yesterday evening.'

'Mr Carver?'

'That is his name, I understand.'

'A delightful young man, I thought.'

'But a dangerous one.'

The waiter had already returned with Ravelstein's coffee and he set the cup down on the table in front of the *Graf*. His hand was trembling slightly and he spilled a few drops of the black liquid on the cloth. He took a quick, gulping breath and began to apologize abjectly. Picking up a napkin, he dabbed desperately at the spilt coffee.

Ravelstein waved him away. '*Es ist nichts*,' he said. '*Verschwinde*.'

Still babbling his apologies, the waiter backed off, turned and fled.

'Dangerous?' Etherege opened his eyes in feigned astonishment. 'Surely not?'

'Perhaps you do not know the gentleman's history.' Ravelstein was now staring fixedly at the small black stain on the cloth as if he intended to make it disappear by the force of his will alone. 'Perhaps you do not know that he killed a man in European Turkey.'

'I did hear stories of his adventures there. It was in self-defence, was it not? The man was a madman.'

'He was a distinguished professor of classical literature at one of your ancient universities.'

'But a madman, nonetheless. He was threatening to murder Carver. The gentleman had no choice but to shoot him.'

'That is not what I have heard.' Ravelstein lifted his eyes from the table and glared fiercely at the English diplomat. 'That delightful young man, as you call him, shot down an elderly scholar in – what is the English phrase? – in cold blood. I was shocked, very shocked when I was told of it.' Ravelstein attempted, not very successfully, to twist his face into an expression to match his words.

It was difficult to imagine what would truly shock the German spymaster. 'And yet,' Etherege said equably, 'no action was taken against Carver either in Turkey or in England, when he returned home.'

'In the new Germany, we are not so tolerant of murderers, Mr Etherege.' The *Graf* paused and tapped his fingers several times on the table. 'We are not, of course, able to prosecute an Englishman for a crime that took place in territory ruled by the Ottomans.'

'Of course not.'

'But we can discourage him from staying here in our capital.'

Etherege said nothing but smiled blandly.

'To put it simply, Mr Etherege, this man Carver is not welcome in Berlin. I would suggest, strongly suggest, that you persuade him to leave the city and return to London.' Ravelstein drank the last of his coffee and pushed his cup into the centre of the table. He stood and nodded his head in the Englishman's direction. 'Good day, Mr Etherege.'

'Good day, Graf.'

Etherege leaned back in his chair, his eyes following the tall figure of the German as he made his way through the noise and bustle of the café. At one point, Ravelstein stopped and bowed ostentatiously to two large men in black suits who were eating Berliner doughnuts as if they feared there was soon to be a shortage of them. They paused long enough in their consumption to haul themselves to their feet and return his salute.

Etherege gestured towards the teenage waiter, who approached cautiously, half an eye still on the *Graf*'s departing figure.

'*Wollen Sie noch etwas, mein Herr?*' the boy asked.

'*Nein, danke. Ich möchte jetzt bezahlen.*'

The waiter dashed off and Etherege watched as the Graf von Ravelstein pushed open the door of the Café Beethoven and stepped into the crowds passing up and down Friedrichstrasse.

* * * * *

'Who's that? Is that you, Harry?'

Adam said nothing. The voice was immediately familiar, and his heart leapt a little as he heard it. He had been both dreading and desiring the moment when he met Hetty again. Now it was here.

The door opened slightly. When Hetty recognized the identity of her visitor, the young woman attempted to slam the door shut but Adam was too quick for her: his foot prevented her from doing so.

'I am sorry to be so ungallant, Hetty, but I must insist on speaking to you.' He pushed hard against the wood and the door flew open as the girl stumbled back into the room. Adam entered and closed the door behind him. Harry Vernon had reserved a suite of rooms at the Deutscher Hof for his mistress. The one into which

Adam now walked was a sitting room, with high windows looking out onto the lime trees that gave Unter den Linden its name.

The girl had recovered her balance and moved behind a large button-back armchair. She glared at Adam.

This was not, he thought, going to be the welcome for which he had been hoping.

'Well, I ain't got no wish to speak to you. What the 'ell do you think you're playing at? Barging into a girl's room like a bull through a five-barred gate.'

'Come, Hetty, there is no point in continuing this charade.' Adam steeled himself to be as brusque as she had decided to be. 'I know why you are here in Berlin. And I know you are not who you claim to be.'

'I don't care a tuppeny damn what you know or don't know.'

'I think you will care when you hear what I have to say.'

'Don't you be so sure.'

'I know that you are no more called Hetty Gallant than I am. I know that you sent me off to York on what you thought would be a wild goose chase. I know that you have travelled here to Berlin with Harry Vernon.'

The girl's face fell. For the first time, she seemed disconcerted rather than outraged by Adam's visit to her room.

'What if I did?' she said, after a moment's silence. 'Ain't no law against a gentleman admirer taking his lady friend on a trip. Not by my reckoning. And whose business is it what I call myself but my own?'

'Agreed on both counts, but there *is* a law against the same gentleman admirer purloining papers from his place of work and taking them abroad.'

'Purloining? What the 'ell you talking about?'

'Stealing.'

'I know what "purloining" means, Mr 'Igh-and-Mighty. I just ain't got the first idea what all this has got to do with me.'

'Harry has left London with some very important documents. He should not have taken them. I have been sent to recover them and return them to their rightful owners. In order to do this, I have to have the answers to certain questions.'

'What's that to me? Why should I care if you want to know all the ins and outs of a duck's arse?'

'I think you will know the answers to some of these questions.'

'Why should I? And, if I did, why should I tell *you*?'

'Well, Dolly – I suppose I should learn to call you Dolly—'

'Or Miss Delaney,' the girl interrupted. 'We ain't that friendly you can be calling me Dolly any time you want.'

'We *were* friendly, Dolly. We were very friendly – for one night at least.' Adam, struggling not to sound too plaintive, could hear that he had failed.

'That was then. This is now.'

'Well, Miss Delaney,' Adam said after a pause, noting that she had decided to drop any pretence of being Hetty Gallant, 'I think you do know, and I think you will very definitely find it to your advantage to confide in me.'

Dolly was now watching him warily. She showed no sign of moving from behind the bulky chair.

'Where is Harry Vernon?' Adam asked.

'I ain't going to tell you.'

'He's staying here in the hotel with you, is he not?'

Dolly was running her fingertips along the back of the chair. She said nothing.

'Have you seen any papers in his possession? Official-looking documents?'

The young woman still said nothing. She was now looking down at her fingers, as if admiring the gold rings that gleamed on two of them.

'Has he spoken to you about any papers? Has he made use of the hotel safe?'

Dolly moistened the forefinger of one hand and used it to polish the rings on the other. She lifted her head and gazed past Adam at the painting of an Arcadian landscape that decorated one wall of the room.

'Very well,' he said. If the young woman could maintain such apparent indifference to their previous relationship, he decided, then so could he. 'Let us start with some questions that I know you *can* answer. Where did you meet Harry?' For a moment Adam thought that Dolly might continue to maintain her silence but she had obviously grown bored with holding her tongue.

'At a party,' she said after another short pause. 'Some toff like yourself had arranged it. We get plenty of invites to parties.'

Adam nodded. He had been to such parties himself. Parties where rich young men could meet women less formal in their manners, less inhibited in their behaviour than those they were likely to marry. Parties where drink flowed freely and dancing girls from the Drury Lane theatres would be very welcome guests indeed.

'And Vernon approached you?'

Dolly laughed mirthlessly. ''E did more than bleedin' approach me. 'E was all over me. Like he 'ad more hands than a shire horse. 'E couldn't get enough of me.'

'And so you bedded him. I am sorry to be crudely direct, but I can think of no other way of putting it.'

'Yes, I bedded 'im. Same as I did you.' The young woman had emerged from behind the armchair. She took several steps sideways, her eyes not leaving Adam's face. 'Not that it was much to talk about. It was all over before you could say Jack Robinson, if you catch my meaning.'

'But you continued to see him.'

''E continued to see *me*. I was working in a show at the Gaiety.'

'With Cyril Montague,' Adam interrupted, further light dawning.

'Cyril?' Dolly was puzzled. 'What's that old Margery Jane got to do with anything?'

'He knew you were Dolly.'

''Course 'e did. Why wouldn't 'e? I was still callin' meself Dolly then.'

'No matter.' Adam waved his hand. 'Do continue with your story.'

Dolly looked at him and then shrugged her shoulders very slightly. 'Harry come visiting all the time, didn't he? After we'd done the business that one time, 'e must have found out I was at the

278

Gaiety. 'E was round at the stage door every night.'

'And you encouraged him?'

'Bought me flowers, didn't he? And jewels,' Dolly said. 'Mind you, some of 'em were logies. He thought I couldn't tell good from bad but I'm sharp enough when it comes to shiners. I've worn enough sham ones on stage to know the difference. But some were the real thing.'

'The ones you sold, doubtless.' The remark seemed cruel as soon as he made it.

Dolly stared unblinkingly at Adam. 'You ain't got no idea what it's like to be poor, 'ave you?' she said, after the silence threatened to grow even more uncomfortable than their conversation had so far been. 'Poor so's you don't know where your next feed's coming from. Poor so's you've been obliged to cut off your hair and sell it to keep body and soul together.' The girl was so carried away by what she was saying that she had lost the nervousness she had earlier shown at Adam's appearance. She had crossed the room and was now standing no more than a foot in front of him. She was a head shorter than the young man but her face was thrust defiantly upwards so that her eyes could catch his. 'Well, I do,' she said, speaking rapidly. 'I've got plenty of idea what it's like. And I ain't 'aving it 'appen to me again. Harry's a rich cove, ain't he? So, if 'e's set on buying me jewels, logies or not, and treating me to other stuff, all so's he can bury his wick from time to time, I ain't going to be saying, "No, take your 'ands off me, I'm a respectable girl," am I?'

Breathless after her outburst, Dolly put her hands on her hips and looked at Adam.

'Put with such eloquence, your case is irrefutable,' he said, only too painfully aware of how pompous he sounded.

'Anyways, Harry is a sweet man. He knows 'ow to treat a lady.'

'So you have come here to Berlin with him.'

'A working girl deserves an 'oliday, same as anyone else. I was fed up of flashing my pins at the Prince Albert.'

'Your story sounds true enough, as far as it goes.'

'Well, thank you for nothing, Mr Clever-arse.'

279

'None of it, however, explains why you changed your name. Or why the girl I thought was Dolly Delaney, the girl I followed to York, was killed.'

Dolly's hands dropped from her hips. Her look of belligerence disappeared and she took several steps backwards. Momentarily she appeared utterly horrified, but she recovered her poise. 'Ain't no 'arm in calling yourself something else,' she said. 'Half the girls in McIlwraith's troupe have got names their mothers wouldn't know 'em by.'

'Perhaps not. But you gave your name to somebody else. And that poor girl ended up stabbed to death on the stage of a York theatre.'

'That weren't my fault.' Dolly suddenly looked close to tears. 'She weren't supposed to end up dead. She weren't even supposed to end up in York.'

'So where was she supposed to be?'

'London. The idea was to fool you. Make you think she'd gone north. But she'd stay in town while you chased your arse around Yorkshire. Gawd alone knows why she actually went. If she'd done what she was told to do, she'd still be alive.'

'I think she went to York because she was scared of what was happening in London. She was beginning to realize that she had waded out into deep waters. Somebody frightened her. So, when the Bascombe woman offered her some money, she took it and fled.'

Dolly shrugged unhappily. 'Well, that weren't part of the plan,' she said.

'And whose elaborate plan was this? Yours? Harry's?'

'Look, I ain't saying no more to you 'less Harry's here.' Dolly was defiant once again, returning her hands to her hips and scowling at Adam.

'And where is Harry now?'

When Adam had asked the question a little earlier, the young woman had been silent. Now she stared hard at him. He felt as if he could very nearly see the thoughts swirling through her mind as she tried to work out whether there was more advantage in answering him or in staying quiet.

''E's away,' she snapped eventually. ''E left me just after we got 'ere.' Dolly did not sound best pleased that her paramour had deserted her. '"I'll be back in a day or so," says he. "Off on business," says he.'

'Did he say with whom?'

'A lord or a count or something. Some German nob.'

'Did he mention where he was going?'

''E talked about an island. Visiting an island.'

'An island? There are dozens of islands around Berlin. Did he say which one?'

'Something about peacocks. An island with peacocks. He didn't want to tell me. 'E got shirty when I asked him more questions.' Dolly continued to glare at Adam. 'And I'm gettin' pretty shirty meself with you and all your bleedin' questions. Chargin' into a lady's boudoir and badgerin' 'er with gammon and spinach about changing names. What d'you think the manager of the 'otel would think if I was to tell 'im you've been pestering me?' She moved towards the wall where there was a bell pull that could summon the hotel staff. ''E's took a real shine to me, 'as 'Err Müller. "*Sherner Frow*", 'e calls me, according to Harry. That's "beautiful lady" in case you ain't up on the lingo 'ere.'

Dolly reached out her arm towards the pull. Adam forced himself to laugh. He held up his hand in mock surrender. 'There is no need to trouble Herr Müller.' The young man still had questions in plenty for Dolly, but they would have to wait. He even continued to harbour the faintest of hopes that she might rekindle the desire for him she had shown in London. However, there was no point in instigating a scene in the woman's room when, he had to admit to himself, it would be difficult to explain his presence there. 'I am leaving. But it is of vital importance that I speak to Harry. When he returns, you must let me know. I am in room twenty-eight on the first floor.'

Adam bowed politely to Dolly Delaney, who raised her eyes to the ceiling and, with a swish of her skirt, turned her back on him. He smiled bitterly and left the room.

CHAPTER TWENTY-EIGHT

The man from the embassy was standing where they had agreed to meet, under the trees to the west of the Neue Wache. Karl Friedrich Schinkel's neoclassical guardhouse on Unter Den Linden, built half a century previously, was one of the landmarks of the city's grandest street, and Etherege had assumed that even a first-time visitor to Berlin such as Adam would have no difficulty in locating it. He had been correct. The portico of Doric columns that faced the street was unmistakable. Soldiers were lined up outside the guardhouse, an officer barking instructions at them. As Adam approached, they wheeled smartly to the right and marched off in the direction of the Brandenburger Tor, leaving only two of their number still standing to attention in front of the columns.

Etherege held out his hand as Adam walked towards him. He had eschewed the smartly tailored suit he had been wearing on their previous meetings in favour of the black jacket and trousers that were standard dress for Berliners. In striving to look as much like a native as he could, Adam decided, the man had succeeded only in emphasizing his essential Englishness. After they had shaken hands, Etherege gestured in the direction of the *Stadtschloss* across the bridge. 'Shall we walk towards the castle?' he asked, setting off before Adam had chance to reply. The young man followed in the diplomat's wake, obliged to quicken his pace to draw level with him. 'A stroll in the Lustgarten would be pleasant. Have you seen the fountain? One of the wonders of the city in my estimation. How they propel the water so high in the air is a mystery to me. By steam,

I am told, but I fail to understand exactly how it is done.'

Chatting amiably but inconsequentially, Etherege seemed to require no response from his companion, guiding Adam into the small park opposite the castle. Within a few minutes they were standing side by side before the famous fountain, watching its waters shoot forty feet into the air. Around them, Berliners of all classes walked the paths that criss-crossed the park, some hurrying to another destination, others enjoying a leisurely promenade.

Adam moved backwards to allow a young woman pushing a per-ambulator more room in which to pass him. Etherege made no such move and the woman, clearly exasperated, was forced to swerve the baby carriage to avoid him. The diplomat, still staring up at the fountain, was oblivious to the manoeuvre. Adam waited for him to speak but he seemed to be lost in wonder at the sight of the jetting water. A slight breeze caught the spray and a few drops were blown into their faces. Adam decided that Etherege must be waiting for him to take the conversational initiative.

'Have you heard any word of Harry Vernon?' he asked him.

Now Etherege did take a step back, so that he and the young man were once again shoulder to shoulder. 'In a manner of speaking,' he said. 'The chap who lost sight of Vernon in the Gendarmenmarkt found him again. Sadly, he proceeded to lose him again as well. I am beginning to think he is not cut out for the kind of work for which we are employing him.' Etherege continued to watch the fountain, apparently entranced by it. 'However, our man did discover one interesting thing about Vernon before he mislaid him for the second time. You remember Ravelstein? The fellow with the Mensur scar at Frau Kestelmann's?'

Adam nodded.

'Of course you do. He is not an easy man to forget. And I warned you against him, I recall. As you know, Vernon met Ravelstein in the Alexanderplatz. They went off together in the German's carriage.'

'But you do not know why he met him? Or where Vernon is now?'

'The why is easy enough to guess. Vernon has brought something to Berlin in which the *Graf* is interested. The other question is not so readily answered. How are your own investigations progressing?'

'I have found the young woman who accompanied him. She is staying in the same hotel that you found for me.'

Etherege laughed briefly. 'A happy coincidence. And she has not been able to point you in the direction of Vernon?'

'She claims not to know where he is. I am inclined to believe her. She says that he left her in the hotel the day after they arrived in Berlin. He told her that he had important business to conduct and that he would return in a day or so. That is the last she has seen of him.'

'Not very gentlemanly behaviour on his part.'

The two men had moved away from the fountain and were walking in the direction of Unter den Linden. Adam glanced briefly over his shoulder at the water still shooting in the air and, behind it, the columns of the Altes Museum. He turned back to his companion. 'Perhaps not.'

'Or perhaps,' Etherege said, 'he wishes to protect her from knowledge of his more dangerous pursuits. Such as selling his country's secrets to a foreign power.'

Adam did not reply immediately. For some time he had assumed that it would be impossible to keep so intelligent and well informed a man as George Etherege in ignorance of the true reasons for his visit to Berlin; now that he had guessed correctly what was happening, Adam felt no need to confirm his conjecture. Silence was his best option.

They had reached the entrance to the garden. Another troop of soldiers, heads held high, strode past in the direction of the Brandenburger Tor. The diplomat watched them as they went, a look of quiet irony on his face. 'Very fond of marching, the Prussians,' he remarked, once they had gone. 'They can't seem to get enough of it. Particularly after their triumphs over the French. The city is forever echoing with the sound of tramping feet.'

They turned in the opposite direction to the one in which the soldiers were travelling.

'Do you know of an island near the city with peacocks on it?' Adam asked as they crossed the Spree.

'Peacocks?' Etherege looked surprised. He paused to consider his reply. 'There is Pfaueninsel, of course. It takes its name from the bird.'

'And where is Pfaueninsel?'

'In the Havel. As it makes its way towards Potsdam.'

'Are there buildings on it? People living there?'

'It belongs to the king. The emperor, as we must learn to call him. He has a small *schloss* there – a folly almost. Built as if it were a ruin. There is a palmhouse on the island as well, I believe. But why do you ask?'

'The woman spoke of it. She said that Vernon had mentioned an island with peacocks. Would Ravelstein have access to it?'

'He might,' Etherege conceded. 'I doubt if Wilhelm uses the place very much. It is an out of the way spot.' He looked sidelong at Adam. 'Ideal for your friend's purposes, I would say.'

The two men had stopped on the bridge across the Spree. Adam asked a few more questions about Pfaueninsel which his companion answered. Eventually Etherege turned away and both of them gazed down into the waters of the river below.

'I bumped into Ravelstein again, by the by,' the diplomat said. 'Yesterday, at the Café Beethoven.'

'The place we met?'

'Yes, on Friedrichstrasse. I say "bumped into", but I doubt if the meeting was fortuitous. Ravelstein does little without a purpose.'

'And his purpose in speaking to you in the café—? Let me guess.' Adam ran his gloved fingers along the bridge's iron railing like a pianist starting a sonata. 'It was to warn you that I was a dangerous miscreant whose presence in Berlin could not be tolerated.'

Etherege laughed. 'More or less,' he said. 'And just as bluntly expressed, which I found surprising. Ravelstein more usually employs the rapier rather than the bludgeon. He made it very clear that your visit to the city does not delight him and that he would be more than happy to see you bring it to a conclusion.'

'And what did you say to him?'

'I made it equally clear that I could not interfere in the travel plans of a private British citizen.' As they continued to stand at the bridge, Etherege rested his hand briefly on Adam's arm. 'I must reiterate what I said to you at Frau Kestelmann's, Carver. Ravelstein is a dangerous man. Probably one of the most dangerous men in Germany. You must take care. You will be aware, no doubt, that he has men following you?'

'I have seen someone at the hotel.'

'There will be others. If you go anywhere, you will be watched. And I suspect that there are other places in Berlin you will wish to see before you say farewell to the city.'

Adam nodded once more.

'Pfaueninsel, perhaps?' Etherege asked.

'What I hear of it makes it sound only too interesting.'

'Well, be sure that you do not have unwanted company when you visit.'

'I will make certain to take only my manservant Quint.'

'That would be wise.'

The two men said their goodbyes and moved away from the bridge, Adam turning right towards the Brandeburger Tor and his hotel, Etherege walking briskly in the opposite direction towards Alexanderplatz. As they parted, rain began to fall.

CHAPTER TWENTY-NINE

The boat collided gently with something. Quint released his hold on the oars and Adam leapt onto a small wooden jetty. Using a length of rope, he tied their small craft to a stanchion. Quint hauled the two oars out of their rowlocks and laid them in the bottom of the boat. They were on Pfaueninsel.

Quint began to pat the pockets of his grubby corduroy jacket. 'As if we ain't got enough in the way of troubles,' he muttered in disgust, 'I'm short of baccy.'

'Never mind that now,' Adam said. 'We have more pressing concerns than your tobacco, or lack of it.'

His servant, looking unconvinced that more pressing concerns than his desire for a smoke could exist, levered himself onto the jetty as Adam tugged briefly at the rope to ensure that the rowing boat was safely moored. The two men set off on a narrow path that led inland.

Thanks to the well-informed Etherege, Adam knew that the island was no more than three quarters of a mile long and a third of a mile wide. The emperor's *Lustschloss* was at its south-western corner, looking towards Potsdam. They had rowed across at what was very nearly the narrowest point between the mainland and Pfaueninsel, and could not be far from the *Schloss*. It had to be somewhere to their left.

Adam beckoned to Quint and turned in that direction. Almost as soon as he did, he noticed the house through the trees: it was little more than a hundred yards away. The building was designed more to be seen from the water than approached inland, but Adam could make out the white stonework shining in the light from the half-moon. The *Schloss* was a scaled-down version of the kind of fairytale castle he remembered from illustrations in the books of his childhood. Elaborate crenellations decorated the top of a square keep. Two circular towers rose from the corners facing the river.

Adam and his servant stopped beneath the wall of the *Schloss*.

''Ow we aimin' to get in?' Quint asked in a low voice, squinting up at the tower on the left. 'Some dollymop goin' to let down 'er 'air?'

Adam laughed quietly. 'I would not have put you down as a reader of the Brothers Grimm, Quint.'

'I don't know anything about any Brothers Grimm. I seen a picture outside a place in the Mile End Road, ain't I?' the older man said belligerently, as if his master might be prepared to argue he had not. 'Christmas before last. Tower just like this 'un and a cove in red tights swarmin' up this judy's 'air like a monkey up a stick.'

'I doubt there is any young woman in the castle tonight, Quint. And the story of Rapunzel reminds me rather too much of our admittance to the Greek monastery last year.' Adam shuddered briefly as he remembered the way the monks of Meteora had hauled him, like a fish in a net, up the cliff on which they lived, whilst an unknown marksman had peppered the rockface around him with bullets. 'Anyway, unlike Rapunzel's tower, this one has a means of entrance.' He pointed to the white stone wall.

Half-hidden behind a thickly proliferating bush was a wooden door. The young man approached it and tried the handle. To his surprise, it turned and the door opened. He looked at Quint and raised an eyebrow.

'Mebbe they're expecting us,' the manservant muttered.

'I hardly think so,' Adam said in an undertone. 'Ravelstein may even believe we have returned to London. Etherege tells me he has tried to circulate that story.' He pushed the door further open and peered cautiously into the building. The door opened into a dark passage, and he could see very little. He withdrew his head and turned to his servant. 'You will remain here, Quint, while I see where this door leads,' Adam whispered. 'Keep a weather eye open for Ravelstein's men. If any of them approach, you must let me know.'

"Ow in 'ell am I s'posed to do that?' Quint hissed back.

'Don't make difficulties, man. Yell loudly. If I hear an eldritch shriek pierce the night, I shall know it is you.'

Not waiting to hear any further complaints Quint might have, Adam entered the building. The darkness seemed complete at first but, as his eyes grew adjusted to what dim light there was, he began to make out his surroundings. A staircase spiralled upwards to his left, leading, he presumed, to the top of the tower. He could see no reason to climb it. He was no knight errant in search of an imprisoned damosel. To his right, a short corridor led further into the building. Cautiously, he began to make his way down it. On one wall hung a large painting of slaughtered game birds, piled high and dripping with blood, which the artist had realized with painstaking attention to detail; against the other stood a full suit of polished armour, like a frozen medieval warrior standing guard. Both walls were further decorated with the spoils of the chase. Adam noticed a boar's head that jutted out into the corridor as if the beast had charged through the wall and somehow become lodged there. Its dead eyes stared glassily at him as he passed.

Adam had walked no more than a few yards when he froze: from behind him came the click of boots on stone. Somebody was descending the staircase from the tower. He quickly wondered if he had time to retrace his steps and leave by the door he had entered, but decided he had not. His only option was to shrink back into the shadows and hope that he would avoid detection. But it did not seem very likely that whoever was approaching would miss him, and his discovery there, a trespasser in the emperor's *Lustschloss*, would be dangerous for him. He doubted he would be able to persuade Ravelstein that he was an innocent visitor.

Adam watched the light from a lamp grow stronger as the man carrying it came down the stairs. He could now hear the voices of two men in conversation. One, he was certain, was Ravelstein. The other he could not identify. They were speaking in German, in low tones, and Adam, whose knowledge of the language was not much better than elementary, could not understand most of what they were saying. Something about '*Der Engländer*' – Harry Vernon, he assumed. And what did the word '*lügner*' mean? It was repeated several times. 'Liar', was it?

Adam stretched out his hands behind him, expecting to touch only the wall of the passage but, to his surprise and relief, he felt a doorknob. The two Germans had now reached the bottom of the spiral staircase. They could not help but see him at any moment. He turned the doorknob and the door opened noiselessly. He had no time to enter the room fully but he was able to draw further back into its shadows as the Germans passed.

Intent on their conversation, Ravelstein and his companion clearly had no suspicion that anyone else was nearby. Still speaking in swift words, they moved along the corridor and through another door at its end.

Adam could feel sweat dripping uncomfortably down his neck and forehead. He waited until he was breathing easily once again, then turned and peered into the room behind him. It was little more than an oversized cupboard, filled with the equipment used to keep the armour polished and the animal heads free of moth for the emperor's infrequent visits.

Nerving himself once more, Adam left the small room, softly closing the door behind him, and walked gingerly along the corridor to the door through which Ravelstein and the other man had just passed. He put his ear to the wood and listened. There were definitely people in the room beyond. He could hear their conversation.

Suddenly, the floorboard beneath his foot made the slightest of creaks. Adam froze in position. He could feel his heart pounding in his chest, but there was no change in the sounds coming from the inner room: he could still hear the low hum of voices. They had not heard him. He listened for a minute. There were at least two, probably three, different speakers, he decided. Adam cursed his ignorance of the language. Words were difficult to distinguish and those few that he could make out he could not translate. From the tone of the different voices, he guessed that there was a fairly heated debate going on. One man – he assumed it was Ravelstein – appeared to be laying down the law. Another was speaking occasionally.

Suddenly there came the sounds of what could only be a scuffle from within the room. There was shouting, and the noise of something crashing to the floor. A chair? A table? Adam could not be sure. More shouting followed. '*Tragt ihn zum Turm!*' The voice was undoubtedly Ravelstein's, raised in anger and coming closer to the door. Now Adam understood what was being said: they were going back to the tower. He had just enough time to retreat down the corridor and enter the tiny room he had found earlier.

Adam pulled the door almost closed and placed his eye to the thin crack that was left. After a moment, a small procession moved past his narrow viewpoint. At its head was Ravelstein. His chin was held high and he was scratching his beard. After him came two burly men in black. They were frogmarching another man between them. Adam recognized him immediately.

It was Harry Vernon. He had slumped in the hands of his captors and looked exceedingly miserable. There were marks on his cheeks and upper lip which suggested that he had been struck. The men passed quickly out of sight, and Adam risked opening the door a little further so that he could continue to observe them. They had reached the spiral staircase and now began to climb it, Ravelstein still in the lead. Vernon was being pushed after him by the other two men. The young man briefly wondered what he should do. If he followed them, there was the danger that he would be trapped on the upper floors of the *Schloss*. If he did not, he might miss something of great significance. He decided to follow them.

Adam emerged cautiously from his hiding place and began to mount the spiral stairs himself. As he reached the top of them, he was faced by a heavy wooden door. The Germans, with their prisoner, had clearly used it – there was nowhere else they could have gone. To the left of the door was a small mullioned window of dark glass. Adam pressed his face to the glass and could just make out what was happening in the room beyond.

A wooden chair had been placed in the centre of the room, and Harry Vernon was tied to it. His head had fallen forward and his chin was resting on his chest. At first, Adam thought he was unconscious but, as he watched, the other Englishman raised his head wearily. He was listening to Ravelstein, who was standing by his side. The German count was speaking rapidly and angrily. Vernon was now shaking his head from side to side, as if trying to clear it. Ravelstein gestured to one of his confederates and said something in a low voice. Vernon looked up in fear and surprise.

One of the men in black had raised a gun and was pointing it at him. There was a swift exchange in German between the count and his captive. The Englishman continued to shake his head. Ravelstein turned to his confederate. '*Bringe ihn um*,' he said.

There were two shots and Adam almost cried out in shock. He moved back from the window. He had seen enough. It was time to leave. He was about to turn around and retreat down the stairs when, to his horror, Adam felt something prod the small of his back.

Another of Ravelstein's men had climbed the stairs unheard and was now behind him. '*Herein*,' the man said, '*schnell*.'

Adam had no option but to obey. With what he could only assume was a gun pressed to his spine, he was obliged to open the heavy door and enter the room at the top of the tower.

The men in the room, all but one, looked in his direction. The one who had shot Harry Vernon raised his gun, but Ravelstein, who seemed unperturbed by Adam's appearance, gestured to him and he lowered it again. Vernon's body, still bound to the chair, was now lying on the floor. Either the impact of the bullets had propelled it there or it had been pushed. Blood was pumping from Vernon's chest.

'*Er war draussen*,' the man behind Adam said to Ravelstein.

'Ah, the young English gentleman from Frau Kestelmann's.' The count smiled amiably, as if the two of them had just been reintroduced at another social gathering. 'I thought that perhaps you were not quite the innocent traveller that you claimed to be. And, despite what George Etherege wished me to believe, I was certain that you had not left Berlin.'

Adam could still feel the gun pressed to his back. Ravelstein nodded to one of his associates, who stepped forward and punched Adam in the solar plexus. The young man doubled up and fell to the floor, writhing and gasping.

'What is that excellent English proverb I have heard?' Ravelstein continued to speak as if they were exchanging pleasantries at a dinner party. 'Ah, yes. "Curiosity killed the cat." We have a similar saying in our own language. "*Neugierige Katzen verbrennen sich die Tatzen*." Curious cats burn their paws.' He bent down to look into Adam's face, which was still contorted with pain from his henchman's blow. 'You have been far too curious a cat, Mr Carver.' Ravelstein motioned to his men, who hauled Adam from the floor. 'And now we must decide how to punish your curiosity. Shall we just burn your paws? Or shall we be obliged to kill you?'

He spoke as if this were a genuine philosophical problem which he was debating with himself.

'Poor Mr Vernon here, he has had an accident.' Ravelstein was inspecting his fingernails as if trying to decide whether or not they required trimming. 'It is so dangerous to handle a gun when you are not used to weaponry. Are you used to weaponry, Mr Carver? You do not look like an expert with the pistol.' The count gestured to the man who had escorted Adam into the room. 'Otto here, he is an expert with the pistol.'

'*Soll ich ihn abmurksen?*' Otto enquired. His eyes had been darting between Ravelstein and Adam, but it was clear that he had not understood what his master had been saying.

'*Nein, nein. Noch nicht.*'

'Etherege knows I have come here.' Adam, still gasping for air, had pulled himself to his haunches. Now he stood up, warily eyeing Otto and his gun. 'You will not be able to avoid a scandal if you kill me.'

Ravelstein laughed. He sounded genuinely amused. '*Ach*, Mr Carver,' he said, 'you would be surprised by the scandals I have already avoided. Another would be no matter.'

CHAPTER THIRTY

Left to his own devices outside the castle, Quint soon grew bored. He looked up at the tower. He could see lights at several of its windows. One of the lights was moving and clearly came from a lantern which someone in the building was carrying. Quint watched as it threw the shadows of two men onto the wall of a room within. He strained his eyes to make out more, but could not, and the shadows passed out of sight.

He walked away from the tower and approached the water of the Havel which had, at this point on its journey towards its conjunction with the Elbe many miles away, opened out into what was, in effect, a lake. The half-moon shone an uncertain light onto the water's surface and Quint could see the dark shapes of trees lining the distant banks. He was no great admirer of nature and soon tired of the view. He wondered if he could risk a smoke. Turning back towards the white towers of the *Lustschloss*, he fumbled in his pocket for the little tobacco he had left and the clay pipe he always carried.

Returning to his sentry duty near the door through which his master had passed, he leaned against the cool stone of the castle. He had begun to push the baccy into the bowl of the pipe and was anticipating its rich savour when an arm shot out of the darkness and seized his throat.

'*Was machen Sie hier?*' a harsh voice hissed.

Pinned to the wall by a large and powerful hand, Quint was unable to make more than choking noises.

'*Sie sollen nicht auf der Insel sein.*'

A face pressed close to Quint's and the Englishman could smell beer and wurst. He wriggled in his captor's grasp.

'*Wo kommen Sie her?*'

The German, realizing perhaps that it was futile to ask questions when his prisoner was physically incapable of answering, released his grip very slightly. Quint spluttered and coughed and then took the opportunity to drive his right knee hard into the man's crotch. With a howl of distress the man doubled up and Quint used his fist to strike him ferociously on the back of the neck. The German slumped to the grass, out cold.

A rifle, which he had been carrying on a strap over his shoulder, fell with him, and Quint picked it up. He felt his throat where the man had seized him. It was tender and he coughed again, still struggling slightly for breath. He took the strap off the rifle and used it to bind together his victim's hands, then he tore a strip from the man's shirt and tied it around his mouth as a makeshift gag. With his foot, he rolled the unconscious man onto his back and then into the bushes.

The German looked as if he might be out for some time, but, Quint reasoned, there were almost certainly more of his comrades in the vicinity. It was time for departure. He could not, however, go without his master.

'I reckon it's time we cut and run, guv,' he muttered to himself as he opened the door through which Adam had passed some twenty minutes earlier and entered the *Lustschloss*.

* * * * *

In the room at the top of the tower, Adam was being interrogated by Ravelstein. The count was not a kindly questioner. Whenever he was dissatisfied with an answer, he nodded to his associates and one of them punched the young man. Battered by half a dozen blows, Adam was struggling to stay on his feet and think about what he could do.

'The plans, Mr Carver,' Ravelstein said now, repeating words he had already used several times. 'Where are the plans?'

'What plans? I do not know what you mean.'

'I think you do.' Ravelstein gestured again to the man called Otto, who struck Adam across the face with a blow that was half-punch and half-slap. 'Why would you come here if you were not in league with Vernon? You have seen what happened to him. Answer my question.'

Before Adam could make any attempt to do so, the door was flung open and a man burst into the room. It was Quint, the rifle he had taken from the guard at the foot of the tower levelled to shoot. Otto swung round to face him and Quint fired the weapon. The German screamed, dropped his gun and fell to the floor. He clutched convulsively at his thigh, which was now spurting blood. Quint was yelling like a madman in English. The other two Germans held their hands in the air.

Adam, bruised though he was by his beating, was swift to seize his chance. He moved to his servant's side and the two of them backed out of the room, Quint still waving the gun. Once through the door, Adam slammed it shut and they raced for the staircase. Behind them, they could hear Otto's cries of pain and Ravelstein shouting out instructions. The Englishmen took the stairs two and three at a time as they clattered down them at speed.

As they came around the last curve of the spiral staircase, they almost went headlong into the figure of another man, who was standing at the foot of the staircase. Bewildered by the noise from the upstairs room, he had obviously been uncertain what to do, and in the weak light of the corridor he did not at first recognize Quint and Adam as intruders.

'*Was ist los?*' he asked.

The realization that these men were not his colleagues dawned almost immediately, but it was too late. Adam launched himself at the man and, with a solid punch to the jaw, knocked him to the floor. He jumped over the fallen German, but Quint paused and reversed his grip on the rifle with surprising speed. Holding it by the barrel, he attempted to strike the German with the weapon's butt. The man, although still half dazed from Adam's punch, was alert enough to roll away but such was the intended force of Quint's blow that the rifle's wooden butt splintered away from the breech as it connected with the floor. The manservant uttered a brief curse, threw the weapon away and followed his master to the door that led outside.

The cool night air welcomed them a moment or two later, and they moved rapidly away from the fairytale tower of the *Schloss*.

'Back to the boat,' Adam said, panting from the exertion of their helter-skelter exit.

'Where the 'ell is it?' Quint asked, equally out of breath.

They both gazed into the night, straining their eyes to work out where they should go. Angry shouting could be heard behind them.

'Over here,' Adam said. 'It must be in this direction.'

They set off at a slow jog-trot, eager to put distance between themselves and Ravelstein's men and yet anxious not to trip or lose their way. A narrow path opened to their right and Adam thought he could see the glint of the river at its end. He turned onto it and beckoned Quint to follow him. He was right. It was the Havel ahead of them. As they reached the water's edge, Adam stopped and turned. He peered into the darkness, looking back at the *Schloss*.

'Come on, guv.' Quint tugged at his master's sleeve. 'You ain't got time to be standing there, staring like a throttled cat. We've got to get off this bleedin' island.'

From the path came the sounds of Ravelstein's men shouting to one another.

'What about Harry Vernon?'

'If that was 'im on the floor in the tower, then 'e's dead. Ain't no 'elping him now. We've got to 'elp ourselves.'

The crash of a body through vegetation indicated that at least one of the Germans had left the path and was making his way towards them. Adam and Quint moved as swiftly as they could along the tangled shoreline.

'Where is that damned jetty?' Adam hissed. The night enveloped them and the only light came from the moon, as it emerged intermittently from behind drifting clouds. As he spoke, it did so briefly and shone upon the water to their right. 'This way,' Adam said. 'We must follow the river's edge.'

They blundered on. The half-moon disappeared behind the clouds and they were plunged once more into darkness. They could still hear the sounds of the men following them, and it seemed they were coming closer.

'I reckon we've missed it,' Quint whispered. 'It's as black as the Duke of 'Ell's riding boots when that moon ain't out.'

His servant's words merely confirmed what Adam had already suspected. Somehow, in the dark, and with Ravelstein's men in pursuit of them, they had blundered past the jetty where their boat was tied. Thick vegetation had also driven them inland and they had lost sight of the water. They were now making their way ever further northward on the island.

'Mebbe we should turn back,' Quint suggested.

'We cannot do so,' Adam said. 'We shall merely run into the arms of our pursuers.'

As if in confirmation of his remark, the sounds of two men calling to one another in German could be heard on the path behind them.

'We must go this way,' Adam whispered, pointing ahead. The two men set off again. Several hundred yards to their south, their boat swung quietly at its mooring.

CHAPTER THIRTY-ONE

'Hark, Quint.' Adam pointed to his left. 'The voices are coming from that direction.'

'We'd best go in this 'un, then,' the manservant said, beginning to move off in the opposite direction.

Adam reached out a hand to stop him. 'No,' he said. 'We are only travelling further and further away from the boat. And the boat is our only way off this wretched island. We must turn back.'

'Right into the path of them Prusskies.'

'It is dark. We can avoid them.'

'I thought you said we couldn't turn back.'

'I have changed my mind. We have no other option.'

There was a sudden, unearthly scream from the darkness ahead of them. Adam felt the hairs on the back of his neck rise.

'What the bleedin' 'ell was that?' Quint asked, his voice trembling slightly.

The eerie screech, like a banshee keening for a death foretold, was repeated. Adam released his breath in a sigh of relief as he realized what the terrible sound was. '*Pfaueninsel*,' he said. 'Peacock Island. The noise is a peacock.'

'That's a bleedin' bird?' Quint was disbelieving. 'I thought it was a cove getting 'is pills cut off.'

'Come, perhaps those terrible peacock cries will distract our pursuers. We will head back towards the boat.'

The two men turned and now moved warily along the path they had just traversed. Behind them the peacock, disturbed by their presence, was emitting its appalling shriek at regular intervals.

Meanwhile, the moon had once again emerged from behind the clouds and was shedding light on the water of the Havel to their left.

Minutes passed, and Adam suddenly realized that he was alone. Turning to find out what had happened to Quint, he looked back along the path. The man had disappeared. Adam peered into the semi-darkness but there was no sign of his servant. He was about to call out as quietly as he could when he heard a rustling behind him. He swung round to find that a dark figure was standing in the path about a dozen yards ahead of him. He could not make out who it was. He took a step or two nearer. 'Is that you, Quint?' he hissed.

'*Wer ist da*?' the figure asked. '*Hans?*'

Adam began immediately to retreat. The shape in front of him started to raise what looked like an arm holding a gun but, just then, another figure suddenly emerged from the shadows by the side of the path and struck the German behind the head with a length of wood. The man crumpled to the ground without a sound.

'That was a bit of a near go,' Quint said quietly, throwing the branch he was holding to the ground. 'I reckon that cove 'ad you in his sights.'

'Where the devil have you been?' hissed Adam, more relieved than he cared to admit at the sight of his manservant.

'Got something stuck to my boot, didn't I? Stopped to see what was wrong and saw the Prussky ahead of you. So I sneaked round and come up behind 'im. Just as well I did.' Quint prodded the fallen man with his foot. 'I've given 'im one hell of a wallop. 'E'll be as good as dead for hours.'

Adam approached and stared down at Quint's victim. 'Yes, but he has companions,' he said. 'He thought I was one of them. They must be close.'

The two men looked about them but there was no sign of anyone nearby. Judging by the sound of voices calling out, the Germans who had been following them had moved inland a little. In the distance the peacock continued to screech.

'Ravelstein's men must have lost the path but they will find us before too long,' Adam said. 'Let us go this way.' He pointed to his left and, deserting the rough track, headed off into the long grass. Quint followed him. Within little more than a minute they had reached the edge of Pfaueninsel and were peering down a muddy incline to the river.

'We shall have to swim for it,' Adam said. 'It is not far to the opposite bank at this point. No more than a couple of hundred yards. Then we can disappear into the woods opposite.'

'I ain't getting in there,' Quint replied.

Adam looked at his servant, whose face was chalk-white in the moonlight. 'We have little choice in the matter.' His master spoke quietly but urgently. 'There is no sign of the boat. It is beginning to look like a midnight dip or throw ourselves on Ravelstein's mercy. And that, I suspect, is not a quality the count possesses in abundance.'

'I ain't getting' in that bleedin' water, I tell you.' Quint had begun to step back from the bank, slowly shaking his head from side to side to emphasize his unwillingness to do what had been suggested.

'For God's sake, Quint, this is our best chance of getting off this wretched island!'

The manservant continued to shake his head and back away. 'I ain't doing it,' he hissed.

'Why on earth not?' Adam hissed back.

'I just ain't.'

There was silence as Adam gazed at his servant and Quint stared truculently back at him.

'You cannot swim, can you?' the young man said after a few moments.

'Well, there ain't much call for it in the smoke, is there? 'Oo needs to doggy-paddle up the bleedin' Thames? There's boats everywhere.'

'You could very nearly wade across at this point.'

'I ain't getting in that water.'

Adam sighed in exasperation. He was about to embark on further discussion when there was shouting in the direction from which they had come. 'They have found the man you struck down,' he said. 'There is no time for argument. We will have to continue to make our way as best we can towards the jetty. It must be this way.'

Half crouching, the two men hugged the shore of the small island as they continued westwards. This time they were in luck: after a few minutes, they were in sight of the place where they had tied up the boat. They stopped and squatted on their haunches behind a small thorn bush.

'Can you see anyone at the jetty, Quint?' Adam asked in a whisper. The moon had been behind cloud for some time.

'Dark as a coal 'ole,' his manservant muttered. 'I can't even see the bleedin' river.'

Adam rose to his feet just as the moon emerged again and silhouetted two men standing, like soldiers to attention, by the small wooden pier. Adam quickly settled on his haunches again. He nudged his servant in the ribs and pointed towards the boat. Quint nodded to indicate that he had seen the men standing guard. Thirty seconds passed and Adam again risked rising a little to see more clearly what was happening. He ducked down swiftly as one of the men appeared to turn in his direction.

'If you goes on bobbing up and down like a sparrer in a mud puddle,' Quint hissed, 'one of those Prusskies is bound to see us.'

Adam crouched further down behind the bush but continued to watch the two men as best he could. One now looked to be pulling at the rope that tied their boat to the wooden post at the jetty's end; the other, standing nearer the bank, was leaning forward and peering into the semi-darkness that surrounded them.

'Well, if you got any good ideas,' Quint added after a while, 'now'd be a good time to let me know what they are.'

Adam made no reply but continued to peer at Ravelstein's two men. The one who had been tugging at the boat's painter had now moved to join his companion. They stood at the point where the wooden planking of the jetty joined the island and gazed inland, speaking in low voices. The taller of the two men lifted his arm and gestured in the direction of the *Schloss*. He seemed to think that he had seen something to which he needed to draw his colleague's attention.

Hunching over again, Adam began to make his way towards the jetty, keeping an eye on the two Germans. Quint followed him. The men at the jetty continued to stare towards the castle. It was evident that they had no idea anyone was in the vicinity. The taller man, still waving his arm, made another remark to his companion. The two Englishmen had now reached a point about twenty yards from the jetty.

Adam leaned to his right to whisper into his servant's ear. 'I will strike the man on the left,' he said, indicating his target. 'When I make a move, you must simultaneously disarm the other man, or all is lost.'

Quint nodded and the pair, still stooping low, moved forward another ten paces. There was no indication that their presence had been detected. Adam signalled to his servant.

At a run, they emerged from the darkness and barrelled into the two men guarding the boat. Both were immediately knocked off their feet. The one on the left let out a half-cry as he fell, which Adam, tumbling on top of him, immediately stifled by thrusting his hand over the man's mouth. Taken completely by surprise, the German nonetheless continued to struggle. Even as he strove to overpower his opponent, Adam was aware of the noises of a similar tussle coming from his right where Quint had hurtled into the other German.

The man Adam had attacked, although winded by the initial assault, was proving a stubborn adversary. He was also exceptionally strong, and he succeeded in freeing one arm from beneath Adam's body, using it to lever the young Englishman off him. Adam was pushed backwards and eventually thrown sideways into the mud and grass by the river's edge. The German leapt to his feet and fell upon him. It was all Adam could do to reach out a hand and grab the man by the throat.

The German was now on the attack himself. While holding Adam down with the weight of his body, he was fighting to pull something from his pocket. The young Englishman was certain that it was a weapon. He let go of the German's throat and struggled desperately to seize the hand that was reaching into the pocket. Suddenly, as Adam fought to keep his opponent at bay, he felt the man's body go limp in his grasp. He slumped to one side and Adam was able to disentangle himself from his adversary and rise unsteadily to his feet. He turned to find Quint standing close by, nursing his right fist.

'I give 'im a nobbler on the 'ead,' the manservant explained, miming a downward blow to the man's skull. 'That's the third time I've saved your bacon tonight.'

'Thank you,' his master said, struggling to regain his breath. He nodded in the direction of the man Quint had attacked, who was also stretched unconscious on the ground. 'We must tie both of them up before we leave. There is rope in the boat.'

Adam hobbled down the jetty and reached into the boat. Within minutes, the two Germans were trussed like turkeys. One of them was beginning to come round and was emitting low groaning noises – Quint walked over to him and kicked him hard in the back of the head. The man ceased groaning immediately. Quint then turned his attention to his companion.

'Leave him be, Quint,' Adam called softly. 'The man is dead to the world.'

'Ain't no point riskin' it,' Quint hissed back. 'The other one was grunting like a pig under a tub. This one might do the same.' He aimed another kick.

The two men then made their way to the boat and climbed in. They untied it from the wooden post at the end of the jetty and pushed off. Reaching down to the bottom boards, Adam found the two oars and silently passed one to Quint. Weary and mud-spattered, they began to row away from the island.

Within a few minutes, the boat hit the mud of a bank on the opposite shore and stuck fast. They were back on the mainland, Pfaueninsel little more than a dark shape behind them. They hauled themselves out of the boat and onto the bank.

As they did so, three men burst from the undergrowth on the island. There were sudden popping noises which, Adam realized after a moment of puzzlement, were the sounds of pistols firing. Nature was on their side. Clouds floated once more across the face of the half-moon. Ravelstein's gunmen could no longer see their targets but they continued to blaze away into the darkness.

With Quint at his heels, Adam disappeared into the woods that fringed the banks of the Havel.

CHAPTER THIRTY-TWO

'**Y**our friend is dead. Perhaps it is for the best.' Etherege glanced sideways at Adam, as if to judge the effect of his remark. 'I do not wish to sound heartless, but it will be easier for us to deal with Harry Vernon the late hero than Harry Vernon the living traitor. And his death will mean that it is easy enough to present him as a hero.'

'He was not my friend. I spoke to the man on only one occasion. Yet I am sorry that he is dead. I am pleased that you will report back to London that he died a hero.'

'It will be simpler that way. We will thus avoid the asking of too many awkward questions.'

The two men were walking in the Tiergarten. It was the morning after Adam's adventures on Pfaueninsel. His body ached from the beating administered by Ravelstein's thugs but a doctor summoned to the Deutscher Hof had confirmed that no serious damage had been done.

In the light of what had happened, Adam had decided that his best option was to seek out the diplomat and tell him much of what he knew. He had even wondered if he and Quint should seek refuge in the embassy, but had decided against that. As Adam had expected, Etherege had not seemed entirely surprised by his revelations: 'We knew that Vernon must be in Berlin for more than social reasons,' he said. 'Sunman had hinted as much and, forgive me, I did not entirely believe the story you told me when we met at the Café Beethoven.'

They had circled around the trees and bushes so neatly planted in the Königsplatz and were now standing side by side, looking across at the imposing bulk of the Kroll Opera House.

'I do not think I expected you to believe it,' Adam replied. 'Not all of it, anyway.' He watched the flight of half a dozen crows which had taken off from a lime tree in the centre of the square and were heading towards the Krolloper. 'Is there nothing we can do to bring Vernon's killer to justice?'

Etherege shook his head. 'Nothing at all,' he said.

'But it was the most cold-blooded act of murder. Ravelstein simply ordered his man to shoot Harry. And I witnessed everything. I would be prepared to testify to what I saw.'

'It would be of no use, Carver. You can have no conception of the influence the count wields. We would be wasting our time *and* compromising our standing with Bismarck and the Wilhelmstrasse – and the emperor.'

'And the emperor would not be troubled that one of his own properties had been the scene for murder?'

Etherege waved away the remark. 'It is an indication,' he said, 'of Ravelstein's confidence in his own immunity that he was prepared to use the *Schloss* on Pfaueninsel for the purpose he did. He believes he is above the law and, to all intents and purposes, as long as he retains Bismarck's trust, he is.' The two men resumed their walk. 'The curious fact about last night's events is not so much that the count had a man killed at the *Lustschloss*,' the diplomat said after a short silence. 'It is that he chose to have him killed at all. Why would Ravelstein wish to kill Vernon?'

'I have asked myself that question,' Adam said. 'Presumably Harry had cheated him of what he wanted. But murdering him would serve no purpose other than to punish him for his treachery. The count would be no nearer to getting his hands on what he expected to receive.'

'And what, I wonder, did he expect to receive?' Etherege asked, as innocently as if he were inquiring the time of day.

An elderly man, wrapped in a fur-lined coat more suited to winter than spring, was approaching them, heading towards the Krolloper.

He raised his hat as he passed and wished them good morning, giving Adam a little time to formulate an answer to Etherege's question. What should he tell him? Sunman had advised – indeed, almost ordered – him to say nothing of his true reasons for coming to Berlin. But now? The circumstances had changed so dramatically and he had, in effect, admitted to the diplomat that he had been lying to him earlier. He had told him a good deal of the truth but by no means all. Was it now the time to make a clean breast of everything? Etherege had all but guessed the reasons behind Vernon's flight from London already, had he not? As he was thinking matters over, Etherege began to speak again and, in doing so, relieved Adam of the responsibility of a decision.

'Let me propose a hypothetical answer to my own question,' the diplomat said. 'Harry Vernon abstracted some document of major significance from the Foreign Office. For the purposes of my hypothesis, it is not important to know exactly what the document is – in some ways, I prefer not to know. He brought it to Berlin with the idea of selling it to the Germans. This document is what Ravelstein expected to receive. Does this sound at all plausible to you?'

Adam inclined his head slightly to indicate that it did. He was still debating with himself how far to take his companion into his confidence as Etherege continued to speak.

'In the meantime, you arrive in Berlin, despatched by our mutual friend Sunman and the FO in hot pursuit of Vernon, and the missing document. Although I *am* a little unclear as to why you were chosen to follow him – as far as I can discover, you are no more than a traveller and writer with an amateur interest in photography. You have no connection with the FO, although you were at school and Cambridge with Sunman. However, that little mystery is not one of any great significance. The important fact is that you *were* sent, and that you were able to locate Vernon at the *Schloss* on Pfaueninsel. However, Vernon – and now I am venturing even further into the realms of hypothesis – was so foolish as to believe that he could play tricks with Ravelstein. He tried to betray him in some way.' Etherege paused and looked at Adam. 'What do you think of my theory so far? Does it hold water, do you think?'

'Perhaps,' Adam conceded, 'but we are still no nearer an explanation of why the count murdered Harry.'

'Ah, but I think we are.' Etherege had slowed his pace as they walked and Adam, in order to keep in step, did likewise. They were now barely moving. 'I would suggest that Ravelstein felt free to kill Vernon because he knew that someone else was involved in the game they were all playing. And because killing Vernon would demonstrate to that other person how serious he, Ravelstein, was about playing it.'

The thought that Harry had a confederate, and that the count knew this, was obvious enough. If the German count had thought Harry was acting alone, why would he have been prepared to kill the only man who could hand over the submarine plans to him?

'What of the girl at your hotel? The one with whom Vernon travelled.' Etherege had now stopped on the path and was gazing down at his brilliantly polished shoes, as if admiring their sheen. 'Could she be the other player in the game?' The diplomat turned his eyes to Adam. 'I can see that you do not think she is.'

'On Pfaueninsel, Ravelstein seemed to be of the opinion that I was.'

'He will be of that opinion no longer. We have sent a message via an agent whom the Germans think is working for them but is actually working for us. You travelled to Berlin to dissuade Vernon from his treachery.'

'And the count will believe this?'

'He trusts the agent. You and your servant are no longer at risk from Ravelstein and his men. However, the girl is another matter. He will be aware, of course, of her existence. I do believe she might be in some danger.'

'Danger?' Adam had not considered the possibility.

'I think we can assume that the count knew from the start that she and Vernon arrived in Berlin together. He may also have concluded that she knows more than she does about her lover's scheme. He may intend to' – the diplomat paused to choose the right word – '*persuade* her to tell him what he thinks she knows.'

'Where is she now?' Adam asked.

'In her room at the hotel. At least, she was there an hour ago. I have a man on the staff who reports to me.'

Adam raised an eyebrow. 'You seem to have a small army of men who report to you,' he said.

'It is as well in a city like Berlin to know what is going on.' Etherege replied with a smile.

'So Dolly is still at the Deutscher Hof. And ignorant of what has taken place.' Adam turned to look at his companion. 'I do believe it is my responsibility to tell her what has happened.'

'Advise her to leave the city, Carver, as swiftly as she possibly can. In the light of what has happened, we cannot guarantee her safety.'

'I shall do so immediately.' Adam cursed himself for not thinking earlier of the peril Dolly might possibly face. He was now eager to make amends for his negligence.

He nodded briefly to Etherege and began to stride determinedly in the direction of the Brandenburger Tor. The diplomat watched him disappear into the distance, and then followed him at a much more leisurely pace.

* * * * *

The lobby of the hotel on Unter den Linden was filled with people when Adam entered it soon after midday. A group of military officers in uniform surrounded the reception desk. Prosperous and well-fed gentlemen, together with their elegant wives, criss-crossed the black-and-white marble floor on their way to their rooms.

Politely offering apologies as he did so, Adam pushed his way through the crowd and reached the stairs. Dolly's rooms were, like his own, on the first floor. He walked along the well-lit corridor until he came to the door he recognized from his previous visit. He tapped quietly on it three times. There was no sound from within. He put his ear to the door but could still hear nothing. He tried the handle and, slightly to his surprise, it opened.

Once more in the sitting room of Dolly's suite, Adam discovered it unoccupied. As he looked around, however, he heard a sound from behind another door which, he assumed, led to Dolly's bedroom. He was about to call out to the young woman but thought better of it. He moved across the room and pushed the inner door very slightly. It swung back a few inches and allowed him to see what was happening within.

Dolly was standing by her unmade bed, her hand resting on the coverlet. She was dressed in a nightgown as if she had just risen from sleep. She was staring in fear at a man in a black jacket and grey trousers, his back to Adam, who was pointing a gun in her direction.

The man spoke a few words in German.

'I tell you I ain't got the first idea what you're saying.' Dolly's voice was trembling. 'If it's gelt you want, I ain't got any.'

Frozen in the doorway, Adam was struggling to decide his best course of action. Should he retreat while he could? Or attempt to disarm the man?

'I got some jumbaree you can 'ave,' Dolly said. 'Rings and brooches and stuff. They're in the flash box over there.' She gestured towards her dressing table. The German made no response. Dolly had now seen Adam, and her eyes must have betrayed the fact as the man with the gun began to turn to his left. It was now or never.

Adam hurled back the door and threw himself forward. As he did so, he heard the gun go off. There was a scream from the young woman as Adam crashed into the intruder. He seized the man around the waist and propelled him to the floor. The pistol skittered across the floor.

The German was quicker to recover than Adam. He swung his fist towards the young man's jaw and made contact. Adam's head snapped back and he felt close to losing consciousness. He could only watch dumbly as the intruder pulled himself to his feet and looked around for his gun. It was not immediately in sight. He must have decided that he had no time to look for it, as the man turned and fled.

He left Adam half stunned on the floor, and Dolly on her bed, blood seeping from a wound in her chest.

CHAPTER THIRTY-THREE

'**H**err Doktor Brandt, at your service, sir.' The man who had stopped in front of Adam clicked his heels in a way that suggested the military profession more than it did the medical.

'Adam Carver.' The young man bowed his head in reply. He had just arrived at one of the buildings of the city's Charité hospital. Dolly, Etherege had told him, had been taken there. When he had enquired for her in broken German, a nurse had left him and returned with the elegant, black-coated gentleman who had just introduced himself.

'You vish to see Miss Delaney?' Brandt was tall and thin, with a pointed beard of sculptured neatness.

Adam agreed that this was exactly what he wished to do.

'You are the lady's lover, perhaps?' Dr Brandt pronounced the word as 'luffah'.

Adam was slightly taken aback by the doctor's use of the word at all, although he acknowledged to himself that it was not an inappropriate one. 'No, I am just a friend,' he said, after a brief pause. 'From London.'

'Ah, from London.' The doctor spoke as if he had certainly heard of the city, but only as a kind of old, half-fabled metropolis such as Troy or Babylon.

'Miss Delaney is well enough to see me?'

'Vell?' The doctor sounded personally affronted. 'She is not vell. Not vell by any means. She is badly vounded.' He seemed suddenly to grow less fierce. 'But she is vell enough to see a friend from London.'

They walked together down one of the hospital's long, grey corridors, Brandt's shoes beating out a rhythm as he went, just as if he were one of the soldiers forever marching down Unter den Linden. After thirty yards, he stopped abruptly at a door outside which a man in a dark blue uniform sat on a chair, a peaked helmet perched on his lap. The man, whom Adam took to be some sort of policeman, stood up and smartly saluted Brandt. The doctor nodded briefly at the guard, who then threw the door open.

Adam peered in and could see Dolly lying in a bed, apparently asleep. He was surprised at how agitated he felt. 'May I speak to Miss Delaney alone?'

'It is most irregular,' Brandt said, 'most irregular. But I haff been told to allow it.'

Adam wondered who had told him. He assumed that Etherege had been in contact with the hospital but he could not imagine why the hospital authorities should particularly wish to accommodate the requests of the British Embassy. And what of Ravelstein? Surely he had not spoken to anyone here? Adam nodded his thanks to Brandt and walked into the room.

'I vill be outside,' the doctor called after him. 'You haff five minutes to speak to your friend.' He closed the door.

The girl was lying on a vast bed beneath the only window in the room. She was propped up by several pillows. As Adam came closer, he could see that she was not, as he had first thought, asleep: her eyes were half open, and she was staring out of the window at the blue sky above Berlin. The whole of her upper body was heavily bandaged. She was as pale as parchment, Adam thought.

She turned as he approached, her face pinched with pain, and gazed at him as if she were unsure who he was.

'Good day to you, Miss Delaney,' Adam said, 'I trust they are looking after you here.'

'I ain't got too many complaints,' the girl said in a whisper. 'The head nurse is a bit of a bleedin' tartar, mind.'

'I am sorry to intrude upon you at a time such as this, but I have a number of questions to which I must have answers.'

Dolly made no reply. She continued to look emptily at him.

'I have to know what Vernon told you about his reasons for coming to Berlin.' Adam paused, but the young woman said nothing. 'And I need to ask you why you changed your name.'

Dolly made a noise that might almost have been a bitter laugh. She was clearly no more inclined to acknowledge any lingering fondness for Adam than she had been at the Deutscher Hof.

'You still badgering me about that? Ain't I ever going to get any peace?'

'You can prevaricate no longer, Miss Delaney,' Adam said, suddenly formal in his address. 'As you know, Harry Vernon is dead. Someone has tried to kill you. You must tell me all you know.'

The girl closed her eyes.

For a moment Adam thought she would say no more. A clock on the wall of the room ticked noisily; there was no other sound.

Adam was about to speak again when Dolly opened her eyes and glared furiously at him. 'We went to Boulogne, didn't we?' she said. 'Not that long before we started at the Prince Albert. The two of us, and Harry. We go as Dolly and Hetty and we come back the other way about. Harry give me papers that proved I was Hetty Gallant. I've still got 'em. Back at the 'otel.'

'What about the other girl?'

'She got papers that proved she was Dolly.'

'But why did she agree to the deception? I can just about understand your motives for changing your name – you would be able to start upon a new life with Harry Vernon, with a new identity. And the papers to prove who you were should you wish to travel. But what were her reasons?'

'Rhino.' Dolly held her hand out of the bedcovers and feebly rubbed her finger and thumb together. 'Wotcher think? Harry 'anded her thirty quid.'

Adam was astonished. The sum was an enormous one. It was very nearly as much as he paid Quint in a year. 'And yet a few weeks later,' he said, 'she was posing naked for money and applying for subsidies from Miss Bascombe. How could she have spent so much in so little a time?'

''Er mother.'

'Her mother spent it?' Adam was finding it difficult to follow what he was being told.

''Er mother 'ad the phossy jaw. Remember what I told you about my Aunt Loo and the matches?' Adam nodded. 'Well, it wasn't my aunt I was talking about, it was 'Etty's ma. 'Etty spent a fortune on doctors and 'ospitals and med'cines. And then 'er ma died anyways.'

'And so poor Hetty lost both her money and her mother.' Adam was abashed to hear what Dolly was telling him. All the elaborate stories of blackmail and skulduggery that he and Quint had concocted, and the simple truth was that the girl needed money to buy treatment for her sick mother.

Dolly was now attempting to pull herself up in the bed. She was unable to do so and sank back onto her pillow with a cry of pain. The sound brought Dr Brandt into the room. He took one look at his patient and then turned to Adam.

'Did I not tell you that your friend was not vell?' he said sternly. 'I must now insist. You vill leave her in peace and kviet.'

Adam had no option. He glanced briefly at Dolly, only to see that she had closed her eyes again. He raised his hat to the doctor and left. As he walked back down the long corridor, he wondered what exactly his feelings were for the wounded girl in the room.

* * * * *

'Damn you, Quint. Have a care with that razor.' Adam was sitting in a chair in his hotel room and staring into a large mirror. A towel was draped around his shoulders and his face was half covered in shaving soap. Behind him, he could see his manservant holding aloft a razor dripping with white lather. 'I want my chin shaved, not my throat cut.'

Quint grunted and dipped the razor into a bowl of water that was sitting on a marble-topped table to his right. 'Less chance of that,' he said, 'if you was to sit still in the bleeding chair and not fidget like a dog with fleas.'

Adam peered into the mirror. A tiny rivulet of blood was running down his neck and drops were falling onto the towel. He lifted a corner of it and wiped the blood away. 'I should have entrusted my whiskers to some Teutonic Figaro,' he said, 'rather than allowed you near my chin with such a lethal weapon.'

'Nothing more than a drop of the ruby,' Quint said. 'No 'arm done.'

'You would not be so blasé if the ruby in question was yours and not mine.'

'Anyways, you're finished now.'

Adam stood up, continuing to dab at his chin with the towel, and began to walk about the room. Quint took away the bowl of water and then returned to perch on the arm of a chair. He lit a cigarette and began to scatter ash on the floor.

'You found cigarettes, I see,' Adam remarked, still examining his face in the mirror. It seemed to have stopped bleeding. 'You were complaining of running low.'

'German ones,' Quint said, waving his hand in the air and depositing more ash on the plush carpet of the hotel room. 'Ain't much of a smoke. Three draws and a spit and they're done.'

There was silence in the room as Adam began to tie a white cravat around his neck and his manservant continued to smoke.

'This bint in the 'ospital,' Quint said eventually.

'Dolly,' Adam said.

'This bint, Dolly. She took the name of the other bint, right?'

'That is correct.'

Quint stubbed out his cigarette and immediately lit another. He looked thoughtful.

'And this dead cully, Harry Vernon. He was doing the four-legged frolic with Dolly.'

'He and Dolly were lovers, yes.'

'And he come here to Berlin to flog something 'e'd stole.'

'Correct again.'

'But 'e ain't the one whose idea it was to filch whatever it is 'e filched. Which you ain't about to tell me.'

'No, I do not believe that he is the mastermind behind the plot.'

'So 'oo is?'

'The answer to that question lies in London. We have done all we can here in Berlin. Dolly will be cared for in the Charité. When she is well enough to travel, Etherege has promised to arrange her journey home. It is time for us to return to Doughty Street.'

'Owf weeder sin to the Prusskies, then.'

'Precisely. I could not have expressed it better myself, Quint.'

PART FIVE

LONDON

CHAPTER THIRTY-FOUR

'So, poor Harry is no more.' Adam and the Honourable Richard Sunman were walking together in St James's Park. The man from the Foreign Office sounded genuinely distressed when he spoke of Vernon. 'We received news from Etherege, of course. He had been informed by the authorities in Berlin that Harry died in a shooting accident near the Grünewald hunting lodge. Had we not had his more private report and your eyewitness story, we would have not known the exact circumstances leading to his death.'

'Can nothing now be done to hold the people responsible for his murder to account?'

Sunman waved his hand impatiently. 'Not a thing,' he said. 'Unfortunately, we must accept what they have told us. Ravelstein is too close to Bismarck. We cannot afford to make waves.'

'That is precisely what Etherege said.'

'He was correct.'

The two men stopped. Adam glanced at his companion, who was prodding his silver-topped cane into the gravel of the path on which they were standing.

'Poor Harry has been laid to rest in the Protestant cemetery in Berlin,' Sunman said. 'Half of his mother's family are already there, it seems.'

'And this sorry saga will be laid to rest with him?'

'Of course it will not,' Sunman snapped.

'I thought as much.'

'How can it be when one outstanding question remains, the most important question of all. The submarine plans. What has happened to them? Ravelstein cannot be in possession of them. They were not in Harry's room at the Deutscher Hof when Etherege's men searched it. Nor in the hotel safe.'

'Perhaps Vernon did not take them abroad at all.'

'Perhaps not. But I shall not sleep soundly in my bed until their whereabouts are ascertained.'

'Actually, I think that I can hazard a guess as to where they are.'

Sunman looked sharply at Adam. 'This is not a time for idle jests.'

'I am not jesting.'

'My God, Adam,' the young aristocrat said, swinging his stick like a rustic scything corn, 'if you know anything more about these damn plans, you must tell me.'

'Bear with me, old man,' Adam said, taking a step back. There was no doubt about it: he was once again rather enjoying Sunman's discomfiture. 'All in good time. I have some further enquiries to make before I can be certain.'

'You must tell me immediately if you learn any more about the blueprints.' Sunman was in a state of nervous agitation now, shifting his cane from one hand to the other as they walked. 'It is impossible to overemphasize the importance of recovering them.'

For the country, Adam wondered, or for the future of your career at the Foreign Office? Both perhaps, he concluded, trying to be as charitable to his friend as he could be. The two men continued to walk, now in silence, along a path that ran parallel to the Mall.

'Etherege seemed to think that Harry will be remembered in the FO as a hero rather than a villain,' Adam said eventually.

Sunman shrugged. What did it matter, his attitude seemed to say, how Vernon was remembered? 'For most people, he will have been the victim of a tragic shooting accident abroad. There is no reason for us to say more. There are, however, small numbers of people within the FO who cannot be fobbed off with such a story.'

'So you will fob them off with another?'

Sunman ignored Adam's facetiousness. 'We will tell them that he

322

travelled to Berlin in order deliberately to mislead the Germans,' he said, 'and that he was killed when his subterfuge was discovered. The fact that he absconded to the Continent with the intention of betraying his queen and country will be conveniently ignored.'

'And all the alarums and excursions of the last few weeks will be forgotten.'

'If you can do as you say and locate the plans,' Sunman said pointedly.

'Oh, I think I can do that.'

'I pray to God that your confidence is justified.'

There was another silence. Adam could see the roof of Buckingham Palace in the distance and a flag fluttering on its pole.

'It is fitting, I suppose,' he said.

'What is fitting?' Sunman was sounding increasingly exasperated.

'That the end of Vernon's life should be the subject of such invention. It seems appropriate.'

'I do not follow you, Adam. Why should this fable that I have been obliged to construct to explain Harry's death be in any way appropriate?'

'Do you not see, old chap? Harry's whole story has been an illusion, a theatrical effect.' Adam took his friend's arm as they turned towards the lake. 'Have you heard of Pepper's Ghost?'

'I cannot say that I have.' The young aristocrat's mouth was pursed in disapproval. 'I am no great habitué of the theatres.'

'Professor Pepper is a lecturer at the Royal Polytechnic Institution in Regent Street. He has used a clever arrangement of mirrors to make audiences believe that they see things which are not there. What they believe is in front of their eyes is nothing more than a reflection.'

'I am sure the good professor is a very ingenious man, Adam, but I cannot see the relevance of his ingenuity to the matter in hand.'

'You still do not understand, Sunman, do you?' Adam unhooked his arm from that of his friend. 'You have been deceived from beginning to end of this matter. So have I. Poor Harry Vernon and his love affair, the search for Dolly Delaney, Vernon's flight to Germany

– they have all been like Pepper's Ghost. They have been shadows designed to keep our attention occupied while the real business takes place behind the scenes.'

'Designed? Designed by whom?'

Adam had already turned to walk away. 'When I am certain of the answer to that question,' he called over his shoulder as he strode towards Horseguards Parade, 'you will be the first person to know.'

* * * * *

'Do they never clean their drinking vessels here?' Adam wondered aloud. The Three Pigs seemed no less filthy a den on his second visit to it than it had on his first. He inspected his gin and water more closely. 'I swear I can see the fingermarks of the last ten people to use it on this glass.'

'Fingermarks ain't going to be the worst of it, guv,' Quint said, nodding in the direction of the bar. ''Ere comes trouble.'

The squat figure of Jem Baines was making his way towards them, pushing his way through the crowd of drinkers. He was wearing a shabby blue jacket and what had once been, long ago, white duck trousers but were now an unappetizing shade of brown. Together with a rolling gait, they gave him a distinctly nautical air. His arm was clamped around the waist of the red-haired woman named Kate who had been his companion before.

'Look at our old pal Quintus, Kate,' Baines sneered. 'Sitting there with his dandy chum. 'E's so flash these days, it's a wonder 'e knows 'isself in a mirror.'

Quint made to rise from his seat. 'You'll be findin' your bleedin' eye in a sling,' he said, 'if you ain't careful, Jem Baines.'

'Gentlemen, gentlemen, let us have no more vituperation.' Adam held out his hands soothingly. 'We have not come here to quarrel, Mr Baines. We have come here to reach a mutually beneficial agreement.'

'I ain't got the first bleedin' idea what you're talkin' about, fancy boy,' Baines said. 'You and your five-guinea words.'

'Ah, well, I shall endeavour to use less complicated language.

Will you not join us, Mr Baines?' Adam gestured to an empty chair at their table. 'We have much to discuss.'

Baines looked at Adam, and then at the chair, as if he suspected that either or both might suddenly attack him. 'I ain't got no call to join you,' he said.

'No matter. If you wish to stand, you are free to do so.'

''Course I am. I can do what I wants 'ere.'

'But not everywhere else in London.'

'What the bleedin' 'ell d'you mean?'

'There are some things you have been doing – away from the confines of this delightful hostelry – in which the police might well take an interest.'

'You can fry in your own grease, fancy boy. I ain't done nothing to catch a bluebottle's eye.' Baines sounded defiant but his confidence was slightly dented. He pulled back the chair and sat in it. 'But whyn't you tell me what I'm supposed to have done?'

'By all means, Mr Baines.' Adam relaxed back in his chair. 'I will relate a little story, to provide some background detail. It begins with a gentleman named Job Benskin. You know him, do you not?'

''Course I do. He was 'ere the first night you and Quint come visitin'.'

'He was here at your suggestion, I think. You and Benskin were in alliance. He had told you about me and his previous acquaintance with me. He had told you of his plans to extort money out of me. Why not, you said, invite him to the Three Pigs? So you both asked the landlord if you could make use of the room at the back' – Adam nodded in the direction of the door through which he had exited in a fury some weeks earlier – 'and he agreed.'

'Ain't no harm in that,' Baines said belligerently.

'None whatsoever.'

'Using a room in a pub.' The pickpocket laughed derisively. 'The blues ain't likely to be after me for that.'

'No, they are not. However, our friends in the police might be more interested in your activities in Doughty Street.'

'Doughty Street? Is that round this neck of the woods, then?

Ain't ever 'eard of it in Whitechapel. What about you, Kate?' He turned to his tipsy doxy, who tried her best to focus her eyes on him. 'You ever 'eard of a Doughty Street in these parts?'

'It's odd that you should forget your visit there, Mr Baines, because you left a little memento of it behind you.'

'Memento? What's a bleedin' memento?'

'An item belonging to you. An item of clothing.' Adam gestured to Quint, who reached inside a carpet bag they had brought with them and extracted something from it.

Baines glanced at the battered article, reached towards it and then stopped himself.

'That's right,' Adam said. 'Your hat fell off during our fracas at my rooms. And you never came back to claim it.'

'Ain't my hat, cully.'

'Are you certain of that, Mr Baines? It has your initials in it. Much though I have my doubts about Mr Job Benskin, I don't think they are his. Take a closer look at it.'

'Ain't my hat, I tell you.'

'Oh, I think it is.'

'And if it is – which it ain't – what the 'ell's it prove? It's jest a bleedin' 'at.'

'It proves you were in my rooms. And there's more. There's the porter, Mr Knibbs. A fine fellow, Mr Knibbs, a decorated veteran of the war in the Crimea, just the kind of witness a jury likes. He'll swear that it was you he saw going in through the gate at Doughty Street, claiming to be a friend of mine.'

Baines looked at Adam doubtfully. For a moment he was disconcerted, but he recovered his bounce almost immediately. 'Get out of 'ere,' he said, 'afore I gets someone to throw you out. A black billy-cock 'at no diff'rent to thousands of others and an old so'jer who prob'ly doesn't know whether 'e's coming or going? You're joking with me. That ain't going to stand up in court.'

'You think not? Inspector Pulverbatch seemed to think differently.'

Baines, who had been about to stand up, sat down again immediately.

'Did I not mention I was a friend of Inspector Pulverbatch?' Adam asked sweetly. 'He was delighted when I told him about my rencontre with you, Mr Baines. It seems he's an old friend of yours as well.'

'That devil Pulverbatch. If I don't see 'im til 'ell freezes over, it'll still be too soon.'

'Yes, Inspector Pulverbatch was delighted to hear how you and I had made acquaintance with one another. It seems that the police have been interested in you for some time, Mr Baines, but they can only ever indict you for dipping your hand into other people's pockets. They would greatly relish seeing you in court on some more serious charge. Breaking and entering, for instance, or assault and battery. Inspector Pulverbatch seemed as certain as he could be that he would be able to make a successful prosecution in this case. I think it's fair to say that his eyes positively lit up when your name was mentioned.'

Baines took several deep breaths. He rested his hands on his thighs and examined his knuckles. He looked around the room as if searching for a means of escape and then stared downwards again. A minute passed.

'It wasn't my idea to rook you with the yarn about your old man,' he said eventually. 'It wasn't Benskin's neither.' The man's self-confidence had almost entirely disappeared. His only concern now seemed to be to avoid any meeting with Pulverbatch. 'It was a toff like yourself. 'E come in the Pigs one night and spoke to me and Benskin both. Give us two quid apiece to set you up with the story. Later, 'e give me another sov for doing over your rooms.'

Adam wondered how much Baines had been given to attack him with a knife. He was certain that his assailant in the muffler had, on both occasions, been the ruffian in front of him, but he could see little purpose in raising the question. Baines was saying enough as it was. 'And what was the name of this "toff" who employed you?' he asked.

'You think he provides us with a moniker and asks us to sign a contract?' Baines gave a short and bitter laugh. 'I ain't got the first bleedin' clue what 'is name is.'

'But you would know him again.'

'Of course I would.'

'Is this the gentleman of whom we have been talking?' Adam held out a cabinet card. Baines took it in his grubby hand and peered at it. 'That's the cove, right enough,' he said. 'I'd know 'im anywhere.'

'And, tell me, Quint.' Adam turned to his manservant and showed him the photograph. 'Do you recognize this same gentleman?'

Quint made a great show of turning the cabinet card this way and that as he looked at it. 'It's 'im, all right,' he said eventually. 'It's the bloke Benskin met in Regent Street.'

'In which case, I think it is time I went to speak to the gentleman in question.' Adam stood and moved towards the door of the pub.

Quint, tucking the carpet bag under his arm and throwing a look of infinite disdain in Baines's direction, followed him.

CHAPTER THIRTY-FIVE

'When I am certain,' he had said to Sunman. Well, now he was. As Adam sat in a cab taking him to the Albany, he was as certain of the answers to his friend's question as he could be. There was only one man who could have masterminded the plot to steal the blueprints. It was the man whose photograph he had shown to Baines and Quint. It was the man whose rooms in Albany he was about to visit. He touched the pistol in the pocket of his jacket to reassure himself it was still there.

Adam had asked the cabman to drop him in Piccadilly and now he walked along the narrow passage that led to the exclusive block of flats. Once inside, he climbed the stairs to the first floor where he knew, from his enquiries, that his quarry lived. He found the entrance to the rooms and knocked. Hearing footsteps approaching the door, he stepped back as it opened. A tall, gaunt figure was framed in the doorway.

It was Gilbert Waterton.

'Ah, the persistent Mr Carver. After Ravelstein telegraphed me with details of what happened the other day, I thought that I might possibly be receiving a visit from you.' Waterton made an extravagant gesture of welcome. 'Allow me to invite you into my humble abode.'

Adam entered and made his way past his host into a short, dark corridor.

'The first door on the left will take you into my reception room,' Waterton said.

The room was tastefully but not extravagantly decorated. Adam's eyes were immediately caught by two prints of Roman goddesses – Diana and Minerva, perhaps – on the wall facing him. His host moved past him and towards a drinks decanter on a table beneath a tall, eighteenth-century window. For a moment, Adam thought he would be offered refreshment but, instead, Waterton turned suddenly and smiled at him. He was holding a gun.

'I am growing weary of people pointing firearms at me,' Adam remarked.

'Perhaps you should refrain from poking your nose so assiduously into those people's business.' Waterton waved the pistol briefly in the direction of a leather-covered chair. 'Do sit down while I decide what I should do with you.'

'I think I prefer to stand.'

'Your preferences are of no interest to me.' Waterton waved the gun in his hand again. 'Sit down.'

Adam lowered himself into a chair. Waterton bared his teeth in an approximation of a smile. 'Thank you, Mr Carver.' He sat down carefully in another chair, his eyes never leaving Adam's. 'And, now we are both comfortable, we can debate the best method of resolving the tangle in which we find ourselves.' While keeping the gun carefully trained on his visitor, Waterton made a pantomime of pondering what he should do. 'No, I do not think there is any other way,' he said eventually. 'I shall have to kill you.' He grinned wolfishly at Adam. 'But, before I do, I have one or two questions to ask you. Just to satisfy my own curiosity. And if you have any questions yourself, do feel at liberty to put them to me – I should hate you to go to meet your Maker in a state of bewilderment.'

'That is most kind of you.'

'Ever the gentleman,' Waterton said. 'In fact, so much the gentleman that I shall allow you to ask your questions first.'

'Most generous of you.' Adam bowed his head in ironic acknowledgement. 'But you have been the puppet master throughout this play that has been enacted, have you not?'

'I have pulled some of the strings,' Waterton admitted. 'Greed and lust have also had their roles in the drama. Would poor Harry have done what he did had he not been so pathetically eager to bed a beautiful dancer? Would the girls have played their parts if they had not dreamed of gold and jewels? I think not.'

'You corrupted all of them.'

The man laughed. 'How melodramatic your language becomes. You have been tainted, Mr Carver, by your time in the theatre. I did not corrupt them – I merely provided the opportunity for their inherent vices to flourish. Who knows? If I had not shown Harry a way of escaping his tipsy wife and finding some pleasure between the sheets, perhaps someone else would have done so.'

'You make your deeds sound like those of a philanthropist. But everything was planned so that you would have a hold over Vernon. So that you would be able to blackmail him into agreeing to your plans.'

'I needed a scapegoat. Or perhaps "sacrificial lamb" is a better term.' Waterton spoke as if he believed that any reasonable man could only agree with him. 'Harry was so obvious a choice for the role that casting him in it was easy.'

'You compromised him with Dolly and forced him into stealing the plans for the submarine. Then you arranged for him to travel to Berlin to deliver them to Ravelstein. I have no doubt that you emphasized his knowledge of Berlin and of the German language. Flattered him into further participation. It would not surprise me to learn that Harry Vernon almost came to believe that the whole scheme to sell the secrets was as much his as yours.'

'You are an astute man, in your own way, Mr Carver.' Waterton was staring coldly at Adam. 'Harry's ability to delude himself was astonishing. There were times when he did seem to forget that what we were planning was treason and that he had had to be, shall we say, coaxed into joining me. And he did indeed begin to assume that we were equal partners in the enterprise.'

'He was wrong, of course.'

'Oh, entirely. But Harry made very many unjustifiable assumptions. He assumed, for instance, that Dolly was wildly enamoured of him.'

'Whereas, in truth, she was besotted with you.'

'It would be immodest of me to agree with you,' Waterton said, looking far from modest as he spoke. 'But she was prepared to go to great lengths to please me.'

'Including seducing Harry at your request.'

'Including that.'

'And so she travelled with Vernon to the Continent.'

'Yes. He was still under the impression that the girl adored him. He wanted her to go with him. It seemed easiest to tell her to accompany him.' There was a pause as Waterton continued to stare at Adam like a stage hypnotist endeavouring to influence a member of his audience. 'How, I wonder, did you guess that Harry had fled the country?'

'I found a scrap of paper hidden in one of the song-sheets at Dolly's lodgings. It had times on it which could only have referred to the boat trains. It was in Harry's writing.'

Waterton smiled mirthlessly. 'I told her from the beginning to destroy any communications she received from him,' he said. 'And I suppose it was an obvious assumption for you and Sunman that he would make his way to the land of his birth.'

'Obvious enough. Where else would he go?'

'Where else indeed?' Waterton gave another ugly smile. 'One of Harry's characteristics on which one could always rely was his predictability.'

'And the blueprints . . .'

'Harry *thought* he had them with him.'

'I am sure he did. But in fact they were in your possession. What did poor Vernon take so trustingly to Ravelstein?'

'I believe it was the designs of a new breech-loading cannon. Mildly interesting, perhaps, but scarcely worth the money the Germans had offered to pay for the submarine plans.'

'So, when Ravelstein came to believe that he was being tricked, he ordered his men to kill Harry. You would have come along a little while later, with the real plans, taken the money and returned to London. Everybody would have known that the plans had been sold to Germany but everybody would have assumed that Harry Vernon – the late Harry Vernon – was the traitor. You would have continued your life in London just as before. Except that you would be, say, ten thousand pounds better off. And free to do further business with Ravelstein and the Germans.'

'Something like that,' Waterton agreed. 'Although I could not be certain that Ravelstein would do away with Harry. However, I know that the count is not a man who likes to be crossed. It seemed to me very possible that he would. And, if he did not, the plan would still work. I could still make my appearance with the submarine designs and Harry would still be blamed for everything. He could babble all he wanted about my treachery but no one would be likely to believe him.'

'There is only one thing I do not quite understand,' Adam said. 'Why did the women need to exchange identities? Why did Dolly have to become Hetty and Hetty become Dolly?' Yet even as he asked the question, he suddenly knew the answer. 'It was done to protect the real Dolly, was it not? Just as Harry was to be the scapegoat for your crimes, so the other girl was to provide camouflage for your lady friend.'

'How *clever* you are, Mr Carver.' Waterton spoke with a sneer. 'You are correct, of course. The original plan was merely that she could hide behind a new name. In addition, I thought that changing the girls' identities might sow extra seeds of confusion. More smoke and mirrors. It has turned out rather well. With the false Dolly dead, it will become even easier for the real Dolly to embark on a new life.'

'With you?'

Waterton shrugged. 'Perhaps,' he said. 'I am not a sentimental man, but I admire Dolly Delaney. She has intelligence, spirit and ambition. All qualities to be applauded. And, like me, she knows how to protect her own interests. She was eager to gain her new identity. Indeed, she insisted on it as a *quid pro quo* for her participation in the plot.' Adam had his own reasons for admiring the girl, but he said nothing of them. 'And yet in Berlin,' he remarked, 'you arranged an attempt on her life.'

'That was not I.' Waterton was angered by the suggestion. 'It was

Ravelstein. He believed at first that she knew more than she did. In any case, his plan was not to kill her. His agent arrived at the Deutscher Hof to abduct her. Your arrival in her room threw everything into confusion and poor Dolly was shot accidentally.'

'So it was my fault?'

'In a sense.'

'And the death of the false Dolly? The girl in York. I suppose that too is my responsibility.'

Adam spoke with heavy sarcasm but Waterton, pretending to think the matter over, agreed with him. 'A modicum of the blame can be attached to you,' he said. 'It was mostly the girl's fault for deciding so precipitously to travel north. I was happy for you to chase around London in pursuit of her. London is a large place, so there was little chance that you would catch up with her. But when she went to York and you followed, I thought it only too likely that you might find her and speak to her.'

'So you also travelled to York and you killed her.'

'That was not part of my original plan.'

'But you murdered her. Tracked her to the theatre, chloroformed her and stabbed her to death.'

'If you say so.' Waterton shrugged. 'It was better that she be hurried off to meet her Maker than loiter around York making a damn nuisance of herself.'

'And, of course, you killed poor Cyril Montague.'

'Poor Cyril Montague, as you so naively call him, was a malicious little opium-soaked nancy boy who was too greedy for his own good. He came calling upon me when he returned to town. With ridiculous threats and demands for money.'

'That was the worst mistake he ever made, I suppose.'

Waterton smiled as if enjoying some private joke. 'I could not take the risk that he would speak unwisely to other people. To your good self, for instance. I'd already guessed when I was in York that the girl might have been indiscreet in her discussions with him. I wanted to speak to him to learn how much, if anything, he knew. I tried to find his address from the theatre records.'

'It must have been you that Quint saw in the office in the York theatre.'

'I saw no one in that office.' Waterton sounded surprised. 'And no one saw me.'

'That is where you are mistaken. Quint was under a table at the time. He heard you coming and hid himself.'

Waterton laughed. 'So all the time I was looking for something which would tell me where Montague was, your little homunculus was crouched under the furniture, was he? How amusing!'

'But you were unable to find him?'

'I had so little time. I needed to be back here. I came to the conclusion that Montague in York represented little threat to my plans. But then I saw that he was in town once more, having read about it in one of the papers—'

'—and you decided to kill him.'

'Only after he began to make a nuisance of himself. If he had not had the gall to approach me with a demand for money, he would be alive today and spouting Shakespeare to his heart's content. He knew, of course, that the Dolly in York was not who she claimed to be. He had been in the same theatre company as the real Dolly.'

'At the Gaiety.'

'If you say so. I am not such a devotee of the stage as you seem to be.' Waterton continued to sound as if he was enjoying the conversation. 'He had not only realized that Dolly was not Dolly but he had learnt that she had been paid money to change her name. This had aroused his curiosity. He had wheedled more information out of the girl, I think.'

'He knew of your connection to her?' Adam was puzzled.

Waterton shrugged. 'Not at that point, no,' he said. 'I assume that the wretched girl spoke of Harry in York. Montague visited Harry when he returned to town and the fool panicked. Not only blurted out far more than he should have done about our scheme, but mentioned my name.'

'And Cyril sealed his fate when he approached you demanding money to keep quiet about what he'd learned.'

Waterton nodded. 'I couldn't run the risk that that opium-soaked board-treader knew enough to scupper my plans. I followed him to the theatre in Holborn one afternoon. He thought I had come to pay him off. I brought a bottle of wine with me. We drank several glasses. Or rather, he did and I pretended to. The wine had been liberally dosed with laudanum.'

'There was no wine bottle in his dressing room.'

'I took it away with me. And the two glasses. I had to wait a confounded age before the drug took effect. Montague's constitution must have become so inured to the intake of opium that it needed enough laudanum to fell an elephant before he succumbed to it.' Waterton was still holding his pistol but he seemed relaxed. He had the air of a popular clubman recounting a favourite anecdote to a gathering of his friends. 'But he did so eventually and I left, clutching the evidence of my crime. No one saw me go save some strange urchin who was loitering in the theatre lobby.'

Billy Bantam, Adam thought. That had been what the belligerent little man had been trying to tell him that night as he had left the Holborn theatre.

'So,' Waterton continued cheerfully, still the amiable raconteur, 'the girl and the nancy boy were both dead. They were no longer in a position to open their mouths and ruin everything. You were a minor irritant, but I was confident that you knew only a little. All could go ahead as planned.'

'Harry Vernon could travel to Berlin.'

'Exactly.' Waterton smiled. 'Anything more you wish to know? Or is all adequately explained?'

'I do have one or two questions,' Adam said, wishing to keep Waterton talking as long as he possibly could. 'Was it you who persuaded Job Benskin to approach me?'

'Ah, the bitter Mr Benskin. I have long known him – from those happy days when he was general factotum to your father. Would you believe that I once invested money in one of your father's many railway schemes? I lost it all, of course, but I made acquaintance with Benskin at the time. Imagine my pleasure when I bumped into

336

him in the Strand one afternoon. And realized how useful he might be to me.' Waterton moved the gun from one hand to another. He stretched the fingers on the hand that had been holding the weapon before returning the gun to its original position. All the time he did this, it continued to point at Adam. 'He needed little persuasion, incidentally. Poor Benskin. He really does hate you. I thought that his story about your father's demise might, if suitably embellished, distract your attention from the search for Dolly. I underestimated your determination to find her.'

'I found it odd that Benskin should suddenly appear from nowhere, after so many years, and confront me.' Adam shifted slightly in his seat. 'And what about the attempts on my life? That was the man Baines, I assume?'

'A fool as well as a rogue.' Waterton sniffed in distaste. 'I found him through Benskin. I gave him money to threaten you on the night you visited the East End.'

'And the night I was leaving the German Gymnasium?'

'The man was a loose cannon. He seemed to think that, since I had paid him a certain amount to knock you down and wave a knife in your face, I would necessarily pay him even more if he actually used the knife on you. I had to disabuse him of that notion. By that point, you seemed little more than a harmless distraction. I had even decided that you might be useful to me insofar as your investigations could lead me to the girl in York.' Waterton sat back in his chair, but the gun remained half pointed in Adam's direction. 'So, now I think you know everything, Mr Carver,' he said. 'It is a pity that the knowledge can be of no benefit to you. And now there remain only the questions I wish to ask you before I dispose of you.' Waterton leaned forward slightly in his seat. 'I am curious to learn . . .'

His words were interrupted by a furious knocking on the door, and several raised voices could be heard in the corridor outside. One of them, Adam recognized with relief, was that of Inspector Pulverbatch. Quint had, for once, done exactly what he had asked of him: he had gone to Scotland Yard and summoned help.

'The game is up, Waterton,' Adam said. 'That is the police.'

CHAPTER THIRTY-SIX

he hammering at the door continued. Waterton turned in the direction of the sound, looking suddenly panicked and unsure of himself. He stared at the print of Minerva on his wall as if the goddess might provide him with the wisdom he needed to make a decision. Standing up, he moved a step or two towards Adam, who remained seated. 'I should destroy you for the interfering devil you are,' Waterton said. The two men gazed at one another as the noise from the door increased. Waterton raised the pistol and aimed it more deliberately at the young man's head.

Adam felt his heartbeat rise and his pulse pound. 'There is no point,' he said, his throat dry and his voice croaking. 'You might escape the noose for the murders you have already committed, but you would scarcely do so if you killed me with Inspector Pulverbatch and his men as witnesses outside the door.'

There was a long pause and Waterton dropped his aim. He had recovered something of his aplomb. 'You are right, of course,' he said. 'The temptation to put an end to you is strong, but your death although it would afford me great pleasure, would bring me no advantage.'

'Your best course of action is to surrender yourself to the police.'

'Perhaps.' Waterton backed away, still holding the gun.

Adam heard behind him the sound of the door to the flat beginning to splinter under the assault of Pulverbatch's men. He turned his head briefly and, as he did so, Waterton ran into his bedroom and slammed shut the door. The key turned in the lock just before a thunderous crash came from the entrance hall. Two uniformed constables, one wielding a fireman's axe, charged into the reception room.

'He's in there,' Adam shouted, pointing at the bedroom door, 'and he's armed with a pistol.'

The policemen stopped in their tracks and looked over their shoulders, awaiting instructions. Pulverbatch strolled through the door with the ease of a pub regular approaching the bar of his local hostelry. He nodded amiably at Adam as if greeting a fellow drinker. 'Ain't seen you in a month of Sundays,' he said. 'I understand from your man you've caught us a murderer.'

'He's in there,' Adam repeated, nodding in the direction Waterton had gone.

'Well, what you waiting for?' Pulverbatch addressed his constables. 'Christmas? You've got that bloody axe, ain't you? You made matchwood of the other bleeding door, didn't you? Knock this one down so's we can get the cuffs on this murderous toff and all go home.'

The constable with the axe, a large man almost bursting out of his overstretched uniform, took a step forward and struck the lock a sharp blow.

'Hit it again, Garforth,' Pulverbatch advised, 'and this time put your back into it.'

Garforth raised the axe far above his head and brought it down on his target with tremendous force. The lock and the wood surrounding it broke into a dozen fragments and the door flew open.

There was a pause, and then Pulverbatch moved forward and stuck his head warily into the room.

'Nobody in here,' he said, taking several paces into the bedroom.

Adam followed the inspector inside. The policeman was correct. Waterton's bedroom was almost spartan in its lack of furnishings and it was, indeed, empty. Looking around, Adam could see that there was nowhere to hide save under the bed. He was about to motion to Pulverbatch to indicate this when he felt a breath of air on his face. 'The window,' he cried.

The constable named Garforth had now also entered the room, still holding onto the axe, and he moved swiftly to the window, one sash of which had been pushed open. Garforth thrust his head through the gap. There was the sound of a pistol shot and the constable fell back into the room, blood streaming from his forehead.

Pulverbatch, galvanized by the injury to his officer, rushed forward to help him. 'Ain't nothing but a scratch,' he said, relief in his voice, as Garforth looked at him with dazed eyes. 'The bullet's done no more than crease the skin. Stand back, for God's sake. Ain't you got the sense you was born with?' This last remark was addressed to the second constable, who was approaching the open window 'Take care of your pal,' Pulverbatch said, pushing Garforth, still confused and bleeding, into the other constable's arms.

The inspector then picked up the axe, which the wounded constable had dropped as he fell backwards, and held it at arm's length out of the window. There was the sound of another shot and the ricochet of bullet off iron axehead. Pulverbatch pulled the axe back into the room and stared at the dent in the metal. 'This bugger's as mad as a striped adder, ain't he?' he said, conversationally, to Adam

'He will escape,' Adam said.

'We're two floors up,' the inspector said. 'How's he going to do that, then? Come to that, where is he? A-hanging in mid-air?'

At first, Adam had no answer. He had heard strange stories from a gentleman of his acquaintance of an American spiritualist medium named Home who had, it was alleged, hovered in the air outside a third-storey window, but he doubted that Waterton possessed such supernatural powers. The solution to the mystery came suddenly to him. 'The portico,' he said. 'There is a pillared portico at the main entrance to the building. He has dropped from the window onto the top of it. He will be endeavouring to make his way from there to the ground. We must stop him.'

He moved to the window and, very gingerly, peered through it He was right. Waterton was crouched on top of the portico, looking down towards the cobbled courtyard below. The drop was more than twenty feet, and he was clearly seeking a means of scrambling safely down one of the white Doric pillars that framed the entrance. Indeed, he was now too involved in his search to pay attention to the window above him.

Adam leaned a little further out. Out of the corner of his eye, he noticed that a new complication had been added to the drama. The courtyard had been empty save for a stray dog, but now a dishevelled figure ambled onto it from Piccadilly. It was Quint. Adam had been so intent on Waterton's escape that he had not noticed his manservant's earlier absence. Pulverbatch and his officers must have left Quint to follow them. Now, here he was, turning up, as so often in his life, at exactly the wrong moment.

The manservant stopped in the centre of the cobbles and, shading his eyes against the spring sunlight, looked up.

'Take care, Quint,' Adam shouted. 'He has a gun.'

The scruffy figure below seemed bewildered. He looked up at the open window, as if awaiting further instructions. He had still not, it seemed, seen the man on the portico. Waterton, however, had seen him and he had heard Adam's call from above. Caught in two minds, he fired his gun at Quint before twisting sharply around to point it upwards at Adam. As he did so, however, he lost his footing. He flailed his arms wildly in an attempt to recover his balance but was unable to do so. Adam could only watch as, with a shout of horror, Waterton toppled backwards and out of sight. There was a moment's silence and then a howl of pain.

'He has fallen,' Adam said to Pulverbatch as he pulled his head back into the room. 'We should go.'

Leaving his colleague to tend the still-bleeding Garforth, the inspector raced out of Waterton's rooms with Adam and down the stairs. As they reached the main door, which was open, they could see Quint standing in the courtyard, staring down at a broken figure on the cobbles. They joined him.

A sheaf of papers had fallen from Waterton's jacket pocket and was lying on the ground. Adam reached down and picked them up. He glanced briefly at one of them to confirm that they were the blueprints for the submarine, and then thrust them into his own pocket.

'You took an enormous risk in bearding the lion in his den, Adam
Sunman was stretched out in a chair in his room at the Foreig
Office. He looked more relaxed than he had done for weeks.

'It was not so great,' Adam said. 'Waterton is no senseless man o
violence. He committed his murders for a reason. I knew that there
would be no advantage for him in killing me at the end. Indeed, i
would be a positive disadvantage, with the police clamouring fo
entrance to his flat.'

'It was a gamble none the less, and a brave one.'

Adam waved away the praise with an air of faint embarrassment
'Waterton should have stayed and tried to brazen it out,' he said
'There was little real evidence against him other than the admis
sions he made to me. His mistake – nearly fatal as it proved – was t
attempt that escape.'

'How is the man? Do you know?'

'He is still in the hands of the doctors. He has broken both hi
legs, but they believe he will survive.'

'It is a terrible thing to say, but I rather wish he does not. He ha
caused us so much trouble already. If he lives to stand trial, he wil
cause even more.' Sunman sighed and stared up at the stucco ceil
ing. 'Ah well, we will cross that bridge when, or if, we come to i
Perhaps something can be arranged.'

Adam smiled to himself. It was so very like Sunman to believ
that something could always 'be arranged'. In his world, perhaps i
always could. They sat in silence.

'You know, I'm still not sure exactly what really happened
Sunman said eventually. 'Perhaps you could oblige me with som
further explanation.'

Adam sat forward in his chair. 'In a nutshell,' he said, 'Waterto
persuaded Dolly to seduce Harry Vernon. Once Vernon was in
position to be blackmailed, he could be forced to acquiesce in th
plan to sell the submarine plans to Germany.'

'Yes, I understand that well enough.' Sunman sounded exas

perated, as if Adam were deliberately and maliciously casting aspersions on his intelligence. 'But why, in heaven's name, did they come to me and enlist my assistance in finding the girl when she disappeared?'

'It was *Harry* who came to you, was it not? Waterton did not. I think Harry was struggling to escape the coils in which he found himself.'

'He could not see any means of revealing the plot himself, but hoped that I would learn something of what was happening and put an end to it?'

'Exactly. Waterton, I have no doubt, was furious when he discovered what Harry had done. But then he was arrogant enough to believe that he could turn the pair of us into pawns in his game.' Adam sighed. 'In one sense, he was right. I became his unwitting accomplice. I led him to York. I led him to the girl. And he killed her.'

'And what of all Harry's tearful remorse – the scenes we both witnessed in which he bewailed his fate. That was all an act?'

Adam nodded. 'Although,' he said, 'in all likelihood, he *was* remorseful. But, other than by approaching you, he could see no means of extricating himself from the web Waterton had woven around him. And it was only in Berlin, at Pfaueninsel, that he would have realized the full extent of the treachery his supposed friend had planned. But by then it was too late. Ravelstein had him in his power.'

'And the real Dolly Delaney? The one who called herself Hetty Gallant—?'

'Dolly, I think, was motivated mostly by money. She wished for a life of ease and luxury. Who does not? She saw Waterton as a means to that end. I do not think she appreciated how dangerous a man he was. She was accustomed to controlling and manipulating the men in her life. She made the error of assuming that she could do the same with Waterton.'

Sunman reached for the square silver box on his desk and extracted two cigars from it. He offered one to Adam. Adam took it and leant forward as his friend struck a wax vesta. Both cigars were soon lit and plumes of smoke rose upwards.

'By the by, Adam, I have heard from Etherege.'

'About Dolly?'

Sunman nodded. 'The girl is still in the hospital in Berlin, although the doctor is very happy with her progress. Young chap from the embassy called Bury pops in to see her regularly. Seems he's quite smitten with her. Wants her to stay in the new German Reich, but she's eager to get back to London.'

'She's a remarkable young woman.'

'And you found her, Adam. I asked you to find Dolly Delaney and you did.'

'But not the one you originally wanted.'

Sunman made a slight motion of his shoulders as if to suggest that it was all one to him. 'It has worked out well enough in the end,' he said.

Adam watched the smoke from his cigar drift towards the window. Not for everyone, he thought. Not for the girl who died so pointlessly in York. Not for poor Cyril Montague, no longer able to dream his opium dreams of new triumphs on the London stage. Not for Harry Vernon, dead and buried in a Berlin cemetery. Things had not worked out well enough in the end for them. Adam determined to shake off the melancholy and regret that such thoughts engendered. He remembered what Cosmo Jardine had said to him: 'Ladies of the chorus. They provide the solution to our problems.' His friend had not been entirely correct, he thought. One lady of the chorus had done as much to create new problems for him as solve old ones. But there was no denying that knowing Dolly Delaney had added excitement and intrigue to his life. Before he had heard her name, he had been directionless and dull. Now, he felt his spirits revived and his energy renewed. If she was returning to London, as Sunman said, Adam was impatient to see her again.

HISTORICAL NOTES

The Prince Albert Theatre in Drury Lane, the Royal Pantheon in Holborn and the Grand in Goodramgate, York, have never existed outside my imagination, but theatres a little bit like them certainly did. In Berlin, Pfaueninsel exists and is well worth visiting, although I have made a number of small changes in its geography to accommodate my story. The *Lustschloss* on the island can also be visited but its internal architecture is (for the most part) unlike the descriptions in the book. I have tried to make my specific references to facts about Victorian England as accurate as possible but, in a small number of cases, I have changed details very slightly to suit my fiction. For instance, in the opening scene, I have my characters musing on mortality at the grave of one James Dark. There was, indeed, a James Dark who was a cricketer and proprietor of Lord's cricket ground. He is, indeed, buried at Kensal Green Cemetery where his grave can still be seen. However, I have placed him in that grave one year earlier than he died in reality in order to provide a topic of conversation for Adam Carver and his friend Sunman. I hope that readers (and, in this example, the shade of James Dark) will forgive me these minor changes.

ACKNOWLEDGEMENTS

My first thanks go to my editor Angus MacKinnon who has contrib
uted so much to both my novels. His encouragement, suggestion
and advice have made an enormous difference to this second adven
ture of Carver and Quint. At Corvus, Sara O'Keeffe and Louis
Cullen have been unfailingly friendly, helpful and efficient. Belind
Jones proved a meticulous and imaginative copy editor. Friend
and family have offered support, reassurance and words of wisdor
throughout the extended process of writing *Carver's Truth*.
would like to thank particularly my sister Cindy Rennison, m
brother-in-law Wolfgang Lüers, my nieces Lorna and Milena Lüers
my mother Eileen Rennison, John, Michael and Andrew Thewli
Jenny Thewlis, John and Karen Magrath, Anita Diaz, Kevin Chap
pell, Hugh Pemberton and Susan Osborne, Andrew Holgate, Stev
Andrews, Graham and Margaret Eagland, and Gordon Kerr.

As always my unending love and gratitude go to my wife Ev
without whom nothing is possible.